DEAT
OF A
DYING MAN

By the Author

Death by the Riverside

Deaths of Jocasta

The Intersection of Law and Desire

Lost Daughters

Death of a Dying Man

Visit us at www.boldstrokesbooks.com

Acclaim for J.M. Redmann's Micky Knight Series

Advance Acclaim for *Death of a Dying Man*

"Set with wrenching reality against the backdrop of a city whose soul has been ravaged by Hurricane Katrina, Redmann's…*Death of a Dying Man*…is a riveting and emotionally complex novel—weaving together a dying man's poignant last wish, the pain of a crumbling lesbian romance, and (of course) a murder—is a virtuoso literary whodunit." —Richard Labonte, *Q Syndicate*

"Mickey Knight is back and how! J.M. Redmann is one of the top mystery writers today, bar none."—Greg Herren, author of the Scott Bradley mystery series

Death by the Riverside and *Deaths of Jocasta*

"Maybe we should call J.M. Redmann 'Lady Spillane'…When this woman puts up her dukes, you'll put everything else down to follow her."—Vicki P. McConnell, author of the Nyla Wade mystery series

"One of the best mystery debuts of this or any year, J.M. Redmann's page-turning *Death by the Riverside*, featuring a fabulously sexual, all too fiercely independent lady dick to rival any hetero or homo counterpart on the market, female or male."—Helen Eisenbach, *QW*

The Intersection of Law and Desire

"A gritty, involving mystery. Pretty good for a woman!"—(Sneaky Pie Brown) Rita Mae Brown

"J.M. Redmann is simply a wonderful writer. And Micky Knight is a terrific character. I enjoyed this book immensely."—Sandra Scoppettone, author of the Lauren Laurano series

"Superbly crafted, multi-layered…One of the most hard boiled and complex female detectives in print today."—*San Francisco Chronicle* (An Editor's Choice selection for 1995)

"J.M. Redmann once again keeps you at the edge of your seat. A gutsy, fast-thinking PI in the Raymond Chandler tradition, Micky Knight is a detective mystery fans both gay and straight will want to see again and again."—*Booklist*

"Fine, hard-boiled tale-telling."—*Washington Post Book World*

"Imagine Kinsey Millhone as a lesbian and you've got Micky Knight."—*The Nation*

"An edge-of-the-seat, action-packed New Orleans adventure... Micky Knight is a fast-moving, fearless, fascinating character...*The Intersection of Law and Desire* will win Redmann lots more fans."
—*New Orleans Times-Picayune*

"Crackling with tension...an uncommonly rich book...Redmann has the making of a landmark series."—*Kirkus Review*

"Perceptive, sensitive prose; in-depth characterization; and pensive, wry wit add up to a memorable and compelling read."—*Library Journal*

"Powerful and page turning...A rip-roaring read, as randy as it is reflective...Micky Knight is a to-die-for creation...a Cajun firebrand with the proverbial quick wit, fast tongue and heavy heart."—*Lambda Book Report*

Lost Daughters

"Few writers understand the human heart as well as J.M. Redmann. *Lost Daughters* manages the rare trick of being a mystery packed with surprises as well as a moving exploration of the pain of loss between parents and children."—Val McDermid, Gold Dagger–winning author of *The Mermaids Singing*

"As tightly plotted a page-turner as they come...One of the pleasures of *Lost Daughters* is its highly accurate portrayal of the real work of private detection...and Knight is a competent, tightly wound, sardonic, passionate detective with a keen eye for detail and a spine made of steel."—*San Francisco Chronicle*

"For finely delineated characters, unerring timing, and page-turning action, Redmann deserves the widest possible audience."—*Booklist*, starred review

"...tastefully sexy..."—*USA Today*

"Like fine wine, J.M. Redmann's private eye has developed interesting depths and nuances with age...Redmann continues to write some of the fastest-moving action scenes in the business."—*New Orleans Times-Picayune*

"An admirable, tough PI with an eye for detail and the courage, finally, to confront her own fear. Recommended."—*Library Journal*

"The best mysteries are character-driven and still have great moments of atmosphere and a tightly wound plot. J.M. Redmann succeeds on all three counts."—*Outsmart*

DEATH
OF A
DYING MAN

by

J.M. Redmann

2009

ISBN 10: 1-60282-075-9
ISBN 13: 978-1-60282-075-3

This Trade Paperback Original Is Published By
Bold Strokes Books, Inc.
P.O. Box 249
Valley Falls, NY 12185

First Bold Strokes Edition: April 2009

CREDITS
EDITOR: SHELLEY THRASHER
PRODUCTION DESIGN: STACIA SEAMAN
COVER DESIGN BY SHERI (GRAPHICARTIST2020@HOTMAIL.COM)

Acknowledgments

No one writes a book without support. For this one, that is especially true.

About ten chapters into this manuscript, I had to pack up my car and drive out of New Orleans. It was August 28, 2005. I spent the next few months on the road, finally returning in early November. New Orleans had changed; the failure of the levees covered 80% of the city with water. The book I had been writing was no longer possible, that city no longer existed. Clearly, the book did get written, since you're reading this. A number of people helped me in my journey back to New Orleans and to completing writing this.

As the storm approached, Connie Ward and Shelley Thrasher offered me a place to stay. Thinking that East Texas would be close and I could get back quickly after the hurricane passed, I took them up on their offer. They were incredibly kind and generous for what turned out to be a three-week visit; including ceding me a laptop as e-mail was one of the few ways us refugees could communicate. Their kindness and being able to talk about books and writing helped keep me sane while watching the horrific images on CNN. I also need to thank Connie and Shelley for their continued friendship, their work for Bold Strokes Books, and especially Shelley for her considerate and thorough editing.

My next home away from home was with my friend Jeanne Harris in Jonesboro, Arkansas. Among many things, Jeanne was also generous with her computers. She gave me carte blanche with her desktop, which allowed me to work via long distance at my day job and get back to writing. A good portion of the manuscript was typed at her desk.

In my refugee road tour, a number of people kept me sane. I met up with Cherry Cappel, the goddess of all things Internet, and her partner Beth Blankenship in Texarkana (don't even ask) where we drank a lot, ate sushi, and generally reminded ourselves that we would get through. (Also Peewee and Bailey for the barks.) True friends travel to small towns in Texas to spend a few hours together, and Beth and Cherry are some of the truest of friends.

Greg Herren and I explored beautiful Hammond, LA, as he was kind enough to let me use the place he was housesitting as a way station on my first trip back to New Orleans. (Many thanks also to Michael, whose house it actually was.) Also credit to Greg for gossip and gym torture.

Thanks go to Paul Willis, a longtime friend, gym buddy, and the founder of Saints and Sinners. Thanks also to the crew from the best little book club in the world emeritus, Barb, Candy, Yvonne, and Marie. We know where we were the Friday before Katrina.

I need to thank all my friends and co-workers at NO/AIDS Task Force, especially those of us who crammed into the CAN office shortly after we came back after Katrina. And re-crammed in after the electrical fire at the main office. Everyone there has been a tremendous support at the day job and for my writing. It's a long list of wonderful people: Noel, Enrique, Josh, Mark, Allison, Ked, DJ, Greg, Brian, Kathy, Pam, Mary Ellen, Seema, Jeannette, Lisa, Abe, Narquis, Tia, Diane, Heidi, TJ, Chad, Doreen, Tina, Larry, and everyone else.

Gratitude to Katherine V. Forrest for being a friend, mentor, and pioneer and helping me tame an unruly manuscript. Also to other writer friends who've helped along the way, especially the New Orleans writers as we struggled to tell the stories of what happened to our city.

I deeply appreciate all my readers; books are ultimately a partnership between those of us who write them and those who read them. Your support, from writing to me, showing up at a reading, passing a book to friends, has been vital in helping me put the words on the page.

Of course to Rad and Lee and everyone else at Bold Strokes for giving this book a very welcoming home.

And finally to Gillian for the cooking, decorating, and music education, even if she is a little taller than I am.

Dedication

To the friends who came back after the flood.
And to the ones who could not.

CHAPTER ONE

I was hearing a confession, I realized.

It should have been a simple case—to find Person X, last seen on this date and at this time. I'd ask a few questions. Person X's birth date, Social Security number (that only happened if I was very lucky), any distinguishing features, that sort of stuff.

But our lives are never simple, so the cases were never simple. Mine—life and cases—were a wide and deep river away from simple. I had arrived at my office shortly before ten just in case Shannon Wild, a journalist who was one of my life's current complications, came by and—because it needed to be done—started on my tasks of filing and finishing up paperwork, everything from ordering paper clips to sending out bills. A little after lunch, I had even finished the things I needed to do and was starting on the things I wanted to do. Ms. Wild had not shown up, but my desk was beginning to appear from under the paper when I received this phone call.

And even as lapsed a Catholic as I am will admit that listening to confessions is better than doing paperwork.

"I was a real jerk," my new client, Damon LaChance, told me. "Didn't believe her. I mean, I'm a gay man, right? Go figure that the one time I do it with a woman, she gets pregnant. Of course, birth control never entered my mind. Sex equals babies just wasn't part of my reality."

Damon was a dying man. He wanted me to find out if he had, indeed, fathered a child seven years earlier, sometime in the late 1990s. And to hear his deathbed confessions. He had already told me about his wild youth, drugs, sex, circuits of parties that ended the next afternoon. He had told me about the time he thought he got infected with the hepatitis C that would kill him in the next six months as his liver failed. When he got infected with HIV, which was making the hepatitis C kill him even more quickly. The times he got gonorrhea—orally, genitally, and rectally. The drugs he used, from skin-popping cocaine and heroin to the expensive wine, bottle after bottle every night.

Damon was a successful man, if you define success as money. He owned four bars in the French Quarter, and Damon may have been decadent, but he was not a fool, and only a fool could lose money in bars in the French Quarter. He'd made his into the kinds of places he liked to go. Three of them were gay bars, and one was a glitzy tourist place that gave people everything they thought they should find on Bourbon Street.

Damon could afford to buy a lot of time in the confessional. "I wrote her back, think I called her a lying bitch. Like I said, a real asshole jerk. I've been hit up through the years by hustlers and money scammers, and I guess I was too quick to lump her in with them."

He hadn't alluded to the one time we met before. Perhaps he had forgotten it. I didn't want to think so, as he had made an impression on me, one that I remembered.

My partner Cordelia James is a do-gooder type doctor, running a clinic in a poor neighborhood, and she was receiving one of those awards that people who do the right thing occasionally get. My spousal duty required that I gussy myself up, paste on my best beatific smile of undying love so no one would suspect that the good doctor rarely remembers to clean out the cat box, hang by her side in case she needed someone to talk to, and not lose the beatific smile as hordes of admirers gushed their congratulations and stepped on my toes as they totally ignored me.

Damon was the master of ceremonies. I knew who he was, or thought I did. Rich, gay party boy. I'd never talked to him in my life, passed him a few times in the French Quarter. But New Orleans has pockets of small town, and the gay community is one of them. Of course I'd heard of him.

But hearing of and actually seeing are different. From behind me, I heard a deep and resonant laugh, the roar of a man who knows how to enjoy life. I turned to see who it was and there was Damon. Tall, movie-star handsome, and in a tuxedo that made him look like he should be pouring martinis out of a silver cocktail shaker for Fred Astaire and Ginger Rogers. Details can tell a story, and the details of the tableau I saw hinted that my quick dismissal of Damon was too facile. He was with a group of women, and at events like this, the girls and boys are often more segregated than at a Catholic middle-school dance. Not just women, but women who wouldn't qualify as anyone's arm decoration. Silver-haired for the most part, and not a single dress or pair of high heels in the bunch. Damon liked women—shocking as it may seem, some gay men are as sexist as the worst of the straight men—and was willing to spend time at a glad-handing event like this talking to them. If he was with those women it was because he enjoyed their company, not because of what they could do for him. They were still talking when Cordelia sent me off to get her something to drink.

When I was coming back, carrying one of those drinks that require a martini glass filled to the rim and therefore the ability of a circus performer to carry it through a packed crowd, Damon and I almost collided. My fault. He was pushing a man in a wheelchair to one of the front tables, and I was so intent on not spilling Cordelia's drink, I didn't notice a man both sitting and moving. I managed to pivot fast enough that Cordelia's pink drink spilled in my direction—direct hit to the cleavage—instead of on Damon or the friend he was pushing.

"I am so sorry," I said, abashed at my inattention and churlish behavior.

"No problem," Damon said, as he wheeled past me. As debonair as Cary Grant, he kept moving and also took a handkerchief from an inside pocket and handed it to me. With a glance at where the drink landed and a rakish smile, he said, "I'm sure one of the women here will help you clean that up."

Then he was through the crowd and I was left with a red face, a sticky pink chest, and his handkerchief. At least I was wearing a black blouse and not the cream one I had considered.

Damon was a smooth emcee, self-deprecating at times, but mostly keeping the focus off himself and onto the awardees. It wasn't his fault that he was taller, handsomer, and wittier than the winners, but the contrast showed. All right, I thought, as one long-winded winner ("And I'd like to thank my parakeet and his veterinarian…") finally exited, I can see why the gay boys like Damon.

Cordelia gave the shortest thank-you speech, taking to heart that brevity is the soul of wit, or at least the less you say, the less chance you have of making a fool of yourself. And she is tall enough that, with dress pumps on, she was almost Damon's height. Then the event was over and I was left trying to manage the beatific smile and watch my toes while hordes gathered around my partner to congratulate her. It was hard with my bra cemented to my chest with triple sec.

An arm was draped around my shoulder. "So, got it licked off yet?" Damon had joined us, with just a brief enough glance at where the drink had landed to let me know what he meant. Unlike most of the others pumping Cordelia's hand, he was willing to acknowledge my existence.

"Saving it for later," I managed to reply. I was still embarrassed at nearly spilling a Cosmo over a man in a wheelchair because I wasn't paying attention to where I was heading.

Damon must have caught the rueful look on my face, as he gave my shoulder a squeeze. Up close he was still as handsome as at a distance—dimples, a roguish grin, full, wavy brownish red hair, well over six feet tall. His arm over my shoulder felt friendly, not invasive, a simple gesture that both let me off from our almost-accident and included me in his congratulating Cordelia, instead of cutting me out as many of the others did.

His "Well deserved. I was happy to see you getting a Spirit Award" came off as sincere. He then bent to give Cordelia a kiss on the cheek and my shoulder a final squeeze.

I offered to wash the handkerchief and return it, but he waved me off.

"It'll be a favor to call in when I really need it," he said, with a wink that Katharine Hepburn would have swooned for, and then he was pulled into the crowd.

That was about four years ago and our paths had never crossed since. Until the phone rang.

"And maybe I was scared…what the hell had I done? Me, with a child? Never planned that, so it was easy to think it couldn't be true," Damon said.

My other phone line glowed accusingly at me. The answering machine could pick it up. I edged up the volume so I could hear who my second caller was.

"She was very attractive, but in an understated way," Damon continued. "Had a Yankee accent, which I've always loved. Sounds so educated and posh, you know?"

Cordelia's voice came on after my recorded message. "Micky? Are you there? I've got a major favor to ask. I hope you're there and you get this. Lauren and I have been working on the study protocols all day and she mentioned how much she loved shrimp and if I could recommend somewhere to pick some up."

Damon said, "I guess it was the sound of her voice—and the three bottles of wine. Plus, I'd done the fumbling high-school stuff, probably too hurried and ashamed, even if I did like women, to be fun. But only men after I turned seventeen. Part of me was curious. It may sound odd, but I felt like the queerest thing I could do was have sex with a woman. I'd done everything else."

Cordelia's voice carried from the answering machine. "Lauren still seems a bit tired from traveling, plus they're moving into a short-term apartment right now from the hotel—"

"So you invited them over for dinner," I muttered.

"So I invited them over for dinner," my lover continued as predicted. "I mean no one cooks shrimp better than you do, and I know it's fairly easy to do."

"I'm sorry, what was that?" Damon asked. I had muttered a bit too loudly.

"I'm terribly sorry, I didn't mean to interrupt you, but I have another client appointment and they're at the door." I told this lie so often, I could whip it out without even thinking. "Can we set aside some time to talk? If you want, I'll be glad to come to you."

"Nothing really fancy," I heard Cordelia say, as I jotted down Damon's French Quarter address and set a time to meet with him. "Maybe if you could stop and pick up shrimp, we could boil them." We? I thought. Cordelia knows I love her, but I'm still not letting her cook seafood. "And maybe some crabs. And maybe…I don't know, they may be politically correct types who eschew anything that looks like a real creature. I don't think Lauren is, but I don't know about Shannon. Anyway, if you could pick up something safe." I'm open to suggestions, I thought. Tofu and I have only passed in the grocery store; we don't have a kitchen acquaintance.

Damon repeated his address to make sure I had it right. Just as I reassured him that I did have it and he said good-bye, Cordelia ended her long message and also hung up.

I debated whether to call her back. It was a bit late in the day to saddle me with a dinner party, and I wasn't interested in socializing with cocky young Shannon Wild. I wouldn't be a total cad and pretend I'd never gotten her message, but I could let her sweat it for a bit. I also considered stopping by the place that sold turtles and taking one home. No, that was over the top.

I flashed back to the night before and the complications that had just been added to my life.

"You don't really believe in monogamy, do you?" Shannon Wild had asked me.

I glanced around the restaurant. It seemed that she hadn't been overheard. Otherwise a line of both men and women would have been forming at the table. Shannon was a stunningly good-looking woman, with short blond hair, sky blue eyes, a strong jaw, and an expression that gave her a look of sophistication on the border of ennui, but with dimples that hinted she wasn't quite that jaded.

She was seated directly across the table from my lover, Cordelia James. Cordelia, however, didn't hear her question or notice the hand Shannon had put on my thigh for emphasis.

Cordelia was engrossed in a conversation with Lauren Calder, Shannon's presumably not-monogamous partner—Dr. Lauren Calder, the author of *The Vagina Dialogues*, a book that had coasted on the best-seller list for months now. It also managed to be an intelligent discussion of women and their sexuality, what they needed to do to be sexually healthy, and pointed out the gender inequality between men's sexuality research and women's, such as all the money spent to overcome the ageing penis and its erectile dysfunction while we still don't have a better tampon. She and Cordelia had lapsed into doctor speak a while ago and were now avidly discussing Dr. Calder's research.

I had been clearly left the spousal duty of keeping the other spouse occupied.

"Too risky in New Orleans," I answered her. "There are only sixty-four lesbians in this city, and if you don't practice monogamy, it's a mathematical certainty that within six months every single one of them will know just what you do in bed, including how many orgasms you had on Tuesday night."

"And how many orgasms did you have Tuesday night?" she asked, her voice low and teasing.

I had the feeling that her flirting was more sport than any serious attempt to bed me. She, also, had been relegated to the tag-along spouse role, and this was her way of making it interesting. "It was a slow night. Only four." In fact, last Tuesday, the number was zero, as Cordelia had had a cold and gone to bed shortly after I'd fed her chicken soup.

Did I believe in monogamy? More in soul than in body. Cordelia and I had been together for almost a decade, and I had never cheated on her. That's not to say that I hadn't occasionally lusted in my heart or missed the hard, heady passion of a new partner. Before she and I got together, I had been, shall we say, sexually adventurous, in truth, using sex, as well as alcohol, to keep away my demons. I was smart enough to know that the love, stability, and security Cordelia gave me were a large part of banishing or at least de-fanging those demons. I wasn't about to risk all that for a sexual thrill, although I had to admit that the thought had crossed my mind this evening. Shannon's hand was still on my thigh. But it was Dr. Lauren Calder that I'd given my second glance to.

Dr. Calder was tall enough to look me in the eye, and she had a figure that showed the muscles of someone who worked out, but also the curves of someone who wouldn't (and hadn't) said no to the white-chocolate bread pudding that was this restaurant's signature dessert. Her hair was a thick, black mane, shot through with steel gray. Her eyes were a sensual brown, the rest of her face a hard plane that signified she was someone accustomed to being in charge, her expression one of intense observation, as if the whole world interested her. Only when she relaxed into a smile or a laugh did her face reveal a different side, a more playful—and dare I think it—sensual side.

I would have preferred to have her explain the importance of control groups to me rather than discuss the pluses and minuses of monogamy with her partner.

"You still haven't revealed what you really think of being with one person for the rest of your life," that partner persisted.

"I've answered it as much as I intend to with my lover sitting six inches away," I answered. Six inches and worlds away.

"Then I will have to ask it in other circumstances," she countered, finally taking her hand off my thigh.

She would have the circumstances to ask again. The complicating thing that had happened that evening was that Shannon was a journalist and was doing a piece on women in nontraditional careers. I'm a private detective. You do the math. In some burst of Southern politeness, I agreed to let her follow me around. Having forged an alliance between us, our respective lovers felt free to head off into the land of medical jargon.

"Do we start bright and early tomorrow morning?" Shannon asked.

"I started my own business to avoid bright and early," I told her. "And tomorrow will be mostly a paperwork day." Actually, tomorrow was a day for me to decide exactly how to handle this bright and bushy-tailed girl reporter. There were some cases and places I had no intention of taking her.

"Don't trust me, do you?" she said as she gave me a direct stare, one she had clearly practiced to be intimidating. "Think I'll be a bother and a pain, asking your clients in the midst of a dirty divorce how to spell their names for the article I'm doing?"

"No, I assume you're more professional than that," I covered, pissed at myself for being so obvious—and at her for calling me so quickly on it. "You're welcome to come by my office and watch me file paper and drink coffee. I'll start around ten. Coffee and chicory, taken black, is as dangerous as it will get."

"I take my work seriously," she said, her voice crisp and professional, all traces of flirting gone. "And I'm on a deadline. Don't waste my time and I won't waste yours. If you're really going to do it, do it. If not, don't play games."

"Games?" I retorted, then thought better of what I was about to say, that a woman who queried me about monogamy in front of my lover and her lover had no right to bitch about game playing. I did a five count, then said, "I take my work just as seriously as you take yours. You want to watch? You'll do it my way."

"You're right, Shannon. New Orleans does know how to eat," Lauren Calder said.

I couldn't tell if she and Cordelia had come to a stopping place in their conversation and finally decided to recognize our existence or if she had realized that her pretty young thing was close to stepping in it.

Lauren—and *The Vagina Dialogues*—paid the bill.

Cordelia finished the last of her cognac and handed the car keys to me. As usual, I was the designated driver. Since Lauren and Shannon had arrived only a few days ago and still seemed to think that north and south had some meaning in a city carved through by a winding river (there are parts of the Westbank you have to go east to get to), we had picked them up. Everyone was full and tired, and it was a sultry summer night, so the block-long walk to our car had little conversation save for a few comments on the meal.

Lauren and Shannon got in the backseat, Shannon quickly snuggling under Lauren's arm. Being a safe driver, as I pulled out I checked my rearview mirror and got a good view of them having a deep kiss. Monogamy did seem so monotonous. Another quick glance told me that Shannon's hand was heading toward Lauren's breast. Then I was a good girl and kept my eyes on the road.

Cordelia didn't even reach out and hold my hand. Although to be fair to her, it was city driving and my car is a stick shift.

Their hotel was close enough they didn't have time to start the orgasm count.

Cordelia and Lauren spent a few minutes reiterating where and when they would meet tomorrow. Shannon merely sauntered up to my window and said, "Call me when you're ready for me to tag along," then went around to the other side of the car to wait for Lauren.

They held hands walking into the lobby.

I had barely pulled away from the hotel when Cordelia said, "I can't believe Dr. Lauren Calder will be at my clinic tomorrow." She then launched into an explanation—in terms that I could understand—of the project. Dr. Calder was doing research on microbicides or, in real-person speak, a chemical barrier a woman could put in her vagina that could help prevent pregnancy or infection with STDs and HIV. The main advantage to these devices was that the woman controlled them. She could put the gel or ointment in her vagina without her partner knowing. It wasn't very profitable research because most of the need was in the developing world, and many of the methods, such as ways to change the acid balance in the vagina, were not things that could be patented.

That explanation took us to our front door. As I opened it to let her in, she finally broke from her vagina monologue to ask, "I know Lauren and I did get a bit engrossed. Is it going to be okay? Shannon doing that story on you?"

"It's fine. And she's not doing the story on me. I'm probably not dangerous enough for her and will be in a paragraph in the end, if I'm not cut entirely."

"Well, it might be convenient if you keep her entertained while Lauren and I are working together, but you don't have to. She's a big girl and can probably take care of herself." The end of her comment was muffled by a large yawn.

"Tired?" I asked, wanting to change the subject from Shannon Wild.

"A bit. This is a weeknight and I'm usually close to bed by this time."

"Real tired?" I asked, putting my arms around her and starting to kiss her neck.

She returned my embrace, then as my lips traveled down her throat to the swell of her breasts, she said, "What's got into you? I'm the one who had champagne and cognac."

"The champagne and cognac did the trick for the doctor and her young thing."

"You were watching?"

"No, I was driving. That occasionally requires a glance in the rearview mirror."

Satisfied that I had seen only what was required in the line of duty, Cordelia asked, "What were they doing?"

I kissed her nipple through her shirt, then answered. "Heavy kissing by the time I pulled away from the curve. I'm pretty sure I saw a hand heading toward a breast."

"I thought I heard some suspicious rustling back there. Dare I ask whose?"

"Against the odds, Shannon was being the butch." I gently bit her nipple.

"I *am* tired." Cordelia sighed. "That tickles more than it arouses."

"Damn," I said, lifting my head away.

"Tomorrow is Friday. I'll make it up to you then," she said, then took my face between her hands and gave me a good, solid kiss to prove her point. She wrapped an arm around my waist and started pulling me toward the stairs and our bedroom. "And I need my sleep tonight," she continued as we maneuvered up the stairs together, "for tomorrow night."

So it was another night with zero orgasms, at least in my house. But that wasn't something I planned to share with Shannon Wild.

And I had to meet them again tonight.

I finished up the notations I was making for Damon's case and got ready to leave.

Damon LaChance wanted to find out if he had a child somewhere. And if he had infected a woman while creating that child. He hadn't directly said that, only hinted at it with a comment about wanting to make sure she was okay. I would take the case, had already agreed to, but it didn't promise a happy ending. He could be right, that she was just trying to scam him and get some baby bucks. Even that didn't mean that she deserved to be infected with the things Damon was carrying in his body. Or she could have told him the truth. She was pregnant and thought the father should know. That she had disappeared after Damon's jerk letter and sent back the subsequent ones argued strongly for the latter scenario. Which meant that I would find this woman and interject the father who couldn't be bothered to be around in the beginning back into her life. And tell her, by the way, you need to get tested for all the latest and greatest infectious diseases.

Cooking shrimp for Dr. Calder and young Shannon seemed easy in comparison.

CHAPTER TWO

The trunk is going to reek, I thought, as I pulled away from the seafood place. It was late August, the tag end of summer, and New Orleans was doing its best steam-bath imitation. I knew the humid air would capture the odor of shrimp, crabs, and oysters and impregnate the trunk with it. Cordelia owed me for this.

I had called her back, missed her, of course, and had to settle for leaving a suitably vague message. I didn't say, "Yes, honey, of course, I'd just love to whip up an impromptu dinner at the next-to-last minute for people I barely know. No problem." Instead, "Got your message, have to take care of a few things first. I'll see what I can do."

What I did was close up the office and head for the grocery store. Salad stuff, so even the most persnickety PC person would have something to eat. Beer. You can't really drink wine with crabs and shrimp. Also some sodas and fancy water to cover all bases.

Needless to say, when I got home, nothing had changed. The breakfast dishes were still in the sink. The cat box needed some attention to bring it up to company snuff. Cordelia hadn't mentioned cleaning, but that clearly was part of the bargain. My availability had become something taken for granted in our relationship. I could arrange my hours, do errands during the day, leave early, stay at home for deliveries. Sometimes, her easy assumption that I could step in and take care of these areas of our life together rankled. Like tonight. But the reality was that I could and she couldn't. I guess what really rankled wasn't the doing part, but the for-granted part.

As I scooped out the litter box, I thought, well, the sex had better be hot tonight. After our guests left, that is.

The most time-consuming part of this dinner was throwing together the salad. While I was rinsing the spinach, my thoughts returned to Damon LaChance and his quest. I wondered what had really prompted it—his guilt, or his wanting to know, before he died, that some of his genes would travel on. I had asked the question about not using a condom with the woman. Even if birth control was foreign to him, safe sex shouldn't have been.

"The usual stupid reason," he had replied. "I didn't have one, she didn't have one, we were three bottles of wine out of control. I had tested negative about a year earlier, so I could go to that gray area in my head and pretend I was probably still negative and that it would be okay. Sex is such an odd thing. I keep looking back at the things I've done and thinking, I should have been able to impose reason on it—a condom every time, never get drunk or high. Never fall in love and feel that touching that person is the most important thing in the world."

I liked Damon and sensed that he was truly sorry he'd caused hurt along the way. He wasn't a careful man, but he was a kind one. Maybe too late, maybe not enough, but he wanted to make amends.

It was too hot for raw oysters. I eat them, but only in the winter months when the cooler water keeps the bacteria count down. Which was safer for these unknown guests, oyster stew or Oysters Rockefeller? The stew was easier, but Cordelia would have to put out tonight if I did Oysters Rockefeller.

After finishing the salad, I started chopping the green onions, dumping them into the blender with some roughly chopped celery and the spinach. Just as the whirring stopped, a car door slammed. Then two in unison.

The front door opened and Cordelia said, "Hi, come into the air-conditioning. This humidity can take a bit of getting used to."

"I might have it by January," Lauren answered. "Smells good in here."

"Thanks to the slaving chef," I muttered loud enough to be heard from the kitchen.

"Hi, Micky," Cordelia called. "What are we having? Come on back and say hi to the so-called slaving chef."

Cordelia entered the kitchen, trailed by the two women. She and Lauren were in professional drag, Lauren in navy pants and a cream blouse. Somehow, despite the heat, she still looked crisp and fresh.

Cordelia's off-white pants showed a day's wrinkles from sitting, and her raw-silk red shirt was slightly darker under the arms from sweat. Shannon chose slacker casual, but her aiming for New York missed here in New Orleans. Jeans and a black T-shirt wasn't a fun ensemble in the heat. The black didn't show it, but I was willing to bet her armpits were as damp as Cordelia's. I was in cut-off jeans and a lavender T-shirt, slaving-chef clothes. Shannon looked about as thrilled to be here as I felt. Maybe we could bond over the trials of doctor lovers. Lauren was somewhere in her forties, Shannon claimed, and looked twenty-nine. Maybe some of my disliking Shannon was that she seemed like a mere hanger-on to the well-known doctor, a groupie who got invited home.

"You do eat seafood, don't you?" I asked her, reminding myself to be polite. She couldn't be a mere bubblehead blonde. Lauren Calder might like them young and cute, but I couldn't see her settling for stupid as well.

"The cooked variety," Shannon answered, proving me right about the raw oysters.

Cordelia and Lauren were off babbling about what some of the research funding could be used for, like getting all expectant mothers at Cordelia's clinic to undergo testing for HIV. This program was designed to measure how effective voluntary counseling would be, as opposed to mandatory testing, in getting the mothers to the needed prenatal care.

"How are you with a knife?" I asked Shannon, as the medical jargon started to reach the threshold of impenetrable.

"Depends on the context," she answered. "In a kitchen, I do quite well."

"I'll settle for the kitchen context. And stay clear of the sharp edge."

She gave me a wry grin, just enough to let me know that she had been thinking precisely that. "What do you want me to cut?"

I handed her some lemon and celery. "Big wedges are fine. It's to help flavor the shrimp."

Cordelia and Lauren extricated themselves enough from the medical world to join us in the kitchen. Cordelia even managed to not leave all the hosting duties to me and give our guests each a beer. I put the finishing touches on the oysters and slid them under the broiler while I listened to Cordelia give Lauren and Shannon helpful hints on New Orleans survival. Like not being able to make a left turn on Tulane

Avenue for about a hundred miles or that the legible street signs were only in the main tourist thoroughfares.

I was paying more attention to the almost-boiling water that I was about to dump the shrimp into, when I heard Lauren say, "You know, Shannon, since that article assignment went awry, you might pick up some private-detecting tips from Micky. It could be a whole new career."

"Micky has been muttering about needing to take on an assistant," Cordelia ever so helpfully added.

"An assistant who's been in New Orleans three days?" I said.

"There are road maps," was Cordelia's lame reply.

"Not to mention a considerable number of years as a prize-winning investigative journalist," Shannon rejoined. I didn't know if she had any interest in assisting me, but she clearly didn't like being rejected so quickly.

"You're from New York City. Can you even remember how to drive?" I muttered back.

"This from a woman who lives in a town with drive-through daiquiri shops? It's not my driving you should be worried about," Shannon replied.

"We have lived outside the city for the past several years," Lauren pointed out.

"But, of course, I don't want to interfere with your life of guns and cheap whiskey," Shannon said. "I doubt I'd be good at Philip Marlowe games."

"Well, if you think this is too much of a big, bad Southern city for you to handle, you can always sit by the river and paint watercolors."

Shannon glared at me. "I don't paint. But I suppose the kind of assistant you're looking for is the big muscles, no brain. You'd have no use for someone with four years of being a crack investigator, a master's degree from Yale, a year at Oxford, and sterling driving ability. Why have an assistant that's so much competition?"

"Competition? Oh, please. I don't need a Yale snob who thinks she knows it all, when she's really just a clueless Yankee. Hubris is dangerous."

"Micky, the water's boiling," Cordelia pointed out.

"Better start cooking before we have to break out the boxing gloves," Lauren added.

"Yes, hubris is dangerous," Shannon replied. "Better take a good look at whose face is in the mirror."

"Fine, we meet at the mirror in my office at nine tomorrow morning. You can help me track down the possibly dying child of a dying man."

Oh, hell, I realized, we had just backed ourselves into a corner. And why did I have to say meet at nine, like the earlier hour would prove something? Lauren's innocent suggestion had turned into a contest of wills. Shannon was going to prove she could do it; I was going to prove she couldn't, and the end result was that I would have Shannon Wild, with her stop-and-stare good looks, as my assistant.

Chapter Three

I had a good time. I hope working with Shannon is okay for you. It's nice to have such intelligent and accomplished friends. Reminds me that there's a world beyond this boggy city," Cordelia said, standing at the sink rinsing dishes. "But, God, I'm tired."

I moved behind her and reached around to cup her breasts. "Tired? You're tired after Oysters Rockefeller?"

"You know oysters aren't really an aphrodisiac."

"It's not the oysters. It's the effort of your lover in procuring and cooking them that's supposed to fire lust in your loins," I said.

"I do appreciate what you did, but that doesn't make me less tired."

I circled a finger around her nipple. "Dropping everything I was doing, rushing to the store, coming home and cleaning up, cooking a perfect meal, watching you flirt with your new doctor friend—"

"I was not flirting."

"Uh-huh. I noticed how helpful you were in teaching her to peel crabs. How often you had to lean into her and guide her hands with your hands." I was teasing, but I was also trying to get Cordelia riled, a certain kind of riled, that is.

"I really was only trying to be helpful. You know I wasn't flirting."

"Seems to me her Yankee girlfriend was doing fine and could have helped her just as well." I goaded her. Cordelia believes very firmly in monogamy. Her father didn't and it destroyed her family, so she has her reasons. But it was clear to me that she enjoyed Lauren's attention. I didn't feel threatened. I couldn't imagine Cordelia actually doing more than helpful crab peeling. I was amused at how adamantly she denied my charges.

"I was sitting next to her and Shannon was across the table. It just made sense that I should help. Don't read more into this than is really there."

The lady was protesting too much. And I was unscrupulous enough to use her protest to my advantage. "So, it's me you love?"

"Of course, I love you."

"Prove it," I demanded.

For an answer, she turned around, took my face between her wet hands, and kissed me. With just her lips. That didn't satisfy me.

"Cleanup can wait until tomorrow," I murmured in her ear. "Let's go upstairs."

She paused to dry her hands, then followed me to our bedroom.

"If you want, you can imagine dear Lauren doing a very private pelvic—"

"Micky! Not funny. You know I would never cheat on you."

"Not even in fantasy? In a stray thought or two?" I headed into the bathroom, forcing her to follow me. Cordelia still had enough vestiges of "good girl" in her that she could be nonplused by my toying with hints of sex and desire where she didn't think they were supposed to be.

"You know what I mean," she replied. "I like Lauren, but…"

"And you haven't the slightest interest in her other than as a professional friend, and it's me and only me that you love, desire, and pant for—except for tonight, as you're too tired. Right?" I started to brush my teeth. I was hoping she couldn't resist this gauntlet thrown before her professions of monogamy.

Cordelia didn't answer. She just picked up her toothbrush and joined me.

I finished first, then left her alone at the sink. After taking off my clothes, I climbed into bed. I usually wear a T-shirt, but tonight I wanted to remind her there was a willing, naked body in bed with her.

Cordelia emerged from the bathroom, turning off the light. Only the faint illumination of the streetlight was left. I heard the rustling of her undressing then felt the bed shift as she got in. For a moment, she lay still.

"You want proof?" she abruptly said. She swung her leg over

me then straddled my chest. "I'll give you proof." Suddenly leaning forward, she pinned my wrists down, bending over far enough to brush a nipple against my cheek. She moved her hips until I could feel the brush of hair against my breasts. She rocked herself, working my now-erect nipple between her legs. She stayed there long enough for me to feel her get wet, then lowered herself until she was straddling my hips.

I suddenly thrust up against her hands, but she pushed back and held me down. "So you're the butch tonight?" I murmured.

"Thought I'd better be. You used up all your butch points in that pissing contest with Shannon."

Before I could retort, she covered my mouth with a kiss. This time it involved a lot more than just her lips. She finally broke it off, to tell me, "Turn over. I'm going to take you from behind."

I did as I was told. Cordelia and I had been together for a while now. While our lovemaking varied, more often than not I was the aggressor and she followed my lead. Often she was tired and distracted from her work and had the energy to follow, but not lead. Those good-girl vestiges also inhibited her. It had been a long learning curve for her to be able to say, "I want to be fucked and I want to be fucked now."

Her hand went down my back, grabbing my buttocks, a delightfully rough massage of each cheek. Her aggression tonight clearly was meant to prove something. Her hand went between my legs. My brain wanted to hold back, make her work for it, but my body went a different direction, my hips arching up to take in her thrusting fingers. She didn't have to work hard at all. I was so ready I barely had time to bury my head in the pillow to muffle the yelling moan I made as I came.

Cordelia lay on top of me as I recovered, her fingers still buried inside me. After catching my breath, I started to roll over, but she kept me pinned beneath her. "I'm not done," she muttered in my ear, as her fingers began to take me again.

I briefly wondered if my doctor lover was feeling some competition with sexuality expert Dr. Lauren Calder. But my brain quickly dispensed with wondering what had prompted Cordelia's change and concentrated on more important things, like how many fingers she was thrusting into me, the way she was kissing my neck, and how she kept me pinned down so all I could do was lie under her and let her do me.

She did, indeed, prove her lust for me.

However, the disadvantage of my teasing Cordelia about a

possible attraction to another woman was that when the alarm clock rang at seven thirty on a Saturday morning, I hadn't had much sleep. You did this to yourself, I reminded myself. This butch pissing contest was all my doing. Mine and Shannon's, that was. I may have started it, but she'd jumped up and aimed at the mark. I decided it was important to get to my office before Shannon. I didn't want to be standing at the door, fumbling with my keys, juggling a coffee cup in one hand, with her looking on.

By eight fifteen, I was showered and ready to go. I kissed Cordelia good-bye—on both sets of lips, just to make sure she remembered last night. I think I woke her a bit more than I intended, but she could go back to sleep. Then I was out the door.

My office is only about twenty blocks downtown from where I live, in a section of New Orleans known as Bywater. It's downtown of the French Quarter and, as its name implies, bordered by the Mississippi River and the Industrial Canal. I could probably afford something better now, but I didn't want to be an uptown dick. I wondered what Ms. Yale would think of my downtown digs. Might scare her off, I thought. Or maybe the three flights of stairs would wear her out.

I opened the door, turned on the lights, and watered the plants that somehow managed to survive despite my cursory attention. Maybe they would stop drooping by the time she got here.

Next was the coffee. I wanted a half-drunk cup in front of me by the time she arrived. No slacking around this joint—not with a sarcastic Yankee judging.

Only then did I sit down to do some work actually involved with the case. Damon wanted and was going to pay for full attention to his needs. His liver could fail all too soon, and time was the one thing he didn't have. I made a case file, then printed up all the paperwork on my computer to be able to take to my interview with him. As I was debating which task I could safely dump on Shannon, I glanced at my watch. It was a little after nine. Not here yet.

I would have felt all too smug, but I did know how cruel the traffic in New Orleans could be, and for a neophyte, the streets that follow the curves of the river rather than any logical direction and the haphazard street signs could be daunting. She had until nine thirty. Then I was going to head out.

At nine fifteen, I heard a knock on my door. Shannon Wild, brand spanking new girl detective, had arrived. She had learned her jeans-and-black color lesson. Today she was in light khaki pants and a cotton V-neck blue shirt that brought out the blue in her eyes. No makeup, not that she needed any, but some discreet jewelry—small gold hoop earrings and a matching chain around her neck. I noticed she didn't wear any rings. I guessed she and Lauren didn't want to announce their committed state.

"Time to go," I said, getting up. I was pleased to note that my light gray pants and peach raw-silk T-shirt looked more professional than hers—as I intended.

"Time to go? I just got here," she answered with an envious look at my cup of coffee.

"A little late," I pointed out. I grabbed my briefcase.

"Where are we going? Do I get briefed?" She had no choice but to follow me out and down the stairs.

"We're working on a case. And as for briefed, all you need to do is listen and look pretty."

Her muttered reply seemed to contain several obscenities. I ignored them all.

Chapter Four

Damon lived in a perfectly restored three-story townhouse, its wrought-iron balconies gleaming with fresh paint and covered with lush, exotic plants. Off to one side was a covered carriage entrance. Damon *would* have his own off-street parking.

I rang the doorbell. Shannon waited a few steps below me, both of us silently listening to the echoing peal of chimes. I didn't know how sick Damon was and how long it might take him to answer the door.

Not very long and not Damon. The man who answered had an unfortunate resemblance to a chipmunk—a large pointed nose, rounded jowly cheeks, and a chin barely a notch above his collar. His thin hair was receding, accenting his sloping forehead. He wore a conservative and well-tailored suit that did its best to hide his skinny frame. The suit was an almost black charcoal with pinstripes, very tasteful, but out of place on a hot, muggy day in the Bohemian French Quarter. The shirt was, as expected, a starched white. However, the yellow tie wasn't the best color for this man's sallow complexion. *More money than taste* came to mind.

"Micky Knight?" he inquired.

"Yes. And this is my…assistant, Shannon Wild."

"Come in," he said. "I'm Ambrose deVille, Damon's lawyer." He must have been paid major lawyer bucks to be making a house call that included opening doors. That suit couldn't hide reality, but it wasn't an off-the-rack model.

We did the customary round of handshaking, then Ambrose led us to the back of the house, into a room filled with both plants and sunlight. A man who looked a lot more like my remembrance of Damon was sitting on a white wicker love seat. The illness showed, but he was still a handsome man, tall, with a strong cleft in his chin. The hair was thinning and turning gray, but it had a debonair wave. He was dressed casually in a well-worn Hawaiian shirt, its color faded from many washings, hiking shorts, and sandals on his feet.

"Ms. Knight?" he asked, standing up. He did so with some difficulty, but clearly he wasn't sick enough to forget his Southern manners. Even his illness couldn't hide the dazzle of his welcoming smile, the direct look of his eyes into mine that made me feel like I was someone he wanted to know.

I offered my hand as I answered, "Yes, I am. This is my assistant, Shannon Wild." His grip was firm and warm, not the limp shake of his lawyer.

"Welcome," he said. "Won't you sit? What can I get for you?" He sat down, and it clearly wasn't him that would be doing the getting.

"Coffee would be wonderful," Shannon said with relief. My earlier churlishness would be compensated for.

"The same," I answered.

Ambrose deVille quickly said, "I'll have George take care of it." Damon made no request. I suspected that George already knew what he wanted.

"Am I sending you on a fool's quest?" Damon asked me. "It's been seven years. How do you find someone seven years gone?"

"Finding's not that hard. It's what happens after you've found her. Have you considered the consequences?"

"Happy ending, right?" Damon's ironic quirk to his smile told me he didn't think it would be that easy.

"One always hopes for happy endings."

Ambrose returned, followed by a servant, presumably George, bearing a tray with four coffee cups on it. The servant put the tray down, then sat one of the cups on the end table next to Damon. Damon looked up at him and smiled his thanks. Ambrose took another one from the tray, ignoring him. George hovered, until Shannon waved him away and added her own milk and sugar. I left mine black. I also caught his eye and smiled a thank-you.

"Tell me everything you know about her," I requested.

He handed me a picture, a shot of the two of them. The Damon in the picture made clear the toll that disease had taken on the man before me. He was very handsome, the hair in its full, thick waviness. He had a glowing tan, not the current sickly yellow tinge to his skin. His arm was around her and she matched him in animal vitality. She was almost as tall as he was, making her around my height. Her hair was a glossy, vibrant reddish-brown.

"She came to town for Jazz Fest, was traveling through the U.S. by herself. I liked her sense of independence and her willingness to find her own adventure. She was standing at the corner of Ursulines and Royal, and as I came by, she stopped me and asked, 'Where's the best haunted house in the Quarter?'"

"I replied, 'Why, mine, of course,' then added, 'I'm gay.'

"'That's all right, love,' she said in that wonderful voice of hers. 'Everyone's got a right to be happy. I'm just a girl who loves a good ghost story. You look like a man who can tell a few.'

"We stood on the corner for a while chatting, then one of us—it may have been me—suggested finding a coffee place to sit in. The afternoon wore on and we had dinner together."

I didn't interrupt Damon, although the tale of his meeting her wouldn't really help in the search. Sometimes what people want more than anything else is to tell their stories. Damon didn't have much time left for his.

When he came to a stopping place, I asked, "Did you get her full name?"

"Eventually. It took us about three days to get to names. Beatrice Elliot. Told her if she was named Elliot Beatrice, I'd probably like her better."

"You mentioned an accent? Can you place it?" I asked.

"Sounded like Katharine Hepburn. She said she was from Sharon, Connecticut."

I turned to Shannon. "Are you familiar with that area?" Maybe her being a Yankee would come in handy—not that I would tell her that.

"A bit. It's in the western part of the state, near the New York border."

"Good, that's helpful to know." I turned back to Damon. "What else about her? What did she do for work?"

"She was a travel writer, that's what she said. We didn't talk much about work. I got the impression she wasn't settled into a job—maybe hoping to be a travel writer, or maybe tired of it and moving on."

"So, she didn't mention any workplace? Or connections like magazines she'd written for?"

"None that I remember. I think I once asked about reading something of hers and she laughed it off, saying, 'You seriously don't want to wade through my speculation about the next year's best beaches for frat parties, do you?' And I had to admit that I didn't."

"What else? How did you spend the time together?"

"She was visiting here, so we spent a lot of time doing the usual things—driving out to the plantations, eating in various restaurants. I got to spout on about New Orleans, like how Frenchmen Street got its name. She enjoyed the bloody stories."

"How did Frenchmen Street get its name?" Shannon asked.

"From the hanged Frenchmen there," Damon answered. "Where the street meets the river, in those oaks in the neutral ground, one of the Spanish governors hanged several Frenchmen. But I don't guess my history lessons will help you find Beatrice." He gave her a wide smile, as if he'd love to sit and tell her all his stories.

"No, they won't, but thanks for sharing that one with me," Shannon said. "Have to love these quaint New Orleans traditions." She gave Damon a quick grin in return, clearly feeling what I was feeling—seduced by his charm and smile, the warmth in his eyes.

"We just killed a few Frenchmen, nothing as organized as the witch trials from your part of the country," I said. Then, to not give Shannon a chance to retort, I continued. "You don't by any chance have any of the letters she sent you?" I felt a pang of jealousy. I wanted Damon to give me a wide smile and direct eye contact, as if he wanted to tell me his stories.

"No, I don't. I threw them away. Guess I didn't want them around reminding me…reminding me I was an asshole. I guess I had enough sense even back then to feel like a shit. Panicked at the thought of a kid in my life. 'Come on, Junior, let's go with Daddy to his leather bar.' Couldn't see it."

"Can you remember anything about the return address? City? Could she have stayed down here?" I asked.

"I know I got a few postcards from her as she traveled. She stayed an extra week here in New Orleans, but she was meeting up with some friends in New York. So I got a few letters, different addresses, so they kind of blur. I know that sounds crazy. There was a month or two of those postcards, then the letter telling me she was pregnant. I hit the bottle a bit after she wrote—didn't want to consider what I'd done, either in being an almost-father or running away from it."

"No contact since that time?" I asked.

"No, she wrote me off. Can't blame her." Damon looked down, then right at me, as if needing to see what my judgment of him was.

"Do you think she wants to hear from you?" I asked softly.

"Can't blame her if she doesn't. But…she can tell me to fuck off. Or you, I guess," he added with a rueful grin. "This is my last chance. I do it now or I don't ever do it."

"I'm just a detective. I can't write happy endings," I said.

Damon nodded. This sick, dying man knew. He held my eyes, as if we were the only people in the room.

"Anything else? Anything else that might help us?" My voice was still soft and gentle.

"Nothing I can think of. I don't guess I've given you very much."

"Damon," Shannon asked, "did you get the idea that Sharon was her hometown? Or just the place she was living at the time?"

"Hard to tell," Damon answered.

Ambrose, the quiet lawyer, spoke up. "You're looking tired, Damon."

He's in love with Damon, I suddenly guessed. Something in the way the homely attorney gazed at Damon told me.

"I guess I am a bit," Damon admitted.

"I can take care of the business details," Ambrose said. "Why don't you go and lie down?"

"Thanks," Damon said. "And, Micky, Shannon, thank you. If you need anything more from me, please let me know." With that he slowly stood up and made his way into the house. Ambrose stood to help him, but Damon waved him off. It was a brief exchange, but it seemed to me that it resonated with unspoken needs—Damon's to not need help until he had no choice; Ambrose's to be close to Damon, to claim what touch he could, even if all he would get was helping a sick man.

Ambrose remained standing as Damon walked in, as if he needed to watch over him, to take care of him. Only after Damon was safely indoors did he speak. "You did bring the contract, didn't you?" He sat back down.

I had, and we went over the business details. Ambrose wrote us a check for five days, plus an advance against expenses. His expression remained perfectly calm when I pointed out that we might have to travel around the country to find this woman. That taken care of, he led us out. I promised I would call Damon in a few days and give a progress report, even if there was no progress to report. Damon wasn't interested in the minutiae, just the final result.

Then Shannon and I were back out on the street. "So, what did I miss?" I queried her.

"He didn't give us a lot to go on."

"Well, it is nice when they cough up birthday, Social Security number, inseam measurement, and address, but if they have that, they usually don't need a private detective."

"Brilliant point. So, brilliant-pointed one, where do we go from here?"

"Back to my office. I want to check out Damon. Make sure he's for real."

"Can't you just make sure the check clears the bank?" Shannon said as we got into my car.

"Damon is a charming, charismatic man. Even as sick as he is, he could still probably sell heaters that only worked in the summer. Nothing intrusive, but it might be safer to know if there's more here than appears to be. What if he's looking to find the kid to kill him/her/it off and avoid messy inheritance problems?" I zoomed through a corner to avoid getting stuck behind a horse-drawn tourist carriage.

"You think like you drive," Shannon muttered. "Fast and loose."

"Then I'll leave the slow and tight thinking to you." I maneuvered around a few walking tourists who seemed to believe that a historic district like the French Quarter wouldn't have anything as modern as cars. After getting us safely out of there, I said, "We can also try the quick and easy, and this is where you might actually be useful."

"Do tell."

"Take that upper-class Yankee accent of yours and call up directory assistance, or whatever you call it up there, and see if you can get an address for Beatrice Elliot in Connecticut."

"It's maritime."

"What?"

"My accent. It's a working-class accent. My grandfather was a fisherman. I realize you're probably too invested in that war we fought over a hundred years ago to know the difference, but you can always start to learn the basics."

"Thank you for the education. Bright and early Monday, you also get to scout around city hall and the courthouses to make sure Damon actually owns the property he says he owns."

"And what will you be doing, besides sitting in your office and drinking all the coffee?"

"Other than the major work of keeping you out of trouble and into actually earning your keep, I'll be chatting up my French Quarter bar buddies. Seeing if any of them remember this woman. Not likely, but I can also ask them about Damon. Don't worry. I earn my keep, also." With that I pulled up in front of my office.

"Do I get a few bus tokens out of the expense advance or do you expect me to walk everywhere?"

I got out of my car and looked at Shannon over the roof. "Can you drive a stick?"

"Can I? Of course. My working-class family didn't get an automatic until I was in college."

I worked two keys off my key ring and tossed them to her. Shannon grabbed them both, one-handed, no less. "See that lime green Datsun?"

She looked across the street at the car I was pointing to. Then she looked back at me. "You can't tell me that piece of junk will make it around the block."

"It's always got me where I've wanted to go. And should you forget that this is a town full of drunken tourists, it has enough scratches and dents in it that adding a few more won't matter."

Shannon gave me one last look, then muttered, "If detecting means no coffee and driving lime green junk heaps, it's back to tabloid reporting for me."

I turned and headed into my office. I wouldn't give her the satisfaction of watching me watch her. As I opened my door, I did hear a strangled curse, then the noisy roar of my old car starting. Shannon Wild, girl detective, in her roadster.

CHAPTER FIVE

When the phone rings brutally early on a Sunday morning it's for Cordelia, so I automatically passed it over to her. I had just started to roll over and go back to sleep when she handed it back to me.

"Good morning," Shannon Wild brightly greeted me.

"Did I mention how much I hate morning people?" I muttered into the phone.

"Especially Yankees who have not only tuned the engine of that junk auto of yours—can't have the perps hear me roaring down the street—but who have also done an Internet search of possible Beatrice Elliots in the northwestern Connecticut area."

"And you got way lucky, found her, and had to call me before the crack of lark fart to let me know." That would really ruin my Sunday morning.

"Alas, not. I did find out that if she was ever there, she's not there now. That took a bit of doing, as Elliot is a somewhat common name in that part of the world. I talked to over ten Elliots yesterday, and one vaguely thought she might have had a cousin named Beatrice."

"And you called me this morning to tell me you called ten people yesterday?"

"Aren't you proud of me?"she said in a voice so cheerful, it had to be deliberately sadistic. "No, I called because yesterday I also e-mailed my journo friends and asked if they'd ever heard of a travel writer by the name of Beatrice Elliot, that she might have written about New Orleans. One of them e-mailed me back and said he thought she might have written something for the rag he works on. He was going to go through the records and see what he could dig up."

I was awake enough to stop myself from letting out the "fuck you" that I was thinking. I was going to be majorly pissed if this blond, Yankee amateur found Beatrice within forty-eight hours. "Good work," I rasped. "When do you think you might have something?"

"Depends on how quickly Chuck does his digging. A day or two."

"Wonderful. Shannon, be a good girl and take the rest of Sunday off. Or at least don't call me." I started to put the phone down, but couldn't resist an offstage mutter, "Those legs had better still be spread," before the receiver quite hit the base. It seemed a fair return for having had to watch Shannon's hand on Lauren's breast.

Luckily for me, Cordelia had fallen back asleep and didn't hear my intimation that we were lustily doing it when Shannon phoned. She might have labeled it childish, and my Sunday morning was already ruined enough without that—especially as she would have been right. Damn Shannon's butt, I thought as I glanced again at the time. The best way to annoy her back was to make her look like a sluggard on the case. I let Cordelia sleep a bit longer as I headed into the kitchen to see if there was anything I could throw together that might qualify as brunch. Breakfast in bed was the easiest way for me to tell her I'd be working today.

As I had hoped, the freshly ground and brewed coffee, cheese-and-mushroom omelet, and sliced melon were my ticket out the door. Cordelia took it as a given that I had to work today, never once suspecting that I was choosing to be on the mean streets instead of cuddling with her.

Okay, we solve this case, I prove whatever point I'm trying to prove to Shannon and then get back to my life, I bargained. My first stop was a coffee shop in the Marigny, a few blocks out of the Quarter. Time to catch up on some cousin gossip. Fate was kind to my obsession. Torbin was there and he was, unnaturally, sitting alone. My cousin Torbin is tall, blond, blue-eyed, and we probably would have hated each other if he'd chosen football and sports cars over mascara and high heels. Instead we'd banded together as the lavender sheep of the family. Today he was sedately dressed in cut-off jeans, an AIDS Walk T-shirt, and what he would call dyke sandals—practical and comfortable.

"Hey, big boy, can I buy you a cup of something strong?" I called out to him.

"What? Not home nesting like a good lesbian? A cup of the Jamaican would be lovely. Especially if I have to listen to your side of the argument that's got you out of the house by yourself on such a beautiful day."

I bought two cups of the Jamaican before settling myself at Torbin's table. "All is bliss at our house. My darling love is right now luxuriating in a scented bath after having had breakfast in bed cooked by my own loving hands."

"Bliss? So, why aren't you in the bathtub with her?"

"The call of work. Besides, she needs a few hours to recover from last night." Not giving Torbin time to respond to that, I said, "What do you know about Damon LaChance?"

"Party-boy Damon?"

"Sounds like the one."

"What don't I know," Torbin said, in his element. "Owns four bars in the Quarter, everyone predicted that all his profits would go up his nose or at least into his drinking glasses, but he proved them wrong. His parties are legendary."

"Do you go to them?"

"Some. But too, too much for me. As you well know, I'm not a prude, but if it could be ingested, snorted, or injected, someone was doing it somewhere at his parties. His booze was good, but not good enough to risk spending some vacation time in jail."

"Was he ever caught, that you know of?"

"No. Probably had everything paid off properly. Or had pictures of enough people in high places doing low things."

"Tell me about the parties you did go to."

"At the first one, someone said, 'Look what the cat dragged in, a drag queen.' I was about to turn around and leave—too A Gay for me—when Damon came up and put his arm around my shoulder and said, 'I caught your show last week. And, damn, I needed that. You had me laughing my ass off in the first minute.' The way he said it, the way he looked at me made me believe he really meant it. He took me around and introduced me to everyone. It's so intangible, but that was his genius. He just knew how to make sure everyone else was having as much fun as he was.

"I did some shows at his bars and one night it was miserable. The audience was small, mostly tourists who didn't know what to make of us, or they'd been snowed-in in Wisconsin so long they forgot how to laugh. A gang of straight boys came in, clearly looking to hassle the queers, and they started heckling me. 'Hey, faggot, I got a knife. I can make you a real girl real quick.' Of course I had the mike, so I gave it back. 'So you want to cut me down to your size?' They didn't like that. They got really nasty and threatening, saying they'd be waiting for me. One of them jumped up on the stage and tried to grab the mike.

"Suddenly just about every security guard from every bar Damon owned surrounded those guys. Damon jumped up onstage with us, twisted the punk's arm behind his back. He took the kid's wallet and read his name and address off his driver's license. Then he said, 'If anyone gets hurt anywhere in the Quarter tonight, I'm calling the cops and giving them this information. And you better hope they get there before we do.' He let go of the kid and shoved him offstage and one of the biggest security guards caught him. Then the guards grabbed all of them, one or two guards holding each punk, while another took their pants off. That scared the shit out of them. One even peed himself. Then the guards gave them whatever was in their pockets—wallets, keys, used tissues—threw their pants in the trash, and marched them out of the bar. They got to go home in their underwear." Torbin laughed at the memory and took a sip of his coffee.

"Nothing like Bourbon Street justice," I said.

"Damon came back to my dressing alcove, carrying a bottle of top-shelf Scotch. Poured us each a glass. He asked a few questions, but mostly he listened, let me get it out—being scared, angry—until we both got to laughing at the picture of those four straight boys wandering around the Quarter in their ratty Jockeys. He said he did it because he thought that after being humiliated like that, they would feel they had to beat up someone just to prove something. But if they were in their skivvies they'd be a lot less likely to hang around.

"When he got up to leave, he told me to keep the bottle. Two of the guards were waiting for me and they walked me home."

"He was kind and thoughtful."

"My knight in brown suede. Damon always seemed to be one of those lucky ones, right time, right place. Until now, of course."

"You know he's ill?"

"He's being quiet about it, but even without the rumors, just his absence would tell anyone looking that something is going on."

"Did you ever see him with this woman?" I showed Torbin the picture of Beatrice Elliot.

"Ah, Beatrice," he said. "I don't recall seeing them together. Why?"

"You knew Beatrice Elliot?" I almost slopped coffee down my nice white shirt at his announcement.

"Just as Beatrice. We ended up one night sitting next to each other in a bar and did the whole life-story thing. Strangers in the night. I didn't know her last name and never saw her again, but she…just made an impression. Together and tough, but open and vulnerable."

"She and Damon had an affair."

"What? Damon slept with a woman? I'd need proof beyond a reasonable doubt before I'd believe that." Now it was Torbin's turn to almost have to mop up his sloshed coffee.

"According to Damon, proof exists and should be about six or seven years old right now."

"I've heard that Damon was a daddy, but I never thought he was that kind of daddy. Where's the kid now?" Torbin carefully set his coffee cup down, shaking his head incredulously.

"That's my job. To see if there really is a child and to locate her or him before Damon goes to the big party on the other side."

"So, how can I help? I'm trying to remember what Beatrice told me, but we talked more about growing up and being different. Me gay and she wanting to travel the world, escape the life of a proper career and house a few blocks away from the parents."

"I'm doing the background fishing right now. I'd like to know some more about Damon. If you can tell me anything about Beatrice, that's a bonus. First, do you think it's possible any of this is true?"

"With Damon, anything is possible." He wrapped his hands around the coffee cup as if to make sure it wouldn't tip over on its own from what it was hearing. "I wouldn't be surprised if he kept eunuchs in the basement. The more I think about it, the more I think, yeah, might be. Damon is wonderfully charming and someone who'd do anything once. Even have sex with a woman. What'll happen to the terms of his will, if you find the kid?"

"Why do you ask?"

"With Damon ill, more than a few people are making plans about what to do with what they're expecting to get. I suspect some of them will be unpleasantly surprised to find another heir suddenly appear."

"Tell me what you know."

"A caution." He leaned and lowered his voice. "You know you can tell your cousin Tor anything, but I'd be closed-mouthed about your kiddy hunt."

"I intend to be anyway, but tell me why."

"First, Bruce Payne—his real name—is the manager of The Outer Limit, Damon's bar in the lower Quarter. He's counting very heavily on inheriting it, for reasons both legal and illegal."

"Give me the illegal first," I said, flashing him a quick grin to let him know how much I appreciated his gossip talents.

"Drugs, of course. Damon is smart enough to not let dealers hang in his bars, but Bruce is skirting that because he gets a big cut. No bar, no cut. Legal is that he owes a bit to the casinos over on the coast and is using the assumed impending ownership of the bar as a way to keep the hot breath of bankruptcy off his neck."

"Okay, who else?"

"Crescent City Care Coalition. Damon is leaving them a nice bequest. Gossip in the streets has it the board consists of three friends of the chair, none of whom can add, and they hired a supposedly hotshot out-of-towner for the top slot at a big-buck salary. Rumor is his leaving California was more about nose candy than a career challenge. The only way they'll end up in the black is if Damon dies before the fiscal year ends."

"So if he keels over at the next AIDS fund-raiser, we'll know they did it."

"Also, Perry Thompson, Damon's most recent boy toy. Major uptown A-list gay. Chiseled good looks, real pretty boy, very good at impressing the 'right' people. But I'd hate to be his maid. Major asshole if he doesn't think you rate. I have to suspect that Damon has told him he can expect something, just to make him stop asking for money all the time. Perry is very good at keeping Damon happy, I'll have to admit. It's been Damon's deep pockets that have allowed Perry to live in the style that he thinks befits him. If Damon cuts him out or even down, he might have to settle for domestic champagne, and that would make Perry very unhappy."

I stated the obvious. "You don't like Perry much, do you?"

"Perry hates women, drag queens like moi, gays that are too 'out,' and anyone who doesn't want to go to the best parties and wear designer-label clothes. I know it's a long shot, but if you find the kid and could arrange for me to be there when Perry-boy finds out, I'd love it."

"If I have my way, Perry-boy will find out long after the ink is dry on Damon's new will."

"Ambrose is another one," Torbin said.

I was surprised. "He knows about Damon hiring us to look for the kid. He was there."

"Pompous idiot. He loves Damon, you know. Broke up with his last boyfriend over his always being at Damon's beck and call. He's set to run the Damon LaChance Foundation. Unless the money ends up with the kid." Torbin sighed. "If he wasn't such an A Gay wannabe, I'd almost feel sorry for him. He has to do Damon's bidding, something I doubt Ambrose wants to do. He's one of those closet queens who wants gay men to resemble the Marlboro Man and lesbians to look like hookers at the Dinah Shore golf thing."

"In other words you don't like him," I said.

"He doesn't like me or people like me. No gender-bending allowed in his little world. Although I have to admit that he's desperate to please Damon, so of course he'll do anything he can to further whatever Damon wishes, even if it means adding a few more people between him and Damon."

"But no matter what happens, he won't have Damon much longer."

"Is Damon really that sick? No one's saying anything."

I looked down at my cup for a moment. I knew I could trust Torbin. "Maybe six months is what they're guessing."

"The new drugs aren't helping him? He can certainly afford the best care."

"Not AIDS."

"Hepatitis C," Torbin correctly guessed. "That's all we need. Another damn epidemic."

We were silent. Then I said softly, "He also wants me to find Beatrice to tell her she needs to get tested." I knew this would not go beyond us, only the two cooling cups of Jamaican to hear.

"Then you do need to find her."

"Think for a bit. If you can remember anything more about her, you know where to call."

Then Torbin and I talked of other things besides dying and diseases and lost children. I bought him another cup of Jamaican before I left.

CHAPTER SIX

Instead of acting like it really was a Sunday and I had a lover at home waiting—well, probably not literally, Cordelia was grown up enough to entertain herself—I headed to my office.

Always do the quick and easy first. I did two Internet searches, one for Beatrice Elliot and one for Damon LaChance. As a number of years had passed and she wasn't local, I doubted that I'd find Beatrice with the quick and easy. But I'd feel really stupid if I bypassed the obvious and went right to the hard and complicated, only to find that quick and easy would have worked just as well.

Damon had a fair number of hits, mostly of his name in various news articles about the Quarter. As Shannon had so astutely pointed out, Elliot was a common name, so I had to scroll through a number of listings to find anything that might be useful, and it wasn't much. There was a link to a short article on New Orleans in a liquor-industry trade magazine with Beatrice Elliot as its author. The article was several years old, no info was listed about the author, and the article itself had apparently been edited to death, with only sentences that referred to alcohol left in. "It's a city of booze, twenty-four hours a day of it, with hundreds of bars concentrated in the French Quarter alone. Hurricanes and hand grenades are some of the drinks marketed to the throngs on the aptly named Bourbon Street, although the name came from French royalty, not liquor" was her opening. From there it jumped to, "After the swamp tour, a stroll down Bourbon Street and into any one of the numerous daiquiri shops is a perfect way to cool down from alligator watching."

I didn't bother to read the rest of it, but printed out a copy because

I'm a thorough detective. And I wanted to show it to Shannon so she could see what the professionals do. I started to print a copy of the search results. Most were probably less than useless. If we really struck out, I'd send Shannon down the list, but I wasn't quite at that cynical level yet.

I sat staring at the computer screen and its less-than-revealing information. Sometimes too much information is worse than none at all. Then I thought of some legal questions and called the one lawyer I could call, without it costing me big bucks, on a Sunday afternoon.

"She's in the middle of the sports section, I'm not sure I should interrupt her," Elly responded to my request. The "she" in question was her partner, Danielle Clayton, one of my closest friends. We'd been lovers for a summer, but that was a long time ago when I was too young and scared to believe that anyone could really love me. I slept around on her, made sure she knew, acted about as unlovable as I could, so when she left me, I could claim reasons other than I just wasn't good enough. Somehow Danny managed to forgive me and even offer friendship.

"Forced heirship?" she responded to my question. "Mick, did you ever notice that I practice criminal law?"

"Yes, Danny dear, I have, but I thought you might be brilliant enough to know some things about other areas of law."

"You can't cut your kids out of the will. That's about all I know." I left a silence, knowing that Danny would most likely fill it with other things she knew. "They did make some changes in the law, even briefly got rid of it sometime in the mid-nineties, then reinstated it. Without a will, a spouse can get nothing. Even with a will, you can't disinherit a kid until they're twenty-four, or at all if they're disabled. One kid gets at least twenty-five percent, and two or more get at least fifty. Why? Is Cordelia thinking of having a baby and you want to know what that'll cost you?"

"No, not quite." Danny and Elly were seriously considering having children and wanted some co-conspirators, or at least people they could swap babysitting with. Cordelia would be a great mother. I might pass as an okay aunt. To forestall any further domestic talk, I said, "It might play into a case I'm working on. Just wanted to know the legal ground I could be treading on. Now you can go back to reading about the Saints' latest losing game."

"Cynic. It's not even football season yet. And this could be their winning year," Danny said, loud enough to make sure I heard it as I put down the phone.

I mused that Ambrose was a good enough lawyer that Damon LaChance had to know how he was changing his estate by seeking out a possible child. Louisiana, unlike the other forty-nine states, operates under Napoleonic code, not common law. Most of the time it's fairly similar—murder is still murder, theft is theft—but every once in a while, we just go our own French-influenced direction.

Damon's will wasn't much my concern. My job was to find the child, but it would be interesting to see the looks on the faces of all the other people waiting for Damon to die when they found out that Mr. Gay Party Boy had a kid and that kid would get a big chunk of his estate.

I returned to what I should really be working on, finding Beatrice Elliot and any child their liaison had produced. My first task was to send off a detailed e-mail to Sarah Clavish. At the improbable age of sixty-two, she had discovered computers and the Internet and was remarkably good at ferreting out all kinds of information. I often used her as a consultant, as she had both the knowledge and the patience that I lacked for these kinds of searches.

Beatrice Elliot would most likely be a challenge to find. She might have married and now had another name. She wasn't from around here, and she seemed like the type who wouldn't end up back close to her hometown. If she had pursued a career as a travel writer, she could even be living out of the country. Still, Damon had a deep checkbook, and with enough money and time anyone could be found.

After sending the e-mail I left my office and started to head home, but instead swung by The Outer Limits, the bar that Torbin had mentioned. Fate obviously meant for me to do this as I found a parking space only a few doors down.

It was Sunday afternoon sports time and the bar was pretty full, mostly men, but a few women. What was I doing here, I wondered as the good-looking, dimpled bartender came over to me. "Draft," I said, deciding that ordering water would be too conspicuous. He was a young guy, not at all my image of Bruce Payne.

In a few minutes I was proven right, as an older man, someone I gauged to be around Damon's age, joined him behind the bar. He had the look of a man who'd seen too many late nights over the rim of a shot glass. His beard could have used a trim and his waist needed a few months of serious sit-ups, though a less tight pair of jeans would have made that not so obvious. His hair was brown, going to gray, and still in the shaggy style of his youth. It only made him look older. He helped himself to the top-shelf bourbon, then lit a cigarette and flicked the ashes onto the floor.

I glanced down at my beer. Just as well it was a prop. Bruce's style of management was obviously the loose variety. I doubted he was keeping a tab on his drinking and deducting it from his paycheck. I was betting he was fudging on some other bills, like having the hot water only lukewarm, to make sure the books more or less balanced. Admittedly I wasn't a disinterested patron, but I'd only been in the place half an hour and I'd noticed that he was raiding the good liquor, coming close to sexually harassing the cute young bartender every time he passed behind him in the bar, and certainly violating some health codes, if not common sense, with his smoking habits. He'd just put down a cigarette far too close to a stack of napkins to be safe or sane.

Then I spotted it in the back corner, the quick exchange of a small plastic bag for a wad of cash. That can happen in any bar, any street corner, or just about any place. The seller had sauntered around the bar for a while, pretending to watch the game. He took a long slow meander, finally ending up near the place where Bruce left his last cigarette. They spoke a few words, and then Bruce leaned in to light his cigarette. The drug dealer put his hand on Bruce's as if this were merely a flirtatious routine, but I saw the money being passed as they did it. They seemed to be more playing a game than making any real attempt at hiding what they were doing. Sure, most bar patrons wouldn't notice. They were more focused on watching the game or drinking their beer. But it wasn't barflies they needed to worry about fooling. It was people like me who knew what to watch for, especially the ones who carried a badge, or the ones who wanted to make this their territory.

Bruce Payne was sloppy and he was stupid. I left my untouched beer where it was and exited the bar. I took a walk around the block to let my clothes air out from the smell of smoke and spilled beer—even sweat and humidity was better than that—before returning to my car.

This kind of stupidity shouldn't be rewarded, I thought as I headed home. I debated telling Ambrose and letting him decide whether to tell Damon. I would be more than glad to find the kid that would make Bruce have to get a real job.

CHAPTER SEVEN

One advantage of Cordelia's doctor hours is that she didn't see me up and about earlier than normal on a Monday morning, a sign of the level my butch-pissing contest with Shannon had sunk to. I would be there before her and again make sure I had a half-empty coffee cup on my desk. I got there at eight thirty. On a usual day, I roll in at ten-ish. It suddenly occurred to me that this was so unusual Cordelia might well suspect me of having an affair with Shannon. I wondered if she and Dr. Lauren had also discussed the monogamy question—and if the good doctor had mentioned that Shannon didn't believe in it.

My musing on monogamy was interrupted by the telephone.

"M. Knight Private Investigations," I answered.

"Hello, didn't think I'd catch you in this early," Damon LaChance said. "Was just planning to leave a message."

"Good morning," I said, trying to sound like I really was up and awake. "Now that you have caught a real, live person instead of a machine, what can I do for you?"

"Had a rough night last night, I just couldn't sleep. So I started prowling around and ended up in the attic. All the little talismans of a life. Mardi Gras beads I thought were special at the time, posters from events at my bars, clothes I haven't worn in so long I'm not sure if they're mine or someone just left them here. Not that any of this matters to you. But I uncovered a box of old letters and photographs. Seems I did keep some things from Beatrice. There's one great picture of her standing with the river behind her, the sun in her hair, a perfect smile on her face. If you find her, can you give her that picture? She can rip it up, but maybe she'll keep it and a few good memories with it."

"If I do, I will give her the picture," I promised.

"And you might be interested in some of the letters and postcards I found, too. Not sure if there's much to help you—"

"But I'll have to see them to know. Besides, sometimes it's hard to know what will help."

"Okay, great." He sounded almost relieved, like he wanted these scraps of paper to matter to someone as much as they now mattered to him. "I'm meeting with Ambrose this morning to talk about some things." Damon paused, then continued. "He's pointed out to me that finding a long-lost kid is going to change a few things—and piss off a few people."

"How do you feel about pissing off those people?" I kept my voice easy and neutral.

"Fuck 'em," Damon said. Then he added, "I don't know. I've known a lot of them a long time, but now it feels like that's all there is, just years of seeing them around."

"Having people around who've been through things with you can be important."

"But they haven't been through things with me. They were just in the vicinity. I've slept with some of them, but I wouldn't tell them my secrets. I can talk to you more about Beatrice and maybe having a kid than any of them."

He paused again, but I didn't fill the silence.

"Or tell them that I'm scared. I'm scared to die and there's not a fucking thing I can do about it," he said, his voice a harsh whisper.

I answered, my voice soft to match his. "No, you can't stop dying, but you can find your child, find Beatrice, maybe mend a few broken places."

"And squeak into heaven, right?" he said, his voice sardonic.

"Maybe, at least move up a few circles in hell." I matched his sardonic tone.

"Will it matter?" he asked, as if he had to know.

"Damon, I'm just a private detective. I might be able to find a child, but I can't find the path to heaven or hell for you."

"But you at least talk to me about it. And your answers are honest. That's what I remember now about Beatrice, and what I forgot when I got scared—she was fun and she was honest and I didn't have to be Damon, party boy, every minute with her."

"Damon, I don't even talk much. I just listen."

"And it's six months to death and I finally realize how important that is. If I didn't have money, I wonder if any of them would even bother with me."

I didn't point out that he had hired me and was paying me money. Maybe because he somehow knew I'd probably look for a dying man's child for nothing if that was what it came to. And that listening to him now wasn't part of what I did as a private investigator, just what I did as a person.

"Kind of a big return on that handkerchief favor, isn't it?" he asked.

He remembered me. I didn't know if I was pleased or discomfited. It hadn't been my best moment. "No, I needed a handkerchief then, you need a detective now. We offer what we can." We were both silent, then I asked, "What do you think they'll do if they find out things have changed?"

"What can they do? Kill a dying man? Make sure I don't get invited to the best parties in hell?"

"Not come by and visit, leave you alone as you die."

"You know, I don't think I'd really notice."

"Then you might as well piss them off and do what you think is right."

He laughed. Then he laughed again and said, "Maybe dying can be fun after all. I can just picture their greedy faces when they see I've changed my will. One big, final shit stir before I head off to the cosmos."

"What about Ambrose?" I asked.

"Ambrose? If I want it, he'll do it. Except see me as anything other than some god he wants a perfect love from. Sometimes I think the best thing I could do for him is to throw him out and tell him to get his own life and stop living in the shadow of mine."

"Will you do that?"

He paused again. "I don't know. I've let him become useful, and he's taking care of a lot of things I don't have the time and energy for now."

"And," I pointed out, "you are leaving him soon, no matter what happens."

"But I'm leaving his fantasy intact—dying won't change that. He'll probably find it easier to live his life for me after I'm dead."

"He can make you whatever he wants you to be."

"Exactly. He'll be the keeper of the flame. 'Damon would have wanted this' or 'Damon would do that,' without me there to point out that he's just doing what Ambrose wants to do. Like this whole kid thing. Ambrose wants the past to be past."

"Beatrice and the child are competition for your attention."

"I didn't even think about it like that. More that everything is set. Ambrose gets to be my executor, and suddenly all those men who passed him by while they were hanging around me will have to be calling him, knocking on his door. He'll get invites to all the events because he controls the estate."

"He gets all the power. And maybe he thinks that's the real difference between the two of you."

"He becomes me." Damon sighed, then said, "And here I am, giving it to him and I realize what a crock it is. I'd have been better off if I'd done the right thing all those years ago. Not to imply that I'd have straightened up and married her, but just paid attention to something more than the next party."

"But Ambrose will never be you, and he'll learn that in a very hard way. I don't know you well, Damon, but you're an open, vibrant man, and that's something Ambrose will never be. It's not just money."

"He'll be here in a bit. I need to decide what to do. Can you drop by this afternoon? I'll give you the stuff I found and let you in on the shit that I've stirred."

I agreed to show up around two, and just as I was putting the phone down, Shannon came in the door.

"Only a fourth of the cup gone," she said with a look into my coffee cup. "Is there any chance I can have some before we must be on the road again?"

"I've been on the phone. Otherwise I'd be on my third cup by now."

Shannon didn't wait for my permission to head for the coffee. She poured herself a generous cup, rummaged in the half-size refrigerator for milk, and was even suspicious, or prudent, enough to sniff it before pouring it into her cup. She then added two packs of sugar.

I suppressed a sigh. What the hell was I going to do with her? The right thing, a little voice in my head told me. I had, I must admit, considered coming up with something truly vile, like doing a tedious stakeout in places where they still fly Confederate flags, or hunting in a garbage dump for some lost papers. But I had no cases that required that kind of effort, and I couldn't bring myself to make one up.

Damon and his quest was the big thing right now. I had other clients, but most of that work was along the lines of randomly dropping by their place of business and observing what was taking place. I'd done those rounds last week. And it didn't sound much like a true test to send Shannon off to sit in a bar or restaurant and try and see if the employees were playing loose with the cash. That left giving her some busywork—but Shannon was smart enough to catch on to that—or finding something she could do, that I could trust her to do that would help the case. Nothing brilliant came to mind.

Shannon sat down, leaning back with her ankle crossed over her knee. "Okay, Boss Mick, what do we do now?"

"What we do now is for you to not call me Boss Mick."

"Boss Ms. Knight?" Her voice was just on the edge of being mocking.

"So your name is Shannon 'Stepping in the Shit' Wild," I retorted, all too easily letting her get under my skin.

"No, actually it's Katherine. Shannon Katherine Wild."

"Nice Irish girl, huh?"

"A bit of a mix really. My mother just liked the name. Yours?"

"Yours what?" I said, to just not answer the question I knew she was asking.

"What is your middle name?" she enunciated very clearly.

Just answer it, I decided, stop playing games. "Antigone. My mother was Greek."

"Ah, that explains your olive skin. I assumed it was from that quaint old Southern tradition known as slave rape." Even more annoying, she calmly sipped her coffee as she said it.

So much for not playing games. It was time to load and lock. "And I'm sure none of the fine gentlemen of the Northeast ever laid a finger on your 'No Irish Need Apply' ancestors. Brief history lesson, Young Shannon. My mother was the daughter of Greek immigrants who came here after the Second World War. If they owned slaves it was during the times of Caesar. More likely they were the slaves. My father was Cajun, from the dirt-poor French who ended up fishing and hunting in the bayous. No slaves there either. If you want to be an obnoxious Yankee bitch and play these games, go to a bar out in the white-flight suburbs, but keep it the fuck out of my office." I glared at her.

She sipped her coffee, but with not quite the assurance she had a moment ago. Finally, she said, "I bet our lovers aren't going at it like this."

"That's a safe bet."

"I don't like being patronized."

"I'm not patronizing you."

"But you are. So is Lauren. Let's park Little Shannon somewhere that'll keep her busy and out of the way."

"Wasn't my idea," I said shortly.

"But you're doing the dirty work."

"With your consent," I reminded her. "You could have picked up the phone this morning and said, 'Hey, I'd rather do plantation tours,' instead of coming in."

She took several long sips of her coffee, her outward cool betrayed by the jiggling of her ankle. "Yeah, I guess I could have."

"But you didn't, Blanche, you didn't."

A puzzled look crossed her face, then she said, "Oh, queer-movie reference, I get it. Do you want me to leave?"

"Do you want to leave?"

"Guess if I really did, I wouldn't have come here," she said slowly.

I looked at her. "Okay, you get one smart-ass Yankee crack per day."

"Same rule applies? You get one smart-ass Big Easy crack per day?"

"Fair enough, but retaliation doesn't count. Some of what you've learned as a journalist might apply, a lot won't. Do what I tell you to do. If you have an idea, you pass it by me first. Fair?"

"Fair enough. So how do we locate this kid?" She leaned forward and uncrossed her leg, putting both feet on the floor.

"Damon did find some of her letters and I'm...we're to go meet him at two this afternoon. It doesn't sound like they'll help much, no guarantee of any address or anyone remotely close to where she actually lived. Nothing really concrete like a Social Security number. Beatrice seemed to be a wanderer, so if she moved around a lot it'll be even harder to find her."

"But no reason to suspect that she's hiding or trying to conceal her whereabouts."

"No. It'd be helpful if we knew for certain if she had the baby. She'd probably go someplace she had some connection to for the birth. Not likely she'd go to a brand-new city for that. We do know about the time she'd have had the child. We could search birth records in those locations."

Shannon flashed me a smile. "You do know what you're doing, don't you?"

"Naw, I just fake it very well."

"Where should I start?"

"I'm going to send you down a side road, one prompted by my curiosity. And instincts. By the way, Damon's rethinking paying for the party boys to keep partying after he's gone."

"Leave it all to the child and mother?"

"Maybe, but I got the feeling more that he's looking at who was just there for the good times—and he had a lot of them—and who was there for the right reasons."

"So, where are your curiosity and instincts sending me?"

"These are some of the names of people who might be affected by Damon's change in affections. Get me the basics on them. Name, rank, and serial number." I handed her the list of names I had gotten from Torbin. Bruce Payne, Perry Thompson, Crescent City Care Coalition.

"Basic background, right? Especially things like criminal records, any kind of legal trouble, debt?"

"Exactly. Damon hinted that he might be stirring some shit."

"And is he talking mouse turds or elephant manure?" She stood up and put her coffee cup down. "Would you care if I do it here or at my place? I've got a lot of bookmarked search sites on my computer there."

"Makes sense. Meet me back here at one thirty if you want to go along to talk to Damon."

"I'll see you then." She washed her coffee cup before she left.

CHAPTER EIGHT

Shannon returned at one twenty-five, carrying a laptop under her arm. Bundled with it, she had a stack of printed pages. "The Internet is a wonderful thing," she said as she made room for her pile on my "file by pile" table in the corner.

"Anything really interesting?"

"Probably nothing that your sources haven't already told you, but it's useful to have rumors backed up by facts. Some party-hearty boys on the list. Bruce Payne has two DUIs. And those are the ones on the record. I'm guessing one or two have been expunged. One drug arrest, but the charges were dropped. Perry Thompson prefers a higher class of nefarious activity, keeps his collar white. He was let go from an antiques shop after a putative misunderstanding about his sales commission—and I'm guessing restitution."

"Misunderstanding?"

"Seems he thought if he sold one, he got one."

"Ah. Such a common misunderstanding."

"Crescent City Care Coalition doesn't seem much of a coalition. In fact they have a list of only five board members, one who must not make it to too many board meetings as he died two years ago. The executive director and his financial assistant have been using the company credit card to help them through times when the city has been slow to reimburse their grant money."

"You've got good sources." Financial info like this isn't supposed to be in the public record like criminal charges or driver's license.

"I had a flash of your curiosity—or intuition. A supposed coalition that seems to have little connection to other agencies, a token board.

Hints at little oversight. So I called in a favor of an ex who works in the financial industry."

"Any evidence they didn't pay it back?"

"I got a list of charges. Two trips to the casinos over on the Gulf Coast. Several car rentals, only one during the week. The rest were weekend. The outstanding balance is still pretty high. I posed as a journo from big, bad New York City, doing a piece on how AIDS is affecting places around the country. I have an appointment with the executive director on Wednesday."

I was impressed. I'd have to look through everything she had, but it sounded like Shannon had done a job and a half. What I'd asked her to do, but also digging a little deeper in the places that seemed suspicious. "Good sleuthing, although it may have little to do with Damon and his quest."

"I know. But tripping over skullduggery gets my adrenaline going. I'll do the interview on my own time. Might be able to turn it into a freelance piece or just use it as background info for something else."

"That is one place you can be useful. I know too many people in this town, especially the gay community, to risk pretending to be doing something like that."

"But they don't know my face. And even if they do look, I check out to be what I say I am."

I tucked that possibility away for later and said, "Shall we go see Damon?"

Just as I was crossing Esplanade into the Quarter, she asked, "If you do find Beatrice Elliot, what will you do?"

"What I've been hired to do. Tell her that Damon is ill and dying and wanted to do what he can to mend what he broke."

"If she slams the door in your face?"

"I'll let you knock on the door." I continued, "Keep my nose out of the way and tell Damon the ending wasn't a happy one."

"What do you think will happen?"

"As the great philosopher Doris Day said, '*Que sera, sera.*'"

Either Shannon was appalled that I put *philosopher* and *Doris Day* in the same sentence or she had run out of questions. We were silent as we made our way to Damon's door. Just as we approached it, the door was flung open.

"You're fucking crazy, Damon!" shouted the man who had opened the door with such vehemence. He was a tall handsome man, but in a bland model way, like he spent hours trying to look like an airbrushed picture instead of a person. "It's a little late in life to turn into some fucking choirboy."

"I was certainly never a celibate choirboy," Damon said from the entryway.

"We were counting on you and now you're just playing with us. I was a fool for love."

"Cause a scene out here on the street and you might get cut out entirely, Perry, dear," Damon replied, his voice impatient. "And you've been a fool for many things besides love."

"Fuck you, Damon," he muttered under his breath, but that was his sole rebellion against the admonishment. Then Perry shoved his hands into his expensive linen jacket and stormed down the street, not even looking in our direction.

"Shit stirred, not shaken?" I inquired as I approached Damon on his doorstep.

"I'm sorry you had to witness that little scene," he said in a voice that implied he wasn't sorry at all.

"Best theater I've seen in a long time. The acting was worthy of a minor regional college stage," Shannon said.

Damon let out a roar of a laugh. "Come in. Who says lesbians aren't funny?"

We followed him down the hallway back to the inner courtyard. It was shaded with leafy banana trees and surrounded by a high brick fence. Several French doors were left open, the cool air-conditioning and shade making it comfortable outside in the August heat. Wicker furniture, faded from the sun, was arranged in several conversational groupings. Damon led us to the one with a love seat and several big comfortable chairs around a low coffee table. Ambrose was there, seated with his back to the door. He looked startled to see us as we came around and sat down. "Michele? I didn't think you were supposed to come by today."

"I called her this morning," Damon said, "and asked her to."

Ambrose let out an audible sigh. It would be so much easier for him when it became just the fantasy Damon. He polished his glasses before saying, "Sometimes it's better to let the past just be past—"

"And do better next lifetime, huh?" Damon interjected. "Sorry,

Ambrose, I know I'm not making things easy for you, but it's my life, my money, and maybe, finally, I need to really think about things instead of just what seems easy. If Kent Richards had said, 'Hey, Damon, instead of always giving me a line of cocaine, why don't you donate the money to CCCC,' they wouldn't be in a financial hole right now. They get half of what I was intending to leave them. They do serve some clients, and those are the people who will really get hurt if they go under, but NO/ AIDS Task Force gets the other part. They do good work. I've actually seen an audit from them, something Kent has promised for a long time but never produced, and I've never seen Noel, their director, with more than a can of beer in his hand, and it's always after work."

Ambrose said, "I have a draft of the changes, but I do think you should think about it."

"I've got two witnesses," Damon said with a nod toward Shannon and me. "I've thought about it all I need to."

Ambrose sighed again.

Damon didn't give him a chance to speak. "Perry gets a fourth of what he was expecting. Too bad if he'll have to get a real job or, horrors, shop at a mall. Bruce gets enough to pay off his gambling debts and get out of town, so he can manage bars in some place where people don't know he has a habit of drinking the profits away. Hell, Ambrose, you ought to be happy. The less for them, the less you have to deal with them." Then he added, "If I can't be a dad, at least I can leave my kid something."

"If there is a child, and if Michele and her assistant find that child," Ambrose said. "I believe you should wait until that happens before you put anything in your will." I might have imagined it, but he had a prim set to his mouth, as if children should be neither seen, heard, nor inherit in the gay world of the French Quarter. Ambrose also seemed to be experiencing a moment of cognitive dissonance. He clearly wanted to do what Damon asked and just as clearly didn't want to do what Damon was asking him to do now. He had a sheen of sweat across his face, a sign of the emotional struggle inside him.

"We'll find Beatrice Elliot and her child," I said. "It's just a matter of how long it takes."

"But you've got very little information," Ambrose said.

"We have enough. Especially if she gave birth to a child, she left a record," I answered.

Ambrose looked almost queasy at the thought of childbirth. He turned away from me as if I'd said nothing and spoke to Damon. "You look tired. Perhaps this can all wait until tomorrow."

Damon waved him off. "I don't feel tired. In fact, I feel jazzed up. Maybe I should disinherit someone every day."

"Damon, this is a serious matter. These are the people who love you that you're throwing away."

"They don't love me enough to clean up my shit when I can't make it to the toilet. Or see me in the hospital or listen to me if I'm not telling jokes or keeping it light and funny." Damon's face was flushed and he was angry. "Do you think that string of visitors would have come by today if you hadn't called them to say, 'Hey, hurry over and make nice or he'll cut you out of his will'?" The only one who hasn't made it is Uncle Raul, maybe because he lives near Breaux Bridge and he's still on the road."

"I didn't call your uncle," Ambrose said, in what I considered a good job of either ignoring or missing Damon's main point.

"Just as well, he hates to drive in the city." Damon sat back as if his sudden burst of anger had worn him out.

"You are tired, you really do need to lie down," Ambrose said, his voice insistent with concern.

"I will, but I need to give Micky and Shannon what I found. And I want to sign the new will." His face was flushed and he was starting to sweat.

"We can come back another time," I offered.

For an answer, Damon reached to the end table beside him and picked up a folder. "This is the stuff I told you about." He opened the folder and took out a picture. Shannon quickly stood, got it from him, and handed it to me.

It was the photo he had told me about and he was right. It was a vibrant picture. The sun was bright and clear, little haze or humidity; the long expanse of the river sparkled in the background. Beatrice had a smile on her face that said the world was perfect. At least in that brief second caught by the camera. She was more a handsome woman than a pretty one, her laughing eyes looking into the lens with an expression that was both seductive and strong. Her hair was a burnished auburn, glossy in the sunlight.

"She is stunning," I said as I passed the photo back to Shannon.

"Give that to her if you find her," Damon said softly, repeating isr earlier request as if the emphasis would help get the photo to her. "Here's the rest of what I found." He put his hand on the folder, but only lifted it a few inches. The flush had left his face and now he seemed gray. I walked the few steps to him and picked it up. He didn't seem able to hold it much longer. As I sat back down, I noticed he was breathing through his mouth as if he couldn't get enough air.

"Let's get this signed," he said, his voice now barely audible.

"Damon, I really think this can wait until tomorrow," Ambrose almost pleaded.

"Tomorrow and tomorrow…" he mumbled. "How does that go?"

"Creeps in this petty pace from day to day," Shannon picked up. "*Macbeth*. Supposed to be bad luck to say the name in a theater. Called 'the Scottish play,' instead."

"I need a pen," Damon said, but didn't move.

Ambrose reluctantly removed one from his inside jacket pocket and slowly handed it to Damon.

"And the new will," Damon prompted him.

Ambrose picked it up from the coffee table in front of him and brought it over to Damon. There was a battle of wills over his will taking place. Ambrose had thought his usefulness had brought him some measure of influence over Damon, and now Damon was proving him wrong.

"Maybe you should read it over—" Ambrose started.

"I know what it says." Damon tugged at the collar of his T-shirt as if it was too tight. He was still breathing through his mouth, and now his breathing was short and rapid.

I'm not a doctor, but I live with one. "Damon, do you have an oxygen tank?"

He looked up at me, confusion on his face. Under the confusion there was fear. "No, I've never needed one." He gasped out a breath. "Until…now."

He hastily flipped to the last page of the will, quickly scrawled his name. For a brief moment a look of relief came over his face, then he dropped the pen and clutched at his throat.

"Lie down," I instructed, as I jumped up and eased him out of his chair onto the ground. "Call 911," I told Ambrose. But as I glanced at him, he seemed as much in shock as Damon was.

Shannon called. I heard her voice behind me giving them directions.

I was holding Damon's hand, trying to keep him as calm as I could. Whatever was happening to him would only be much worse if he went into shock. "I know you're scared," I told him in a quiet voice, "but try and be as calm as you can."

Damon was staring at me, his eyes pleading for some release from the fear that gripped him. "I have months to go," he rasped. He clutched his chest again. "Coke," he whispered. Damon kept his eyes locked with mine, "Coke…rush," he gasped. "But I didn't—"

"What's he saying?" Ambrose demanded, as if his shock had suddenly worn off and he knew he should be doing something.

Damon slowly shook his head once. "Makes no sense…"

Suddenly his hand tightened on mine in a vise grip and his chest arched up. He's having a heart attack, I thought. I had seen my Uncle Claude die from one. Pain was now etched on Damon's face.

"Crushing chest pain?" I asked.

He could only manage a head bob.

"You can survive this," I told him. "The ambulance is on its way. They'll get here in time."

"Coke. Nor. Veer," he rasped out. He was desperately trying to tell me something. "Find who…"

He suddenly jerked again, his breathing a heaving, labored pant. Then it stopped. One breath came out, but he didn't take another one in.

I glanced back at Shannon, desperately trying to remember CPR. "He's stopped breathing."

His eyes were open, but they seemed empty.

Shannon knelt down on the other side of Damon. "Go out front and flag down the EMTs," she told Ambrose. Then she looked at me. "Chest or breathing?"

"Can you do chest compressions?" I asked her. She nodded.

In a clumsy choreography, we moved into position, Shannon poised over Damon's chest, and I had his airway clear. "Ready when you are," she said.

"Let me get some air into him first." I started breathing for Damon. Shannon pressed her ear against his chest.

He gave a jerking spasm, but didn't start breathing on his own. I looked up and was nodding to Shannon to begin the chest compressions when Damon gave a rattling pant.

There was a clatter in the hallway and two EMTs arrived, trailed by Ambrose.

Ambrose was babbling. He seemed a methodical man, and this was beyond both his control and comprehension. Chaos wasn't something he did well.

Shannon and I stopped the CPR to let the EMTs in. One of them gave me a questioning look, making it clear that Ambrose hadn't given them much useful information.

"Might be a heart attack. He's ill, but with hep C and HIV. Should be his liver that goes, not his heart," I told them.

They were a Mutt and Jeff pair, one big linebacker-sized black man and a petite blond woman.

"Come on, sir," the big man said. "You're taking a ride."

It all became a blur, they were quick and professional. Damon was on the gurney, then quickly wheeled out to the waiting ambulance.

I caught a glimpse of him with an oxygen mask strapped to his face. Then the back door of the ambulance shut. The woman climbed around to take the wheel.

"Wait, I'm his lawyer, I need to be with him," Ambrose said, as if finally figuring out his appointed role in all this. He quickly climbed into the passenger seat. He was fumbling with his seat belt as the siren began wailing and the ambulance pulled out.

Shannon and I retreated into the house to get away from the sound. I closed the front door, then locked it.

"This isn't a crime scene yet," I said.

"But you think it will be?" she asked, giving me a look.

"Damon said a few things just before he died."

"I couldn't hear."

"Coke. Nor. Veer. Don't know what the last means, but I think he was talking about cocaine. He asked, 'Find who…' but didn't finish. I think he was asking me to find who jacked up something he takes with cocaine."

"But would that have been enough to kill him?" Shannon asked. "I mean, it's not like he's never tried the stuff. And for all we know, they'll revive him at the hospital."

"I hope they do, but that would change it only to attempted

murder. Even experienced addicts can overdose. And he's not in good health, not able to handle near as much as he has in the past. Let's take a look around, but don't touch anything that shouldn't already have our fingerprints on it."

"Like the door lock?" she said, but was following me back to the courtyard.

"Hey, we were left here alone. We can't just walk out and leave the door open."

The courtyard showed the disturbance of a man dying—chairs pushed aside and over, the contents of Ambrose's briefcase half-spilled onto the ground. The changed will and pen haphazardly flung away, the will half-hanging on the shoot of a potted plant.

I grabbed the small satchel I'd brought with me. Latex gloves—one of the perks of living with a doctor was a ready supply—and a small notebook and pen. I started to do a quick sketch of the scene, but Shannon upstaged me by pulling out a small digital camera from the bag she had with her. I need to get one of those and carry it with me, I thought, as she snapped a few pictures.

"Let's check out the house before anyone gets here," I suggested, handing Shannon a glove.

"And we can tell them we had to use the bathroom, if anyone questions us."

There was a staircase leading off the front hall. I headed for it. If we got the chance, I'd look over the whole house, but I guessed that the downstairs, the most-used part, would hold few secrets.

It had a third floor. I paused at the landing. We might make the bathroom excuse extend to the second floor, but not the third, so I needed to quickly check that area out before anyone got back. "You start here," I told Shannon as I mounted the stairs. "Just be careful if you touch anything."

"Yes, ma'am, boss, ma'am."

I ignored her hint that I was patronizing her by stressing something so obvious and reached the top landing. "Hello, anyone here?" I called, as a precaution. With no answer, I opened the first door. It was a sparsely furnished bedroom, with all the hallmarks of a guest room. I quickly glanced around, even opening the closet door, but saw only some empty hangers.

The next room was a half bath, also used only for company, with no toothbrush or any other sign it was other than a guest bathroom. Beyond it was another bedroom, equally bereft of anything beyond supplies for an occasional house guest. When Damon had been well, these rooms were probably often occupied, I guessed, with visitors or party-goers in need of some sleeping-off time. But, while neat and clean, neither felt like it had been used recently. A third room was a storage room, piled with boxes, some elaborate Mardi Gras costumes and other paraphernalia from years of accumulating memories and the mementos that go with them.

The final room up here was set up as a playroom, in the adult sense. A sling was suspended from the ceiling, an X cross, some handcuffs bolted into the wall, and a queen-sized bed with the head slightly elevated, so someone lying there could view the scene. Like the other rooms, it too didn't seem like it had been used in a while. There was dust in the upper V of the cross, and the air was musty with the smell of a closed room, not the dried sweat of men.

I closed that door and headed to the second floor to join Shannon. I found her in what was clearly Damon's bedroom taking a close-up of his stack of medicines.

"And, no, I haven't left fingerprints all over everything," she said at hearing my approach.

"Good girl. My little Shannon is growing up."

She gave me the finger and took another picture from a different angle. "Trying to get all the labels," she explained.

I left her to her photography and examined the rest of the room. It was large, taking up the same space as the two upper bedrooms combined. Off to one side was a master bathroom. I opened some of the drawers in the vanity there. Damon might well have been using a few fun drugs and the bathroom might be a good hiding place. But the most risqué thing the drawers revealed was a big stack of condoms and about four or five different kinds of lube. The rest of the stuff was the usual bathroom flotsam and jetsam—shaving cream, a stack of hotel shampoos, extra toothbrushes, some reading material consisting mostly of the usual gay magazines like *Vanity Fair*, but also *National Geographic* and *Consumer Reports*. Drugs were of the usual over-the-counter variety—aspirin, nose drops, and cough syrup.

I rejoined Shannon in the bedroom, kneeling down to look under the bed. Several suitcases were stored there, but with enough dust on them to indicate that they hadn't been used in a while. I turned to his chest of drawers and opened the top one. It held only socks, the one below it underwear, ranging from mundane white to satin leopard skin. The next drawer was T-shirts, below that, sweaters. The bottom draw held his toy collection—a pile of dildos, harnesses, and more condoms and lube. But nothing that looked like drugs. The closet was filled with clothes. Damon dressed well, from smartly-tailored suits to several leather jackets—brown, black, and suede. Everything was neatly arranged, and unless I wanted to look through around twenty shoe boxes, nothing seemed hidden.

Shannon had finished taking pictures, and I leaned in for a close look at his medications. There were a number of them, few with names that meant anything to me. I quickly copied down the drugs in my notepad. I could ask Cordelia about them later. I took a final long look around the bedroom, but nothing seemed to be more than it was, then followed Shannon to the rooms across the hall.

One was the entertainment room. A large-screen TV dominated one wall, with several comfortable leather chairs and a matching couch grouped for maximum viewing pleasure. There was a small refrigerator with a few beers, but they were in back and most of the shelf space was taken by bottled water.

The only other room on this floor was a small office. I would have liked to get on the computer, but that would take too long, especially if I had to guess passwords. I had to content myself with glancing at labels on disks and the paperwork visible on the desk. Everything seemed to fit in with the mundane running of a business—balance sheets, schedules, a pile of the normal bills. I opened the top desk drawer but found nothing more telling than a hot pink pen amid the blue and black ones, plus several boxes of paper clips and Post-It notes.

Shannon and I exchanged a look, almost as if to say, "Is this all there is?" I gave a nod and we headed downstairs.

It showed the same humdrum signs of living—some dishes left in the sink, a few bottles of what looked to be decent wine—but I gave a quick swipe with a gloved finger and there was a thin layer of dust on them. Damon had apparently given up on the drinking, just as his doctors had ordered. He was a man afraid of dying. The kitchen opened into the dining room, and a comfortable living room took up the back half of the house, looking over the courtyard. The rooms looked neat, but lived in. A magazine left open on the couch, a pair of loafers under the coffee table, a half-full bottle of water on an end table—all signs that someone lived a quiet life here.

We found ourselves back in the courtyard.

"What were we looking for?" Shannon asked me.

"I'm not sure, something that gives a clue to what happened."

"And did we not find it or did I miss something?"

"Sometimes what you don't find tells as much as what you do."

"Meaning?"

"What happened to Damon was sudden, like something major changed. From what he told me, his liver was barely functioning, but his doctors were giving him six months to a year. He even told me they said everything else was fine. So what changed? Did he ingest something that overwhelmed his system? And did Damon do this to himself, or did someone do it to him? Ours wasn't the most thorough of searches, but if Damon was doing anything other than those prescription drugs on his bed, would he hide them in his own house?"

"He might, especially if he'd been warned about them, given his condition, and didn't want his friends to know."

"True. But he's not drinking, so why take an even greater chance with street drugs? And if Damon didn't even have anything like cocaine here—and it doesn't seem he did—then someone did this to him."

"Right as he was about to change his will," Shannon pointed out. "The yet-to-be-found child is in this new will, I'm assuming. Can it stand under the circumstances?"

"He can't disinherit a child under Louisiana law." I gave her a quick explanation of the forced-heirship law. "But even so, Damon was cutting back on some bequests in the new will, and there were people who would clearly prefer that not to happen."

"So if someone wanted to kill Damon, they were stupid," Shannon commented as I finished.

"Maybe they just wanted to scare him. It would be hard to predict how much cocaine would be needed to kill him. But any amount could be enough to scare him."

"Someone playing with his drugs. And his life."

I pulled my cell phone out of my bag as I listened to Shannon.

"Enough to kill a dying man? Could they have been so desperate for the money that a few months would make a difference?" she asked.

"Time is money." I hit one of my speed-dial numbers and was rewarded with a live human voice instead of the voice mail I had expected.

"Joanne Ranson."

"Joanne, this is Micky. Got a case that might be coming your direction." She listened as I told her what had happened and my suspicions. Joanne was a longtime friend and, more importantly in this case, a detective sergeant for NOPD.

After I finished, she was quiet, then said, "I probably don't need to tell you this, but a dying man dying makes it hard to prove murder. It might be hard to argue even to do the tox screen and see if he was slipped something he wasn't supposed to have. And even if it shows cocaine or some other substance, what proof is there that someone slipped it to him?"

"I know, but I think someone did this. And I think he was trying to make peace with dying and he may not get a chance."

"I'll do what I can, but…"

"That's all I'm asking for." We said good-bye. I looked at Shannon and said, "I'd like to stay here for a while. Ambrose will probably return rather than go home. You don't have to stay—"

"But I'd like to. I think it would be good for me to write this all down. That's usually how I do things if I can. Write down my impressions as soon as possible." She rummaged in her knapsack and pulled out a thick notebook and several pens. "I color-code things," she explained. "Important points, stray thoughts, useful facts all get their own color."

I left her to her writing and decided I could clean up a few things, like lifting the new will out of the potted plant. I looked at it, Damon's hasty scrawl on the last page. Would it hold up, I wondered? And what would happen if this contentious document disappeared? The copy machine was only a flight of stairs away. I made two copies, one that I tucked into a desk drawer and one that I decided to keep. Then it was back down the stairs.

Even if the police turned this into a crime scene, by the time that happened, Ambrose would have returned to fetch his briefcase. I carefully lifted it and rearranged the spilled contents, making sure I got a good look at everything as I put it back. Ambrose was a man of lists. He had a small spiral notebook with different sections devoted to lists. A grocery list, a dry-cleaning list, a to-do today list, a to-do over-the-weekend list, a list of movies to see. There was a Damon section, with lists of his doctors, his medicines, contact numbers for all his bars, several lists of financial holdings, stocks, mutual funds, and bank accounts. Way in the back was a list of Damon's ex-boyfriends, each with a date beside the name, with the oldest starting over ten years ago. Beatrice Elliot wasn't listed, but maybe Ambrose didn't know about her or think he needed to keep track of a woman. I quickly jotted the names down. Despite all the paper in the briefcase, little was personal or hinted at who Ambrose was. The grocery list held no special foods, no craving for dark chocolate, just a list of toilet paper, bread, milk. The movies were the latest big releases, no obscure foreign films or even Disney cartoons.

There was a copy of the previous will. I quickly scanned it, then noted who got what in the first and who lost what in the second. In the latter his child—if found—got half, and the rest were cut to make up for that.

Hearing the front door open and footsteps in the passageway that led to the courtyard, I just had time to close the briefcase, place it on a chair, and move away as if I'd done little more than pick it up, and that a long time ago.

It was Ambrose and he seemed surprised to see us still here.

"Any word on Damon?" I asked.

His mouth opened, but for a long moment nothing came out, as if he couldn't think the words enough to say them. Finally, he said, "He hasn't woken up."

"He's dead?" I asked.

Ambrose shook his head, then sat down heavily in the closest chair. He didn't seem filled with shock and grief, but empty, as if there was nothing to hold him together anymore, as if he needed Damon here to tell him what to do.

"In a coma?" I pushed.

This time Ambrose nodded.

I moved in to take advantage of his emptiness. It's for the right reasons, I told myself. "Ambrose," I said as I put my hand on his shoulder, "I think someone may have poisoned Damon. He seemed to think he had been given cocaine. One of the last things he said to me was to find who did this."

He half lifted his head, his eyes numb and bewildered. "Can you do that?"

"I can try. Even if the police become involved, it's not likely they'll give a dying man much attention. If you want to know who did this to Damon, I'm your best chance. I'm already digging into Damon's life to find his child. I can dig in this direction as well."

"I guess that makes sense," Ambrose said slowly.

"You're his attorney. You have the power to hire me to do this." I added, "It's up to you now to make sure Damon's wishes are carried out." I thought this was a bit much, but it seemed to be the perfect jolt for Ambrose. I might as well get paid for this, I thought, as I pushed. It'll just be a little less for the people Damon already wanted to cut out.

He lifted his head. "You're right. This is my duty. And I owe it to Damon." With that he stood up, transmogrified from an empty man to the anointed keeper of Damon LaChance's flame.

Play it, sister, I thought. "I'll need your help, of course. You probably knew Damon better than anyone. And you know the people around him. Can you make me some lists?"

"List" was a word to warm his heart. He nodded, a man with a mission. "Of course. I would be the best person for that."

"I need to know who was expecting money from Damon, both in the old will and the new one." I had that info, but it wouldn't hurt to cross-check. "I also need a list of people who had access to Damon, who came here in the last few days, if any of them had keys and could come and go as they pleased. Also, and I know this will be subjective, but who do you think might have done something like this? Maybe not even intending to kill Damon, but just to play a nasty joke."

"I can get that for you by tomorrow," he said. Then he asked, "Do you think the police will be involved?"

"It depends on what the tox screens show." I didn't mention my intercession on behalf of those screens. "If they find something that shouldn't be there…"

"What a mess," Ambrose said, shaking his head. "Damon wouldn't like it." He was already settling into his flame-keeping—and Damon might still wake up and live for a few more months.

"Can you make me a copy of any staff lists from his bars?"

Ambrose agreed and was helpful enough to tell me that Damon

had an office here, so we could make the copies right now. He led me up the stairs to the office, making sure to point out the worn place on the rug so I wouldn't trip over it. I considered stubbing my toe just to make it look like I'd never been this way, but that didn't seem necessary. Ambrose copied most of the things on the desk. A lot of them were financial reports from the bars, and I doubted they had much to do with this, but better to have too much than too little. Besides, now Ambrose was a man with a mission, and I wasn't about to slow him down.

I even stayed long enough to talk about what arrangements should be made. Ambrose seemed to want someone to at least back up any choices he made, if not make them outright for him. Several times, I had to ask, "What do you think Damon would have wanted?" or "What have others done at times like this?" to get him to make a decision.

Finally after everything that could be copied was copied and all the major decisions that Ambrose or I could think of were made, I went back to the courtyard and collected Shannon.

"So, we're hired to investigate what happened to Damon?" she asked after we were out on the street.

I thought about saying, "We, kemo sabe?" but restrained myself. "Objections?"

"Think the police will appreciate it?"

"I don't think the police will look very hard at this. He was dying anyway."

"And we still have to find out if there is a child involved."

"We do. What was that quote? The one Damon started and you finished?"

"*Macbeth*. 'Tomorrow and tomorrow and tomorrow / Creeps in this petty pace from day to day; / To the last syllable of recorded time; / And all our yesterdays have lighted fools / The way to dusty death. Out, out, brief candle! / Life's but a walking shadow, a poor player / That struts and frets his hour upon the stage / And then is heard no more. It is a tale / Told by an idiot, full of sound and fury / Signifying nothing.'"

"Cheery thought."

"A tragedy."

"Aren't they all?" I said as I unlocked the door for her. Wasn't Damon? Even if we found his child, would he wake up to even know?

CHAPTER NINE

Who would murder a man about to die? That was the question I asked myself the next day. I was again sitting in my office, a now-empty coffee cup in front of me.

The suspects would be within the circle of people who had something to gain from Damon dying now, rather than after his putative child could be found. Who needed the money badly enough to murder a dying man? Or had he justified his actions by thinking that Damon was so close to death a nudge wasn't really murder?

There was another possibility I had to consider. Perhaps someone had only intended a nasty joke, or a vicious reminder of how dependent Damon was on the kindness of others. It might have been meant as a scare tactic, from someone who didn't know or didn't think about what the consequences might be. It could also have been some bizarre coincidence, someone who didn't know about the child and just happened to strike now. Or maybe Damon had wanted one last ride, was willing to take a chance. Or something that I didn't even know about.

Any of Damon's inner circle, those with the most to lose if a child appeared, would or should have some idea of how ill he really was and that a little cocaine mixed in with his drugs could be deadly. His not-so-inner circle might be more likely to be in the nasty-joke category, but he had a pretty large not-so-inner circle. A lot of names, a lot of suspects, a myriad of motives. Why isn't it ever only enough people to bring together in a drawing room like it is in books?

I looked at the papers spread out in front of me. Damon had done well, made the right investments at the right time, then made the right investments with what he'd earned from the right investments. His inner-circle group all were getting some nice six-figure sums if no heir arrived to take a mandatory percentage of the estate.

Ambrose had dutifully sent in his lists via e-mail, but they told me little other than what I already knew. The top names were Perry Thompson and Bruce Payne, but his list gave no clue as to whether Ambrose just didn't like them or if he really suspected them. I had to wonder if he didn't think the two were the same.

I was again in my office, again with a half-empty cup of coffee in front of me. However, the time was early afternoon. After briefly meeting with Shannon this morning, I had sent her off to dig in the city records.

I was trying to put the so-called gray cells to work and come up with a strategy for which direction we should take. Although we hadn't exactly been lollygagging about finding Beatrice Elliot, I wanted to make that our first priority. If Damon did wake up, I wanted to be able to answer his questions about her and the child they might have had together. Of course, Damon's chances of waking up might be dependent on my finding out who wished him harm and whether they would try again.

I had plowed through everything that Ambrose had given me, making lists and connections. This is a lot of what private-detective work is—actually reading papers no one else wants to read and making sense of them. From these papers I now had a list of the people who were supposed to inherit something from Damon—my suspect pool.

Bruce Payne had been scheduled to inherit the bar he managed, The Outer Limits. But that was it—just the business, not even the building the bar was in. If he lost a chunk of the bar to Damon's heir, he would be forced to sell. Or the same cut might make Ambrose, who was set to get the building itself for Damon's foundation, sell it. Either of those would bring the same bad ending for Bruce Payne—no bar, no flow of cash from both sides of the law. From what I'd seen in the bar, he certainly had access to drugs. Also, from what I'd seen in the bar, Bruce wasn't the most upstanding and moral person in the world— or even in the French Quarter. From what Torbin said, he needed the money and he needed it now.

Next on my little list was Perry Thompson. From my brief encounter with Perry, I doubted that he'd like to share his stash with a bouncing baby, a second-grader by this point. He probably also had access to drugs and to Damon's pill cache. I would guess that Perry-boy was looking forward to having his own pot of gold to dip into instead of having to cadge off Damon. I would also guess that he was good at rationalizing his self-serving life, that he might call it a favor to Damon to help him exit on one last wild ride instead of the slow decline of disease.

The Crescent City Care Coalition was also expecting to do well from Damon. I'd sent Shannon off to dig through their records. She was going to have to charm someone at City Hall to get access to the financial records of the grants administrated through the city; they were public record, but public record buried in a myriad of files. It would be interesting to see how close to the bone they were. Kent Richards, the executive director, had raised a few eyebrows from his high living—he had no rich boyfriend to explain frequent weekend jaunts to Houston or Atlanta and even New York and San Francisco. Torbin had also dug up for me that some of the CCCC employees had gone without being paid for about a month, supposedly because of the lag time in receiving reimbursements from granting sources.

Damon had also left money to an uncle, Raul LaChance. He lived out in a small town around Lafayette, back in the Cajun country Damon left a long time ago. He seemed less likely to have access to drugs, and he'd had to travel a few hours each way to get to New Orleans. Damon had also left something to an aunt with an uptown address. She wasn't getting much, several paintings. From her address, it didn't seem like money would be a pressing issue for her. I considered her unlikely but still would have to check her out.

Ambrose would do well from Damon's death, in addition to running the foundation. It wouldn't be a large charitable trust. The focus was on local arts, especially in the gay community. A rough guess would be that the grants would be thousands or tens of thousands at most. A nice bit of money for something like a film festival or art show, but nothing to live off. It would give Ambrose a high profile in the glitzy arts circle though. The keeper of the flame. But Ambrose loved Damon. I couldn't see a reason for Ambrose to harm him. He'd still have what seemed to matter to him—save for Damon to love him back. Besides, Ambrose had been willing to hire me to find who hurt Damon. He lacked flair and imagination, but he wasn't stupid, and only a stupid man would engage a private detective to look into an attempted murder that would have otherwise gotten a pass.

Another person on the list was someone named Jud Lasser. It was interesting that his name hadn't come up yet, especially as he was getting a chunk of change. He lived on the North Shore, the other side of Lake Pontchartrain, which was turning into an exclusive suburb, the riffraff kept out by a twenty-four-mile drive across the Causeway. I put a check mark next to his name.

NO/AIDS Task Force was getting a nice bequest. But they had been around since 1983, and Cordelia worked with them on a number of HIV issues. Some of their staff did testing once a week out of her clinic. Unlike the Crescent City Care Coalition, even the amount that Damon was leaving them wasn't a make-or-break sum.

The rest of the estate was divided into smaller bequests. I counted twenty-two of them. Something for his employees, at least those who had been around for over five years, including the silent George of the good coffee. He would get a few thousand and any of the kitchen stuff he wanted. None of the sums seemed to be in the murder range, but money could mean different things to different people. However, most of the beneficiaries were bar workers. Few of them would have access to Damon's house, I was assuming. I'd have to see if Ambrose, and possibly George, could give me an idea of anyone coming and going in the last few days.

I took a sip of my coffee, then looked out the window, away from the stack of paper on my desk that seemed to ask more questions than it answered. What if Beatrice Elliot didn't want to be found? Or if the trail led to a grave marker? True, she was young enough, but being young isn't protection. I'd twice had to tell parents that the children they sought had found a home under a tombstone. One was a young man who'd wanted adventure and found it on a motorcycle without a helmet. A thrill of speed, one veer over an oil slick and into the concrete piling of an overpass. At least with him, I was able to tell his mother that the EMTs said death had been instantaneous.

The other was a young woman, and I still wished I hadn't found her grave. She'd run away from home at sixteen. The streets had claimed her. Arrests for prostitution, drugs. She became a Jane Doe thrown down an isolated muddy embankment, left there to slowly bleed to death from the violence of her sexual assault. I left out the worst of it when I told her parents. Six months later, I saw the mother's obituary in the paper.

A cloud passed over the sun, and its shadow moved across the room. Then the sunlight returned. I turned back to the papers in front of me and the questions they asked. I listed the order in which I wanted to interview people. First, Ambrose and George. They had seen Damon recently. Perry Thompson, I knew, was already on that list, so he was next. I put Bruce Payne after him. Bruce was too desperate, and The Outer Limits was just a few blocks from Damon's townhouse. The offices of the Crescent City Care Coalition were also close by, about eight blocks away. I'd let Shannon do that one. Kent Richards, the executive director, knew who I was.

I also made a note to check with Sarah Clavish, although I knew if she had something, I'd have it by now. The next task for Shannon would be to do a birth-records search. I was hoping that most of the last seven years or so would be computerized. If Beatrice Elliot was from Connecticut, maybe that was where she'd had her child.

Speaking of the young girl detective, I heard her footsteps on my stairs. They were a trudge, as if she'd lost her early morning perkiness. I took a sip of my coffee to hide the smile that thought brought to my lips.

The door opened and she entered. The New Orleans heat and humidity seemed to be taking its toll on my Yankee friend. Damp circles were visible under her armpits, and her hair had wilted from its morning spiky assurance.

"It's good to know that tax dollars aren't being spent on keeping your public buildings cool and comfortable," she said as she dumped her satchel on the table that was now her spot in the office.

"Not the areas the grimy public actually uses. They save all the cool air for the inner offices."

She glared as if I were responsible for the stuffy air, then grabbed a paper towel from next to the coffee urn to wipe the sweat off her face and neck. "For some reason, I have no problem believing you," she muttered.

"This is New Orleans. We know how to do corruption right."

With another glare at my coffee cup, as if no one should be drinking a warm beverage within a hundred yards of her, she grabbed a bottle of water from the small refrigerator and took a long swig. "Not only was it hot, humid, and every line I stood in seemed to have the finalist for the dregs-of-humanity contest, I found out nothing."

"Nothing?" I cocked an eyebrow at her. "You found nothing, or you found something, but it doesn't seem to offer much in way of either motive for murder or missing children?"

"What I found was that Damon LaChance does own everything he says he owns. His taxes are all paid, and in short, he seems to be a fine, upstanding citizen. New Orleans style." She took another long swig of water.

"That does mean that Damon—or Ambrose—can pay my bill, and you may consider that nothing, but I happen to think it's important."

She finished the bottle. Her only answer was still another glare, somewhat contradicted by a drop of sweat trickling down her nose.

"And it does tell us that Damon is what he represents himself to be, that we don't have to play games within games."

"Does that happen a lot?" she asked, tossing her empty bottle toward the trash can. It missed, but she left it for the moment.

"Does everyone answer your journo questions honestly, or do they occasionally try to save face?" She gave a bare nod. "Sometimes it does. If the wife is missing, does hubby have any domestic-abuse charges against him? Some people use property mortgaged to the hilt as collateral. Better to look for messes than step into them."

Shannon got up and retrieved her water bottle. I pointed at the recycling bin. She obediently dropped it there. "So, what next?" She got another bottle as if asserting her right to my water.

"I'm planning to talk to Ambrose as well as George and see if they can recall anyone who visited Damon in the last few days. That might help narrow down the suspects."

"What about the cops? Won't they be pissed if you're stepping on their turf?"

"If this were clearly an attempted murder, yes. But they won't have anything even pointing in that direction until the tox screens come back. And even then, if it's cocaine, Damon's not exactly a virgin on that count."

"So you don't think they'll even look into it?" Half the bottle of water disappeared in one gulp.

"At this point, no. Or at least not very far. And I think more important than finding out 'whodunit,' we need to dig enough to scare anyone off from doing it again. Damon may only have six months, but I think he deserves them."

"What if they come after you?"

"That's TV or the movies, not real life. Even if this was done in anger, it was still planned. Chaotic anger is scary, the meth head who goes off. But this person had access to Damon that they don't have to either of us. So, if he—and I'm guessing it's a he—isn't likely to just lose it and if he can't get to us, he'll just lie low. And even if I figure out who did it, for Damon's sake, it might be hard to get anything approaching evidence."

"Do you really believe that or are you just trying to reassure me?" Shannon looked directly at me, her eyes seeking the answer in my face.

"Mostly I believe it." I shrugged and didn't return her look.

"Reassuring me isn't a priority for you, I gather."

"Not especially. Finding something useful for you to do is."

She finished her water and threw it in the garbage, hard enough to suggest she was close to disgusted.

I ignored it. "Try to think like Beatrice Elliot seven years ago. Pregnant, quite unmarried. Do you have the child or not?"

"If she was going to abort, why even tell Damon?"

"To help with the costs?"

"She was in her thirties at the time. Not a babe in the woods. Why wasn't she using birth control?"

"Maybe she didn't expect to be having sex with a gay man. Or maybe she didn't have any handy. Even for people who are supposed to know what they're doing, sex can be complicated."

"Or, maybe, Beatrice's biological clock was ticking and she decided to let fate make a decision for her. Roll the dice. From the way Damon told it, it seemed like she was saying that she was having his child, did he want to be involved."

"So, your guess is that she did have the baby?"

"Just a gut feeling."

"So follow your gut," I told her. "Babies leave records. See if you can find one."

"Connecticut, right? She went home."

"Or she probably had friends there."

"It's a start. Can I do it from the cool of my apartment?" Shannon stood up and started to gather her things.

"Be my guest."

She snagged another bottle of water from the fridge, gave me a mock salute, and headed out. I gave her five minutes and a few more sips of my coffee, then headed out the door myself.

My destination was Damon's townhouse in the French Quarter. It would probably just be a short drive past an empty building, but I wondered if anyone would be there, and if so, why. Middle-of-the-weekday parking isn't the tedious hunt that weekend parking is, but I still ended up three blocks away. The afternoon heat was almost enough that I wished I'd followed Shannon's example with the water bottle.

Sweat was running down my back as I rang the doorbell. At first, there was only echoing silence, then I heard footsteps in the hallway. A moment later, the door cracked open.

"I'm sorry, Miss, Damon isn't here." It was George, and that was the longest sentence I'd heard him utter.

"Still in the hospital?" I asked in a kind voice.

"Yes, ma'am." Then he was silent again.

"Actually, George, if I could I'd like to talk to you for a few minutes."

He looked surprised. "Me?" he finally said, as if he wasn't someone to be talked to.

I looked at him. He wasn't tall, but he was muscular, probably about the same age as Damon, early forties, but age hadn't been kind to George. His hair was thinning. There was still a thatch on his forehead, but then it V-ed back sharply, its uniform color giving away the dye job. But it was his face that aged him—a thick, blunt nose that had perhaps been broken, eyes with bags as if they'd spent too many nights in smoky bars with cheap beer and cigarettes.

"Yes, you," I answered. "Did Ambrose talk to you?"

"Ambrose?" he said slowly, as if working out who Ambrose might be and why he would talk to him. Then he shook his head and added very softly, as if this was something he didn't want to admit, "Ambrose almost never talks to me. Orders coffee, whiskey. That's all."

"May I come in?"

"Of course," he said, seeming to suddenly remember the rules of politeness.

The cool air that had been wafting out the door enveloped me as I stepped in.

"Would you like something to drink, miss?" he asked.

I started to say no, but I was thirsty and I also suspected that George needed to be in his customary role before he could step out of it. "Yes, please. Something cold, water or a soda. And get yourself something, too, if you like."

George ushered me to the living room before going to the kitchen. It had been cleaned of its few remnants of someone being in the room. The shoes were gone, the magazines neatly stacked and fanned in display. He returned in a few minutes with bottled water and a glass of ice for me, and a can of Dr Pepper for himself. After serving my drink, he hesitated, then seated himself on the opposite end of the couch.

"You probably overheard some of what was going on. Tell me what you know."

George didn't demur, so at least he was an honest servant. He slowly answered, "The will. Damon wants you to find his child."

I said, "Originally Damon hired me to see if he had fathered a child. But when he collapsed, he was able to talk for a few minutes and he seemed to think that someone had tampered with his medicines. He asked me to find out who might have done that."

"Someone wanted to hurt Mr. Damon?" George asked. He seemed genuinely shocked and surprised at the idea.

"Maybe," I hedged. "That's what I'm trying to find out." I realized George was not just silent, but his thoughts moved slowly, as if some damage or deficit was part of his life. "What are your duties here?"

"Well, some of everything. Cleaning, picking up. I take care of the plants. Answer the door, some cooking, not much. I run out and get things to go mostly."

"How long have you worked for Damon?"

George thought for a second, then unobtrusively tried to count on his fingers. "Long time. Maybe ten years?"

"That is a long time. Do you live here? Some helpers live in," I clarified, as he looked puzzled.

"No, I live uptown."

"How much time do you spend here looking after things?" I asked.

"Well, now afternoons, most days. I do stuff for Miss Carlotta, mostly her yard, the rest of the time. That's where I live. Small place behind her garage."

"Can you remember who came and visited on the days just before Damon got sick?"

"You did," he said.

"Yes, I did. And Shannon, my assistant." I didn't get the feeling he was giving me a smart reply, but instead giving me a literal answer to the question I asked, as if that was the only way he knew to answer.

"Yes, her. Mr. Ambrose." He paused to think. "Perry." It was slight, just a bare wrinkle of his nose and the fact that he didn't use a title.

"You don't like Perry, do you?"

"No."

"I saw him briefly, out on the street. He didn't seem very nice."

"He isn't nice. Not to me. He's nice to Damon. Mostly. Sometimes he even yells at Damon."

"What sort of stuff does he yell about?"

"I try not to listen. When he yells at Damon, I know he'll yell at me."

"About money? About Damon giving him things?" I asked.

"Perry complains. Wearing the same clothes to different parties. His car is five years old, he'd like a new one. Damon doesn't appreciate all Perry does for him. But it's mostly Perry coming here to complain." George seemed to be opening up, as if not too many people listened to him.

"Can you remember how long he was here that day?"

"It was a little over half an hour because Damon likes his water really cold, so I put some in the freezer for half an hour until they're almost ice. I just put one in right after Perry arrived and took it out right before he left."

Half an hour was certainly enough time to slip something into Damon's drugs. "Who else was here?"

George was silent, then said, "Mr. Jud was here. Miss Carlotta, but she just stepped in, and she mostly came down to drop me off. Bruce from the bar came by. He argued with Damon, too, about bar stuff."

"What kind of bar stuff?"

"Something about bottles not matching, something about money."

"Always seems to be about money," I said almost to myself.

It wasn't a question, but George answered. "Not always. Mr. Ambrose argued about honesty. About how he thought Damon was misleading people."

"When was this?"

"That day. Just before Perry came."

"So was Mr. Ambrose here when Perry was here?"

"Only a minute. They don't like each other. So when I let Perry in, Mr. Ambrose left."

"When Jud came, who else was here?"

"Me. Damon."

"Ambrose wasn't here yet?"

"No. He didn't come until a little later."

"Who was here first?"

"Me. Miss Carlotta, too."

"When was that?"

"Around eight thirty in the morning."

"Jud was here next? About what time?"

"I think around nine." George picked up on where I was going and continued. "Bruce came right after Mr. Jud left, almost like he was watching. Then Mr. Ambrose at eleven. Perry came around one. Then you and your girlfriend came."

I didn't correct him about Shannon. "Do you know what he and Jud talked about?"

George hesitated for a moment, then said, "Jud's nice. Nice to me." He hesitated a second time before continuing. "Damon told him there might be a kid. Jud asked him if he was doing the right thing. That's all I heard." He looked down, then took a nervous sip of his soda. It seemed he didn't like revealing things about Jud, almost like a betrayal of a friend.

I changed the topic. "Who does the grocery shopping?"

"Me. Damon gives me a list and taxi money. He used to go but not anymore."

"So you do all the shopping and put things away?"

George nodded.

"How about his medicines? How does he get them?"

"Mostly I get them. They know me."

"Where's that?"

"At Royal Pharmacy. They're nice to me. It's just a few blocks away."

I knew the place he was talking about, at the corner of Royal and Ursulines, an old-fashioned mom-and-pop store. "Does anyone else get his medicines?"

"Mostly me, but sometimes Mr. Ambrose does. That's where he went when Perry came. I was going to do it, but Mr. Ambrose didn't want to be around."

"Where does Damon keep his medicines?" I had a good idea from our snooping, but I wanted to see what George would say. Maybe there was a place we hadn't found.

"Mostly upstairs. He takes some in the morning and some before bed, so he keeps them close to the bed."

"Does Damon usually take them on his own or does someone help him?"

"Sometimes Damon asks me to get them, if he's downstairs and tired." Then he added as if not wanting to admit it, "Sometimes Mr. Ambrose does it instead. He told Damon that I don't read good enough to know the bottles." He started to take an agitated sip of his drink, but instead said, "But I do. I can tell the shape of the pills, too."

Mr. Control Freak Ambrose.

George said, "Mr. Ambrose likes to help with the other things as well."

"Like what?"

"When Damon's really tired, Mr. Ambrose helps him in the bathtub. Also putting things up...well, you know, the behind."

I must have looked a little surprised, as George continued. "What do you call them? Superities? Super something?" He looked a little embarrassed talking about that with a woman, so his embarrassment made the discussion seem dirtier than it was turning out to be.

"Suppositories?"

"Yeah, I think that's it."

"So Ambrose helps Damon with that? How often?" Mr. Major Control Freak, I thought, then had to wonder if this was as close to physical intimacy as Ambrose ever got with Damon.

"It depends. When Damon feels sick to his stomach."

"Did Ambrose help him that day?"

George thought for a moment, then said, "Yes, he did. He came back while Perry was still here and interrupted them. He told Damon he had his medicine and the sooner he took it the sooner he'd feel better."

"So in the middle of Perry's whine about money, Ambrose got Damon away to help him insert a suppository?"

"Yeah, he did. Perry didn't like it."

I'll bet he didn't. Of course, that left Mr. Unhappy Perry alone and unsupervised with whatever Damon had been drinking or any medicines he had with him, and from what we'd seen as he stormed out, he was angry enough to do just about anything. "Can you think of anyone who might put something like cocaine in Damon's medicines? Maybe someone upset about the idea of Damon leaving part of his estate to a child?"

George was silent, as if thinking. "Some people were upset. But who would want to hurt Damon?"

"Maybe not hurt him, maybe just scare him?"

George was again silent, then slowly shook his head. "Not even scare him. Why? Why scare Damon?"

I let the silence hang, but clearly George couldn't imagine anyone harming Damon. I stood to go. "You've been a great help, George. You've given me a good idea of who was here and the time frame of how things happened."

George also stood, then for a moment he looked like a lost boy. "He'll be okay?" he asked softly.

Cordelia is good at this kind of thing. Answering the questions when it won't be okay. Cancer, HIV, all the won't-be-okays. I didn't know what to say to this lost boy in a man's body. "I don't know. Damon is sick and—"

"He's not coming back, is he?"

"He may be back for a while. He may get through this, but...he *is* sick."

George didn't answer. His only response was a tear slowly sliding down his cheek. I reached up and caught it with my finger, resting my palm against his cheek. It wasn't the kind of gesture I usually make.

"I'm sorry," I said. "What will you do when Damon's gone?" It wasn't a question I needed to ask, and I suspected the answer would be hard to hear.

"Miss Carlotta will take care of me." He was silent for a moment more. "But I'll miss Damon." He briefly covered my hand with his, then turned away. "I'll walk you out, miss."

I followed him to the door. With his back to me, he brusquely rubbed his hand over his face.

"Thank you, George," I said as he opened the door for me.

"You're welcome, miss. You have a good day."

"You, too, George. You, too," I said as he closed the door behind me. I stood in the sun, the heat a wave I could almost touch. But it was heat only, and no warmth. I headed for my car.

Perry was now at the top of my list. He had a motive, he had access, and the timing was right. Although it was also possible that whatever had been added had been done earlier. So that still left a long list of suspects.

I pulled my notebook out of my bag. Torbin had mentioned that Perry had "a gentle-faggot's job" as a partner in an antique store on Royal Street. It was about ten blocks from here, but I wouldn't find closer parking without paying for it. Besides, ten blocks in the heat would make me look like a properly wilted tourist.

I stopped at one of the little corner groceries for a bottle of water, then headed down to Royal to cover the distance. It was hot enough that even the tourists had enough sense to stay inside, probably in the frozen-daiquiri shops on Bourbon Street. Royal, below Jackson Square, is mostly residential, but from there—actually the back of St. Louis Cathedral, as the square only goes from Decatur to Chartres Street, where the cathedral sits and goes back to Royal—turns into art galleries and antique stores. There is some beautiful stuff here, but it's not the place to find a bargain.

I sucked down the last of my water just as I got to the address Torbin had given me. After backtracking a few steps to throw the bottle away, I sauntered by the windows, pausing to look over what was displayed. Most of it was too rococo for my taste, not to mention pricey. The window displayed a massive dining-room table, set with china so delicate it couldn't possibly hold anything heavier than air, and still air at that. The table, on the other hand, looked sturdy enough to float through hurricanes with nary a hair disturbed on the round-cheeked cherubs carved in every space a cherub could fit. I suspected that the only thing possibly linking the table and the china was price—other than that they were an unappetizing odd couple.

Still, I tried to put an interested look on my face. Sneering at the merchandise does little to loosen the owner's tongue. I glanced farther into the shop but could see no one about. I was almost hoping Perry Thompson wouldn't be here, as I might find out more from one of his business partners, especially as Torbin had hinted that it was as happy a marriage as the table and the china. Something about Perry thinking that scheduled hours and deadlines didn't really apply to him—but woe betide anyone who was thirty seconds late relieving him or being tardy in something he needed.

I quietly opened the door, wanting to give myself a few more minutes of looking around before being looked at. A bell was attached to the door, but by closing it gently, I avoided tripping it. The store seemed less than organized, with several unsorted boxes shoved against the counter where the cash register was. No one seemed to be around. There was a musty smell, and by running a finger around the lower edge of a desk, I noticed that dusting was not a top priority here—or that it was a top priority, in that only the tops of things were dusted. The faint sound of voices came from the rear. I drifted back in their direction, still being quiet. Two men, and one sounded like Perry. Not that I'd heard his voice other than the shouting match outside Damon's, but Perry had a distinct whine.

"I can pay you in a few weeks" had the same whine as Perry's.

I edged closer to hear what his companion was saying.

"…said that a few weeks ago. Time is money, dear boy."

With my eyes now fully adjusted to the dim interior, I could see light spilling around the edges of several folding screens, indicating a back room with the door open enough for me to hear. I also noticed a mirror on the far wall through the crack between screen panels. From this angle, the mirror gave me a partial view into the back room.

My whine sense was indeed correct. I saw the profile of Mr. Perry himself. His companion was an older man, probably late sixties or early seventies, but too many years of tanning made his skin look almost mask-like, with several ugly reddish splotches that hinted of skin-cancer lesions cut off. He wasn't a handsome man, but his clothes and the look in his eyes said he had money and power and that pretenders like Perry were toys to him.

"This time is different. I'm about to make a big sale," Perry pleaded.

"Every time is different. You've said that for too long. I'm tired of words."

Perry was silent, then he said, "I don't have it now. What do you want me to do?" A sullen tone crept into his voice, seemingly because his companion wasn't letting his excuses get by.

In a bored tone, that companion replied, "I want you to repay the money you borrowed a year ago and said you'd repay in a few weeks. Clearly I'm not going to get that right away, so we need to work out some way for you to at least cover the interest until your big sale, of course."

Perry was being toyed with, and sadly, he didn't seem to know it.

Grasping at this straw, Perry replied, "I'm sure we can work out something, and I really will have it soon. There are a couple of pieces here that I'm sure you'll like and we can—"

"I have more antiques in one of my homes than this entire shop. I'm not interested in helping you cheat your partners again."

"Then what can I do?" Perry asked, his usual whine back.

I could guess where this was going.

"What do you think you have that I could possibly be interested in? And I'm only talking of covering the interest here, not the principal."

"I'm not sure what you mean," Perry said, as if he was genuinely puzzled and not merely playing coy.

"Oh, come on," the older man said dismissively, "you've sucked a few cocks in your lifetime, haven't you?"

"You want me to suck your cock?"

"What else do you have to offer me?"

I craned my head a little to be able to see Perry's reflection in the mirror and his expression. It was a mixture of sly and repulsed. Clearly Perry had some inkling that he was being treated with the respect due a hustler in a back alley. Just as clearly, he had the instincts of that back-alley hustler. This was a solution to his putative cash-flow problem.

"So, if I suck you off, you'll forgive the interest?" Perry bargained.

"Three times a week, until I'm paid back in full."

Perry was silent, thinking, if his brain churnings could be called that. "Uh…how about twice a week?"

"Three. Take it or I'll have some of my associates communicate with you." Then he added, "Not that they'll say much."

Perry got the picture. "Uh…okay, three times a week."

"Starting now." I heard the sound of a zipper being pulled down and caught a brief glimpse of Perry getting to his knees.

I turned and walked quietly back to the front door. I carefully opened it, then slammed it shut as hard as I could, making sure the bell jangled loudly. Ignoring the heat I walked as quickly as I could to get away from that shop.

I didn't stop until I got to my car, the sweat dripping down my back. I sat there, then realized that the only thing hotter than outside was sitting in a car that had just spent an hour locked up in the sun. I quickly wiped the sweat off my nose, then started the car and kicked the AC on high. I had to rub my hands on my pants to get them dry enough to grip the steering wheel.

Perry had pissed me off. Even if he hadn't given Damon a little push in the direction of death, in those few minutes in that shop I had learned that he scammed his partners, had run up his credit cards to the point of getting loans from men who had associates who didn't talk much, and had no qualms about prostituting himself for a quick buck. And his opinion of himself was so warped that he'd never see how well that word fit what he was doing. I intended to rattle Perry-boy's cage and to rattle it hard.

One more pass of the hands over my jeans, then I gripped the now merely searing steering wheel and headed downtown to my office.

I managed to get there long enough to wash my face, hands, and neck and down half a bottle of water, three gulps' worth, before I heard Shannon coming up the stairs. I noted that she'd been here enough for me to recognize her footsteps.

Framed in the doorway, she said, "Jane Elizabeth Elliot, seven pounds and twelve ounces. Born on the fifth of July, 1998. That makes her seven years, one month, and nineteen days old."

CHAPTER TEN

Shannon's face was red and sweating. At least she's not perfect, was my first oh-so-charitable thought after her announcement. My second and the one I voiced was, "Not bad. Good work, even. If Damon wakes up, you get to tell him." I glanced at the calendar. August 24, 2005. Even her counting was correct. For a second she was silent, then we clearly both wanted to elide over whether Damon would wake up or not. "Good day to be born. It's the same birthday as my friend Larry, Mr. Frog Man."

"Excuse me. Did you just say 'good work' in reference to something I did?" Shannon crossed the room to help herself to my expensive bottled water.

"Sorry, heatstroke or LSD flashback. I meant to say, what the fuck took you so long with that amateur crap?"

Shannon took a long swig then sat down before replying. "I took a break and ate lunch, had phone sex with the girlfriend, for your benefit, I'll have you know—to keep her sated enough to not make a go for your main squeeze—had to do a few of life's little errands like groceries and picking up dry cleaning. Otherwise, I'd have been back here hours ago."

"I appreciate the phone sex. I know what a burden that must have been for you. Tell me what else you found out about Jane Elizabeth Elliot."

"Mother listed as Beatrice Elliot, no father listed. She was born," Shannon pulled a notebook out of her carryall and glanced at it, "at one fifteen a.m.—almost arrived with the fireworks. Place of birth was New Haven, Connecticut."

"Didn't get her Social Security number, did you?"

"No, that wasn't conveniently listed on her birth certificate."

"Amateur city," I mumbled.

"Right, and I presume you solved Damon's attack ages ago and have been filing your nails for the last two hours."

"Yep. Gotta keep 'em clipped. Cordelia's not much into phone sex, so I have to always be prepared for the real thing."

"So, who did it?" As Shannon said it, she stood up and reached across my desk to take one of my hands. Holding it, she made a pretense of examining my nails. "The middle on your right is a tad long." She held my hand for a moment longer, until I pulled it away.

I couldn't quite read her expression, whether she was flirting or challenging me. Then I wondered if she was seriously worried about Lauren and Cordelia. I would let her worry a bit, before cluing her in that Cordelia was Ms. Monogamy of the Millennium. "Finish telling me about Jane Elizabeth and I'll tell you what I have."

"It took me a while trolling Lexis and Nexus. She was born in the Yale–New Haven Hospital. I even called in a favor. An old college roommate works there at the muckety-muck manager level, so I convinced her to pull the old chart for an address. But it's out of date."

"You tried it?"

"Yep, rang the number, answered by some twelve-year-old on a cell phone, so I did the cross and looked up the address, found that phone number, and rang it. This time got a chatty yuppie. Whatever had been there was torn down and he insisted on describing his new condo. Told me he thought girl dicks were sexy and asked me to look him up next time I was in New Haven."

I had to give it to her, she'd crossed her *t*'s and dotted her *i*'s.

"Then I did a run of Elliots in the New Haven area. Fourteen of them. Maybe one of the messages will give me a call back, but of those I talked to, no one knew a Beatrice with Child Jane in tow. Yuppie Boy did tell me he thought the old building had been torn down four years ago. So the address I got was probably at least that much out of date."

I took a sip of water, hoping to cover what I suspected was an expression of annoyance on my face—as well as grudging respect. Shannon knew what she was doing, and she did the follow-through that made the difference between mediocre and excellent.

"What's your next step?" I asked her.

"You're the big dick here, aren't you supposed to tell me?" she retorted.

"The phone sex wasn't good for you, was it?" I countered.

"Are you ever going to stop pissing on me?"

"Sorry, you'll have to get Lauren for that. Not in my repertoire."

"Fuck you, Micky Knight." The red seeped back into her face, not from heat, but anger. "I'm doing your fucking legwork, and you can't even manage a 'thank you.' Just give me shit like I'm some—"

"Fresh in the city twentysomething?" I knew I was pushing it, that I should just end the butch pissing contest and acknowledge that Shannon was pulling her weight.

"Double fuck you. I ought to just tell Lauren to go for it. Have another vagina dialogue. You'd deserve whatever shit you get."

Something in her expression hinted this wasn't just about my being churlish with my praise on her investigative skills—which I was, admittedly. I wondered if Shannon was having a few second thoughts about nonmonogamy, or if she was insecure enough to feel threatened that her lover was spending so much time with Cordelia—another doctor and someone who shared a big part of Lauren's world, one that Shannon never would.

I leaned back and put my feet on my desk. "Let me get this straight, Shannon. You're pissed at me because I didn't lavish praise on you, so you're threatening—if that's the right word—to have your lover seduce my lover?"

She glared at me for at least a full minute. I took a couple of sips of water. Finally she said, "I'm trying to tell you to look where you're heading. You might not like where you end up."

"You're really trying to threaten me, aren't you?"

She looked away, took a drink of her water, then muttered, "Just a warning."

I stood up, strode around my desk until I loomed over her. "This is how you do a threat." I leaned in a little closer, so she had to shift away. "Don't make little pissant 'warnings.' Don't toss around my lover like she's some pawn in whatever sexual games you play with Lauren. Don't piss me off any more than you already have. Understand?"

Shannon made a point of not looking at me. She even started to take a sip of her water, but realized she didn't have room to lift the bottle up with me so close. "You're a macho turd, you know that?"

I grabbed the water bottle out of her hand and threw it across the room. Then took a final step so my legs were against her chair, her knees between mine. She couldn't stand up because I had taken that space. Shannon pulled away, pressing into the back of the chair. It was fleeting, but a look of fear crossed her face. I stood there, keeping my face expressionless. I didn't want Shannon to catch the internal debate I was having. This is stupid, I told myself. If you haven't crossed the line, you're damn close to it. I wasn't even as angry as it probably seemed to her. There was some kind of point I was trying to prove. Then it hit me. Shannon reminded me of myself at her age—brash, smart, and too well aware of it. Except she had a lover of several years, a career she cared about. When I was her age I'd had none of those things. No one had helped that young Micky Knight so I was damned if I would help young Shannon Wild. Maybe Cordelia was right and a few more years of therapy wouldn't hurt.

I leaned over, bracing my hands on the back of the chair, then said very quietly to her, "Scared you, didn't I? Don't worry. I don't expect you to admit it." With that, I stood up and crossed back to my desk.

Shannon bolted out of the chair. "That's it. I'm the fuck out of here."

"Sit down," I said calmly.

"The fuck I will," she said as she started grabbing her things.

"Then don't sit down," I said just as calmly. "I'm sorry things aren't going well with you and Lauren."

Shannon stopped and looked at me. "Who the fuck said things weren't good with me and Lauren?"

"You did."

"I did not," she rejoined, but she didn't resume gathering her things.

"Shannon," I said, as gently as I could, "you did. You told me you're worried about her spending so much time with another doctor, someone her professional equal. You told me you're scared Lauren will dump you for Cordelia and there's nothing you can do to change that."

"I didn't say anything like that."

"Not in words."

"Fuck," was all she said, but she dropped her things and slumped back into the chair. She was silent, then said, "Fuck…you." Another moment of silence passed and she said, "That bloody obvious, huh?"

"No, I'm just discerning."

She gave me a wry smile. "I should warn you, Lauren usually gets what she wants."

"And she told you she wanted Cordelia?"

"Not in words," she echoed, "but I can occasionally be discerning, too. This isn't the first time and I know the pattern by now." She slowly sat up, leaning her elbows on her knees. "She gets busy, no time for me, seems distracted. I can never quite decide if I prefer her being discreet or if it would be better if she just said, 'Hey, I'm off with a new one. I'll let you know when it's over.' Or 'Let you know when I'm ready to leave you,'" she added softly.

"I thought nonmonogamy was your choice."

"No…it was Lauren's requirement." For a brief second she seemed very young and exposed, then her face closed away that young self. "And I thought, hey, why not? Best of both worlds, right? Variety and stability. I also thought, at least she's honest about this whole sex bit. I hate finding out after I've moved all the furniture that it was just a short-term lease. Love forever after a week, only it changes three months later."

"So nonmonogamy didn't quite turn out to be the perfect fantasy?"

"We doing therapy now?"

I just shrugged. It was her choice to answer or not. I was even kind enough not to point out that she was the one who let her anger at Lauren seep into our work.

She chose to answer. "For me, it was either impersonal or messy. One-night stands when I'd never see them again. Hell, my vibrator was often more satisfying. Then messy. Well, she starts to fall in love or want something there isn't enough time in the day to give her."

"But it seems to work for Lauren?"

"Yeah, it does. But I think…because she avoids the consequences. She can be…so ardent, focused on you like you're the only person in the world. She asks about the things that no one else seems to care about. She can make you feel interesting and alive. Lauren just brings that out in people. I don't think she really understands how seductive she is. The thing is, she really is interested…for a while, but…"

I left the silence.

Shannon finished. "And you feel so alone after she's gone. More alone than you ever knew you could be."

"But she hasn't moved, you're the home port."

"Not at first. No. I was happily coupled with someone I'd met in grad school. Two cats, one bed, buying furniture together, when I started doing a story on the famous Dr. Lauren Calder." Shannon paused. "She had a partner, too, of course. She always does. First it was just the frisson of someone really smart, funny, the aura of ambition and success. Then…then she seemed to want to really know me, what made me want to be a journalist, what I went through to become who I was. Then we were in bed together—hot, heady passion. Nothing else in the world mattered." Shannon paused, as if remembering. "But that was only to us. Her partner left a message telling me I was just another one of Lauren's flings and the sooner I crawled back to where I came the better. And she was right. I was just a fling."

"But you're with Lauren and she's not."

"You noticed, huh?" Shannon said with a dry smile. "My partner wasn't so, shall we say, understanding. She got the cats and all the furniture. I managed to get most of my books and my computer and a few hundred out of the checking account before she closed it."

"Hard on you."

"Not fun, but looking back I can't blame her. I was a self-absorbed lout. Not that I quite admitted it at the time. I thought I was pursuing the grand, fated passion. Being doubly dumped and doubly alone, I decided I had nothing to lose by wooing the great Dr. Lauren Calder. I sent her articles I knew she'd be interested in—made sure not to do it too often, just enough to keep her interest. I left flowers anonymously, but we had talked about how much we loved the blue in irises so she knew they were from me. When she broke up with her then-partner, I was there, more than willing to move my computer and books in with her."

"How long ago was that?"

"Three and a half years."

"And she's been with other women in that time?"

"Have I caught her in the act? No. But…I know. I was the other woman once, so I know how she acts. I also now know what I put her partner through. Sometimes I think she really only wants that passionate first rush, when everything is possible and the world is new and you don't have to make compromises with a flawed human being. But mostly I tell myself, this time is different, she'll always come back to me. No matter what, she'll always come back to me."

There seemed little I could say to that. Maybe she was right—and if she wasn't, she had enough insight to see the hurt coming. "In this case you don't have to worry about her coming back since she's not leaving. Cordelia's picture is in the dictionary next to the definition of monogamy."

"Lauren can be very tempting," Shannon said, a rueful smile on her lips.

"I think it might be good for Cordelia to find herself a little tempted. Cordelia even frowns on the fantasy fuck—you know, if you find that Sally Ride is a lesbian and says she's always lusted after you, you're free to go."

"Have you ever cheated on her?"

"In deed? No. Occasional lust, but nothing I can or would act on."

"But that doesn't stop your brain from roving."

"No, but the heart and the body stay put."

Shannon shook her head, then finished her water. "I don't get you. From macho butch turd to Ms. Rock Solid Partner. So, what was that little threat thing about?"

I was hoping we'd moved beyond my churlish acting out of a psychodrama with my younger self. But Shannon didn't let the details go by. "Training. Even you pantywaist journalists might need to make a credible threat someday."

"Training. Right."

"Maybe I wanted…" What did I want, and if I could figure it out, would I tell Shannon? "…wanted to be a macho turd. I guess I felt like you were playing games with me. And Cordelia. And this is my space and my life…and Macho Turd Woman can be a bit territorial." I got up and crossed the office to retrieve the water bottle I'd thrown. I put it away, took another one from the small refrigerator, and handed it to Shannon.

"Just a bit territorial," she said as she took the water from me, her fingers briefly touching mine, as if claiming back some territory.

I sat behind my desk. "You did a good job tracking down Beatrice's bouncing baby. Short of a paternity test, the timing and the circumstances indicate that Damon has a daughter."

"Yeah. I think I'm more sorry for him than her. Jane's never known him, she won't miss that he's not there. But Damon…he was so close to an answer he desperately wanted."

"He may get it yet. It's only been a short time, he may regain consciousness." I said it with more conviction than I felt.

We were both silent. I was guessing Shannon couldn't muster any more conviction that I could.

"So where are we on the 'whodunit' part?" she asked.

I told her about my sordid antique shopping.

When I finished, she said, "Does that put Perry at the top of the suspect list?"

"I'd like him to be."

"Like? You mean he's not?"

I voiced what was troubling me about Perry as suspect number one. "Perry is a 'today and tomorrow' man, not a next-week or next-month man. He only plans far enough ahead to solve today's problem. He wants to go off to the latest circuit party, so he borrows money without really considering how he'll pay it back, or that he might need the money for other things. Today's problem—wanting to go someplace new to party—is solved. But next week's—how to pay the money back—is only made worse. He might have done it, but I'm guessing he'd have had to have the cocaine on him—certainly possible—and that he was handed the opportunity. I just feel this was planned more carefully than that."

"Why do you think that?" Shannon leaned forward. She seemed interested in what I was saying. I even caught a hint of reluctant respect.

"Timing. It's just sheer luck for Perry to spike Damon's drugs almost in time to stop the new will from being signed. The timing is so close it feels like it had to be someone who knew Damon's routine and when they could do what they did."

"He did sign it, but will that will stand?"

"That's for the lawyers to decide. Even if it doesn't stand—and he did sign it, we did witness it, along with Ambrose, so it's got a decent chance—forced heirship still applies."

"But can't they dispute that Damon is the father?"

"Only if the paternity test backs them."

"If there is a paternity test."

"With this kind of money in play, Ambrose has to ask for one, even if Damon doesn't wake up. Damon wanted to find his kid. Beatrice would have one hell of a civil suit if Ambrose doesn't ensure there's enough blood in some freezer somewhere for her to do that. Try that with a jury. Abandoned child, father finally wanting to do the right thing, and uncharismatic lawyer thwarts them by letting them put Damon in the ground without taking a tube of blood."

"And even then, they could exhume him. It'll be years before his DNA is all gone."

"I want Perry as a suspect because I don't like him. But seemingly nice people can also do despicable things. I think we need to look into the rest of the people on the list."

"I've got that journalist appointment with Kent Richards tomorrow. Anything I should ask him?"

"Where he gets his cocaine."

"That's subtle. I'd never have come up with a question like that."

"You can ask about how party drugs are affecting HIV, steer it to what he's seeing locally."

"And throw in some sympathetic ones about how hard it must be in these times to keep the money coming in."

"Got it in one," I told her.

"What will you be doing?"

"I'll talk with the others on our list. Right now I'm going to hold off that the presumed heir actually exists."

"Use it strategically—that might come as an unpleasant surprise."

"It also might keep Damon alive. Maybe it was a bad and nasty joke, but there's a real possibility that the intent was to murder Damon. Whoever did it may try again."

"Another reason to be discreet about finding Jane. He might not stop with just Damon."

"An ugly thought. But not one we can ignore." Shannon was right. While it might be that whoever tried to kill Damon justified it as not really murder, not with Damon so close to death, it could be foolish—and lethal—to underestimate what desperation might drive someone to do.

"What should I do besides the interview with Kent Richards?"

"Find Jane and her mother. Do a quick rundown on the ex-boyfriend list. And if you get a chance, check out the finances of those expecting money from Damon. It would be interesting to see who's the most desperate."

Shannon nodded and stood up. With a glance at her watch, she said, "Our girlfriends might be home by now. Don't want them wondering what we're doing working late." She gave me a roguish grin as she said it. "Is it okay if I start off working at home tomorrow? I'll continue the online sleuthing in the morning, then I talk to Mr. Richards at one. I'll come by after that."

"Call first," I instructed. "I'll be out and about. Let's tentatively plan to meet at the end of the day."

"Have cell phone, will travel." With that, she sauntered out the door.

I needed to be following her, but I wanted to make a phone call before I did that. It was cheating a little bit since this was ostensibly a professional call, but I used her cell number as my first choice.

Obviously Joanne had caller ID, because she answered, "It had better be good—and brief. Alex and I are about to be seated for a major wine-and-roses romantic dinner."

"Say hi to Alex for me, Joanne," I responded. "Briefly, Damon LaChance. The more I look into this, the less it looks like he did this to himself."

"Any concrete reasons?" she asked. I heard Alex in the background saying, "Hi, Micky."

"Timing. He was about to change his will, and too many slimeballs around him need the money they thought they were going to get before he changed it."

"Okay, come by sometime tomorrow. We can talk and I'll try and make a few suggestions to the right people."

Joanne made it clear that this was not an evening during which she wanted to discuss the details. But I'd gotten what I wanted, which was to get my suspicions about Damon headed in an official direction. "Thanks, Joanne. I'll see you tomorrow. Enjoy your dinner."

And with that, it was time for me to head home for what I hoped might also be a romantic dinner. No wine and roses, but a bedroom right upstairs.

CHAPTER ELEVEN

As I entered the door, I realized it wouldn't be a romantic dinner unless we would be having a ménage à trois. I heard two voices in the kitchen.

"Micky, is that you?" the more familiar of the voices called to me.

"No, it's the local neighborhood serial killer come over to borrow a cup of sugar."

"I don't think we have any sugar unless you picked some up," Cordelia answered.

"I only kill those I can't get sugar from," I replied as I stuck my head in the kitchen door.

Fortunately for everyone concerned both Cordelia and Lauren were fully clothed, belts buckled and shoes tied. Not that I had taken Shannon's quasi threat with any real seriousness. Even if Lauren was having a bit of the three-year itch, that didn't mean she would do more than use it as leverage with Shannon, and even if she did anything, Cordelia would have to be willing. I didn't see that happening.

"I couldn't see cooking," my innocent lover said, "so we decided to stop and get Chinese." An explanation that was hardly necessary as the containers of food and the aroma of fried rice easily gave it away. "Can you hold off on the killing if we feed you shrimp with roasted pecans?"

"Hi, Micky," Lauren chimed in. "Our temporary apartment is not set up yet, so I bribed my way here with sweet-and-sour pork."

"Shrimp and a kiss," I said, interrupting Cordelia's unpacking the food to claim the latter. She didn't quite kiss me back the way I kissed her, but then she's not one for public displays of affection. "More later," I whispered to her, loud enough for Lauren to hear. I didn't mind her seeing me kiss Cordelia or getting a hint that she needed no rescue from "lesbian bed death." "What about Shannon?" I asked, to bring the conversation back up to company level. "Does she have to live on peanut butter?"

"No, I called her on her cell and she's on her way here," Lauren said.

I realized that I'd prefer to have spent some time away from Shannon—because I'd been a macho-turd jerk and now I'd have to spend the whole evening wondering if and how she might bring up my display of macho turdiness.

Cordelia and Lauren went back to their conversation. "We can do the attachments to the protocol while we're waiting for IRB approval," Cordelia said.

"What's an IRB?" I asked.

"Institutional Review Board," Lauren answered. "Any research involving human subjects has to be approved by an IRB to ensure that it's ethical."

Cordelia sighed ever so slightly, my hint that she didn't want to educate me on things I'd shown little interest in before now. I took the hint and edged her away from the food. Even if it was takeout, we could still be civilized and eat with real knives and forks, and folded napkins even.

Just as I finished getting everything arranged, the doorbell rang. "Good timing," I told Shannon as I let her in.

She had two bottles of wine. "One red and one white," she said. "I didn't know what kind you drink." She followed me into the kitchen.

"We can present this at USCA," Lauren was saying. She didn't feel a need to kiss Shannon hello and settled for a brief wave as she continued, "or the National Prevention conference CDC does in Atlanta."

"That's why they need all those years of education," I told Shannon, "to memorize all the different acronyms."

Lauren clearly overheard me. She flashed a quick smile and said, "USCA is the United States Conference on AIDS and the CDC is the Centers for Disease Control."

Cordelia didn't smile.

I turned to Shannon and asked, "Which would you prefer?" as I took the corkscrew out of the drawer.

"Whatever you're having," she replied.

"I'm having water."

"Then I'll go with the red," she answered. "Do you not like wine or do you not drink?"

I hated answering this question. I'd yet to come up with a quick, flip answer to explain what a mess I'd made of my life with the aid of a bottle. I wanted to say "You don't know me well enough yet for the answer," but instead I replied, "I like wine, I don't drink." I put the corkscrew into the bottle.

"Should I have not brought any?" Shannon asked softly, although our lovers were lost in their medical world of acronyms and jargon.

"No, it's fine," I said, pulling the cork out. "I'm used to it. Can't live in New Orleans without alcohol at every party." I took three wineglasses from the cupboard and took them out to the table.

Once we settled down to eat, the conversation moved to more normal topics. Books, movies, restaurant recommendations for Lauren and Shannon. Lauren was even polite enough to ask me about what I was doing.

As I answered, I realized that Shannon was right. Lauren had an ardent interest that could easily be seductive. The most beguiling thing was that it was real, or at least it seemed so to me. She asked me what I did and how I felt about what I did. What was it like uniting a lost daughter with a mother seeking her for a decade? What happened when I didn't find the person I was looking for? What cases haunted me? I told her about the young woman who died in a ravine, bleeding to death from her attack. I hadn't even told Cordelia about that case. But Lauren wanted to know about me—why I told her parents what I told them, why I withheld what I didn't tell them.

"How did you keep that secret without telling anyone?" she asked, her eyes holding mine.

I couldn't answer for a moment. Lauren reached out and held my hand until I found a response. "She wasn't my daughter. It will haunt me, but in the way we should all be haunted by common, unnecessary cruelties. Her parents knew she died young, that she was murdered—that was pain enough."

"That must have happened before we got together," Cordelia said. "I don't remember you ever telling me about it."

"No," I said slowly, "it was several years ago. It was a few weeks after we visited my mother in New York for the first time. You were very busy because you'd taken so much time off from the clinic. Working late most nights. I didn't want to burden you."

"I guess I was busy," Cordelia said. "I'm sorry." Her tone was more perfunctory, her voice the one she used when she didn't want to say what she was really thinking. I wasn't sure what emotion it was hiding—hurt that I hadn't told her, but now let it out at this dinner party? Or did she not like that I was monopolizing Lauren?

"It's not that big a deal," I said. "Lauren just asked me about some of my cases."

"The ones 'that haunt you the most,' if I recall," Cordelia replied. Then she stood up and began clearing the table. "We have fresh blueberries and ice cream for dessert," she said as she headed into the kitchen.

"Let me help," Lauren said, grabbing my plate and hers. She followed Cordelia to the kitchen.

"Maybe we should all help," I muttered. I started to corral the salad bowls, but Shannon put her hand on my arm.

"There is helping and there is helping," she pointed out. "Let the old ladies serve us for once. Besides, you did the setup."

"In other words, I should let Lauren clean up the mess between Cordelia and me."

"No, or not quite. Cordelia could have asked the same question Lauren asked," Shannon pointed out.

"You think she should have?" I retorted, not liking the implied criticism of my lover.

"You seem to. She seems to. What I think doesn't really matter."

"I should have told her. She shouldn't have had to ask." I didn't add the obvious. That she shouldn't have found out in front of company, hearing me talk to someone I barely knew. Cordelia had been busy and tired, she had gone out of her way to make time for me to be with my mother, and the long hours were her cost for doing so. I came home one night wanting to talk, having just told the dead woman's parents, but Cordelia was already in bed and asleep when I got there. Time passed and other things crowded in.

I heard laughter from the kitchen. Lauren had already worked her magic.

"Don't tell me that you and Lauren share every detail every day, all the time," I said to Shannon.

"Just the important ones," she rejoined.

"Cordelia's never cheated on me," I shot back. That wasn't fair. Shannon had let down her guard with me, revealing that their nonmonogamous relationship wasn't her choice but Lauren's requirement. My remark had its effect, a fleeting grimace, then she turned away from me.

I covered her hand with mine. She didn't respond to my touch. "I'm sorry," I said. "That wasn't fair."

"All's fair in love and war, isn't it?" She still didn't look my way.

"This isn't love or war."

She turned to me and took my hand between both of hers. "Are you sure?"

Lauren and Cordelia came back into the dining room with the bowls of berries and ice cream. Just in case they somehow missed our handholding, Shannon jerked away as if caught at something.

"Glad to see you missed me," Lauren said in a wry tone.

Cordelia put a bowl down in front of me, but said nothing.

"I love blueberries," Lauren said as she took a bite.

I was pissed at Shannon, Cordelia. Oh, yeah, and myself. I was pretty sure Shannon was playing a game, taking my hand to prove something to Lauren. My back was to the kitchen, Shannon to my left—she could have seen them headed this way. Cordelia was overreacting and I was overreacting to her overreaction. You're not guilty of anything, I told myself, so don't act like you're guilty of anything.

I took a bite of ice cream, then decided to break the silence. "I do have a doctor question about a case I'm working on right now."

I gave them the quick rundown about Damon—not his name, of course. HIV positive, but dying of hepatitis C. His sudden downturn and his suspicions that someone had given him cocaine. I also mentioned that he had the kind of money people would be angry about losing, angry enough to play a nasty joke, maybe even angry enough to kill. Halfway through my narrative, Cordelia relaxed enough to start eating those antioxidant blueberries she was always preaching about to me.

When I finished, Lauren was even astute enough to say to Cordelia, "This is more your area of expertise. Penises, drugs, and infectious disease are things I mostly left behind in medical school."

Cordelia would think about it just for me, I was pretty sure, but now she could also show off for Dr. Lauren.

"Any chance he missed the fast lane and took coke himself?" Cordelia asked.

"I don't think so. He's an intelligent man. He had to have a good idea of the risk in taking some party drugs. He was scared of dying. He had some things he wanted to finish before he was gone, and... he seemed so surprised when it happened." I remembered the look in Damon's eyes, the startlement and confusion.

"Any idea what kinds of meds he was on?" Cordelia asked.

"I took a picture of his pill bottles on my digital camera," Shannon put in. That led to her retrieving her camera from her car. Both Lauren and Cordelia crowded around her to get a good view.

I cleaned up the dessert bowls. Cordelia had finished the blueberries, but left most of the ice cream. Since she had served herself, she had presumably wanted it before she caught sight of Shannon holding my hand.

After several minutes of looking at the images stored in the camera, everyone realized that the pictures were too small to read the drug labels. I halted the discussion of whether our computer had the capability to display Shannon's pictures by finding the list I had written down. The low-tech pen vanquishes the high-tech camera.

Cordelia peered over my shoulder. I saved her the indignity of finding her reading glasses by reading to her. "Rebetol, Kaletra, Combivir, Diflucan, Bactrim DS."

"Nothing there that I'd really question," Cordelia said. "I wonder if he knew about Kaletra and what it would do."

"What would it do?" I asked.

"It's a mix of two protease inhibitors, ritonavir and lopinavir. Ritonavir is one of the early ones and quickly fell out of use until it was discovered that it greatly increased the bioavailability of other drugs," Cordelia explained.

"In English," Lauren added, putting her hand on Cordelia's shoulder to make her remark friendly, "ritonavir is a crank."

"If he took cocaine it would increase the effect," Cordelia added.

"If he knew that, then that's pretty strong evidence he knew how risky taking any street drug could be, and further proof of your suspicion that someone did this to him."

"But there's not much way to know that, is there?" Shannon mused. "Unless he wakes up and tells us."

I had no answer to that question. We were all silent. But I wanted to keep talking about Damon and medical issues, instead of risking heading into emotional shoals. I said, "It's probably nothing, but he said something that sounded like 'nor veer.' Does that mean anything to anyone?"

Lauren shook her head.

But Cordelia said, "He gave you the answer. Norvir is the brand name for ritonavir. He was seeing what was happening. Someone had slipped him the cocaine and he realized that the Norvir would crank it up. To the point his damaged body couldn't handle it."

"Damn," I said.

Shannon echoed it with her own "Damn."

"Now the question is, did the person who gave it to him know?" I asked. "If he did, then his intent was murder."

On that high note, the evening wound down. Lauren and Shannon helped clear off the few things left on the table. Then we walked them to their car, Cordelia going with Lauren to the driver's side as they talked about where and what time they would meet tomorrow.

I watched the way Lauren hugged Cordelia good-bye. If she's not tempted by that, then she really is Ms. Monogamy USA, I thought, with a fleeting wish for Lauren to give me that kind of hug.

Lauren got in the car and Cordelia bent down to make some final comment through the window. I became aware that Shannon had been watching me watching them, the shadows not quite hiding her sardonic smile. She shrugged, made a half turn for the car, then turned back, took my face in her hands, and kissed me on the lips. She quickly let go and got in the car.

Cordelia straightened up and came around to join me. We waved as they drove off, but she didn't say anything as we walked back to the house. We both headed to the kitchen to finish cleaning up. I was trying to come up with some way to say "It's not what you think it is" without making it seem like I was protesting far too much.

Cordelia stood at the sink as if she was about to finish rinsing the dishes and put them in the dishwasher. Finally she sighed, turned to me, and said, "Is there something you want to tell me?" Before I answered, she added, "Or something I should know?"

I fumbled with putting away the soy sauce, then said, "I think Shannon's games are for Lauren's benefit. I'm sorry you're getting some of the fallout."

"What do you mean?"

"To make Lauren jealous and pay attention to her. The hand-holding. The kiss."

"She kissed you?"

Cordelia had missed that. Damn. I had assumed she'd stood up just in time to catch a glimpse.

"Yeah, just now out on the sidewalk."

"Did you kiss her back?"

"No, of course not."

"Did you want to?"

I didn't answer quite quickly enough. Cordelia turned back to the sink.

"No, I didn't want to. I didn't…" Don't protest too much. "Look, Shannon's good-looking and she's smart, and if you didn't exist, I'd want to kiss her." I came up behind Cordelia and put my arms around her. "But you do exist and I do love you and I don't want that to change."

She remained stiff in my arms. I was silent, just holding her. Finally, she covered my hands with hers. But she said, "What would you say if you were really sleeping with her?"

I wondered what I would say. But I wasn't cheating on Cordelia and I didn't have to lie. "I don't know. I hope I don't ever know what I would say."

She turned in my embrace to face me, her arms lightly around my waist. "Just don't lie to me." The look on her face was almost beyond fear into resignation, but it was fleeting, and she hid her expression from me by resting her head on my shoulder. I tightened my arms around her.

"I need to go to bed," she mumbled into my neck. "I'm tired."

"I'll join you." But her brief distrust made me add, "If you want me to."

"It's your bed, too." Cordelia let go of me and headed up the stairs to our bedroom.

I followed and climbed in beside her, hesitated, then curled beside her.

"It is so damned complicated, isn't it?" she murmured, then lifted my chin to kiss me.

I kissed her back, wanting to banish any stray thought of Shannon's brief touch of lips.

She kissed me for a moment more, then broke it off. "I'm tired."

"Can we go out tomorrow night?" I asked. "Just the two of us? Someplace nice for dinner?" I usually grumbled about getting dressed up for someplace fancy, and it was something Cordelia wanted to do more often than I did.

"Yeah, we can do that," she mumbled sleepily. After that all I heard was her regular breath of sleep.

She was tired. But I had to wonder if being tired was a way to avoid the doubt and distrust that had crept in between us.

Chapter Twelve

I lay awake for a long time before finally falling into sleep. When I woke, I was alone in the bed. A glance at the clock told me Cordelia was long gone. This, I told myself as I flung off the covers, was just another of our ups and downs.

I was a little disappointed to not find a note from her, but I did notice her coffee cup on top of the dishes from last night. A washed coffee cup meant she was in her usual morning routine, an unwashed one meant that she was late and in a hurry. I hoped she remembered we had a dinner date tonight.

I'll call her sometime today and remind her, I thought as I added my cup to hers. I was also late and in a hurry.

Shannon wasn't at my office, which I was glad for, although I hadn't been expecting her. I left her a note on top of the small refrigerator—to let her know that I knew she would be drinking my water—explaining that I was heading to the North Shore, the far side of Lake Pontchartrain, to talk to Damon's ex, the one George had mentioned.

I also called Cordelia's clinic. She was busy with patients. The somewhat-new receptionist I was talking to didn't seem aware of my special-privileged-lover status. I left a message. "Remember we're having dinner tonight."

After that I grabbed a bottle of water and headed out.

The Causeway over the lake is twenty-four miles long, so for a good portion it's just you, the road, and the water. Lake Pontchartrain is shallow and only slowly recovering from years of pollution, so it's not the sightliest body of water. But then, I wasn't looking at the scenery.

I stopped for gas in Mandeville, the first land at the end of the Causeway, and also to consult a map and figure out just where Jud Lasser lived. I'd done the handy computer thing of letting the digital age give me directions from here to there, but I'm a great believer in the familiar, and I'd been to Abita Springs, the town listed, several times. It's most well known as the place where a local favorite, Abita Beer, is brewed. In my younger years I went to the brewhouse restaurant more than a few times.

I filled my car, emptied my bladder, and headed out to find Jud. I hadn't called ahead, which would give me the element of surprise. The only question was whether it was his at me showing up or mine at making this trip for nothing.

His place was on the outskirts of town, a rambling old house with several leafy oaks and magnolias in the front yard. A weathered bench swing hung from one of the oak branches, and on the wide porch was an arrangement of wicker chairs, also weathered. The place looked comfortable and lived in.

If Jud wasn't home, someone was. As I got out of my car, I heard the buzz of a power tool and a whistled tune. I followed the sounds around to the back of the house. The noise covered up my approach, and I was able to observe the man I guessed to be Jud Lasser.

He was sanding a table, one that when finished would be worth a few thousand dollars. Jud was a tall, handsome man; his hair had sawdust in it and was just on the border between blond and brown, with highlights of both. It could have been dyed, but it had the look of a man who spends time in the sun. His face had a few lines and seams, some from his age, which I guessed to be either late thirties or early forties, but also from the weathered tan from working in the sun. As he moved to put his sander down, I noticed a tan line at his sleeve, so clearly he was not a sun bunny striving to bake evenly.

In the quiet he realized he was being watched. I hadn't stirred or made a noise, that I was aware of. An observant man. He didn't seem particularly startled to have a strange woman appear in his backyard. He brushed the sawdust out of his hair, then said, "Can I help you?"

"I'm looking for Jud Lasser," I replied.

"You're looking at him. What can I do for you?"

Jud seemed friendly and open. This was the part of my job I didn't like. It would have been nice to be friendly and open back, but I needed to question him about an attempted murder and get him to reveal more than he intended.

I brandished my PI license, trying to make it look as official as I could. "My name's Michele Knight. I'm an investigator from New Orleans. Tell me what you know about Damon LaChance."

Jud looked at me for a long time. Finally he said, "That's a long order. I know a lot about Damon. What are you investigating about him?" He seemed more perplexed and curious than hostile or defensive.

I decided that friendly was probably the better way to go with him. I actually preferred an honest antagonistic questioning to a fake friendly one. "I'm not investigating Damon, but what happened to him."

"That he collapsed?"

"How do you know that?"

"George called me, so did Miss Carlotta."

"What did they tell you?"

Jud again brushed the sawdust out of his hair. "Let me take a break. We'll be more comfortable on the porch with some iced tea." He didn't wait for my answer, but led me back around to the front and up the stairs to the porch.

I followed him into the house. The door opened to a comfortable living room, which was open to a dining area with an example of what the unfinished table in the back would look like when it was done. It was a deep burnished oak, in a simple style, as if the wood needed little adornment. The chairs matched the table, also clearly handcrafted.

"Beautiful work," I commented.

"Thanks. That was one of the first tables I made. I gave it to my grandmother. When she passed away, it came back to me. Lot of her good cooking is now part of the spirit of that table." He led the way back into the kitchen. Like the rest of the house, it wasn't picture-perfect but had a comfortable, lived-in look.

Jud washed his hands, then took a big pitcher of tea from the refrigerator, grabbed two large tumblers, sugar bowl, lemon and knife to slice it, and put them all on a platter. He easily hoisted the platter with one hand and with a nod of his head pointed me back out to the porch.

"No air-conditioning, I'm impressed," I said as we sat down.

Jud started slicing the lemon. "Don't be too impressed. Got a big old compressor out back, but I don't see much point in running it all day when I'm mostly outside."

"So, what do you know about what happened to Damon?" I asked. The day was still hot, but it was comfortable on the porch with the shade and a breeze.

He poured a glass of tea and put it in front of me, then did the same for himself. I didn't fill the silence, waiting for him to do so.

"Miss Carlotta called me, she was worried about George."

"She wasn't worried about Damon?" I asked. "And how does Miss Carlotta figure in all this?"

"Carlotta LaChance, Damon's aunt. She's a bit crusty, but she's entitled, I'd say—outlived her husband by twenty-five years so far. She's worried about Damon, too. But George called her from Damon's place. No one told him what happened, so he went to work there as usual, only to find an empty house. He waited a bit, called Miss Carlotta. Her car was in the shop. So I drove into town, picked up George and her, and we went to see Damon in the hospital."

"That didn't upset George more?"

"No, George is easier with things he can see than things he can't. He could see that Damon was well cared for. Ambrose bustling around telling us we could only stay a few minutes didn't help, but that's Ambrose."

"You don't like Ambrose?" I made it more a statement than a question.

"Not really dislike, we just live in different worlds. He likes power and control. I walked away from it."

"How so?"

"I used to be a lawyer."

"Now you're a carpenter?"

"After I got diagnosed, I took a long look at my life, decided I didn't want to sit at a desk with a tie around my neck worrying about billable hours."

"Diagnosed?"

"HIV. Something to remember Damon by."

"He infected you?"

"Can't say a hundred percent, but most likely."

"Good reason not to like a man."

"Yeah, but I was a big boy and I had my eyes open. Or should have. Everything we did I agreed to. Damon was honest. Condom broke once and we didn't use it for oral."

"Still, HIV is a hell of a parting gift."

"I won't say that HIV is the best thing to happen to me, and I wish to hell I'd learned the lessons it taught me in another way. But I'm doing what I want to now, making myself happy instead of anyone else. My friends are now my friends because they like me, not because of what I might do for them."

"Happy ending all around?"

"You think something happened to Damon?" Jud was a smart man, and he caught the slight sardonic note in my voice.

"Damon thinks something happened to him. I was there when he collapsed. He was just signing a new will. It was sudden."

"You think someone poisoned him? He was dying."

"What I know is that Damon is a very rich man and he was changing his will. When that kind of money is involved and something happens that wasn't supposed to happen, it raises suspicion."

Jud was silent. He was HIV positive, so he probably knew about the medications, and he used to be a lawyer, so he would be at least passing familiar with forced heirship.

Finally he said, "That's not a pleasant thought. I suppose I'm on the suspect list."

I didn't respond to that and asked, "What if that did happen? Who do you think would do that?"

"How about whoever mentioned my name?"

"You're in Damon's will."

He took a moment, then said, "It would depend. I'm presuming tests are being run on Damon to determine if he was slipped anything. Who would know he was signing a new will? Was the motive money? Jealousy? Something else?"

"Who would be jealous of a dying man?"

"Perry. Kent. Bruce. People I don't know. Even Ambrose."

"He's in love with Damon," I pointed out.

"You think it's love? I'd call it control. Or maybe that's what love is to him."

"What would cause Ambrose to kill Damon?"

"Maybe if Damon cut Ambrose out—not of the money, per se, but pushed him to the side. But...I don't like Ambrose, yet I can't see him doing something like this."

"So that's love, or what passes. Who would kill Damon for money?" Before he could answer, I asked, "How much are you getting?"

He gave me a sharp look, a smart man and enough of a lawyer to know he was being interrogated. "Not enough to even consider murder. I have what I need, and what I want, here," he said, his eyes sweeping across the shaded lawn. "I can afford the AC if I want to run it. The water is hot when I turn it on. I can buy a good cut of steak if I like. Have a truck that's fairly new and in good condition. Will I turn down Damon's money? No. It might come in handy with medical costs down the line, and I think he owes me that. Will it make me happier? No."

"What if it's twenty-five percent less because Damon fathered a child?"

"It won't make the sun stop shining."

"Who would murder Damon for money?"

"Well...I'd like it to be Perry. Him I really don't like. He has the morals to run over crippled children if they got in his way, just not the organizational skills. He has to have a maid to boil his water."

"What if he got someone to help him?"

Jud finished his tea and poured more. "That's possible. Perry would do it out of spite. He's the bitterest queen in the universe. Bruce Payne would do it out of desperation. Everyone knows about his money troubles. He's been digging himself further and further into gambling debt, maybe deep enough to realize that the blackjack table won't get him out."

"What do you know about Kent Richards and the Crescent City Care Coalition?"

"Kent? A little too fond of nose candy. On the path to hell paved with his good intentions."

"So, I should put him off the murder-suspect list?"

Jud gave me a wry smile. "Would it matter who I told you to not suspect?"

"George?"

"No, not George. George might lose his temper and punch someone, but not Damon."

"Did Damon ever mention possibly having a kid to you?"

"He did. Once, when he was somewhat drunk. It was his hard-edged kidding, what I came to recognize as his behavior when he was dealing with something he didn't want to deal with."

"What did he say? Do you remember?"

Jud gave a rueful half-smile. "Remember hard-edged. Something along the lines that his dick could take on anything, including a woman, and he had a kid somewhere to prove it."

"That was all?"

"Well, we hadn't been together long then and…I don't think we talked much more after that. But he brought it up later, just a few months ago."

"Really? In what way?"

"Asking my advice, or at least just running it up the flagpole. If I thought it was a bad idea then everyone would think it was a bad idea."

"And did you think it was a bad idea?"

"Oddly, no, I didn't. I could see how it might disrupt life for both the child and the mother. But…Damon would be a good father. He hasn't been a perfect person, by any means, but fooling around and fathering a kid, only to walk away, was low. He needed to say he was wrong and that he was sorry, for himself, if not for them."

"So you encouraged him?"

"I guess I did, although I gather I was a minority."

"Who was opposed?"

"Perry screeched about it. I think for him it was both the money and the thought that a penis he touched had also touched a vagina. His uncle thought it was a 'damn fool thing to do,' according to what Damon told me. Ambrose listed every legal reason to be 'cautious' about it. That's all I heard directly."

"What did you hear indirectly?"

"The usual gossip. Some titillated at the idea of Damon having a kid, which turned into a wife and kids somewhere along the line. Others enjoying the comeuppance of those expecting money and how that would change it."

"So was it common knowledge among Damon's circle?" I asked.

"That's an interesting thing. Damon said he didn't really tell anyone, save for some close friends, but about three weeks ago, I was in town for a birthday party and it was the topic of conversation. I think someone in the inner circle leaked."

"Why? Any ideas?"

"Anything from the usual, having a story to tell that will get you attention, to trying to make a mess. Bruce Payne was really agitated at hearing it, and of course Perry had to smear it in his face. 'There goes your bar, little Brucie boy.' Royce, his head of security for the bars, wasn't happy either. Perry started his shit with him, and Royce slammed him against the wall and told him to shut the fuck up."

"Do you know Royce's last name?"

"No. It might be Royce, but that's the only name I have for him."

I nodded. It would be easy enough to find out. And another person to question. "Any other likely suspects?" I asked.

"The shifty-eyed guy in the raincoat?" he said with a crooked smile. Men would swoon for it. Even I found him attractive.

"No credible evidence he was in the area," I replied, straight-faced.

Jud was silent for a moment, then said, "I don't want it to be someone I know. Even someone I don't like. It's one thing to be greedy or self-serving…but murder…"

"Being greedy and self-serving can be the hallmarks of murder. Remember the banality of evil." Jud was a smart man, he would understand my reference—Hannah Arendt's famous remark on the Nazi bureaucrats, the ones who made sure the trains taking the Jews to the concentration camps ran on time.

"Yeah, it's not convenient when they're not monsters, when they resemble the guy next door." He took another sip of tea, then said, "Damon is special, and everyone wants a piece of that special."

"Including you?" I asked quietly.

"At first, yes, oh, yes. I fell really hard for him…and stayed around long enough to see a real, flawed man behind his Mardi Gras mask of a life. I still loved him, even now I still do. He's funny and charming and generous. He makes me laugh more than just about anyone."

"Was he in love with you?"

Jud took a long time before finally answering. "I think so…but I'll never know for sure. Damon called love, those first few heady months, the electric touch. So he said love, but love doesn't just disappear. At least that's the way I see it."

"Was that how it was for you? Just disappeared?"

"Guess Damon got to know me as a real person, too. Why settle for a flawed human when you can move on to the next fantasy man?"

"Who did he move on to?" I asked.

But Jud didn't directly answer. "The party was fun until I got that test result. Then I realized life can be short and I wanted to do other things than stay up all night drinking. I suddenly felt like all the beer tasted flat and the conversations were just the same thing over and over again. But Damon lived for the attention, all the pretty young boys vying to get a piece of what was special about him."

"So who broke you up?" I prompted him.

"We didn't really break up, just drifted apart. I bought this place, started spending more time out here working with the wood and less time driving over the bridge to party. Found out that I preferred the trees and the breeze to the boys and the bars. But you asked for suspects, not my happy ending." He gave me his crooked smile again, one I couldn't help returning. "Damon shined oh, so bright a light on people when he gave them his attention. Then he left them in the dark. Some people… might do anything not to be left in the dark."

"Murder?"

"Yes. I can only name the people I knew when I knew Damon. There might be others."

"In the darkness?"

"You mentioned love earlier. Maybe the reason is money, but don't overlook love."

I finished my tea and thanked Jud for his time. He shook my hand, then was back to his unfinished table, whistling and sanding by the time I started my car.

I thought about the darkness as I drove across the lake. Money was the obvious motive, but being given love—or what you think is love—then having it taken away is painful. It seemed that Damon had caused a lot of that pain for others.

I liked Jud and, as did he, wanted the monsters obvious, not someone I enjoyed drinking tea with on a comfortable porch.

CHAPTER THIRTEEN

I made a quick stop by my office. Shannon still wasn't there, which was still fine with me. Joanne had left a message asking if I could stop by in what was now a half hour from now. I told my grumbling stomach that it would eat soon, but duty called. I didn't think this would be a long meeting.

I was right. The detective Joanne introduced me to was polite, and she listened carefully to my story and speculation. She seemed to think some form of foul play was more than possible, but added, as I almost knew she would, "We have to have more evidence than a dying man seeming to die a little sooner. Get me a gun, it doesn't even have to be smoking, and we'll look harder at it."

Then I was back out in the heat, asphalt heat, no shade, no breeze, and not a glass of iced tea in sight. I called in an order for a fried-crawfish wrap at one of my favorite little bistros in the lower end of the Quarter, turned the AC in my car on high, and headed back downtown. The parking gods were cruel, and my quick stop to grab lunch required me to park two blocks away. Someday this steam-bath summer has to end, I told myself. Even the windows rolled down and the AC on full blast got only the worst of the heat out of my car before I got to my office.

My car, my old one that Shannon was driving, was parked out front. I hope she's had lunch, I thought as I mounted the stairs, because I'm not sharing mine.

She was sitting at my desk, drinking my water and eating a messy-looking oyster po-boy. She glanced up when I entered, but wasn't going to be interrupted mid-chew to acknowledge me.

"Gosh," I said, "and here I thought that a smart Yankee girl like you would know that the desk is for working and this table," I said as I moved a stack of paper as if it had no business being there, "is for eating." I put my food in the now-cleared space, sliding it a little so as to rub away the dust outline left from the paper.

"Was making phone calls," Shannon mumbled as she swallowed.

"Your cell phone doesn't work over here?" I crossed to the refrigerator to get some water, knowing there was only one there when I left. I was coming up with the perfect stinging rebuke as I opened the door. Shannon had bought more water and stocked it.

"A couple in the freezer, they should be good and cold."

They were there and they were cold.

"What did you do today?"

Shannon finished chewing, then had the good sense to pick up her food and join me at the table. I pushed aside another stack of paper to make room for her. She even picked up a plump oyster that fell out of her sandwich and put it on my take-out container. Crawfish and oysters can go a long way to making a frustrating day bearable.

"What did you find out?" I asked, taking a bite from my wrap. I didn't want to hastily gobble the oyster, no matter how much my stomach suggested otherwise.

"More than I want to know and not much to help this case."

"What's the more-than?"

She put her po-boy down to answer. I kept eating.

"Kent Richards is a smarmy slimebag. Even had the nerve to ask me to 'skirt' for him at some uptown party. I replied with surprise that anyone would think he was straight. So he explained that the idea wasn't to fool anyone really, just to obey the social rules and make nice."

"Are you going with him?"

"Hell, no," she answered. "I asked some questions about drugs and where to get them, and he offered to introduce me to his dealer."

"That was pretty blatant," I said, finally succumbing to the oyster.

"He didn't quite say the words, but his intent was clear. He could introduce me to someone who would 'take care of anything I wanted,' and he put in a long pause before adding 'to know.' The whole time I was there, I didn't see anyone who looked like a client of the agency. I did see a fair number of friends, most young, good-looking men, drop by. He acted more like it was a bar at happy hour than a workplace."

"Were you able to work it around to Damon and the money?"

"You betcha. Kent acted like he's used to journalists on a daily basis, but he didn't have a clue how an interview of this sort would really go. And he never once asked me anything, like where I got my information, that kind of stuff. So, I asked questions about funding, all that sort of thing. He bitched about grants, said they didn't add enough for expenses like copy machines, all the admin stuff—like his salary. From there I moved to fund-raising, then sucker punched him with a question about Damon's money and the rumor that it was all being left to a child."

Shannon took a sip of water, enjoying the attention I was giving her. I looked away from her to my crawfish wrap and took another bite.

"He tried to cover, but turned a little white and started blustering that it had to be just some stupid rumor. He knew Damon well enough to be sure there was never a child, that Damon was a great supporter of CCCC and was confident his money would be used for the right things."

"Better or worse acting job than Perry?" I asked.

"Worse, if you can believe that. Of course, Kent was the star in this little drama. Perry was just a bit sidewalk player." Shannon took another sip of water, barely suppressing a big grin. "So I told him I had it on good sources that Damon'd hired a top-notch private investigator who was now looking for an actual child." She was no longer suppressing her smile. "He sputtered that it couldn't be true and then said he'd heard who that top-notch PI was." Shannon put her hand on my arm for emphasis. "I quote, 'that bull dyke, Micky Knight, who couldn't detect her way out of her Bywater office,' end quote."

I threw my wrap down. "That does it. He has to be the murderer," I fumed. "I am not a bull dyke." I do get shit like this more often than I'd like. Some comes from being a woman, some from being lesbian, and then being a lesbian woman in a man's job. It might not really prove Kent Richards a killer, but it did prove that he was a grade-A jerk.

Shannon was still grinning. "So I gave Mr. Kent Richards a lesson in doing interviews with reporters. I told him I was on my way down to your office to talk to you next, and as he hadn't gone off the record, I'd see how you responded to his comment."

I briefly covered her hand with mine, then remembered I wasn't supposed to like Shannon Wild this much and instead picked up my wrap again. "No digital pictures?" I asked between chews.

"Alas, no, but he was pretty close to beet red. By that point, I didn't like him very much, so I twisted the knife a little bit more and told him I'd also be talking to all the city officials he'd trashed, as well as looking at the financial records. Which I had to remind him were public."

"I'm glad you're on my side," I said. Then added, "I think."

"So, Madame-Not-a-Bull-Dyke, what did you do today?"

I ignored the title and told her about Jud, giving her a chance to eat.

"Left in the darkness," she mused after I'd finished. She bunched up her sandwich paper into a small ball that she crushed in her hand. "I wouldn't have murdered to get Lauren back after that first time, but I wasn't the most honorable person either. I wonder if he could be right."

"About someone trying to kill Damon for love instead of money? Could be. But it makes sense to me to look at those who had dual motives—they were involved with Damon and expecting money."

Shannon, as if letting go of something, threw the paper across the room into the trash can. "I've got an update on Beatrice."

"Where she is?"

"Where she was. She went back to college, got a PhD in English from the University of Connecticut. Tomorrow I'll try and track her down through the alumni office. That's as far as I got with her today. Also got through at least some of the ex-boyfriend list. Boring, boring, then bingo. One of them just got out of jail."

"Local?"

"Angola."

"That's local enough." Angola was a couple hours' drive north of New Orleans, in the middle of cotton fields. "How long has he been out?"

"About two months. Nothing beyond that. Just out of jail and into the air. I couldn't get an address or any idea where he ended up."

"Not a bad day's work," I allowed. I balled up my trash and threw it toward the can. Mine hit the edge and bounced back to the floor. I picked it up and put it where it belonged. Then I brushed off my desk, as if I had found crumbs there. "If we keep up this pace, we might be done before Southern Decadence."

"Before what? You mean there's a specific time for it?"

"You probably call it by the more prosaic Labor Day weekend, but down here in New Orleans it's a party centered around the quaint tradition of men dressing up in drag, parading around the Quarter, and doing their best to scare the tourists. The weekend after next."

"I don't suppose it will be any cooler by then."

"No, cher, it probably won't break below eighty until early October."

"And here I packed some sweaters, thinking it might be cool at night."

"Only in the air-conditioning."

"Did you call me 'cher'?"

"Sorry, the Cajun coming out."

"It was kind of cute, sounded almost natural."

I knew I had to bring up what happened last night, and I would have preferred to avoid it.

"Ah, you silent butch types," Shannon said, filling the stillness. "You just need to dust the table a bit more if you want me to believe it's where you always eat your lunch." With that, she got up and started gathering her things. "I presume that having done a decent day's work, I can now go home for the two-hour shower it will take to get the sweat off me."

Just say it and get it out, I told myself. "Shannon, I like you and you do good work, but I'd really prefer not to be caught up in whatever games you're playing with Lauren."

Shannon hefted her bag over her shoulder, then turned to look directly at me. "What do you mean?"

"Last night? Remember kissing me?"

"That's what you think? That I'm playing games?"

"What other reason could there be?"

Shannon looked away, then her gaze was again on me. "Maybe I wanted to kiss you." She turned and walked out the door. I heard her steps hastening down the stairs.

Oh, fuck, I thought. I should have listened to my instincts and avoided all this emotional stuff. Shannon playing games was one thing. Shannon actually attracted to me was another.

The phone rang. I picked it up. Cordelia. Of course.

"Hi," she said. "I'm guessing you've already made the dinner reservation."

Well, no, I hadn't. But I wasn't about to let her think I'd forgotten to do that. "Yes, I have, what's up?"

"What time?"

"Uh…seven."

"Can we do it earlier? Say around six?"

"Uh, yeah. I can call and change it."

"I may have to go to the hospital, there are a…lot of things up in the air."

"Okay. Should I meet you at the clinic?"

"No, I'll be home a little before six. See you there."

I put the phone down for a second, then picked it up again. "Torbin," I said as his answering machine picked up. "Romantic dinner. Tonight. At six. Suggestions?"

He picked up. "The Lavender Cross to the rescue. Dare I ask just whom this romantic dinner is for?"

"Cordelia, of course," I quickly answered.

"I didn't think it was you and anyone else. I just thought it might be another romantic couple altogether." Torbin knew me far too well. "Patching up a little altercation, are we?"

"No. Well, not really. Just we've been busy and I wanted some quality time."

"Ah. So it is true that she's been spending the days with the famous Dr. Lauren Calder. Is she as attractive as she looks in her pictures?"

"Torbin, just what would you know about *Vagina Dialogues*?" I asked, ever so cleverly avoiding his question.

"Two sisters, one mother, and a bevy of lesbian friends. I can dialogue with a vagina as well as any man. So, I'm gathering that the answer to my question is yes, she is stunningly attractive, as charming in real life as she appears on the talk shows, and has been spending a good deal of time with your true love."

I did avoid answering the question because Torbin did it for me.

"Time's wasting. She wants to meet at six, and I'm supposed to be calling to change the reservations from seven."

"The reservations you haven't made yet merely lied about."

"Exactly, those reservations."

"On a scale of Commander's to Bywater Bar-b-que, where do you want to end up?"

Commander's Palace is one of the top restaurants in New Orleans, Bywater a funky, good burger and bar downtown where I once saw a cook wearing an apron that said, "Don't make me poison your food."

"Something that will impress her, yet not too snooty."

"To which I have the connections to get you in at the last minute. How about Bacco or Bayona?" Torbin knew better than to leave that opening too wide. "Good," he went on without pause. "I'll call and let you know where you're eating."

Two minutes later, the phone rang again. "Bayona at six p.m. and you owe me. There's a large convention in town and places are booked."

"Who would dare come to New Orleans in August?" I inquired.

"Damn Yankees. And there's a hurricane heading for the Keys and probably into the Gulf. They could have the full Crescent City treatment."

"Busy season. We're already into, what, J, K, L now?"

"K something, I think. Let's hope it heads to Texas."

"Thanks, Tor. I'm sure you'll keep in mind that I owe you."

I stared at my desk as if it would give me an answer about any of this. Maybe part of the game is that Shannon doesn't want to admit that it's a game, I told myself, still thinking of her parting remark. I mused on telling Cordelia, but then had to wonder if she would believe me that I hadn't…what? Encouraged Shannon's attraction? I hadn't, or at least didn't think I had. Well, I hadn't exactly jerked away from her kiss.

I focused again at the piles on my desk. Find who tried to harm Damon, find his daughter. Say good-bye to Shannon Wild. And hope that Cordelia says good-bye to Dr. Lauren Calder. I told myself I was feeling guilty if I was letting myself think Cordelia would even flirt with Dr. Lauren. Let alone allow a hasty good-night kiss. As I had.

I'll make love to her tonight for so long she won't need sex for a year, I told myself. And maybe convince her that I really have been faithful to her for the last nine-plus years.

I did manage to find out that Royce, the security head Jud had mentioned, was on vacation in Australia during the pertinent times, and well before and after, in fact.

A little after five, I headed home. The heat suggested a shower for me if I wanted to carry out my major romantic-evening plan. I even went as far as putting on the little black dress, sleeveless and summer weight. Then perfume and earrings. I looked at myself in the mirror. Not bad for a bull dyke. A few gray hairs, the lines at the corner of my eyes didn't disappear as they always had in years past. I began to think I looked like a little girl overdressed—albeit with gray hair. A glance at my watch told me it was too late to change. Well, Cordelia loves me, I thought as I turned from the mirror. She'll at least appreciate the effort.

At five minutes to six the phone rang.

Cordelia. "Micky, I'm sorry, I'm running late. Can we meet at the restaurant?"

"Of course. Do you trust me to order for you?"

"That'd be good. Sorry, things are crazy here. I'll see you in a bit."

"Bayona," I got in before she hung up.

"What?"

"The restaurant we're meeting at. Bayona, 400 block of Dauphine."

"Thanks, see you soon."

Cordelia would clearly need to be steered in the romantic direction I was hoping to go.

I didn't bother to look again at the mirror, as I grabbed my keys, cell phone, and wallet and threw them in the little black purse I kept around for pocket-less ensembles. I'd really owe Torbin if I didn't show up after the strings he'd pulled.

I was seated with a menu in front of me by a little beyond a quarter after. I took my time, to give Cordelia time as well. A before-dinner drink would be helpful, I thought as the waiter refilled my water glass. At a quarter to seven, I went ahead and ordered for us both.

Two minutes later my cell phone rang.

"Micky, I'm sorry," Cordelia said. "I…just can't get away. You're at the restaurant, aren't you?"

"Well—"

"I'm sorry," she repeated. "I know this isn't…I'm sorry." She sounded tired, upset even.

"It's okay. Things come up, you can't help it."

"Yeah, they do. When you least expect it." She was silent for a moment, then said, "I may be late getting home."

"I'll be up."

"No, don't. It may be late even for you. I've got to go. I'll talk to you later."

She was gone. I stared at my cell phone as the waiter put the salads on the table. I stared at my phone another second, then dialed Torbin. Without preamble, I said, "I've been stood up and they just served the salads. Are you hungry?"

"Your treat?"

"No, my trick, I'd say."

I guess Torbin heard the dejection in my voice. "Ten minutes max. Don't let the salad wilt." He lived close enough that ten minutes was realistic.

I'd barely picked a few lettuce leaves from my salad when he arrived. Torbin, in boy drag, as he calls it, is a tall, stunning blond. He was dressed in a white summer suit, with a light gray V-necked shirt under it, stylish and casual. I felt such a wave of relief at seeing him that I jumped up and hugged him.

Must be close to my period, I thought as I sat down. My emotions were unexpected. Yes, I was disappointed. However, I also knew what kind of hours Cordelia worked when I married her. But I'd been sitting here alone in a crowded restaurant, and much as I knew that I hadn't been abandoned, the appearance that I had been had seeped into my thoughts. A no-longer-young woman by herself, that was what I looked like.

"Is Andy upset that I pulled you away at the last minute?" I asked Torbin about his partner.

"Andy doesn't know," he said. "Poor boy, he's at a computer-nerd conference in San Francisco. Called me last night to rub in that it was in the low seventies during the day and then had the gall to complain about having to wear a jacket at night."

"So, we've both been abandoned?" I let slip out. "In the temporary sense."

"Gives us a chance for a girls' night out," he said in a conspiring voice. Torbin then launched into both his salad and the latest gossip from the bars of the Quarter.

Even when he's not trying, Torbin can get me to laugh. Tonight he was trying. After about half an hour in his company, I was having a good time and feeling sorry for my girlfriend, still at work and probably grabbing a sandwich in the cafeteria.

Cordelia would be late, so we lingered, Torbin sipping cognac while we considered dessert. "How's the case of the missing child progressing?" he asked.

"Might have it done before Decadence."

The waiter came and we decided to split the chocolate tart.

Torbin was quiet for a moment, then said, "I like Damon, but he was flame and he singed a lot of moths."

"Someone else said something like that, that Damon's attention was like a spotlight, and when he turned away, he left people in the dark."

"Maybe…but Damon didn't intend to hurt anyone. I don't think he understood the effect he had on people and didn't see why they were so hurt when he wasn't there for them anymore."

"But he still hurt people along the way."

"Yes, he did. But there are people who are cowards or slimy on the way out the door."

"Yeah, I've known a few people like that. Sometimes we lied because we couldn't think of how to tell the truth."

Torbin covered my hand with his. "I'm not talking about you. In your younger days, you were more like Damon than the cowards I'm talking about. I never saw you pretend to love someone you didn't love. It's not a kindness to claim love when it isn't really there."

"Still—"

"This isn't about you, keep to my point. When love isn't equal it will hurt, but there are those who still care enough about the person to be decent and kind as they leave. If you're a real bastard, it leaves a festering hate. If you're decent, only the few who are desperate for what they can't have will continue to pursue a failed love affair."

"Obsessive? Crazy?"

"The ones who never stopped wanting what Damon couldn't give them."

The waiter brought our chocolate tart. It was too good to talk about murder.

Torbin walked me to my car, holding my hand as we strolled in the quiet of a late summer night in the French Quarter. In the distance, we could hear the clop of the carriages and a fog was rolling in. With gaslight flickering, I could almost feel the centuries that this patch of land by the river had endured. Through storm and fever and fire and war, it had endured.

I offered Torbin a ride the few blocks to his house, but he declined, as if the history were calling to him, too. He hugged me tight and for a long time. Then I watched his white suit until he turned the far corner.

When I got home, Cordelia's car wasn't there. There was no message on our answering machine. She did say she would be late, I reminded myself.

I hastily changed out of the dress. Torbin had told me I looked good. Better than nothing. I lingered a while, reading a bit, until almost one in the morning. I tried to quell my worry. Cordelia could, and did, often work late, but this was late for even her. Two possible reasons came to mind, neither happy thoughts. The first was that whatever was keeping her at the hospital was seriously bad, people so ill or hurt that she couldn't leave. That was the best option. The other was that she had left the hospital and something happened to her. No, she's okay, I told myself. If something happened other than her still being in the hospital, I'd have heard by now.

I remember the clock blinking something like one thirty, but nothing after that.

CHAPTER FOURTEEN

When I woke, Cordelia was in bed beside me, fast asleep. She didn't budge when I got up. I looked at her for a moment; even in sleep she seemed tired or worried. Or maybe, I thought, like me, she's getting older, and I haven't paid enough attention to notice. I was greatly relieved that she was here. At least I knew that whatever had caused her long hours away, it was someone else's calamity. And maybe her being there had made a difference. Selfishly, I thought, to stand me up she should have at least saved all the orphans and their puppies, too.

I gently kissed her on the cheek then quietly got ready. I even waited until I got to my office to make coffee, so as to make sure I didn't wake her with either noise or the smell of freshly brewing caffeine.

Shannon wasn't there and I was faced with a far-too-clean desk. I skimmed the Internet for news, but it was late August, too hot for much to happen. The hurricane was a category one, barely huffing and puffing at the lower end of Florida, and predictions had it headed for the Panhandle.

Time to talk to a few more people. I left the office, got in my car, and slowly drove by Damon's house. I wondered who might be hanging out there, but it seemed empty. It was too early for either Perry Thompson or Bruce Payne. I headed uptown to talk to Damon's aunt, George's other employer.

She lived in an old Garden District home, with several large oak trees shading the front lawn. It had the requisite white columns and generous veranda. A big boat of a Cadillac, pink, no less, was parked in the driveway. I pulled out my license as I mounted the stairs. This wasn't the kind of door that opened to just anyone, and my twill khakis and polo shirt—dressed up from my usual jeans and T-shirt—didn't scream fancy-pants professional.

The door opened just as I put my foot on the porch.

"You must be Micky Knight," a tall, gray-haired woman announced from the open doorway. "I was wondering when you'd get around to me."

"Money talks," I said as I took her proffered hand. "And yours seems to say you don't have a major motive for trying to hurt your nephew."

"Well, if you're going down the major-suspects list first, I'll be mollified. I didn't want you passing me by because you thought a little old lady like me wouldn't be of much use." She stood back and ushered me in.

The house was beautifully furnished, with antiques that had been handed down, not bought. They showed the nicks and scars of generations of use as well as the loving care of those generations.

"A Walter Anderson?" I asked, noting one of the paintings on her walls.

"Yes, I bought it because I liked it, before he became famous around here. Let's go to the kitchen. The coffee's brewed."

Miss Carlotta was probably somewhere in her late sixties or early seventies, but looked younger, her handsome jaw and brow the same as Damon's. Her hair was a silver white, thick and full, also like Damon's, but his would never have the years to turn to silver.

She made strong coffee. Her offer of "Milk?" was almost a challenge, as if only wimps or less-than-true-New Orleanians would need to dilute her black chicory mix.

I smiled and declined. We seated ourselves at her kitchen table. "So, who would want to try to kill Damon?" I asked.

"That's getting to the point," she said, taking a sip of her coffee before telling me, "I love my nephew. It's not a fair life that I'll go to his funeral instead of him to mine. If Ambrose does something foolish like pulling you off this case, I'll pay you."

"Did Ambrose say anything about that to you?"

"Ambrose treats me the way men who don't really like women

do—as if whatever he gives me is more than I deserve. He makes the decisions and his sole responsibility is to tell me."

In less than five minutes with Miss Carlotta I knew better than to patronize her. It was telling that after years of knowing Damon—and presumably seeing how Damon treated his aunt—that Ambrose hadn't figured that out.

"I'm guessing that bothers you?" I said, in a tone that made it clear there was no guessing on my part.

"First of all, Damon isn't dead. I'm of no mind to hurry him to the grave. Oh, yes, I know, it doesn't look good. Still, Ambrose seems to have forgotten how often Damon rejected his advice.

"Second, I'm the actual executor for the estate. Ambrose is Damon's lawyer of, I'd say, more convenience than choice. Once Jud started making furniture full-time, Damon ended up with the B legal team."

"Ambrose gave the impression that he was the executor."

"Not legally." Miss Carlotta snorted. "He'll manage the foundation, parceling out a few thousand here and there. Mostly I'd expect to the more handsome of the artists, not the most talented."

"Do you think Ambrose would harm Damon to get this a little sooner?"

She pursed her lips. "No. Too weak for murder. Or too fastidious. I'm not even sure which. And I think that he—in his odd way—cared for Damon too much to consider hurting him."

I remembered the flustered man Ambrose had become after Damon collapsed and found myself agreeing with Miss Carlotta. Ambrose was too weak and too much of a control freak for the chaos of attempted murder. "Has he talked about taking me off the case?"

"He had the nerve to tell me he didn't think searching for the missing child was a good idea. Like I wouldn't want to find the child almost as much as Damon wanted to. Then when I made it clear that I strongly disagreed with that, he suggested that 'we' bring in a real private-detective agency, a big one from someplace like Atlanta or Houston."

"They might have resources I don't have," I said mildly.

"And they wouldn't have a clue about New Orleans, especially the gay world that Damon lives in. No, thank you. I trust Damon's judgment more than Ambrose's, and Damon picked you. I think it was more Ambrose's way to give me—and Damon—what we want, while doing his best to thwart us."

"Why? What does he have to gain by thwarting you?"

"It's not about gain. It's about power and control. Add a child, and her mother, and Ambrose loses a lot of control. Plus, a mother is another woman. You're a woman. Far too many women for him."

"He'll have another one to deal with. Damon has a daughter."

For a moment, Miss Carlotta said nothing. Then she brought her hands to her face, as if to feel the surprise of joy that suffused her features. "A daughter? Are you sure?"

I had dropped that information to see her reaction. Anyone can claim to want something, but the truth was in her emotions. Miss Carlotta wanted to see her nephew's child, even if it was likely that he would not.

"We've tracked down birth records that fit what Damon told us. Beatrice Elliot did have a daughter, Jane Elizabeth. You're the first to know and, given everything, it's best to keep it quiet for now. We haven't uncovered her current whereabouts or contacted her yet."

"But you will? You must," Miss Carlotta decided.

I smiled. Jane Elizabeth had a doting great-aunt she hadn't met yet. "I will do my best." Then I had to add, "I can't predict how Beatrice Elliot will react. She may not want any contact."

"We'll worry about that when we get there. I can be as charming as my nephew if I put my mind to it."

I had no doubt of that. "What can you tell me about Damon, about those around him?"

"Like who do I think would hurt him?" She got to the point.

"That might be useful."

"Damon had good taste in women and horrible taste in men. Pretty Boy Perry is a ratter. I guess I can see it clearly because I didn't have that sex thing blurring my vision. Sex just turns men into idiots."

"Why would Perry murder Damon?" I asked.

"Oh, damn, maybe for money or because Damon wouldn't buy him a new designer suit. He'd have to think of it first, though, and that would tax his brain. But, as much as I don't like him, I'd have to put him in the same category as Ambrose, too weak. He'd sneak money out of Damon's wallet, but murder?"

"Even poison, the so-called woman's crime?"

"What was the poison?"

"Probably cocaine. Mixed with the other drugs Damon was on, it could easily be fatal."

She gave a harsh laugh. "Couldn't see Perry using his fun drugs for anything other than himself."

"Maybe he had a lot, thought he could spare some."

"Not the Perry I know. He always cadged from others. The grasshopper in the story of the grasshopper and the ant would be a prudent planner compared to him."

"So who would slip Damon cocaine in an attempt to kill him?"

"A little sooner than life was going to?"

"Yes, why kill a dying man?"

"Because he could give you something in death that he couldn't in life."

"What about his uncle, the one who lives out by Lafayette?"

"Raul? No, not likely. Raul doesn't have much, but he has what he needs and he's a smart enough man to know that. He loves Damon, although he doesn't understand him. Besides, he will do anything to avoid traveling into Lafayette—too much traffic, too confusing. You can imagine how he feels about New Orleans."

"If you had to pick someone, who would it be?" Miss Carlotta had good instincts and I was interested in which way hers pointed.

She briefly thought, then answered, "That ragtag bar manager. Bruce whatever his name is."

"Bruce Payne," I supplied. "Why?"

"He's desperate, lucky that Damon felt sorry for him. He won't get that lucky again."

"Does he know that?"

"It's what makes him desperate. He knows it the way an animal knows it. And he might think that killing Damon before you find the child will make a difference."

"Any other likely suspects?"

"Damon told me a lot about his life. More than you'd think he'd share with an old widowed aunt," she said with a faint smile. "No one else stands out."

"George?"

"No," she said with a vigorous shake of her head.

"Why not?"

"Have you ever talked to George?"

"Yes, he's a…damaged man."

"Drugs. He was an average young man, new to being gay and to the party life, not as smart as some, perhaps. Certainly not as lucky as some. He took the wrong ones and came out of the coma with the damage you noted. He never blamed Damon."

"Why would he blame Damon?" I had a good guess, but wanted to hear from her.

"It happened at one of Damon's parties." I left a silence. She said, "I love Damon. I don't excuse him."

"What if George didn't know? Came out of the coma without being aware of what happened and only recently found out?"

"Possible if it happened that way. But it didn't. Damon told him. He thought it only fair that George know what took so much away. Damon is very good at talking to George in a way that George understands. And Damon did everything he could to give George dignity and value in his life, patiently trained him so he could work, talked me into letting him live in the cottage behind my garage. Damon can be reckless, but he can also be very kind. It redeems him in some measure."

"Does he need redemption?"

"Don't we all?" Miss Carlotta looked directly at me, as if she knew too much about sin, mine included.

"What about Jud Lassar?"

She stood up. "Come. Let me show you something." She led me around a corner and into the formal dining room. A beautifully made oak table stood in the center of the room. She gestured to it. "Could someone who made that be a killer?"

"Yes."

She cast me an annoyed look, like I was being too literal when I should be subtle. "Point given," she admitted. "Jud's harm to Damon was to be too late in holding up a mirror with other choices for him to look at. If Jud had shown up ten years earlier and given Damon a view of life with meaning outside the party life…"

"Do you blame Jud for that?" I asked.

A wash of sorrow etched her face. "No, I blame myself. I lived the same life for so long. Parties and balls, a new dress, good champagne.

The consequences were different for me. I got enough years to get a good long run at redemption. Damon…"

Will not. I didn't say it for her.

She regained her composure. "While I would call Jud strong enough to kill, I can't see him having the heart or soul for it. He likes women and children. I think he'll like that Damon has a child more than he cares about money."

That was what I wanted to believe of Jud Lasser as well. But it didn't make it true.

"What else would it help me to know about Damon?" I asked.

She gave a slight smile. "I think I know too much about him to know what to sort out. I can show you pictures of him as a newborn to a month ago at my birthday. I was twenty-eight when he was born. I can't quite believe…" She was silent, finally finishing with, "that time has passed so quickly."

"Let me know if you think of something," I said, digging in my wallet to give her a card.

"Or if I need to hire you myself," she said, taking the card and walking me to the door.

I asked her one last question as we stood on the porch. "Are you sure it's not the weak men who turn to murder?"

She looked at me for a long minute before answering. "No, but I don't want Damon taken by a weak man. Apollo should be taken by another god, don't you think?"

I nodded and she softly closed the door.

A glance at my watch as I got in my car told me it was late enough to return to the antique store and possibly find Perry there. Weak men could murder and he was a very weak man.

Like most of us who actually live in Orleans Parish, I tend to think that only tourists and people from the suburbs pay for parking in the French Quarter. However, today I put my snobbery aside and pulled into a parking lot close to Perry and partner's antique store. I didn't like Perry as it was, and a long hot walk wouldn't make me like him any better.

The massive rococo table with its dainty china was still displayed in the window. A small measure of my faith in humanity was restored by it not having been bought yet.

I pushed open the door.

Perry Thompson was behind the counter, reading a magazine. He glanced up as I came in, obviously assessed me as being a tourist looker rather than a buyer worth his time—gave me a bare nod—and went back to his reading or, from the quickness of the turning pages, his looking at pictures.

I used his inattention to glance around for any of his other partners, including a quick glance in the mirror that reflected the back room. It seemed we were alone.

I strode to the counter and put my license on it. I gave Perry enough time to notice I was shoving something official under his nose, then put it back in my pocket. "My name is Michele Knight and I'm investigating the attempted murder of Damon LaChance."

That got Perry-boy's attention. He actually put down the magazine. "Murder?" He blinked at me. "But Damon is dying. Why would anyone need to kill him?"

Miss Carlotta was right; thinking was heavy labor for Perry. I could almost watch the thoughts forming and moving across his brain, down his face, and into his mouth.

"Damon was changing his will, making some people—like you— less well-off than they thought they'd be. He was also looking for a child he possibly fathered, which would cut down the amount even more. Maybe someone thought that killing him now would prevent those things from happening."

"But murder, isn't that a stretch?" Perry's voice was taking on that whining sound I found so annoying. How could Damon have overlooked that? Perry was tall, with a perfect nose, a very good blond dye job, big brown bedroom eyes, and the body of someone who spent more time working out than reading or thinking. Maybe they didn't talk much.

"Attempted murder and, no, it's not a stretch."

"Oh, please, this is a waste of my time," he said peevishly, reaching for the magazine.

"You're at the top of the suspect list, Mr. Thompson," I informed him. "I can arrange to have your time 'wasted' down at the station if that's what you'd prefer." I didn't cross my fingers because I might be able to arrange it, plus I hadn't really defined "station." It could be gas.

"Me?" He tried to look shocked, but good acting requires thinking and, as already noted, that was not his strong point. "Why would I want to hurt Damon?"

"Because you desperately need the money you were planning to get from him. You're way over your head in debt. The sooner he dies, the sooner you get it. And it would be helpful if he would die before changing his will and before finding his child."

His lips turned down and he spat out, "Rubbish. Damon and I are very close. He has no reason to cut me out and therefore I have no reason to hurt him."

"I've seen the two wills. I know exactly how much you stand to lose," I informed him.

Perry was used to getting away with his lies, so he had little idea of what to do when called on one of them. A sheen of sweat appeared on his upper lip. He was silent. It looked like no thoughts were moving through his brain. Finally he said, "Well, this is the first I've heard of it."

"Then why were you fighting with him about his will shortly before he collapsed?" I questioned.

"Wha… Who told you that?" He was clearly flustered.

"Several witnesses."

"That stupid George." He snorted. "He's an idiot. You can't trust what he says."

"Several witnesses," I repeated.

"Well, no…yes, I guess, but not in the way you're implying." His leg was jiggling rapidly. "I mean, we had a little fight. But nothing major. Not major at all."

It was time for me to be silent and let Perry talk. People talking faster than they think often let things out they shouldn't. By this point, I was guessing that his mouth was about a week in front of his brain.

"These things can get twisted, you know. Damon and I, well, we might fight, but it never meant anything. Damon always came around. I was very good to him and he appreciated that. I'd go with him wherever he wanted to go—the best parties, good restaurants, any vacation he wanted company on."

"Damon paid?" I interjected.

"Well, yes, of course. That was the deal."

"What did you provide?"

He stood up, almost preening, so I could get a good look at him and his body. He even flexed an arm for me.

I kept an expectant look on my face as if waiting for his answer.

He sighed, a whiny sigh if that's possible. "Most men would give their eyeteeth to be with me."

"Damon wasn't most men," I answered.

"What are you, a lesbian?" he retorted.

"Yes." Then I stated, "So you worked as an escort for Damon?"

That ruffled his fine feathers. "It wasn't like that at all."

"Damon got tired of you, but he was leaving you something in his will. Then he decided to leave you a lot less."

"Well, let me tell you, Miss Dyke, I didn't do it, but Damon deserved what he got," Perry retorted. "We'd all planned what we'd do with the money, made promises about it."

"Counting coins on his grave?" I cut in.

"I gave him the best years of my life!"

I stared at him, wondering if he knew what a cliché he had just become. "Really? From what you told me, it sounds like you sold him the best years of your life. At a pretty high price."

"You don't understand," he huffed.

I wasn't interested in understanding. "Who else was there?"

"Well, George, of course. He could have done something. He's so stupid, he could mess anything up. That stupid prick Ambrose was there. Just waiting for a chance to remind me he'd control the estate once Damon was gone. He hates me because he knows Damon likes me more than he likes him."

I understood his convoluted sentence to mean that Damon had sex with Perry, but not with Ambrose. "So were Ambrose and George there the whole time you were?"

"Well, George went to the kitchen to do whatever he does there. Ambrose looked like he was all set to be his usual prick self and park himself between Damon and me, but I was better than that pantywaist dick, and this time I ran him off."

"How'd you do that?"

Perry blinked. "Well, I just told him to go, that I was tired of looking at his ugly face...or something like that."

It seemed more like Ambrose was tired of Perry than Perry actually being manly enough to run the pantywaist lawyer off.

"So you scared off the big, bad lawyer? In other words you were alone with Damon and had the perfect opportunity to slip him enough cocaine to blow out his damaged heart. And don't tell me you don't have access to more than enough cocaine to do that."

Perry finally seemed to understand that he'd put a noose around his neck. The sheen of sweat covered his face. "But…but," he sputtered. "I didn't do it. Really."

"So who did do it?"

Again, I watched the thoughts as they slowly furrowed his brow, then stumbled out of his mouth. "Well, George and Ambrose were there, they could have done it."

"What's their motive?"

That stumped him. Finally he said, "Well, anything. Money, just like mine."

"Damon wasn't cutting them out," I noted.

"Well, then the ones he was cutting out. Any of them."

"Most aren't as in debt as you are."

"Oh." The brow furrowed again. He would need a shot of Botox by the time I got through with him. "Well, some are." A little more thinking and he said, "I know—Bruce, that bar manager. He had gambling debts. He needed the money."

"How do you know that?"

"I get around," Perry said, as if he was proud of how well he knew the party scene.

"Tell me more."

"I heard him cursing Damon out, saying something like he'd throttle the kid himself if it could keep the money coming." Perry leaned a little closer. He seemed to like trashing other people, especially when it could save his butt. "Little Brucie was also teetering on the line of being fired and cut out completely, close to washing dishes in Biloxi for the rest of his life."

"How'd he get put in the will in the first place?" I asked.

"Bruce used to be a hard worker. Not smart, just hard." Perry didn't seem to be making a pun. "Came from some bumfuck town in the lower parishes, wanted to be part of the scene, got a job as barback, stayed late, worked hard. Used to be able to count on him to make things happen. He'd get the ice through during Mardi Gras, make sure the beer truck showed up. That sort of thing. Useful little fellow." Bruce wasn't small, and I doubted that Perry called him Little Brucie to his face.

"So why did he get unuseful?"

"He started thinking he deserved things, that he made Damon's bars work, so he was owed. He'd already paid in time, and he didn't think he needed to pay anymore. Plus he fell in love, or lust, with some new boy bartender. They were hot and heavy for a few years. Then the boy dropped him like a lead balloon for something better, so Brucie started drinking off the top shelf. Drowned his sorrows."

"Who was the something better?" I asked.

Perry managed a smug little smile that told me exactly who the "something better" was, at least in his estimation. "That would be telling."

"How'd you do it?" I asked.

"Do it?"

"Break up Bruce and his boyfriend."

He seemed to forget that he said he wasn't telling. "The poor boy was young and new to town when he fell for Brucie. He wised up, saw his prince was really just a frog. That and a few hints of indiscretion on Brucie's part and they were splitsville."

"You lied and told him Bruce was cheating on him?"

"Not lied, exactly. Maybe Bruce was."

Perry was doing something I thought would have been very hard, making me like him even less than I already did. "Just a little Iago, huh?"

"What?"

"Never mind. Maybe Bruce had the motive, but no one saw him at Damon's place that day. Who else?"

"Oh. Everyone Damon is cutting out." A moment of heavy thinking. "Jud Lasser. You need to look into him."

"Why?"

"He and Damon used to be together. I know Damon would have left him a lot. He's a carpenter, so he would need the money."

Jud had probably sold that table I saw in Miss Carlotta's dining room for enough money to pay off most of Perry's debts.

"Jud used to be a lawyer," I pointed out.

"Yeah, I guess he couldn't take it. Not much of a success and I never did trust him."

"Why not?"

"Well, he just wasn't trustworthy," was the best answer Perry could come up with.

"Damon dumped you to take up with Jud," I guessed.

"Jud was an evil, manipulative bastard," he spat. "He probably told Damon lies about me to break us apart. Damon was a fool to give me up." Then his eyes brightened in glee. "And I saw him there that day."

"Where and when?" I asked, surprised.

"That day," he repeated, as if that was all the answer I needed. "I think it was him."

"You didn't see him inside Damon's house? Just someone you've now suddenly decided was him?"

"Do you believe me or not?" Perry whined back.

No, not at all. "Just the facts, sir, just the facts."

"I wasn't the only boyfriend Damon dumped. You ought to talk to Kent Richards. He can tell you where some bodies are buried."

"Why would Kent know that?"

"He was one of them."

"And he knows where the 'bodies are buried,'" Perry didn't seem to notice how inapt his metaphor was, "but you don't?"

"Well…I've heard rumors that Damon wasn't always careful with using a condom. Kent might know about that." He said it with a sly look on his face that made me think he was being as honest with me as he had been with Bruce's boyfriend. Plus, even if Kent did know, he'd be breaking all kinds of confidentiality laws to say anything to me.

"Are you saying he didn't use a condom with you?" I asked him directly.

"Well…no, of course we used them. But I'm just saying—"

"Anything you think you can get away with," I retorted.

He actually stamped his foot. "Look, I'm trying to help you. I'm giving you information you wouldn't get any other way."

"You're trying to do anything you can—including telling vicious lies—to point me away from you. Why are you so desperate, Mr. Thompson? What do you have to hide?"

The tips of his perfectly dyed hair were turning damp with sweat, and his leg was almost beyond jiggling to jerking. "I am not hiding anything, and I am not lying and I…oh."

The door to the shop opened. A very well-dressed older man entered. I hadn't seen his face clearly, but from Perry's reaction, his gentleman caller had arrived.

I wanted to believe that Perry was as guilty as the sins he committed. But, "You've got drugs on you, don't you?"

"No, of course not," he lied, not even thinking enough to stop himself from giving his pants pocket a quick pat.

"I'll be back," I said. I turned and walked around the older man. He barely glanced at me. His face had the expression of someone carrying out a minor business detail. I didn't think he'd be giving his eyeteeth for Perry. As I closed the door behind me, part of me wanted Perry to be guilty. But part of me also agreed with Miss Carlotta. Someone as petty as he was shouldn't have been allowed to bring down Apollo.

I crossed to the shady side of the street. It was just past noon and the sun was searing. Compounding my tourist's errors, I stopped and bought a bottle of water from one of the street vendors. Better overcharged than overheated, I thought as I took a swig.

Next stop, Bruce Payne. I hoped it was early enough for him to be sober.

The Outer Limits, the bar Bruce managed and hoped to inherit, had only a few people in it—two men in a corner and a woman at the bar. The men looked like tourists getting out of the heat, the woman like a fixture. It was cool and dim inside. Bruce was sitting at the far end of the bar, talking to the very young, very good-looking bartender. I stood just inside the door, letting my eyes adjust and watching him. It seemed that the conversation was mostly one-sided, with the bartender doing the listening of someone who has to listen. He seemed relieved when the woman signaled him for a refill.

I slowly made my way to Bruce, giving the bartender time to move away to the tap to draw a beer. As I drew near, Bruce looked at me, watching me approach him.

"You're the dyke dick, aren't you?" he said, busying himself with lighting a cigarette to show he wasn't really interested in my answer or worried about being questioned by a private detective.

"And what if I am?" I sat on a bar stool beside him.

"Nothing to me." He shrugged, making a point to blow smoke in my direction. "Damon's money is his business. I just run the bar."

"If you don't get fired for drinking from the top shelf," I replied, ignoring the smoke and matching his bored tone.

His bored tone disappeared. "Who the fuck told you that?" Bruce stabbed out his half-smoked cigarette and then promptly lit another one.

"Or arrested for the drug dealing," I added, using the same neutral tone.

He stared at me for a long stretch. "Bullshit." He finally exploded. "Only drug here is booze." He started to stab out the just-lit cigarette but stopped himself just shy of the ashtray.

I didn't say anything, letting my silence tell him how much I believed him.

"Who the fuck told you that?"

"You should be more careful, Bruce. Anything goes here, but only as long as it doesn't go too far."

"What the fuck does that mean?" he demanded, blowing a stream of smoke directly at my face as punctuation.

"It means that I spent half an hour in this bar and saw the drug dealing and the booze pilfering myself. You wouldn't fool a rookie undercover cop, and I can promise you that sooner or later one will be in here."

"What the fuck is this? Blackmail?"

"I work for Damon," I answered. He stabbed out the cigarette. I continued as he again lit another one, "And it's a good thing for you that he hired me to find his missing child and to find out who slipped him something to prevent his signing a new will."

Bruce took a long drag on his cigarette. His hand was starting to tremble. He said, "Yeah, that's what I heard, that he was about to sign the will and, bam, something happened. Like the hand of God." He blew smoke in my face.

"He did sign his will."

"Bullshit! Ambrose told me he didn't sign it."

"I witnessed him signing it."

"What the fuck!" Bruce ground his cigarette into the ashtray, hard enough to send shreds of tobacco onto the bar.

"Ambrose told you Damon didn't sign the will before he collapsed." I made it a statement and not a question.

"Ambrose told me…said he didn't think Damon would sign it, or he was sure Damon wouldn't really sign it. Something like that." He got up and went behind the bar, avoiding looking at me. He dug around under the bar, then brought out a new pack of cigarettes. He lit one and took a long drag before coming back around the bar to again sit. "I don't really remember. Just talked to Ambrose one day, he mentioned the damn will. Likes to remind me he's the executor and we're all gonna have to suck his dick."

"When did he tell you this?"

He shrugged. "Don't really remember. He was in here one day."

"Ambrose comes in here so often, you can't remember when?" Bruce was clearly lying about something.

"Kent Richards warned me about you," he said in a nasty tone.

"So you're his dealer."

"I don't know what the hell you're talking about," he said, so quickly it was clear he knew exactly what I was talking about. "I don't sell drugs and I pay for the booze I drink."

"Bruce, Perry calls you 'Little Brucie.' Is that your nickname?"

That got the expected reaction. "That cunt!" He stabbed out his cigarette so forcefully that it sent the ashtray skittering down the bar. "I'll break that fuckin' pretty-boy face of his one day soon."

"Get this clear, I'm investigating Damon's attempted murder. What I'm finding out about you isn't pretty. Lot of motives for you to go after Damon. Debt—you're up to your nose hairs in it. Revenge— you're about to get fired with nothing. When I'm done, and I'm close to it, I'm handing everything over to the police. You'll have a jolly time when they come in every day to question you, your staff, every customer in here."

"What the fuck do you want, bitch?" he growled at me. He was angry, and behind that I caught a fleeting look of desperation.

"You think because I'm a woman, I'll be fooled by your stupid lies. All you're doing is pissing me off."

"Yeah, well, you're pissing me off pretty good, too."

"Perry fingered you as the person most likely to go after Damon."

"Goddamn him!" Bruce slammed his fist down on the bar.

The tourist couple got up and left. The bartender stayed down at the far end of the bar, watching the woman drink her beer.

He spat out, "Goddamn motherfucker bloodsucker! He thinks his big cock lets him get away with anything."

"Even telling the truth?" I said, twisting the knife.

"That cocksucker wouldn't know the truth if it mugged him! He's lying if he said I did anything other than... If he said I did anything at all. Lying motherfucker."

"Did anything other than what?" I pushed.

"I don't know what you're talking about," Bruce muttered. "I didn't do anything. I got witnesses to prove I wasn't anywhere near... fuck...fuck." He seemed to realize he was spewing out things he didn't want to tell me. He lit another cigarette, took a deep drag, then said, "Look I got work to do, okay, so you go play somewhere else."

"Like the 5th District Police station?"

"Fuck. Don't threaten me, bitch. You could get something nasty slipped to you, too."

"Like you did to Damon?"

"Fuck!" he yelled. "I didn't do anything to Damon. Can't you get that through your stupid head?"

"I didn't tell you someone slipped something to Damon. How else could you know?"

"Guess I just guessed." He lit another cigarette, ignoring the one burning in his ashtray. "Wait, I think Ambrose told me something. Yeah, I think he mentioned it."

"During one of his frequent visits here?"

"I got work to do." Bruce stood up and stalked into a little office in the back, slamming the door hard enough to make the woman slosh her beer at the noise.

I slid off the stool, pulled a five-dollar bill out of my wallet, and left it on the bar as a tip.

"Hey, thanks," the bartender said, surprised.

"Can't be the easiest boss to work for," I said as I walked out the door.

I was hungry and it was way past my lunchtime. Instead of heading to my car, I stopped at the Nellie Deli to pick up a po-boy. As I waited, I wondered how involved Bruce was. Did he do it, or did he merely provide the cocaine? I'd have to have Shannon go by there later with a picture of Ambrose and find out if he'd actually ever been seen in the bar. If he had, that wouldn't really prove much, but if he hadn't, then Bruce was a liar and probably a murderer.

With my sandwich tucked under my arm, I was headed back to my car when I realized I was only a few blocks from Damon's house. It was hot and I was tired, yet I still found myself heading that way. I wasn't even sure why, save that sometimes unexpected visits have unexpected results.

Or sometimes expected results that you're hoping for. Ambrose himself was fumbling with the lock on Damon's door. His fumbling turned into a free fall when he noticed me standing there looking at him. "Michele, what are you doing here?" he said as he scrambled for the papers that had slipped from his arms.

"Walking from the deli back to my car," I said as I started to help him gather the scattered documents.

Ambrose was trying to look dignified and also retrieve his papers and was mostly succeeding at neither. "I didn't expect to see you," he explained, as if he needed to.

I gave each page a glance as I picked it up. Ambrose was taking all of Damon's business papers. I wondered if Miss Carlotta was aware of this. Given Ambrose's reaction, I suspected not.

"I'll take those," he said peremptorily, his hand out for the documents I had gathered. I gave them to him. He then cleared his throat as if preparing for a speech. "There are some things that perhaps we should have a conversation about."

"Like replacing me with a large firm from Houston?"

He was silent before saying, in his lawyerly way, "Well, not exactly, but it couldn't hurt to have some additional resources for the job. It's not like you've solved anything."

"No, but I'm getting close. We've discovered that Beatrice Elliot did have a child. The timing fits in with everything Damon told us. Now it's just a matter of locating her current whereabouts."

"Why are you telling me this only now?" he demanded, something between anger and fear skittering across his face.

"It's a recent development." I was hedging. I was still working for Damon, not Ambrose, and it wasn't clear that he was the person I should report to, with Miss Carlotta as the actual executor. Something he had neglected to tell me. It seemed we were both holding back in some ways.

"There can't really be a child, can there?" he said skeptically.

"It appears there is."

That seemed to discomfit him, as if he had never considered that this could really happen. "Are you sure?" he asked sharply.

"Short of actually seeing the child and getting a DNA test, yes."

Ambrose's dignity—what there was of it, was rapidly melting as he stood here in the sun in his suit and tie. The sweat was dripping down his nose, and his face was red and flushed. He seemed reluctant to invite me in, preferring to stand out here and sweat. He chewed his lip, then said, "Well, perhaps we should consider a quit claim. Give her ten thousand and tell her to go away."

Ten thousand would be a fraction of what she'd get from the estate. Damon's being gone had freed something in Ambrose and it wasn't pretty.

"Shouldn't that be Miss Carlotta's decision?"

He looked at me sharply. "Have you been talking to her?"

"Yes, of course."

"I don't want you doing that sort of thing without my permission."

"The only way I can investigate this is to talk to the people who knew Damon and who knew the people around him. Do you want me to solve this case or not?"

Ambrose regarded me, a big drop of sweat rolling down his nose. "Damon would have wanted it solved, but not at the expense of upsetting his aunt."

"You can talk to her, but I don't think she was upset at my questioning her."

"Still, I need you reporting to me on a regular basis," he ordered. "And it might not be a bad idea to bring in some help."

I thought it would be a bad idea, but it seemed Miss Carlotta was right. If Ambrose couldn't have Damon, he would have control of what was Damon's. "Fine by me. If you want, I can give you some suggestions of agencies I'm familiar with." I was guessing that seeming to cooperate would undercut his need for control.

He blinked several times. "Ah, I'll consider that." He quickly wiped the sweat off his nose, started to turn away, then turned back to me. "Miss Carlotta is very charming, but she and Damon weren't always as close as she pretends they were."

"Oh?" I let it hang, wondering what he had to say.

"They had a big falling-out years ago. She pretends it never happened, but I was there."

"What was it about?"

"The paintings Damon is leaving her, they've been in the family for years. She didn't know much about handling money, and after her husband died, she didn't handle it well. She had to sell some of the heirlooms. Damon offered to buy the paintings. He'd always liked them as a kid, but she wanted to get as much as she could for them, so she put them up for auction. Damon was furious that he had to bid against strangers and furious that he had to pay so much to keep them."

"But he got the paintings."

"Yes, and she had the nerve to ask for them back. Said that since they'd remained in the family, they should hang where they'd always hung." He again wiped the sweat off his face.

"Damon held on to them," I prompted.

"He told her she could have them back over his dead body. I think leaving them to her is his way of making his point."

"I take it they're worth a lot of money."

"A few hundred thousand back then. I haven't had the heart to even have them appraised now. Miss Carlotta will do as well as, if not better than the rest of us. I tried to talk Damon out of it, tried to point out how valuable they were, but he was adamant. 'I said she'll get them over my dead body, I intend to keep my word.' The money didn't matter, he wanted to make his point."

"But if he were really still angry at her, he could leave the paintings to a museum or somebody else."

Ambrose blinked, then rubbed his hand over his face. He said quietly, as if not wanting to admit this, "Miss Carlotta is charming and entertaining. She knew how to win her nephew over again." He sighed, wiped his nose again, and said even more quietly, "I can marshal the facts, know the law—I can be useful, but Miss Carlotta doesn't like me. I'm boring and plain. No fun at parties. She can sway Damon in ways I can't." He took off his glasses, purposefully wiped them, as if gathering his control after this moment of being vulnerable. He turned back to the door and said, "Now if you'll excuse me."

"Miss Carlotta is very charming," I said. "But charm isn't enough for me to give anyone a pass."

He brusquely nodded and looked at me. "Good. My thought in bringing in someone else was to ensure that this investigation isn't… swayed by personalities." He put his hand on the door.

"One question," I said. "Bruce Payne says you told him Damon didn't sign the will."

Ambrose turned back to me. "He said what? That's not right. I never talk to Bruce. If I can help it, that is."

"So you never went to the bar, even to check him out, make sure he was doing his job?"

Ambrose sniffed. "I didn't need to do that. I knew he wasn't doing his job, and I don't go to those kinds of bars. Why would I tell him anything about Damon's affairs?"

"He seemed to think you did."

"Well, he's wrong," Ambrose retorted. "Now, I don't want to keep you from your lunch," he said, dismissing me and turning back to the door.

His controlling persona annoyed me and I considered doing the "one more question" thing, just to annoy him back, but it was too hot and what would I gain anyway? If you're not charming or fun, what's left but control? Annoyance gave way to sympathy. Ambrose was the ugly duckling surrounded by swans, and he desperately wanted to be one. And was just smart enough to know that he never would be.

I sauntered to the shady side of the street. Why was Ambrose going back into the house? It seemed that he was on his way out. I suspected it was just more control. He could go in the house, but keep me waiting on the sidewalk. I'd let him have his control; he had so little else. But his revelations about Miss Carlotta perturbed me. She had been charming and I did like her. She seemed genuinely fond of Damon and, also, even if she did need the money from the paintings, she seemed to have enough wherewithal to hold on until disease took him. Still, it would make sense to look into her financial state, if only to firmly close that door.

I might have Shannon check out the bar, but I suspected that Ambrose—as annoying as he was—was telling the truth. If he went to the Outer Limits, he would be noticed, and he wasn't likely to lie about something that could be so easily found out.

When I got close to my office I drove around the block, checking for my old car. All clear. I parked under a tree in hopes that the shade would keep my car a little below broiling.

When I got upstairs I found a note from Shannon. "Stopped by to look for my cell phone. Have a lead I'm working on at home. Will call later." If she finds her cell phone, I thought. It seemed we both needed a little distance. Or I did, and she was smart enough to notice it.

Water, air-conditioning, and food went a long way to making me feel human again. As I ate, I started to pick up the phone to call Cordelia. I realized that I had expected to find a message from her and was just a little irritated that she hadn't called to explain what happened last night. It wasn't like her not to call by now. She's tired and busy, I told myself—and showing off for Dr. Lauren, my not-nice voice added. She'll call when she can. I left the phone alone and finished eating.

Chapter Fifteen

As I was putting away my lunch trash, I started thinking about garbage. Ye shall know them by what they throw out. I wondered if someone had gone back to take the trash out. I stood for another few minutes in the air-conditioning, then finished clearing up my lunch stuff and got some latex gloves and a couple plastic bags for any booty I might find.

And I was back out in the heat, driving by Damon's house again. No sign of anyone. I didn't see it at first, but a small white trash bag sat off to the side of the stairs. I cursed myself for not thinking of this earlier, because I couldn't be sure that bag hadn't been here.

I quickly snagged it and threw it in the trunk of my car. It's not stealing to take something that someone is throwing away, but better not to have to answer questions. As I was driving away, I caught sight of someone who looked a lot like Bruce Payne coming up the block. I stayed at the stop sign to see if he went to Damon's place, but a big truck pulled up behind me, blocking my view and forcing me to proceed through the intersection. I drove back around the block, but he was gone and I could see nothing beyond closed doors and shuttered windows.

I drove back to my place and again parked under the shady tree. I took the bag out of my trunk and placed it on the sidewalk. After putting on the gloves, I opened it, then the empty garbage bag I had brought, and started moving the contents of one bag to the other.

It was mostly just garbage—banana peels, some frozen dinner trays, plastic water bottles, junk mail. It's bad enough to deal with my own junk mail, but this was someone else's—smeared with garbage and hard to read far enough to be sure it wasn't something useful. The bathroom trash had obviously been dumped in here as I found a layer with an old toothpaste tube, used-up deodorant, several cardboard toilet-paper tubes, a few miles of dental floss, the usual bathroom detritus. At least it was a man's bathroom and I didn't run into any used tampons. Garbage diving isn't one of the more glamorous parts of PI work.

Bored, I was hot and getting hotter. I chunked a half-eaten apple into the second bag, then noticed a tag of plastic stuck to it. Peeling it off—there are reasons gloves are required for this activity—I realized it was a wrapper for a suppository. Obviously it had to be anal, not vaginal. I tossed it back to the apple. And I had thought that tampons were the worst I'd have to worry about.

At the bottom was a stack of papers, covered by chicken bones and the fast-food wrappers that had held them—the chicken, not the documents. The pages were stuck together with various garbage gunk. I leafed through business papers, copies, things like invoices for the bars. I sighed and put those into one of the booty bags. I could look through them in a more comfortable place.

Under another layer of reeking food was a plastic sack tied shut. I carefully opened it to find another plastic bag. Opening that produced several sex toys—two big dildos, what looked like anal beads, some padded leather handcuffs. I used a chicken-drumstick bone to poke around. Gloves can only go so far. I only looked long enough to be sure that the bag within a bag contained nothing other than adult playthings. Then I tied the bag back up and threw it into the second garbage bag. Well, what else do you do with a used dildo?

The rest of the original garbage had more chicken bones, soppy paper towels, plastic shrink wrappers from things like toilet paper to bottled water, and a few candy-bar wrappers. I wadded up the first sack, put it in the second, then pulled off my gloves to add them to the mix. I then tied up everything and placed it in my garbage can.

I was hot and sweaty and wanted nothing more than to take a long cooling shower. I went back upstairs to my office to do a thorough hand washing until I could get to the shower. The phone rang just as I finished rinsing the soap off my hands.

"Michele, this is Carlotta LaChance," my caller said. Miss Carlotta.

"Hello, how are you? Oh, and I did run into Ambrose and he mentioned bringing in outside help to assist me. So I told him that might be a good idea and I'd be happy to recommend several firms."

"Yes, a good response. It's not control if you agree with him. But Ambrose is not what I'm calling about."

"What's happening?"

"I'm at the hospital," she said, "and I just spoke to Damon." To make sure I understood, she added, "He's woken up. Still very groggy and out of it, but clearly awake."

"Oh, wow! That's great news." I didn't add "unexpected." Then I asked, "Who else have you told?"

"Well…actually you're the first. I wanted to know if you'd found his daughter yet. That seems so important now."

"It might be a good idea to not tell too many people," I said.

"You think someone doesn't want Damon to wake up," she said somberly.

"I think someone tried to harm him and I can't be sure they won't again."

"And there is a chance that person is the kind of supposed friend who would want to see Damon if he was awake."

"That's possible," I confirmed.

"I can hire a guard," she suggested, "but that will be hard, it's keeping out friends. Damon will soon be awake enough to object."

"He might also be awake enough to help solve this. Right now Damon might have the best idea of who would do this. He had only seconds before he collapsed, but give him a day or so with a clear head and the answer might be apparent to him."

"That's very true. All right, this will be the only call I'll make until Monday. People will find out, and I'd prefer to have some control over when so as to be prepared. This is the weekend and it's less likely anyone will come by. I'll make it a point to be here as long as I can."

"We'll work over the weekend," I promised for Shannon and myself. "It's likely that we can locate Damon's daughter by then."

As I put the phone down, I couldn't keep a smile from my face. Damon waking up was very good news—for him and the case. But it would also give him a chance to meet the daughter he'd never seen and get to know her, even if just for a short time—a lot better outcome than never.

I was frustrated not to know what Shannon had been doing today, then decided that could happen with a phone call this evening. The news about Damon seemed like a high note with which to end the work day and get to my much-deserved shower.

The house was dark and the cats hungry when I got there. Cordelia often worked late, but rarely on Fridays. No note or messages on the answering machine, so I assumed she'd be home soon. I headed upstairs for the bathroom and my shower.

I took a long one, cool at first, until I was chilled enough to turn up the hot water. It felt like such relief as the water cascaded down my back, washing away the tensions of the week. Damon would be okay—for as long as possible. Shannon only had a minor crush and would get over it, and Cordelia would be waiting for me when I got out of the shower and we could make up for last night's lost romantic dinner.

But as I toweled off, I didn't hear anything that indicated another person in the house. Cordelia is not the kind of person who comes in and turns on the TV or stereo, so quiet didn't mean she wasn't downstairs reading. Or even napping on the couch.

I put on a robe and went down; a glance out the window showed an empty space where her car usually was. Sometimes when she worked late, I'd go by the office and meet her, although I hadn't done that lately. We'd fallen into our routines. I let her work late, it gave me some alone time. Too often? Maybe she thought I didn't care whether she came home or not.

I was also a little worried that she hadn't called. It's crazy, but I almost felt like she was evading me—guilt from standing me up? Or guilt because she'd found herself attracted to Dr. Lauren, something that, according to her, doesn't happen once you've found your true love. Or maybe if that happens it means it's not your true love. Don't be so insecure, I admonished myself. If Cordelia is avoiding me it's because she thinks I'm pissed about dinner. And the best way to handle that is to seek her out and make sure my kind, understanding side is present and accounted for.

I went back upstairs and got dressed, no black dress this time, but a pair of jeans just tight enough in the butt to show it off and a V-necked T-shirt that gave a nice hint of cleavage, at least as much cleavage as my scrawny shape could manage.

I even stopped at the little flower shop on Rampart, getting there just before closing, to pick up a bouquet of flowers, a mixed bunch of irises, day lilies, some others I didn't recognize.

Blasting the air-conditioning in my car so my shower wouldn't be for naught, I headed to her clinic. The late-Friday-evening traffic was sparse, and I was there in five minutes. Cordelia's car was still in the parking lot, but hers was the only one.

Gathering my flowers, I trotted up the front steps. The door was locked, which made sense if she was the only person here. However, I had a key and, since I'd set it up, the alarm code.

All the lights were turned off in the lobby and the reception area, giving the place a deserted look. I wondered if Cordelia had fallen asleep in her office. Then I felt uneasy. Something wasn't right. She should have called me if she was going to be this late. I slowly crossed the lobby, and when I got to the reception area, I realized I had gone on alert, my heart beating faster. I heard nothing beyond the drone of the air-conditioning. I went behind the reception area, holding the flowers at the ready, as if they could be any kind of weapon.

This is silly, I told myself. My first scenario was the most likely, that Cordelia had stayed after work to catch up on a few things and, after her late night, had nodded off. She was probably just now waking up, realizing what time it was, thinking that I'd be worried, and would be leaving a message for me on our answering machine just as I came around the door to her office to give her the flowers.

I quietly made my way to the hallway that led to the offices and exam rooms. I didn't want to wake her with the sound of footsteps in an empty building, nor announce my presence should I be walking into anything nefarious.

The lights were out back here as well, although I could see that at the far end of the hall the door to Cordelia's office was cracked open. She had to be in there, she wouldn't leave without locking her office.

As I made my way down the hallway, I heard a slight rustling sound. Then what sounded like a gasp of breath and a soft exhale. I stood stock-still, forcing the fear away to think what would be the best plan. By the book would be to go back out and call for help. But I knew I wouldn't leave Cordelia.

I wanted to put the flowers down, but couldn't risk the crinkling of the paper. I didn't have my gun—not even my cell phone; I had left it in the car. I told myself, find out what's happening, then use surprise to…I didn't even know.

I heard the rustling sound again as I crept down the hallway to Cordelia's cracked door.

The lights were out in her office as well, and I could see little through the slight opening in the door, save for a bright slit of light through the window blinds.

I stood just outside her door. I think I knew before I knew, one kind of fear replaced with another. Perhaps some part of me recognized the rustling sound. I put my fingertips on the door, slowly inching it open.

Cordelia was there. So was Lauren. They didn't see me.

What I was hearing wasn't pain or fear, but desire. I was numb, unmoving as if desperately trying to find some other way to explain what I was seeing—my partner of over nine years in the arms of another woman, their clothes disheveled.

Then the numbness was gone, anger—and a desperate fear—in its place.

"Goddamn you!" I screamed, hurling the flowers at Cordelia. "God-fucking-damn you!"

I couldn't bear to be here, to hear whatever she might say. I spun around and tore down the hallway. I heard Cordelia cry, "Oh, no… Micky…"

If she said anything else, I couldn't hear it over the pounding of my blood and running feet. I don't even remember crossing the lobby, just shoving open the main doors with the panic bar, probably setting off the alarm, but I didn't give a damn.

I peeled out of the parking lot, tires squealing as I swung into traffic. It would serve her right, I thought, as I ran a yellow light turning red, if I got hurt in an accident. But I finally forced myself to drive like other cars were on the road. It might serve her right, but it wouldn't do me any good.

I pulled up in front of our house, then thought, what am I doing here? I don't live here anymore. But I tore out of the car and inside. I ran upstairs, snatched a suitcase out of the closet, and started throwing clothes in it. I blindly grabbed what was handy, tossing the dress I'd worn last night—was it only a day ago?—onto the floor, the rest into the suitcase. Then I was in the bathroom and just swept everything that was mine into a bag. Enough, I told myself, and was back in my car, driving again.

I couldn't bear to see Cordelia and didn't want to be there when she returned. *If* she comes back, I told myself. I wanted her to search for me, to find that I was gone. I wanted her…I didn't even know.

The streets were familiar and I realized I was heading toward my office. I stopped in front, but sat in my car, trying desperately to think what I wanted to do. Beat the shit out of Lauren Calder came to mind. I even pictured myself taking a punch at her and for a moment that was satisfying, but then it slipped away. I knew enough about physical fighting to know that I'd just end up with a sore hand and nothing solved.

Oh, hell, I thought, as my bladder prompted me to get out of my car. It seemed so mundane that I should still have such bodily functions right now. As I climbed the stairs, I had the thought: I can't stay here, she might find me. And, of course, some part of me wanted her to find me, but I didn't want to make it easy.

"Miss Goddamned Fucking Monogamy," I cursed as I opened the door to my office.

Shannon was there. Damn it, I hadn't bothered to look for her car.

We stared at each other. Then I walked over to my desk, trying to hide what had to be clearly showing on my face.

"Hey, good news, I found—" she started, but must have read my expression anyway. "What's the matter?"

"I suppose you knew," I spat out. "You could have told me."

"Told you what?"

"Or maybe you're so used to being nonmonogamous that little things like this don't matter to you."

"Like what?" she said. But she was smart. "What happened?"

I took it out on her. "Can't you fuck your girlfriend enough so she doesn't have to get it elsewhere?"

"Cordelia and Lauren?"

"Who the fuck else!" I shouted back.

"What happened?" she asked again, her expression a mixture of disbelief and resignation.

"I walked in on them, what the fuck do you think happened?"

"Are you sure?" Shannon asked. She jammed her hands in her pockets as if she didn't really want confirmation.

I just stared at her. "Sure?" It was a shout. I strode over to her and pushed her against the wall, then shoved my body against hers, my hand down her pants, and kissed her hard, my mouth open.

Shannon jerked her hands out of her pockets, one bracing against the wall, the other on my shoulder as if undecided whether to hold me at bay—or in an embrace.

I didn't stop there. My hand went between her legs, my fingers pulling away the elastic of her underwear. Abruptly I stopped and pulled back.

"That's what I saw. Oh, both shirts were open. Lauren has big, brown nipples."

Shannon's hand just hung in the air as I moved away, as if she couldn't think of what to do with it. She was quiet. I wondered if I had bruised her. "I guess that's sure," she said slowly. "What are you going to do?"

"How the fuck should I know?"

Shannon turned away from me and I finally got a glimpse outside my pain. I selfishly assumed that she knew, but maybe she didn't and I had just walked in, announced that her lover was cheating on her, and blamed her for it.

"I don't know what I'll do," I said. Then softly asked, "Did you know?"

She took a deep breath, then said, "I guess I did, I suspected something. But...no smoking gun. And I wasn't looking for one."

"Are they in love?" I was disconcerted to hear my voice break.

Shannon kept her back to me. "Lauren is always in love. The thief of hearts. She's ardent and vibrant and pledges love with utter passion. She believes it, so you believe it. And tomorrow she loves someone else with just as much ardor and doesn't understand why you're standing there with a broken heart. It's just the way she is. But, love forever, or for today? I don't know."

"Has she said anything to you?"

She finally turned around, not looking directly at me, brushing her hand over her face. "Like, pack your bags, get the fuck out, it's over? No."

The phone rang. I stared at it as if it were a coiled snake. "Shit,"

I said. I turned first one way then another. I wanted to stop the phone from ringing and I also wanted it to be Cordelia calling to say... The answering machine picked up. We both stood still and silent as the message played, then a voice came on, "Is this Joe's Cozy Corner?"

"Fuck," I let out. All that tension for a wrong number. Then a streak of anger. Why wasn't she calling me? Was she just going to let me walk in on that and not do a damn thing? I suddenly decided that I needed some time away, a few days to sort myself out. I'd need a few years for that, but would take a few days to think about what I wanted. Right now all the choices were Cordelia's and I needed to make some of my own and I was too confused to do that.

I switched my office answering machine to pick up without ringing and then, for good measure, switched off my cell phone.

"What will you do?" Shannon asked, watching me.

"Go away for a few days."

"I'm coming with you," she announced.

"I'd prefer to be alone."

"You're in no state to be alone. And where else am I supposed to go?"

"I thought that nonmonogamy was okay with you. Or at least you'd already made the deal with the devil about it."

"This isn't okay with me," she said bitterly. "She's hurt me, she's hurt you, and she'll hurt Cordelia."

"Right now that's a pleasant thought," I replied, matching her bitter tone.

"Right now."

"Yeah, right now. Cordelia has preached monogamy, trust, respect at me for the last nine years. And then she's the one who cheats on me. Fuck, just fuck her!" I threw the car keys at Shannon. "Just don't say I invited you along."

Shannon grabbed some water from the refrigerator. I straightened up the things on my desk while waiting for her, throwing everything that seemed important into a briefcase—all the open files, my checkbook. I wasn't sure what I was doing, maybe just trying for order and control in a life that lacked both. Right now I needed my professional life to hold on to, since my personal one seemed in shambles. In the bathroom I grabbed the extra shampoo I kept here—I wasn't sure I'd taken any from home. It was all a blur.

As we headed for the door, I said, "Damon woke up. His aunt called me this afternoon."

Shannon opened the door. "And I found Beatrice."

I locked the door, both locks, the one Cordelia had the key to and the one she didn't. If she came by here, I wanted her to know she wasn't welcome anymore.

We headed down the stairs.

"At least someone gets a happy ending," I said as we left.

Chapter Sixteen

Where are we headed?" Shannon asked, as I directed her to Claiborne and from there over the bridge to the other side of the Mississippi River.

Should I go there? I wondered. I was heading for the now-defunct shipyard that my father once owned and was now mine. Cordelia knew where it was and would probably know I might head there. I glanced at my watch. It was almost eight, the last gloaming of the evening fading to black. She'd look for me in the city first. If she looked for me at all.

"A shack out in the bayous where I grew up."

Shannon didn't say much, as if she knew that I did want to be alone. Or maybe she had her own thoughts to preoccupy her.

I couldn't think of more than the next minute, the next turn in the road. Tomorrow was too far and too forbidding.

The lights of the city faded behind us and the night was dark. No, Cordelia wouldn't follow me out here; she doesn't like driving at night. And she might not follow me in the daylight either.

"Let's stop here," I said as we came upon the lights of a small grocery store.

Shannon pulled in.

"Get what you'd like to eat and fill the tank. Not too many gas stations out here," I told her. This was Louisiana; I knew they'd have what I wanted. I left Shannon at the fuel pumps and headed for the liquor. One of the unique features of our peculiar region is how easy it is to get booze—gas stations, drug stores, every grocery. They didn't have a great selection, but one or two decent bottles of Scotch was all I needed.

I joined Shannon at the counter as she was putting her food there. I added my two bottles. "It's together," I said to the clerk.

"Gettin' ready, huh?" she asked as she rang up the bottles.

I didn't reply. Shannon cast me a glance but said nothing. I threw down several twenties and let Shannon get the change as I hurriedly bagged our groceries and took them to the car.

She got in, but sat still. "Are you sure this is a good idea?" she asked.

"Just drive."

She started the car and pulled out, but said nothing further save responses to my directions. And I said nothing beyond giving them.

"Slow down," I said. It was easy to go past the driveway to the shipyard in the dark. "It'll be up here on the left." The sides of the road were overgrown, the lushness of late summer taking the brush to the very edge of the asphalt. Then a slight gap in the brush appeared. "Turn here."

Shannon slowed even further, as if wondering if she could fit the car through the small opening. She carefully turned in, but still the car bumped down from the road to the oyster-shell drive. It probably needed some refilling, I thought. Shannon suddenly slammed on the brakes as the gate to the property appeared in the headlights.

I got out, sliding between the shrubs and the car to get to the gate. After opening it, I motioned Shannon to drive through. She did and I relocked it. Another key Cordelia didn't have.

I got back in the car. "We're here," I told her.

Shannon gave a dubious look. We seemed to be on a dark, rutted track, with the trees and brush almost growing over the car as we sat. She shifted into first and slowly drove forward into the dark. She tried not to show it, but I could tell she was relieved when the oppressive overgrowth gave way to a clearing and then the headlights picked up the house.

It was made of weathered barge boards, cypress wood impervious to most of what south Louisiana could throw at it. The house was raised a good five feet up from the ground and surrounded on three sides by a wide porch. It was too dark to see, but beyond this clearing were the unused buildings of a shipyard, slips with rotting slings that had brought the boats out of the bayou that ran beside the property.

I grabbed my suitcase and several of the bags, making sure

I got the ones with my Scotch. I didn't trust that Shannon wouldn't "accidentally" drop them. She got the rest of the bags and followed me up the stairs.

"Where did you find her?" I asked as I unlocked the door.

"What? Find who?" She followed me in.

"Beatrice and Jane. The case. What I have left to do with my life." I turned on the lights. "Bathroom and kitchen that way," I said, pointing to the far end of the large room we were in. "Two bedrooms on the bayou side." I dropped my suitcase, then kicked it in the direction of the bedrooms and took the grocery bags to the kitchen. Shannon followed me, putting hers down as well. She started putting the water and some cold cuts into the refrigerator. I stepped around her and went to the bathroom, dumping my bag of toiletries there.

Shannon was at the door when I turned to leave. She held up one of her grocery bags. "Toothbrush," she said. I let her pass and went back to the kitchen.

I just stood there, as if I couldn't move. Then fury coursed through me, and I grabbed the kitchen curtains and ripped them down. Cordelia had picked them out.

"Didn't like that pattern, did you?" Shannon asked. She picked them up off the floor and put them under the sink, as if she understood it would be too much for her to throw them away, but knew they needed to be out of sight.

"How the fuck can you be so calm?" I spewed at her.

She sighed. "I'm not calm. Resigned. There *is* a difference. I guess I hoped Lauren wouldn't do this, but suspected she would eventually. I saw it coming, you didn't. That's the only distance between us."

I found a glass in the cabinet, then got an ice tray from the freezer and cracked it over the sink.

"I'm hungry, I'm fixing some sandwiches," Shannon said.

"I'm not," I replied, half filling the glass with ice.

"You might want to eat anyway," she suggested.

I just shrugged, opened one of the bottles of Scotch, and filled my glass.

Shannon put her hand on my arm, a gentle touch. And a brief one, as if she knew she couldn't stop me, only pick up the pieces later. She looked at me, then turned away, gathering the things to make her sandwich.

I took a sip. It burned, an old familiar burn that promised a blurring, a blunting of the sharp edges. I took another swallow, a long one, almost half the glass. I left Shannon in the kitchen, taking the bottle with me as I went out onto the porch. I sat on the side facing the bayou. As my eyes adjusted to the night, I could make out its dark waters, a bare glimmer of light from somewhere reflecting on the glass surface. The night was dense, birds and insects constant in their callings, the faint light from the window cast over thick overgrowth, with shadows that seemed to stretch into dark holes, the heavy mantle of humid air enveloping me, an embrace of indifference.

I finished the glass in one last gulp, then filled it again.

At some point Shannon came out and joined me, handing me a sandwich. I ate part of it, then forgot to eat the rest. She came and took the plate away later.

I remember hearing somewhere in the distance the bellow of an alligator. It silenced the croaking of the frogs. Then the night blurred, the Scotch delivering its promise.

Shannon's hand was on my shoulder. I knew time had passed, whatever light had glimmered off the bayou had been turned out, and the call of birds was now muted.

"Come to bed," she said. She took the glass from my drooping hand. The bottle was almost half empty.

I groggily stood up, letting Shannon half carry and guide me into the house. She left me in the bathroom and I managed to stumble through brushing my teeth and peeing. Then she led me to the bedroom.

I don't remember getting undressed or going to bed. Sometime when the sky was turning to a bare gray of dawn, I woke, my stomach heaving. I started to roll out of bed and bumped into Shannon, asleep beside me. I woke her up, but didn't care, crawling over her to get to the bathroom.

But I could only manage dry heaves as I knelt before the toilet. I don't know how long I stayed there, my head resting against the cool of the porcelain.

"Can you drink some water?" Shannon handed me a cold bottle.

I stared at it, then gingerly took a sip, then another. I was very thirsty, I realized, but knew better than to guzzle the water. My stomach was too roiled for anything sudden.

Shannon wasn't wearing any clothes. But I was too drunk and my stomach too queasy for any thought beyond that. I took another sip, then slowly hoisted myself up from the floor. "Should try to sleep," I mumbled.

"Sounds like a good idea," she agreed.

We walked back across the big room to the bedrooms. She stayed beside me, as if ready to catch me, waiting for my shambling steps to trip me up.

She had put us to bed in the larger of the bedrooms, the one with the double bed. It was where Cordelia and I usually slept.

"Where did you find her?" I asked, as I pulled the sheet over me. I was still in my underpants, but that was all.

"Beatrice?" Shannon confirmed, as if she was getting used to my disjointed thoughts.

"Yeah, her."

She slid into the bed beside me. "She's teaching at a small college in Arkansas."

"Doesn't sound like the Beatrice of the French Quarter," I mumbled.

"Maybe having to raise a kid makes a difference."

"Where in Arkansas?"

"Northeast corner. Jonesboro. Arkansas State University at Jonesboro. About seventy miles beyond Memphis."

"We'll go there tomorrow," I said. "Finish this up. Damon's awake, Beatrice is found, can finish this." I turned on my side to sleep.

"Probably Sunday. I think tomorrow you might want to take it easy," Shannon said softly.

I felt her turn in the bed, then she curled around me from behind, her arm over me.

"I can't do this," I said, stiffening.

"We're just sleeping," she said. "Okay?"

"Okay," I agreed, both scared and wanting the comfort of her warmth against me. The dawn light caught her arm wrapped around me, pale blond arm hair and light skin. It looked wrong. I was used to Cordelia's arm's holding me, her hair darker, the arm more muscled, with a sparse scattering of freckles.

I closed my eyes and told myself I couldn't think about that. I couldn't think about any of that.

CHAPTER SEVENTEEN

I woke to a hammering in my head. Slowly I realized that the hammering was outside my head. Either that or I also had added a buzz saw to my hangover. Someone had decided to do a weekend project. Several someones, as I heard two hammers pounding at the same time.

I lay in bed slowly orienting myself. It was bright daylight and Shannon was no longer beside me. I ran my hand down my side. I still had my underwear on. Well, at least that didn't happen, I thought groggily—having sex and being too drunk to remember.

I gingerly swung out of bed, then stood there to get my balance. My body wanted to stay in bed, but my bladder demanded movement.

I didn't see Shannon around. It was a beautiful day, hot, of course, but at least this was country hot and not city hot. She was probably outside somewhere. I hoped she wasn't so Yankee that she would stumble into a nest of water moccasins or try to pet a baby alligator.

After finishing in the bathroom, I went to the kitchen, drinking some more water, nibbling half a slice of bread, and downing two aspirin. Then I shut the windows and turned on the air-conditioning. It was too hot to be awake, let alone sleep off a hangover, without chilled air.

I shut the blinds and curled up back in bed. I didn't wake up until sometime in late afternoon. I was hot and sweaty despite the air-conditioning. At first I thought maybe Shannon had turned it off, but after a groggy moment, I heard its mechanical buzz.

Shower. Aspirin. I slowly swung myself out of bed and headed to the bathroom. Shannon was sitting on the couch in the big room, reading a book. She was in a pair of my shorts and a T-shirt.

"Nice outfit," I muttered as I passed her.

She looked up at me, following me with her eyes as I passed. "I like yours, too," she answered.

I was still wearing only a pair of panties. Suddenly self-conscious, I crossed my arms over my chest. Like that'd make any difference after all this time, I thought, as I shut the bathroom door behind me. Shannon hadn't exactly packed any clothes for this trip. She could borrow mine or wear the same ones. Oh, hell, I thought, that means she's probably wearing my underwear as well. I hoped that she'd found a decent pair—some of them were pretty raggedy.

I stepped under the shower, not even letting the water get warm; it seemed too hot to worry about it. I just stood in the water, letting it wash over me. *What am I doing out here, with a strange woman sitting on the other side of the door? And what will I do tomorrow? And the day after that? And...* but I couldn't think of that.

Tomorrow I'd drive up to some small town in Arkansas and find Beatrice Elliot. And maybe the day after that I'd take her to see Damon. Jane Elliot would have a father for at least a little while, enough to have a memory of the man. She'd meet a great-aunt who would be around for a little longer. A happy ending. Or at least as close as life sometime gives you.

Suddenly something flickered across my consciousness. I needed to look through that trash again. Something nagged at me, something that didn't feel right. It would still be there. Trash pickup wasn't until Monday, and even then I had to put the can out for that to happen. I wrinkled my nose at the thought—a few more days in August heat would turn it to a toxic-waste dump. But that's what gloves and masks were for.

The water was starting to run cold. I hastily soaped and shampooed, being chilled before I completely rinsed off. I started to open the door, then realized I was naked. I wrapped myself in the towel, even taking time to make sure it hung low enough to cover what it needed to cover.

Shannon was still reading as I passed her, her legs stretched out comfortably on the couch. Nice legs, I thought, noting that my shorts, slightly hiked up from her position, showed them off.

"How's your head?" she asked on seeing me.

"Fine," I answered shortly. I am not sleeping with her, I vowed. That would be throwing gasoline onto an already roaring fire. But why not, I thought as I closed the bedroom door behind me. It's not like I'd be cheating on Cordelia if I did. Ms. Monogamy was more than willing to sneak behind my back when she stumbled over someone better.

I took the towel off and was at the door on my way to Shannon on the couch before I suddenly wondered if she might turn me down. I hadn't exactly been a pretty sight last night. And…and if Cordelia didn't want me, why would she?

I stood with my hand on the doorknob for so long I made Hamlet look decisive. I finally turned away, leaving it safely closed, and noticed that Shannon had neatly unpacked the clothes I had so hurriedly thrown in the suitcase. I found my underwear in the top drawer. I even put on a bra, something I usually avoid if I can. Then long pants and a T-shirt, a baggy one.

What is going on with me, I wondered, taking a look at myself in the mirror hanging on the closet door. Well, I've just had a gut-punch rejection, fallen off a ten-year wagon, and I desperately want the affirmation and comfort I'd get from sex—and I'm even more desperately afraid of being rejected again. I don't know if I can take even a small one on top of this big one. And the decent part of me realized that if I did have sex with Shannon, it would only be tangentially about her. I'd be sleeping with her to get back at Cordelia and to give my ego the boost that, even if she didn't want me, someone did.

Dressed, with my hand on the door, I also thought, that doesn't mean I won't do it. It just means that I shouldn't.

Shannon was still reading, the shorts still hiked up. She looked at me. "I almost thought you'd gotten lost."

"I'm not used to neatly packed clothes. It took me twenty minutes to find where you'd put my underwear."

She continued to look at me. "No rule says you need to wear any."

Fuck. So much for rejection. I needed a drink, I suddenly decided. I headed for the kitchen. She got up and followed me, watching as I put ice in the glass, then poured the Scotch. I turned to face her. "Look, I'm kind of fucked up right now. You'd do better to stay away from me."

"Is that what you want?"

"I don't know what I want." I brought the glass to my lips and took a swallow.

She looked at me for a moment longer. "You know where to find me." She turned away and went back to reading.

I took the bottle out to the porch and watched the day slide into darkness. I could still hear hammering off in the distance. It seemed to be the weekend for building projects. Then the night was quiet, even the birds seemed to have stilled their voices.

Sometime later Shannon came out with a plate of sandwiches. "You should eat," she said simply, placing the plate on a small table between us.

She was silent while she ate. I finally reached over and took one. I hadn't known how hungry I was until I started eating. I ate that half and took another. After finishing it, I said, "Thanks." Then added, "I'm sorry."

"For what?"

"Being...I don't know...drunk, just sitting here watching the shadows. Barely talking to you."

"You did say you wanted to be alone. Besides, this is hell. You get a few days to fall apart."

"So why aren't you falling apart?"

"I am. Just doing it differently."

"How? How are you falling apart and not...?" I waved my glass.

"Writing. While you're out here or sleeping, I've been madly scribbling in my notebook. I've decided I'll make a short story out of this—that Lauren isn't worth a novel. Calling her every vile name I can think of."

"Sounds like you've had more therapy than I have."

"Maybe. Or maybe drinking only gives me a headache."

I poured another glass of Scotch. "It keeps me from thinking too much." I took a swallow.

"Tomorrow we go to Arkansas," she said, standing up and retrieving the plate.

"Yeah, tomorrow." I took another sip. I didn't mention a possible side trip back to New Orleans to look through trash.

She took the bottle. "It's empty," she said as I gave her a look. "And, no, I'm not bringing you the other one." With that, she went back inside.

I finished what was in my glass and then alternated between just listening to the sounds of the night and considering going inside to get the second bottle. Glancing at my watch, I saw it was a little past midnight. I finally decided against the second bottle.

Cordelia could have driven out here today and looked for me if she wanted to.

Shannon and I would try to find Beatrice Elliot tomorrow. It would probably take most of the day to drive up there. If we got there early enough, we'd search her out in the evening. If not, the next day. Damon didn't have time for me to sit here in my pain. I could hurt here or I could hurt on the road. I had promised to try to find his daughter, so I might as well pack up my hurt and my suitcase and give someone else a happy ending, even if I couldn't give myself one.

I went back into the house. Shannon was no longer writing, but back to reading. She watched me as I walked into the kitchen. I put my glass down and came out empty-handed. There seemed to be a look of approval on her face. Or maybe I needed to think I saw it there.

"We have to leave early tomorrow," I told her, embarrassed that my words were slightly slurred.

"Time for bed?"

"Yeah." I hesitated then said, "We should sleep in different beds tonight."

"Don't trust me?" she asked with an arched eyebrow.

"Don't trust me," I told her. "I can't and I shouldn't and I might… and it's better not to make things too easy. Besides, I'm not too sober and…might not make decisions we'd respect in the morning." With that, I turned from her. It *would* be too easy. I went to the bedroom we'd shared the night before, got some clothes, and took them to the second room. I put sheets on the unused bed. When I had finished, Shannon was in the bathroom.

"Good night," I said when she came out.

"Good night." She came to me, put her hand on my cheek, leaned in slightly as if she was about to kiss me, but then pulled back. "See you in the morning."

I went into the bathroom. When I came out the door to her bedroom was shut.

I went to the second bedroom, shutting my door as well. I got in bed, then curled up, hugging a pillow to me. I buried my face in it, muffling my sobs, feeling hollow and empty. But I stayed in bed and slept by myself.

Chapter Eighteen

When I woke it was early morning. The alcohol was reminding me of its costs. I was thirsty, needed to pee, and had a headache. I glanced at my watch, it was just before seven.

I threw on a T-shirt and shorts and quietly left my room for the bathroom. Shannon's door was still shut. I decided to go ahead and take a shower. It would be a long drive on a hot day, and I might as well start out clean.

When I was done and dressed, Shannon was still asleep. I decided I'd let her have another half an hour. I wandered down to the bayou, about fifty feet beyond the house. A slight breeze was stirring, rippling the usual glassy surface. Something wasn't right. It was too quiet. Someone should be getting ready for a fishing trip, some sounds of human activity.

I went to the water's edge and looked around. The hammering and sawing from yesterday. All the houses I could see had plywood covering their windows.

Damn Yankee, I thought as I strode back to the house. She wouldn't know what this meant. The last I'd paid attention, sometime on Friday, the hurricane was heading for the Florida Panhandle. It must have changed direction. Damn and damn.

I hurried back inside and knocked loudly on Shannon's door. "Hey, wake up," I called.

She opened the door, her hair mussed and her eyes still sleepy.

"There's a radio in the kitchen," I told her. "Turn it on and find out what's happening with the hurricane."

"What?" she asked groggily.

"And get ready to leave," I told her. "I'll secure the house." With that I headed back outside.

First I ran down to the sheds that had been used by the shipyard. I quickly threw everything—some outdoor chairs, gardening things— inside them, then locked them all up. There wasn't time to tape the windows. My father had had sturdy shutters installed on all the windows of the house, so I only had to close and secure them. I also took all the furniture on the porch and pulled it into the big room.

Shannon came out of the bathroom, her hair wet from a quick shower. "How did you know?" she asked me. Then added, "It's not good."

"How not good?" I started moving books from the bottom shelves and putting them up on higher shelves. I glanced at her long enough to see that she was scared.

"A category five, headed straight for New Orleans."

I looked at her for a second as it sunk in. "Oh, hell. That's the nightmare."

"And it gets here before it gets there, right?" she asked.

"Right. When's landfall?" I didn't stop to talk, but kept moving what I could up higher.

"They said early tomorrow, but we'll start feeling the effects this evening. That it's a huge storm, with outer bands covering almost the entire Gulf."

I briefly stopped, to respond to her fear. "We'll be okay. We can get out before then. But the sooner the better."

"What should I do?"

"Empty the refrigerator of anything that can't live for a few days without electricity. It could be weeks before they'll get power back on out here. Then pack our stuff."

I went back to moving things and unplugging everything electrical. The bathroom window didn't have a shutter, so I hurriedly taped that one.

I came back out to the big room and looked around. What would I truly miss if it wasn't here tomorrow? I hastily took down pictures and paintings from the wall and loaded them into the backseat of the car. I remembered to grab the brass nameplate with Knight of Tides on it, taken by my father from his father's shrimp boat.

Shannon had finished in the kitchen and was now in the bedroom packing.

I looked around again. It won't be here after this, I thought. This building had weathered so many storms, but this one felt different. Then I literally shook myself—maybe I was picking up Shannon's fear, or I was thinking that nature was adding a brutal echo of what Cordelia had done to me. It'll be okay. This house, all the memories in the walls, will be here, I told myself.

Shannon came out of the bedroom carrying my suitcase.

"Take it to the car," I told her. I grabbed one of the big flashlights, a large knife, peanut butter and bread, a blanket, several empty garbage bags—a hasty survival kit. And then one last look around before I left, locking the door behind me.

Shannon was arranging things in the car. "Want me to drive?" she asked, her face still pale. My reassurances could only do so much.

"No, I will. I know the roads out here better." I stowed my stuff in the trunk. As I opened the car door, I wondered why no one had called me. Oh, shit, I hadn't turned on my cell phone. It was still in the glove box of the car. I pulled it out and turned it on. Almost immediately it sounded the tone that let me know I had messages. As I started the car, I also fumbled with my phone to check them.

"You have twenty-two messages," the mechanical tone informed me.

"No one called you on your cell phone?" I asked Shannon as I was trying to do too many things at once—fasten my seat belt, listen to the messages, and drive the car.

She gave me a slight, rueful smile. "I forgot it. Was already at the car, but thought I was just doing a quick run downtown."

I let go of the seat belt. I'd have to take it off to open the gate anyway.

My first message was from Torbin. "Mick, darling, you are watching the weather, aren't you? It looks like we might have been right about the tourists and the ever-so-unique hurricane special—the real thing, not the drink." He'd left that late Friday evening.

Danny called early Saturday morning, saying basically the same thing. Then a little later Joanne. Then my mother, offering to let us stay in New York with her, if we wanted. "I love you both, be safe," she finished up.

I hit erase for that one, then jammed on the brakes as the gate was suddenly in front of us.

Shannon gave me a long look. My actions weren't doing much to match the reassuring words I'd said. I got out of the car, quickly opened the gate, still listening to my messages. Most were reiterations from Torbin, Joanne, and Danny about the storm, wanting to know what I was planning to do. "Call me, please," was number fourteen, from Joanne.

I got back in the car and drove though the gate, got back out, closing and locking it. Then I stared back down the drive. I could make out a corner of the roof. In my life this place had always been here, always been the one home I could come back to.

I heard Cordelia's voice. She was message nineteen. "Micky... God, please be okay. This isn't...you don't need to talk to me, but, please, please let me know...that you're okay, that you're on the way away from this monster." Then very quietly, I could barely hear her, "I love you."

I took a deep breath, but it broke into a sob, the tears streaking down my cheeks. It was just too much. I felt like I was being driven away from everything that had defined my life—this place, with a lifetime of memories, a love I had thought even more secure than those sturdy cypress walls.

"Micky?" I heard Shannon's voice from what sounded like a long way away. Then she simply wrapped her arms around me and held me, wiping my tears with her palm.

"It's..." I started, but the words didn't make it through my crying. I finally got out, "It's...everything."

"Too much everything," she said. "Let me drive." She took the car keys from my unresisting hand. For a moment, she tightened her embrace. I responded, holding her to me like a lifeline.

Then I pulled away. We had to be on the road. I felt responsible for Shannon being out here. I was the bayou rat who shouldn't have let a hurricane sneak up on us. The clerk who asked if we were getting ready, the hammering and sawing, the quiet of the bayou, they all should have told me that a hurricane was coming, if I'd been paying attention.

We got in the car. I was still wiping my eyes as I buckled the seat belt. "We'll be okay," I managed to get out.

Shannon took my face between her hands, wiping the last of the tears away with her thumbs. Then she very deliberately pulled me to her and kissed me. She held it for a long time. I let her kiss me. Then kissed her back.

We both pulled away.

"Good thing I'm a journalist," she said as she started the car. "At least I should get a good story out of this."

There was little traffic on the road. Far less than normal. People had either gotten out or were hunkering down. I turned on the radio. "… contra-flow is moving cars out of New Orleans," the announcer said. That meant they had reversed the interstates, so that all lanes headed out of the city. "Both the mayor and the governor are urging all residents to evacuate," she continued. Another announcer added, "Or make sure you have an axe if you need to break through the roof."

"Good Lord, are they serious?" Shannon asked.

"I've never had to use an ax," I said. "But for some people they were handy during Betsy and Camille, I've heard."

"The water gets that high?" she asked, a rising note of worry in her voice.

"In the past, but they built the levees up after Betsy in 1965."

"Out here?"

"No," I had to admit. "The metro area. But we won't be out here when the storm hits."

I tuned back to the radio announcers. "Traffic is moving, slowly, but moving, on I-10. Remember to choose before you get on the interstate. The regular lanes exit north, the reversed lanes go west to Baton Rouge."

"Okay, that decides us," I told Shannon, turning down the radio. "We go back into the city. Better that than trying to squirrel around on this side of the river. No stoplights on the interstate."

"Just tell me where to turn," Shannon said.

We made good time on the back roads leading away from Bayou St. Jack. Traffic was light going into the city. It was almost eerie. Bright sunshine, no clouds in the sky yet, but the city was empty, waiting for an unseen monster.

I considered running by my house—and even thought about the garbage I wanted to look through again. But I knew the streets had all emptied in the direction we had to go and these deserted roads would soon turn into massive traffic jams as we caught up with the rest of the fleeing people.

The Superdome appeared as we crossed above Lee Circle, General Robert E. still calmly at the top of his pole. He was astride his stone horse, atop a tall column, giving him a commanding view of the city. Suddenly, I thought about our cats, Rook and Hepplewhite. Should we go by my house and get them? Cordelia would take care of them. She might cheat on me, but she wouldn't abandon our cats. They're okay, I reassured myself, and there's no time to make what would almost certainly be a pointless detour.

"Follow the signs to I-10," I told Shannon.

"Yeah, I sort of figured."

Soon after we got on the interstate, the line of cars I knew to be there appeared. Shannon had to brake sharply to slow down for the almost-stopped traffic.

"Get comfy," I said as she tucked behind the last car. "It'll be a long ride."

We were briefly the last car, but others quickly queued behind us. It took over an hour to just cross the parish line from Orleans to Jefferson.

"C'mon, drive," Shannon muttered at a sluggish car in front of us. She was gripping the steering wheel as if the tighter she held it, the faster we could go.

"It's okay," I told her. "It won't be fun. A long, slow drive out of here, but we'll be okay."

"Where are we going? I mean, where do we stop?"

"The Pacific Ocean?"

She looked at me. Shannon seemed to have a weak spot with situations where she felt trapped, with no way out. She wasn't in the mood for joking.

"We won't find a hotel this side of Houston," I told her.

She gave me a look of disbelief. "Tell me you're not pulling my Yankee leg."

"No, I wish I were. One point five million people in the metro New Orleans area. That can suck up hotel rooms."

"And every single one of them is on this highway," she muttered, drumming her fingers on the steering wheel with impatience. "I've got friends in some town near the Texas border," she said. "Might be easier to stay there than driving until we can find a hotel room. Can I borrow your cell phone?"

I had shoved it in my pants pocket and left it there, not even checking the rest of my messages. Which I needed to do, but first I handed Shannon the phone.

She started to open it, then handed it back. "Have to get the phone number. It's in my address book in my backpack."

"In the trunk," I finished for her. I glanced at my watch. It was a little past twelve. "There will probably be a point when it's slow enough to get out, or we can pull over after Baton Rouge."

"How long from there to Texas?"

"On a normal day it's about two to three hours. An hour and a half from New Orleans to Baton Rouge."

"So a little over three hours if we call after Baton Rouge."

"If this were a normal day. But add some hours for the traffic."

"Okay. Let's hope my friends haven't already booked the refugee hotel," she said with a note of frustration in her voice.

"Hey, I can see the traffic crossing over to the other lanes." In the distance a snake of cars was traveling to what would normally be the eastbound lanes.

It took us a half hour to get there.

"You would drive a standard," Shannon said, rubbing her left knee.

"I didn't buy the car with hurricane evacuation in mind. Try not to ride the clutch."

We moved a little better after we crossed over, even made it to third gear a few times. I took out my cell phone and listened to the rest of my messages.

Cordelia hadn't called again, but the rest of my friends had—all of them increasingly worried that they hadn't heard from me. I needed to contact them, but I hesitated. Certainly by now they had all called Cordelia. I didn't know what she'd said to explain why we were apart, and I didn't want to deal with it. I sighed. "I don't want to talk about it" would have to suffice until this was over. And until I could talk about it.

I punched in Torbin's number.

"Where are you?" was his greeting. His caller ID had clearly identified me.

"On I-10 heading for Texas."

"So you have noticed that there is a major hurricane with New Orleans in the bull's-eye?"

"It did catch my attention."

"What happened?"

"I'd turned off my cell phone and was out at the shipyard."

"That's not what I'm asking."

I knew that, but had hoped he'd take the hint. "I really don't want to talk about it."

"Andy and I helped Cordelia board up your house. Can I at least call her and tell her you're okay?"

Just hearing her name seared me. "You don't need my permission. Thank you for boarding up our...the house."

Torbin sighed. He knew what my pissy formal tone meant. "We'll talk later. We're in Dallas, about to board a plane for San Francisco."

"San Francisco?"

"Andy's brother is out there. The one smart enough to be a computer genius where they pay well for that kind of stuff. We could stay with my mother, my sisters, their brat children, several cousins in a small shotgun in LaPlace or we could fly to San Francisco. Believe me, it was a hard choice. Oh, they're calling our plane."

"Be safe. Give my love to Andy," I told him.

"Will do. I'll call Cordelia. I'm still friends with her, you know. You be safe, too."

"Wait, where is she?" I didn't want to ask, but I had to know.

"I think she said she was staying at Charity Hospital."

"Thanks, Tor. I love you."

"I love you, too. We'll be back together soon."

Then he was gone. I wanted to ask if she was with Lauren, but I couldn't.

The phone rang as I was holding it. I glanced at the caller ID. It was Joanne. I had to answer this one.

"Hi, I'm on the interstate," I told her with no preamble.

"Fuck, I've been wondering where the hell you were. Look, Alex is on her way to Baton Rouge and I'm worried about her."

"You have to stay?"

"Yeah, we're all on duty until this is over. I'm hoping to hell it jogs over to Mississippi. That'll teach them to put casinos on boats. She left with her brother yesterday. They'll stay with their uncle there. The right-wing jerk."

"Even right-wing jerks take in family during hurricanes."

"Yeah, but he may not be happy. Look, Alex is pregnant. We just got the test back."

"Joanne—"

"We weren't going to tell anyone just yet, in case…she loses this one, too."

Alex and Joanne had been trying for a while to have a child. They had come heartbreakingly close, Alex miscarrying in the third month. They had stopped talking about it after that. I didn't know if they had given up or were just holding it close to avoid the pain of having to tell everyone if they lost one again.

"And I'm scared," Joanne said. "I don't want her to have to listen to his rants about her immoral lifestyle under any circumstances, and… if something happens, this will be hell on her."

"What do you want me to do?"

Joanne was silent, then said, "Oh, hell, I don't even know at this point. I was hoping you'd take her out of the city, but—"

"I'm sorry. I can try and get her in Baton Rouge, but I'm not sure where we go from there."

"No, don't be sorry, this mess isn't your doing. Maybe pick her up when you come back in the city. The shorter her visit there, the better."

"Okay, I can do that."

"Do you have her cell number?"

I didn't. I usually called Joanne, and Cordelia talked more to Alex. On the few occasions I needed to call Alex, I'd just either used Cordelia's phone, or called Cordelia and had her call Alex. "Give it to me," I said, as I rummaged in the glove box for a pen and something to write on.

Then Joanne had to go. I wouldn't want to be a cop in New Orleans during Mardi Gras, let alone during a hurricane.

Danny was next. She and Elly were already in Shreveport, staying with friends there. "Two dogs, one cat, my mom and dad, every cousin in the state. An impromptu reunion," she told me. Then she asked, "Are you okay, Mick?"

"Yeah, just stuck in traffic."

Danny's silence let me know that she knew more. "Just traffic?" she finally asked.

"What did she tell you?" I decided that I at least wanted to know the story Cordelia was telling people. If Danny was going to question me, I could question her.

"What did who tell me?"

"Then I'm just stuck in traffic."

Danny sighed. "We'll talk after this is over, okay?"

"Yeah, we'll talk," I said. "Probably about the weather."

We left it at that, both telling each other to be safe.

Then I needed to call my mother. I decided not to tell her about Cordelia. They had grown close; in fact my mother often said she'd gained two daughters instead of just one.

The little benefit we'd gotten from the contra-flow traffic split was gone. Now we were inching forward five to ten feet at a time. Then stopping before inching another few feet. I looked at my watch. It was close to four hours since we'd left the shipyard, a journey that should take about an hour.

"We should probably turn the air-conditioning off for a while," I said, with a glance at the temperature gauge.

"This is just not fun, is it?" Shannon said. She was still gripping the wheel, so I turned off the controls. She let go long enough to unroll her window.

"It should be better once we get farther along. I just don't want to risk overheating in this mess."

"Yeah," she muttered. "And it'll save gas as well." She cast a nervous glance at the fuel gauge. Three-quarters of a tank.

I dialed my mother's number. Maybe she wouldn't be there and I could just leave a message.

She was there. "Michele!" she exclaimed. She had named me Michele, not Micky, so she rarely used the latter. "I've been glued to the TV, watching what's happening with New Orleans. Where are you?"

"I was out at the shipyard and left my phone in the car. But now I'm on I-10 out of the city."

"Oh, good. I was worried you might try and ride it out, stay because

Cordelia is there. She told me she'll be all right, in Charity. She wasn't just reassuring me, was she?"

Just what I wanted to talk about. "Maybe a little. It won't be a good time, they might lose power, but you've seen the Charity monolith—nothing can move that. She's smart enough to stay away from windows and stuff like that," I hastily finished. I couldn't do it—just talk about Cordelia like everything was okay.

"Is something the matter?" she asked. If I had hoped that all those years we were apart would prevent her from knowing me too well, I was wrong. In many ways—too many, according to Cordelia and Nina, Mom's partner—we were very much alike.

"Other than a category five hurricane being about to wash away New Orleans, being stuck in traffic creeping along at barely five miles an hour, in ninety-five-plus degree heat?" It's not nice to be sarcastic to your mother, a little voice in my head reminded me. "I'm sorry. It's hot, we're moving too slow to turn on the air-conditioning, and who knows when we'll get to some place we can go to the bathroom."

"Who are you traveling with?"

I had let "we" slip out. "A friend, Shannon. She's a Yankee and doesn't know much about hurricanes."

"Good. I was worried with Cordelia staying that you would be alone. I'm glad you have someone with you to share the driving."

"Yeah, it's good." I wanted to yell, Would you stop talking about Cordelia. "Look, Mom, I've got to go. I don't want to run down my cell-phone battery."

"Call me later, please? Whenever you get to where you're going."

"It may be late," I hedged.

"Michele, honey, I love you. It doesn't matter how late. I just want to know you're safe."

"Okay, Mom, I'll call you…and I love you, too." I clicked off the cell phone. I was too close to crying to continue talking. And if I broke down, she'd know for sure that something was wrong. At least now I had a few hours to think of what I would say to her later.

I glanced over at Shannon. Sweat was dripping off her nose. We still had miles to go before we would be beyond the metro area. I rummaged in the backseat and found one of the water bottles and handed it to her.

"Pace your drinking with our ability to take a bathroom break," I reminded her.

She nodded, uncapping the bottle and taking a couple of swallows. She rested the tepid bottle against her forehead. "Remind me to never come here during hurricane season again," she said as she handed the bottle back to me.

The sun slipped away, hidden by misty clouds, and we were still in the city.

It was odd, driving past the backward signs. Not that we needed to know what the speed limit was—there was no chance we would exceed it. About every hundred yards or so, a car was pulled over to the side, some clearly signaling their distress with hoods up and steam coming out.

Slowly, we inched out of the city, over a marshy area called the Bonnet Carré Spillway. If the Mississippi is in danger of overflowing, this area has a floodgate to let the river spill into Lake Pontchartrain. The interstate is a raised causeway, with swampy marsh below and the lake beside it.

If possible, we were moving even slower, and the misty clouds were coalescing, turning a more solid gray.

"How long are we on this?" Shannon asked.

"In normal—"

"Don't give me normal! How long are we going to be stuck over this morass?" She looked in the rearview mirror. "Oh, shit, look behind us."

I turned to look. There were cars as far as I could see. And the horizon was filled with ominous dark black clouds, turning the sky a thick charcoal. We weren't moving. We were over this marsh and not moving.

Shannon suddenly hit the steering wheel. "Why the fuck aren't we moving?"

"Maybe an accident," I guessed.

"Oh, great. We get to ride out the hurricane here." She pounded the dash. "Fuck!"

"Let's get in the trunk and get your friend's number, okay?"

She shot out of the car, as if craving movement. She didn't even take the car key. I pulled it out of the ignition and met her at the trunk.

She hastily pawed through the things we had packed; I tried to put them back again neatly as she moved to the next thing, looking for her backpack. She finally found it. "Okay, let me keep this up front with me." She flashed a rueful smile. "Security blanket."

"Let me drive for a while," I said as she started to head back to the driver's side.

"Yeah, okay. My left leg needs a rest anyway."

Suddenly there was a gust of wind and the rain started. We hurried back into the car.

"This is it, isn't it?" Shannon asked, her voice tight.

"Just the outer bands," I said. "We're still a long way from the—"

"Not long enough," Shannon cut in. "Oh, shit, I'm not handling this well. Damn." She gripped herself with her arms, as if trying to hold the fear in.

A gust of wind shook the car. I looked at my watch. It was around two p.m. The storm was coming ashore; it would start tonight, with landfall sometime in the very early morning. We had been listening to the radio nonstop. I could almost recite the longitude and latitude and progression of Hurricane Katrina.

I had brought Shannon here and I needed to take care of her. I put my arm around her shoulder and pulled her to me. She was breathing rapidly and was covered in sweat, her shirt sticking to her back.

"I know this is scary. I don't like being stuck in traffic like this. But right now, we're just in a thunderstorm. It will just be a thunderstorm for a while." I brushed her hair off her face. "Whatever is ahead of us, they'll get it cleared out. They have to get the traffic moving, and we'll get out of here."

"Shit, I'm sorry," she said, her voice muffled against my chest. "I'm usually Miss Calm and Cool, but when I feel I'm trapped…and powerless…sometimes, I just lose it."

"We'll be okay. I won't let anything happen to you, got that?"

I just held her for several minutes. We weren't going anywhere anyway. Her breathing slowed to a steadier pace.

Shannon lifted her head and looked at me. "You know I'm falling in love with you."

Not a single reply came to mind. I think I started to say something, just to fill the now-dense silence, but nothing resembling a single word came out.

"Shhh," Shannon said, putting a finger on my lips. "I didn't say that to get a response. Or to put you on the spot." She replaced her finger with her lips, kissing me.

Her lips were a little salty from the sweat, but also soft and welcoming. We held it for a moment more, then pulled away.

"Damn, Shannon Wild, you pick the most romantic places," I said as I sat back.

That got a laugh out of her, not a big laugh—we were still stuck over a swamp with a hurricane approaching, after all.

"Let's stop listening to the radio," I said, switching to the CD player. "We know what we need to know." I was hoping I had something decent in the player, that I hadn't been in a weird disco mood or something when I loaded it.

"Yeah, music might help. Let me call my friends and see if they want company."

The Indigo Girls started singing. I turned them down so that Shannon could make her call, relieved that my CD choices were respectable.

"Hey, Connie," she said into my cell phone. "Shannon Wild here. Would you and Shelley be up to taking in some New Orleans people for a day or two?"

As she was talking, the traffic finally started inching forward again. I looked at my watch. We hadn't moved for twenty minutes. The ten miles over the spillway was slow, inch forward and stop, over and over again. We finally got back onto something resembling dry land.

We even started moving enough to escape the rain, as well as turn the air-conditioning back on.

But the dark clouds were still behind us, as if chasing us away from New Orleans.

Chapter Nineteen

As we got closer to Baton Rouge, I decided to call Alex to clue her in that I would be taking her back to New Orleans. The traffic was slow enough that finding the number and reading it as I dialed wasn't a hazard. It wasn't like I was traveling fast enough to do any damage anyway.

"All circuits are busy. Please try your call again later," a mechanical voice told me.

I tried again later and got the same message.

Then, just to be contrary, my phone rang. The caller ID told me it was Torbin. "Where are you?" I asked him.

"At the airport," he answered.

"Still?"

"The San Francisco airport. We just got in. Where are you?"

"Heading for Baton Rouge. Still. Somewhere around Gonzales, I think."

"Don't worry. I won't rub in our respective locations."

My cell phone seconded him. It beeped to tell me I'd lost the signal. I punched his name in again. The call got through. "Did you talk to her?" I didn't want to ask, but I had to know and my cell-phone coverage wasn't going to let me work up to the question.

"No, I didn't, had to leave a message."

Damn. She'll be okay, I told myself...and she doesn't love me anymore anyway, so why am I concerned about her? The answer was obvious, even to me. Because I still loved her.

"Thanks, Tor. Give my regards to the city by the bay."

Then my cell cut out again.

Not that we had been making great time, but on the outskirts of Baton Rouge, we went from our speedy ten miles an hour to about two miles an hour.

Off in the distant west, a red and gold sun was setting, but we were being chased by the storm, and the clouds soon took away whatever daylight might have been left. The rain caught us again, first a steady downpour, then it turned to a fierce thunderstorm, water sheeting down the windshield. I reached over and took Shannon's hand, just holding it. I could see that she was starting to get agitated again.

She grasped my hand tight, saying nothing beyond her hard grip. Then softly, "Lauren had no patience for…this. She'd just tell me to get over it. No hand-holding from Dr. Calder."

"Holding your hand isn't exactly a heavy burden."

"No, but dealing with my shit right now isn't exactly what you want to be doing."

"Right now nothing is exactly what I want to be doing. But that's the covenant—I fall apart, you help. You fall apart, I help you. That's what…friends do." I almost said lovers. I continued, "I probably still owe you some for my drunken performance these past few days."

"You don't owe me."

"Two days versus two hours," I said, braking as someone abruptly changed lanes in front of me, their brake lights a blur in the rain.

"If you insist. How about payment in sexual favors?"

"Don't think we're moving quite slow enough for that." I didn't dare look at her, afraid she would see the confusion on my face. And the desire.

"Later?"

My cell phone rang. I glanced at the caller ID, but it just gave a New Orleans number. I answered it.

Cordelia. "Micky! Are you still in the city?"

"No, driving through Baton Rouge now."

"Oh, thank God." I could hear the relief in her voice. She was genuinely worried about me. She still cared. I jammed on the brakes to avoid hitting the car in front of me.

"I wanted to tell you to come to Charity, if you were still here," she said. "And…" she hesitated in the way that I knew meant she intended to say something hard to get out, "I'm so sorry. I never meant to…do what I did. To hurt you that way."

Damn you, damn you, damn you, I thought, staring at the glaring red lights in front of me, distorted by rain almost to a smear. "What way did you mean to hurt me?" I said angrily. Then added, "I've got Shannon with me."

Cordelia was silent before replying. "I didn't mean to…Lauren went back to New York, and—"

The line cut out again. I hurriedly hit redial. "All circuits are busy," the mechanical voice told me.

I hit redial again and got the same message. "In the glove box," I told Shannon, "there should be a cord for me to charge my cell phone." She found it and handed it to me. I plugged it in. I gave it a minute to charge, then hit redial again. The circuits were still busy.

"I thought you said earlier that you were worried about your cell batteries," Shannon said, running her fingers along the cord.

"Okay, I can strategically have a memory lapse." I tried redial again. Nothing, save the mechanical voice. All the fucking circuits were fucking busy.

Every few minutes, I tried again. In fact, I tried to call just about everyone whose number was stored on my cell phone, including my home number. Nothing got through. I wondered if the winds had already taken the cell towers out.

"Are we spending the night here?" Shannon muttered, not really a question to me, more a comment on the traffic. The rain was still sheeting down the windshield.

"This is how traffic usually is in Baton Rouge," I told her. Even on good days, our state capital wasn't known for its smoothly flowing highways.

"Bullshit, Knight. Hey, where are we going?"

"Over the river," I told her. Shannon had noticed that the highway was rising, now at about rooftop level and still heading up.

"The river?"

"The Mississippi River, Father of Waters, Old Man River."

"Oh, fuck, if we get stuck there, I'll have to start walking and you can pick me up."

Shannon shut her eyes. The bridge is high, hundreds of feet for large ships to pass under. On a miserably rainy night, with wind gusts buffeting the car and all that was between us and a roiling expanse of water was a small slab of concrete, it was scary. A truck in front got hit by a blast of wind and fishtailed, almost hitting a minivan before regaining control. One accident and this will be a nightmare, I thought, glancing at Shannon. She still had her eyes closed and I didn't say anything.

After we crossed the river, enough people had peeled off in Baton Rouge for us to pick up actual speed, even in some stretches something resembling a highway pace. The rain was still steady, but was beginning to seem more like just rain and not the harbinger of a hurricane.

"Atchafalaya Basin," I said, as I took her hand. It was another large swampy area where it was you, your car, an elevated roadway, and swamp below and on all sides as far as you could see—even on a clear day, which this certainly wasn't.

"Thanks," Shannon said with a weak smile. She closed her eyes. "Tell me when we're on dry land again."

I didn't let on, but I found her hand reassuring. It was dark, rainy, and nothing but swamp around, save for a ribbon of blurry taillights in front of me and headlights behind me.

Those other people felt distant, all of us intent on escaping the storm, driving, just driving into the night. Shannon was here with me, her hand warm in mine.

"Dry land," I told her as we came off the bridge. I didn't let go of her hand.

Traffic slowed again around Lafayette. I drove beyond the city, then found an exit. Gas and bathroom time. We hit the bathroom first, then grabbed caffeine and chocolate—the healthy evacuation diet. I let Shannon pump the gas. I tried my cell phone again. I couldn't get through to anyone in New Orleans, or anyone who had a New Orleans area code. I did connect with my mother. Evidently if the cell call didn't have to route through New Orleans, it worked. I managed to keep our call to, "Hey, I'm okay, a little past Lafayette, well out of the storm path. We're on the way to Texas to stay with friends there." The rain had even stopped. Or rather we had driven out of it. I had no doubt that rain was falling and falling hard, back from where we came.

Shannon called her friends to give them a guesstimate of when we might show up. It was now past nine p.m.

"Want me to drive?" she said.

"Yeah, now that we're on dry land and it's not raining," I said, heading for the passenger door.

When we got back on the interstate, she took my hand again. Even now, this far out, the traffic was slow, at some points back to nothing better than stop-and-go. It was almost surreal, surrounded by the dark piney woods of west Louisiana and traffic bumper to bumper. People had fled this monster storm.

"A lot of people are going to Houston, aren't they?" Shannon noticed, as we passed over the lake that gives Lake Charles its name.

"Closest hotel room."

We were both tired, talking little. We'd been on the road for over twelve hours now, with just one stop. Well, one real stop, hundreds of times of sitting stopped.

"This is a hell of a ride," she said, rubbing her neck for a moment, lifting her hand from the steering wheel but still holding mine.

"Here, let me do that." I let go of her hand to use both of mine to rub her shoulders and back.

"I'm just about dead," she said. "How do other people do it? I mean, you and I are in pretty good shape, relatively young. What if you're old, or have a heart condition or something?"

"Probably a lot of them stayed. Or they got friends or family to help. It's a hellish choice. Remember, on Friday, when we left the city, the last we heard was that Katrina was headed more for Florida. She changed direction some time after that. Do you risk your health and safety by going through this ordeal or risk that you'll be better off staying where you are?"

"Not good choices," Shannon agreed. "This is pretty miserable."

"I'll be very happy if this is the worst thing that happens to us," I said.

She looked at me. "You think it'll be bad?"

"New Orleans is a low city, protected by levees and floodwalls. This is possibly the nightmare scenario they've been predicting for years—a major hurricane and a direct hit. If the levees fail, we'll fill up like a bowl, water that's likely to be a stew of chemicals and human waste. It'll flood the sewer system, probably even wash out graveyards." I was quiet, then added with a bitter laugh, "Why do you think we drink so much in New Orleans?"

"You're scared, aren't you?" she asked.

"Yeah, terrified. Good thing I hide it so well." Then I admitted, "I kept thinking as we drove away, is this the last time I'll see this? The shipyard, all the little towns around it, New Orleans, General Lee on his horse in his circle, the Superdome, the French Quarter? My house? My friends' houses?"

Shannon squeezed my hand tight. Then she said, "Hey, we're in Texas."

"Just when you think things can't get any worse, you end up in Texas."

"Good news for us, my friends are the first exit beyond the state line."

"Pity the poor fools who still have another couple of hours before getting to Houston." I looked at my watch. It was well past midnight. Some people would be driving until daybreak.

The traffic was still that of a heavy rush hour, but at least we were now moving at something like rush-hour speeds.

"Orange, Texas," Shannon announced, as she started to slow for the exit.

We pulled off the interstate into a gas station, then she called her friends. We both got out, cramped from the long hours of sitting. I watched the traffic still rushing by on the highway. Car, after car, after car. It was almost one a.m. on a Monday morning, this stream of traffic the only testament to what was happening in New Orleans on an otherwise balmy summer night. Who were those people in the cars? How many of them did I know? Was Miss Carlotta passing by? Ambrose? Or would he stay to guard the myth he'd made of Damon? What about Damon? He'd woken up. Where was he? Evacuated, or riding out the storm in a hospital that was equipped to handle a day or two without power? I still needed to find Beatrice, not lose the one last chance to connect a daughter to her father.

Then Shannon was off the phone and she wrapped her arms around me, both us of hugging tight in the relief of being through this ordeal. She let go, then turned me around to rub my shoulders, saying, "Payback."

"I like the way you do math," I said, relaxing into the kneading of her hands.

It seemed that she had just started when Shelley and Connie pulled up in their car. After a brief hello and introduction, we followed them to their house.

They were kind and gracious hosts, insisting that they were night people and would probably be up anyway. Shelley was tall, silver-haired, and quiet. Connie was shorter, her hair still a rich chestnut brown, and she kept an easy flow of chatter. They insisted on feeding us. Other than the chocolate bar outside Lafayette, Shannon and I hadn't eaten much.

We watched the news for a little while.

"That looks bad," Shannon said on seeing a shot of a flooded highway.

"That's two inches from the Gulf, they flood during a drizzle," I said.

She didn't answer. Either she believed me or decided I was whistling past a graveyard and she wouldn't challenge me tonight.

She'd evidently made the sleeping arrangements, as we got one room—and one bed—to ourselves. But we were both too tired—and on my part, at least, too worried—to do anything more than collapse into bed.

I woke in the middle of the night and started to call out for Cordelia before I realized I wasn't home, but in a strange bed, nor was I with her. I lay still, wondering what she was doing now. Trying to sleep? Listening to the whipping winds? Or too involved with life and death to be aware of them? Then I wondered if I'd ever talk to her and find out.

I curled around a softly snoring Shannon and fell back asleep.

CHAPTER TWENTY

It felt all wrong when I woke up. The wrong bed, the wrong town, the wrong state. The wrong person? I didn't know. I lay beside Shannon taking comfort from her solid warmth. I carefully reached over her for my watch. It was around nine. The hurricane would have made landfall by now. I'd soon know what the damage was. I was hesitant to find out, holding on to a tag of hope that might soon be dashed.

Shannon stirred beside me. She rolled to face me, her eyes open.

"Shower?" I said, starting to get up. Then added, "I have to know what's happening."

"I wake up slow, you go ahead," she offered.

I grabbed some clothes and padded down the hall to the bathroom. Shannon picked her friends well. Not only did they have a spare bedroom, but also two bathrooms, and they had ceded one to us. I took a quick shower.

Shannon was awake and went to shower when I got back. By the time I had more or less organized the stuff we had hastily deposited last night, she was back.

Our hosts were up and, after giving us the breakfast choices, let us turn on the TV. The news was better than I expected. The hurricane had, at the last of the last minutes, jogged east, bad news for the Mississippi Gulf Coast, but a reprieve for New Orleans.

But the news didn't stay good. The city was flooding; one of the levees must have given way. I sat and watched, a dread chill seeping into my heart and lingering there. I watched, desperately wanting to somehow reach out and stop the water. It's just a few yards, I impatiently thought, couldn't something somehow be used to plug that gap before it took the whole city? They are working on it, the news reported. Maybe that will be it, some places flooded, but contained. They have to be able to stop the water.

Shannon and I spent the day alternating between the television and e-mail. I could no longer get or receive calls on my cell phone. Torbin—probably Andy, given their levels of tech knowledge—text-messaged me. "U ok?"

I clumsily typed back, "Yes. In TX. U ok?"

"Fab. In SF. Love u."

I typed back a "Love U," actually "lovd u"—my thumb wasn't used to using a cell phone as a keyboard—then sent a text message to Joanne, wondering if it would get through. Just the basic, "U ok?" After a moment's hesitation, I sent the same to Cordelia.

Shelley and Connie had two computers, a hers-and-hers arrangement. Plus a laptop and wireless in their house. Shannon had her laptop, also wireless, so I had the spare computer to myself. I sent e-mails to just about everyone. My mother, a long one, mostly on the details of yesterday's journey, as reassuring as I could be. Danny and Elly, Alex, Torbin and Andy. I knew Andy would find a computer. Plus I was getting e-mails from just about everyone I knew, asking if I was okay. My asshole cousin Bayard even sent me one. His, I didn't bother answering.

Evening slipped into night and the news that they'd fixed the levees didn't come. Only the water kept coming. Sleep, if it came at all, was restless.

In the morning, I watched the screen, seeing the streets I'd spent most of my life traveling turn to grimy bayous, familiar places turning into some bizarre water world. I desperately scanned the faces of the people in the background of the announcers, looking for faces I knew. Joanne. Cordelia.

But I didn't see them. The camera caught so little, a few feet, yards, of a city I knew with my whole life.

Then the night was so deep, it became time to try for rest. Shannon held me close, sensing the horror that had invaded my world. She kissed me, and part of me very much wanted to kiss her back, to just hold her and make love and forget about the water and the people there. But I couldn't.

"Thank you," I whispered to her. "But I wouldn't be here."

We slept, I restlessly. I woke, thinking I felt Cordelia's hand on my shoulder. But no one was there, nothing, not even the blanket was touching me there.

And then New Orleans turned into a conflagration of flood and fire.

My cell phone told me it tried three times to deliver the text messages I had sent to Joanne and Cordelia, but the delivery failed. I sent them again and a few hours later got the same message—they couldn't be delivered.

All I could do was strain to view the background on TV to see something that would let me know they were okay. But instead it was water, chaos, a city in anarchy, flames, and flood. No one could fix the levees and the city was under water. I watched as boats floated down Tulane Avenue, past Charity Hospital, and remembered the nights when I'd meet Cordelia there, or wait outside to pick her up.

Shannon, and Connie and Shelley, were kind, feeding me at times around lunch and dinner, somehow understanding that this was my city, not theirs, and that I could do little beyond watch the stories on TV, sometimes the same ones over and over, part of me numb, in shock, and another part feeling every inch of the horror of what was lost and would never be again.

Shannon held me again that night, but I was too chilled by the day's events to think of love or passion. She kissed me as tenderly as she could, touched me, but I couldn't respond. I was too heartbroken to love anyone.

"Just hold me," I asked, and she did.

I woke up again in the deep hours of the night, from a dream that I was back in my home in New Orleans and the flood waters were coming. Cordelia was somewhere in the house, but I couldn't find her.

It's only a dream, I told myself. But it wasn't. I couldn't find Cordelia, and the water was too close to our house to know if it had escaped or not.

I had disturbed Shannon and she woke up. "You okay?" she asked.

No, I'll never be okay, I thought. "Bad dream," I admitted.

"Understandable," she murmured.

"Curl around me and I'll go back to sleep," I told her.

I took what comfort I could from her arm around me. Her regular breathing finally lulled me into a restless sleep.

When I woke up the next day I thought it couldn't be worse, but it could. The TV showed scenes that I would be appalled to see in some far-off third-world country, but this was from my home city, streets I had just walked in a few days ago. The TV cameras showed scenes of looting and anarchy.

Alex and I sent e-mails almost every hour. I was scared for Joanne, Alex was terrified. The police force of New Orleans was overwhelmed, first by the fury of the storm, then the fury of people, some desperate, some willing to scavenge off tragedy. And there was nothing either of us could do, save for this electronic reaching out. I offered to come to Baton Rouge to be with her. "I'd love it," she replied, then sensibly pointed out that the hotels, the shelters, everything was full, and "my uncle has only noticed how this has inconvenienced him. He wouldn't let you sleep in his yard because you might kill his grass. His verdict is New Orleans deserved what it got. I vowed long ago that I won't kill him and risk jail, but it took me a long time to work through to that. I can't place you at risk. If I get desperate enough, I'll let you know."

I wanted to pick up the phone and call her, just to hear a voice I knew and loved. I wanted to call all my friends. More, I wanted to be with them, but we were scattered across the country. Torbin and Andy in San Francisco, Alex in Baton Rouge, Danny and Elly in Shreveport, the far northwest part of Louisiana, Joanne and Cordelia in the belly of the beast. Hutch, Joanne's partner, was also in New Orleans. I'd gotten an e-mail from Millie, his partner—domestic, that is. She was in Austin, Texas. Emma Auerbach and her partner, Rachel, had been in Chicago and just stayed there. Karen, Cordelia's cousin, had flown to D.C. with her latest girlfriend. Barbara Selby and her two children Patrick and Cissy to outside of Nashville, Lindsay McNeil to Raleigh, North Carolina. Others spread from Seattle to Milwaukee to Albany. A diaspora.

I finally couldn't sit in front of the TV or the computer screen.

"Okay if I go for a walk?" I asked, a general question.

"Want me to go with you?" Shannon offered.

"No, but thanks. I just need to be alone for a bit."

I left the house. It was one of several in a subdivision north of town. Their owners would have seen the differences in the houses, but to me they were typical suburban, mostly ranch houses and I could be walking in just about anyplace. Although the heat did hint I was someplace in the South. But I had to move, had to just get out and away for an hour. I had to take a break from the horrific images, the flooded houses, floating bodies, the old, the disabled, left to desperately await deliverance that was far too slow in coming. I was alone on the street, people sealed behind air-conditioning or in cars that passed by.

Let them be okay. Joanne. Cordelia. The people I didn't know, trapped on roofs, left in the Superdome and Convention Center. I would have prayed if I thought it would do any good. *Please let them be okay.* And I knew it was too late for many of them. Being okay, at best, would be being alive, everything else gone—every baby picture, every love letter, a faded picture of a grandmother, a football trophy, a flag from a soldier's coffin—lost to the black water.

Let her be okay. I bargained with fate: Cordelia could live happily ever after with Lauren, as long as she was okay. With a stark clarity, I knew that whatever pain I felt at seeing her in the arms of another woman—and that had hurt like hell—that pain would be nothing in comparison to losing her entirely.

"No!" I said aloud, glad that no one was around to hear my anguish, my desperate begging for kindness from some blind, unthinking fate. "Let her be okay." If she was okay, it would take time, but we could be friends, I could have her in my life. Suddenly I just badly wanted to hold her, to have her safe and solid in my arms.

But I would give up that, give up ever touching her again as a lover, just as long as she was all right. And if I couldn't have that— Cordelia as a lover—what could I have? I thought of Shannon. Again, clarity. I wasn't in love with her, but maybe I could be. If I had to turn from Cordelia, Shannon wasn't a bad direction to turn to. I remembered her in the soft light as she sat reading, her long legs. A sudden jolt of desire hit me.

Then clarity left me. Lauren had returned to New York. What did that say about them? I would have pushed hard to stay at Charity with Cordelia and would have left only if she'd told me to, had asked me to look after Alex or told me she'd worry less if I were somewhere safe. What was she planning to say to me when we got cut off? What did I hope she would say?

I walked for over an hour, all the streets of this enclave of houses, the sweat sticking to my back and matting my hair. The only hope I allowed myself was that Cordelia would be okay. I'd made my bargain with fate. If she was okay, other things would matter, but that would be enough.

Shannon was on the laptop when I came back into the living room. She looked up as I entered. I gave her a bare nod and sat down at my computer. E-mail had become a lifeline, the one slim connection to the friends who made up my daily life. Ten messages had piled up in the last few hours. One from Alex, of course, just an update on living with her uncle and the rest of her family in Baton Rouge. I sent her a quick reply. It didn't so much matter what we said, just that we communicated—I'm here and I hear you.

A subject line caught my eye. "Damon's Daughter." It was from Miss Carlotta. She was in Memphis, traveling with George and Jud Lasser. Reluctantly, she had left Damon in Memorial Hospital. He would be safer there than being moved. Damon's last words to her were, "Go, be safe. It's just a few days." Jud was traveling back to his place in Abita Springs and then attempting to see what he could find out about Damon and, if possible, get him moved up to Memphis. Miss Carlotta wanted to know if it would be possible to find Beatrice and Jane soon.

She was polite enough to first say she hoped that I was okay and she'd understand perfectly if I could no longer follow through. But she wanted Damon's daughter located. And she had a point. If they hadn't already evacuated the hospitals, they had to soon. Generators can only power so much, and air-conditioning falls below life-support systems. Ninety-degree-plus heat and being carried through flood waters wasn't helping much to extend Damon's already short life span.

I'd already decided to act, so my answer to her was easy. And to be honest, her request was welcome. I couldn't do anything for Cordelia or Joanne, or for the city that was my life, or the people there. But I could find Damon's daughter, I could do my best to talk Beatrice into letting Jane meet her father. Put some small, very small piece of what had been ripped apart back together again.

Today was Thursday. I looked up distances and driving times. I calculated we could leave Friday. From where we were, it would be a two-day drive—I didn't think that either Shannon or I wanted another marathon trip—to the northeast corner of Arkansas. We'd talk to Beatrice on either Saturday or Sunday. By then, Damon would probably have been moved to Memphis and had enough time to recover from the journey and to be up to the visit. If possible and not too intrusive, I wanted to be there, at least for the initial few minutes. Happy endings were rare, but they were one of the perks of the job.

When I told our hosts my plans, Connie asked why I needed to drive up there instead of just calling on the phone.

"It's pretty emotional to have someone like me show up with this kind of news. Being on the doorstep gives me the best chance to convince her to say yes."

I did offer Shannon the option of not joining me, but, as I expected, she said no way would she miss this. "Besides, I've never been to Arkansas," she added. "This might be one of my only chances."

That sense of purpose was the one bright space in that day. "What the fuck is going on with the assholes in charge?" Shannon raged at the TV as we watched the chaotic events of the day. Thousands still stranded at the Superdome and the Convention Center, no food, no water. I had to get up and leave the room when they reported snipers firing on those trying to evacuate Charity. Then I came back and obsessively watched, trying for a glimpse of Cordelia and listening with dread that I might hear someone had been hurt.

She has to be okay, I told myself, gripping Shannon's hand so hard she finally had to ask me to loosen my grasp. She said nothing beyond that, but she had to know what my worry was, the way I honed in when the announcer said Charity Hospital, or even just hospital. Or sniper. I was worried about Joanne, too, but at least she had a gun and could shoot back. And presumably she was with other people who also had guns.

Later that night as we lay beside each other, Shannon said, "You know, I still love Lauren. It doesn't just go away. I know that I won't go back. But that doesn't mean I wouldn't worry about her or care if she was…"

I rolled to my side, facing her. Wanting her. But I only kissed her on her forehead. I almost kissed her on the lips, but didn't trust myself to stop there. Too much of me was still consumed with what was happening to my city, the people there, the ones in my life. Too much of me would not be with Shannon if I started touching her.

The next morning, we packed up and left for Arkansas. I gave Connie and Shelley a long hug. They had been kind and generous and it wasn't something I would forget.

It was a drive of about five hundred miles from Orange, Texas, to Jonesboro, Arkansas. We decided to break it into two days.

"It's not like we have anyplace we need to be," Shannon pointed out.

The route was the state highway up the east border of Texas to Texarkana, then Interstate 30 to Little Rock, and then one of the smaller state highways to Jonesboro.

"I do love the back roads," she said.

"Not like we have any choice. We're heading places the interstates seem to have bypassed."

In Texarkana we found a motel just off the interstate. It'd do for a night.

We had passed a mall on the way in and Shannon decided to replace her cell phone. "Who knows when I'll be able to go back and snag it? Besides, yours is useless and mine is a New York number."

A cell phone that could take incoming calls made sense. I was seriously considering just buying one, so I could have a working number. I still had received nothing other than text messages and that was getting old.

After accomplishing the cell-phone mission, I made my needs known. "I'm hungry. What do you feel like eating?"

Shannon gave me a mischievous grin. "Let's have an adventure. How about sushi?"

"If you can find a place, we'll go," I offered, thinking I was safe.

However, Shannon was an investigative journalist, and she put her brand-new cell phone to work and somehow managed to find a sushi restaurant.

"I didn't know you Southerners were into this raw stuff," she said as I slurped up some raw salmon.

"Hell, we Cajuns were eating it raw long before you Yankees," I rejoined. "I ate my first raw oyster before you were born. That's what they weaned us with."

After dinner, we went back to the hotel and to the ritual of watching TV. Shannon plugged in her laptop and we checked e-mail.

We watched a snippet from a presidential press conference. Bush did the usual all-is-right-with-the-world crap, saying to the head of FEMA, "Brownie, you're doing a heck of a job." Not how I would have put it. I would have said something more like, "You fucking privileged little shit. Can you get an empathy transplant so you can at least have a modicum of an idea what it's like to be left for a week without food, water, a working toilet, in ninety-plus-degree heat, after your house has been destroyed by the flood?" And probably a few more things, but they didn't ask me.

The hospitals had finally been evacuated. I caught only a glimpse of scrubs that I thought might be Cordelia, but when the clip came by again, I saw it wasn't her. In fact, the figure looked more like a man than a woman. But the news didn't tell me what I wanted to know, where they had been taken. Only "Charity Hospital has finally been evacuated."

I stayed up late, hoping to find out more, but they just showed the same footage again.

Finally Shannon said, "Come to bed. Maybe there will be more in the morning, but not much will happen tonight."

She was right. We were in the same time zone, and wherever those who had been rescued were, they were probably sleeping. I turned off the TV and went into the bathroom to brush my teeth. She was awake when I came out, waiting for me.

I kept my T-shirt on and got in bed beside her.

"Do you not want me?" she asked, her eyes searching my face for any lie I might tell.

"No," I said slowly. "I want you too much. Some for the right reasons. And some for the wrong reasons. And…I think I should work out at least some of those wrong reasons before…"

"Before we make love," she finished for me.

"But how can you feel, watching me watching the TV for any news, any hint of Cordelia?"

She brushed the hair off my face. "Hey, you think I'll love you more if you just blithely toss over a love that lasted a long time, if you don't worry about her?" Then, softly, she said, "I'm hoping you'll care about me the way you care about her." She touched her lips to mine, then added, "I can say I love you, but it's not love if it's only about what I want."

I nestled my head against her shoulder. It would be so easy. And

I wanted to. But still some part of me held back, a chaotic offer to the gods. I couldn't make love to Shannon until I knew that Cordelia was okay. Not just a hollow promise from the TV screen that Charity Hospital had been evacuated, but someone somewhere actually hearing from her.

I couldn't put that into words for Shannon. Instead I just said, "Not yet, okay?"

"Yeah, I do pick the romantic places, don't I?"

"Well, it's not like we've included Paris on our itinerary."

"There is a Paris in Texas, you know," she told me.

"Another reason I don't like this state," I muttered.

We fell asleep in each other's arms.

Morning in Texarkana. The hotel provided an adequate continental breakfast. Savings for Miss Carlotta. Because breakfast was an early affair—if we wanted a free one, that is—I delayed my shower until afterward.

When I got out Shannon was on her new cell phone. "Fifty-two messages," she told me, as she snapped it shut. "And…Lauren called. Wanted to know if we'd heard anything about Cordelia."

"What did you tell her?" I asked brusquely, wondering if part of my bargain for Cordelia to be okay included being nice to Lauren.

"That we hadn't heard anything."

"What did she say?" I demanded.

"Just thanked me for talking to her about this and that she hoped I was okay."

What did I expect her to say—that she and Cordelia had broken it off? Or that Cordelia was supposed to be on her way to meet Lauren, but the hurricane had pulled them away from each other? I sighed and looked at Shannon. She was being remarkably stoic about watching both me and her lover—ex-lover?—both be more worried about another woman.

"How did you learn to be so calm?" I asked her. I strode across the too-small hotel room and jerked the curtain back, staring at the empty parking lot.

"From the sea, I guess. Watching it with my mother for my grandfather to come home from his fishing. On one stormy day, I remember her saying, 'We can worry, but the worry will not change the waves or the wind.' That's the short answer."

"What's the long answer?" I asked, turning from the window to grab our things and start packing them.

"One day he didn't come back," she said, remaining on the bed, her body still. "I watched my mother and my grandmother cry as they sorted the fish at the seafood place where they worked. I watched them cry as they cleaned the house and cooked us dinner. Then they stopped crying and made life go as best they could."

"Where was your dad?"

"He'd left years ago, to get rich in Las Vegas. He was supposed to send child support, but it always had to wait until the next roll of the dice. Even with all that, my mother and grandmother loved me enough to let me go. Guess I learned what's really important at an early age. When you know what's important, you know what to be calm about."

"Good lesson to learn. But it's hard when you're young." I stopped packing, lifted her chin with my hand, and touched my lips to hers, a brief, gentle kiss.

"It's probably hard to learn at any age. And I think it's important for us to leave Texas and go to Arkansas." She stood up, stuffing her cell phone away; her stillness broke, as if wrenched from the memory.

She helped me finish packing, and with one quick turn, we left Texas.

CHAPTER TWENTY-ONE

"Oh, Toto, we're not in Kansas anymore."

"No, we're in Arkansas," I replied. Shannon was commenting on the narrow two-lane road we were on. We passed few cars, more trucks, and more big trucks that didn't look like they quite fit on this small highway.

"Rice," Shannon said.

"What?" I said. Being the driver, I was paying more attention to the big truck coming at us in the other lane.

"We're in rice country," she explained.

"And me without my red beans," I grumbled.

The dusty two-lane finally gave way to a larger road with actual signs of people. The slightly larger road brought us into the booming metropolis of Jonesboro, Arkansas.

"Let's find a motel and get checked in," I told Shannon.

"Think this town is big enough to have one?"

"New York snob. It's a college town, it's got places to stay." We found one off the highway.

"Time to shower and make ourselves presentable," I told Shannon as I opened my suitcase. "I need to look the best I can," I said, surveying my packed clothes, "to be professional and respectable enough for Beatrice to trust us."

I grabbed the most professional of what I had. Just a black pair of pants, slightly frayed on the cuffs, but I hoped that Beatrice would not be looking down, and a V-necked T-shirt, but it was dark and didn't have anything written on it.

Shannon had set up her laptop and was on it when I emerged from the shower. "You smell nice," she noticed.

"Or the motel soap does," I said.

She stood up. "No, I think it's you." She kissed my shoulder as she passed me on her way to the shower. "Definitely you."

The tone of her voice and the hint in it sent a shock of wanting through me. Find Beatrice first, I told myself. I needed not to be alone in a motel room with Shannon right now. I sat at her computer to check my e-mail while she made herself presentable, hoping for a message that would give my brain something other than lust to focus on.

The gods of irony were at play again. One e-mail from Miss Carlotta, this one dispensed with politeness. Damon had finally been evacuated from Memorial Hospital and was on his way to Memphis. She was waiting for him there. Jud, who was traveling with Damon's ambulance, had said little, which meant there was little good to say. Maybe a few days of hydration and care would bring Damon back. And maybe not, maybe the clock was ticking and ticking faster, days instead of months. Maybe even hours.

An e-mail from Alex was brief: "Uncle's coming. CJ text-messaged me. She's at the airport." Nothing more.

That was it. Cordelia was at the airport. Waiting for a plane to join Lauren? Waiting for any plane to anywhere?

Shannon came out of the shower, wrapped in a towel.

I watched her as she started to dress, dropping the towel to pick up a bra. Then I turned my eyes away. Cordelia was okay. That's all that matters, I told myself. You made your bargain. She's okay. Fuck the hell out of Shannon tonight and get on with your life. Cordelia was okay—and she had written Alex, not me.

A sudden wave of grief threatened to sweep over me. Losing Cordelia prompted it, but that pain let in the pain from what I'd seen on the TV, what I knew was happening, what I knew would happen to so many people. The ill, the elderly, the poor, children with everything of their childhood gone.

I closed the computer and got up, walking to the window and pulling back the curtain enough to peer out. The sun was shining brightly, glaring off car hoods. I stared, letting it blur my vision.

"Are you okay?" Shannon asked, her hand on my shoulder.

"Yeah," I said, my voice shaky, then again, stronger, "Yeah, I'm okay. It just…hit me." I cleared my throat. "Let's go." I wanted to kiss her, kiss her hard and long and keep the world out. You will later, I told myself.

Jonesboro is not a big town and Beatrice's house was easy to find. I drove by it and then back around the block, wanting to check out the neighborhood. It was a tidy middle-class enclave, neat houses with trimmed lawns. Hers had several bright flower beds scattered through it, under the windows, along the edge of the driveway, around a tree in the center of the lawn. A car was parked in her driveway.

At my office I had grabbed the case file for Damon and taken it with me. As I came around the block again, I parked several houses down from Beatrice and reached into the backseat to find it.

In it was the photograph Damon had given me to present to her. I looked at it, aware I was about to change this woman's life. Then, "Ready?" I asked Shannon.

"When you are."

I got out of the car, the slam of the door echoing in this quiet corner. Or maybe it was just my perception, the feeling that something more than a mundane knock should herald the news I was bringing.

I paused at the door. I thought I heard the faint sound of voices, perhaps her, perhaps the TV. My license and the picture in hand, I knocked on her door. The voices stopped. Then footsteps crossed to the door and it opened. Beatrice Elliot was in front of me. She still looked like her picture, though a little more subdued in this suburban setting than the flashing sun of the Mississippi River, with her hair shorter, more practical. She wore no makeup, only a few lines added during the years. Her expression was a little puzzled, a little wary. Strange people didn't knock on doors around here.

I held out my license and the picture. "My name is Michele Knight and I'm a private detective from New Orleans. Damon LaChance hired me to find you. And to give you this." I offered her the picture.

She looked from me to my license to the photo. Finally, tentatively, she took the picture. Some memory crossed her face as she looked at it, wistful, perhaps a little sad, even. Then her face was the blank neutral that is almost resentment.

"And how is Damon?" she said, a sardonic smile barely playing at her lips.

"Much…different from when you last saw him. He was evacuated out of Memorial Hospital in New Orleans yesterday. He's on his way to Memphis. He's…very ill."

The smile left her lips.

"May we come in?" I asked.

She looked at me, then Shannon, then back into the house. "My daughter…it may be better for her not to hear this."

"Jane?" I asked.

She looked again at me, as if challenging me that I knew too much about her.

"We're not here to hurt you, or upset you, although I know we're bringing up something that you thought you'd left behind long ago," I said.

"This is about her, isn't it?" she asked.

"It is," I admitted.

"Damon left, why should I let him back in?" she asked, folding her arms, but her gesture seemed more protective than defiant.

"That's not what we're here for. Can I at least come in and talk to you? Shannon can wait in the car." I didn't want her to feel outnumbered.

She glanced at Shannon, then slowly moved away from the door.

It was enough of an invitation for me. I mounted the one low step and entered.

"Let's talk out back," Beatrice said. "You don't need to wait in the car," she added to Shannon, who remained on the doorstep.

We followed her through the small house. It was crammed with bookshelves, including one that was clearly Jane's, brimming with children's books, stuffed animals as bookends. Some toys were scattered around, but in one area, as if they were today's playthings, not just left there. Sprawled out on a throw rug, a coloring book spread open, was Jane, concentrating on the green she was adding to a leafy tree. I was struck by how much of Damon she carried with her. His hair, not only the exact color from the vibrant man in the photos, but also the wave and shape, unlike Beatrice's straighter hair.

She glanced up as her mother, with two strangers, entered the room.

"Hi, honey, we're going out to the porch to talk for a little bit, okay?"

"'Kay," Jane said, putting down the green for a red. She used it to add apples, berries, some splotch of red to her tree.

Beatrice led us back outside, this time to a brick patio. She hastily dusted off a picnic bench, one of a pair complete with table, the only furniture out here. She settled on the far side. I sat directly across from her. Shannon sat at the end of my bench, so it wasn't so directly the two of us on one side against her.

"Okay, let's talk. What does Damon want?"

The heat was heavy, summer still holding tight to early September.

"To make up for his past mistakes," I answered. "When he hired me—us—he had about six months to live."

"But Damon's not old. Six months? From what?"

"This may be very hard to hear and I'm sorry. Damon's liver is failing. He has hepatitis C. He's also infected with HIV."

She took a long moment to absorb that. "Later, after…everything, I wondered about HIV. I got tested before Jane was born." Then she added, "The results were—"

"That's your business, you needn't tell us if you don't want to," I broke in gently.

"But you wondered," she replied. "I tested negative."

"I worried," I said. "For you. For me having to tell you."

She looked directly at me, as if searching to see whether my words were honest or not. "You didn't want to tell me, did you?"

"No," I admitted.

"So why did you? You could have left that for Damon."

"You needed to know," I said simply. I didn't add, *for you to get a chance to get beyond the first wave of anger before meeting Damon.* Part of my job was to take that anger for him. Or, as was more likely now, Miss Carlotta.

"So I should get tested for hepatitis C?" she asked, but it seemed more a question than an accusation.

"Yes, you probably should," I said.

"But hepatitis C is usually spread through blood," Shannon interjected. "Needles. Before testing, blood transfusions. It's hard to transmit sexually."

I gave her a glance.

She added, "I did some research on it recently. I do a little journalism on the side and it was for a story. It also takes a long time to damage the liver, and that's if it's going to. Many people don't get sick."

"Still need to get tested, right?" Beatrice asked, but it wasn't really a question. "So what does Damon want? From me? From…us?" She nodded slightly in the direction of Jane.

"I think a chance to say he is sorry. To have a chance to meet his daughter."

"How ill is he? You said he had six months?"

I wondered how much honesty I could throw at her. Could I tell her someone had tried to kill Damon to prevent him from ever meeting his daughter? Then I decided she needed to know the dangers before she made her decision. I was paid to put Damon's needs first, but Jane had to have first place in Beatrice's heart. "Louisiana has something called forced heirship," I said. "Basically, it means that legally a child can't be disinherited. Damon's child has to get part of his estate, even if he didn't want to give her anything, which he does." I paused, but Beatrice said nothing, as if she knew there was more. "For the HIV and hepatitis C, Damon was on a lot of drugs. Someone slipped him some cocaine and it reacted badly with his medications."

"Deliberately?" she asked.

"Yes, but it could have been someone playing a nasty joke, who didn't know how serious it could be. Or it could have been someone who thought if they killed Damon a little early, before we found you…"

"No kid, and no forced heirship," she filled in for me.

"A lot of people wanted pieces of what Damon had. Bringing in such a wild card as a child at the last minute would change everything."

"You think there is some danger?" she asked bluntly.

"The person slipped Damon cocaine. It was a desperate move, but even so, not one of violence. Could there be danger? Yes. But…I'm sorry. Jane is legally entitled to part of that estate until she's twenty-four, so—"

Beatrice saw where I was heading. "So, I can't just say good-bye to you and make this go away. As long as Jane is around, she's just as much of a threat."

"Only if the killer still has something to lose. If he doesn't, if it's too late to stop Damon's will from being done, then hurting Jane—or you—would gain him nothing. Except the chance of jail. Damon is a dying man. The death of a dying man isn't unexpected, especially one with a reputation for partying who dies from using a party drug."

"What's your point?"

"To harm you or Jane, he'd have to be blatant, take much greater risks than he did with Damon. If Jane already has the estate, then it can no longer benefit him. Hurting her won't bring it back."

"So get the money as quickly as I can. Or renounce it once and for all?"

"You can't renounce it."

Beatrice grimaced. "So, the best choice is to make Jane a nice, visible target and hope the legal wheels turn quickly enough—all the successions signed, sealed, and delivered to keep Damon's money moving in a direction that'll never reach whoever harmed him." She folded her arms over her chest. It was clear that she didn't like the choices she and her daughter were given.

"I know it must be scary to think about exposing—"

"Damn right," Beatrice cut in.

"But the only way to remove the threat is to get things settled. Once that's done and he's cut out, the threat ends."

"Unless he gets pissed and wants revenge."

"While that's possible, giving Damon a drug is cowardly and clever, not the kind of thing someone who gets pissed and wants revenge does. No one has tried anything with me or Shannon. So far the only act was to slip drugs to a dying man. Probably someone who was part of his life and could easily give him the cocaine. This will sound gruesome, but whoever it is can't just kill Jane. You inherit if she dies. He has to kill both of you, and he has to get access to you that he doesn't have now."

Beatrice looked away, her face grim. Then she turned back to me, with a sad half-smile. "Can't I just ignore it for a while?"

I shook my head. "Damon is still alive, but he doesn't have long. The chaos of Katrina had to affect whoever harmed him. You may be able to get things settled before that person recovers enough to do anything. Right now whoever that is may be living in a shelter in Houston and have little time or energy to come after you."

"Or in a motel here in Jonesboro," she added ironically.

"Damon was generous," I said gently. "I think he was trying to make up for all the years when he should have been a father and wasn't."

"Nothing can make up for that."

"No, nothing can. I think he knows that."

"Do I have time to think about this?"

"If you want to see Damon…he had just come out of a coma when the hurricane hit. He's now spent a hellish week in a hospital without power or water. It may be days, at best."

She was thoughtful. "I have to do what's best for Jane."

"Of course."

"So you're not kidnapping us and taking us there?"

"No, you choose to go with us or not at all."

She glanced down at the picture, still in her hand. "He was a beautiful man. Jane asks about her father. This is her one chance to meet him, isn't it?"

"I'm sorry, it probably is."

"Don't be sorry. Better than never." She stood up. "You came a long way to find me."

"We were evacuating anyway. It was Texas or Arkansas," I said.

"Oh, my God, of course," Beatrice said. She reached across the table, her hand on mine. It was spontaneous, a warmth that I could see attracting Damon. "Your broken city, the horror of the storm and the evil of the inaction. What did you lose?"

I was caught off guard by her sudden focus on me and my worries. I had prepared myself to deal with all sorts of reactions from her, but I hadn't prepared for any of my own. I finally fumbled out, "I don't know. I didn't…don't live in the worst part, but with the looting, the water, could be roof damage. I just don't know yet."

She kept her hand on mine, a generous gesture to a stranger. She looked to Shannon, asking the same question with her expression.

"I live in New York, just down in New Orleans for a short stint," Shannon said.

"Still," Beatrice said, "not bearing the full brunt of the horrors doesn't mean you've had it easy. Losing less doesn't mean you haven't lost."

"But we're okay," I said. "As far as we know, our friends and families are okay. If that's all I get, that's enough." I covered her hand with my other one. She, too, was affected by this storm. She'd met a man in New Orleans, had a vibrant love affair, now a daughter from that meeting. Her memories, her destiny were twinned with our city. And the man who might have been a father for a few months now had only days—if that—because of what had happened.

My cell phone improbably rang. Shannon was astute enough to take it from my pocket and walk to the far end of the yard as she was answering it.

"I like Damon," I said. Bringing Beatrice and Jane back into his life was my mission, not what the hurricane had done to me. "That doesn't mean I excuse what he did. That's for you to forgive or not. But I think he's genuine in wanting to make amends."

"You think I should go see him?"

"I do. The choice is yours. If there is no way you'll ever regret it, you needn't go."

Beatrice squeezed my hand. "Regret…there are some regrets I can live with. But I don't think this is one of them. I liked Damon, too. And I can't take this chance from Jane."

Shannon rejoined us. She waited to be sure Beatrice was finished talking, then said, "That was Miss Carlotta. Damon has arrived in Memphis."

"How is he?" Beatrice asked.

"They don't know yet. He…they think he stopped breathing and they got him back, but time…"

"Memphis is close," Beatrice said. "We can go there today. I just have to explain what's happening to Jane."

"Have you met Damon's aunt, Miss Carlotta?" I asked.

"No, I haven't."

"That was who called. You'll see Damon in her. I think she'll be thrilled to have a grand-niece," I said. "And I think you'll like her. I know I do."

"Let me talk to Jane," Beatrice said.

"Do you want us to leave?" I offered.

"No, stay. Maybe fill in…if I stumble." She stood up. "Let's go inside. It's pretty damn hot out here."

Shannon and I followed her back into the house. Jane had moved on to another page in her coloring book, now working on making a sky more blue than it usually was.

"Would you like something?" Beatrice asked us. "Water, milk, beer?"

"Water would be nice," I said. Shannon seconded me.

"I'll be a perfect hostess and add ice, even," Beatrice said, smiling at us.

Beautiful smile, I thought. If Jane got that from her, with Damon's hair, she'd be a heartbreaker without even knowing it.

Just like Damon, I thought. All the hearts he'd left broken because he didn't know he was breaking them. And like Lauren. I'd found myself attracted to her. It was so easy for them, the Damons and Laurens. They didn't know how hard it was for the rest of us, how we struggled to find love, to find the person who would smile at us, and only us, the way Beatrice smiled. The way...the way Cordelia would smile when she caught sight of me unexpectedly. The way Shannon smiled at me now.

Beatrice handed us our water, then got a glass for herself. "Procrastinating," she murmured with a wry smile. She took a sip, then said, "Jane, honey, come here. I've got something to tell you." Following Beatrice's cue, we all sat around the kitchen table.

Jane joined us, coloring book still in hand, her sky just about finished. She shyly glanced from me to Shannon, then fixed her gaze on her mother.

"These women are from New Orleans," Beatrice started, "and they're...they know your dad."

"Daddy?" Jane asked, her face brightening.

Like my face would have, had I been her age and someone mentioned knowing my mother. I'd at least known her until I was five. We didn't meet again until I was thirty.

Beatrice was faltering. It was too hard for her to find the words.

"We're friends of your dad," I stepped in. "He asked us to find you. He wants to meet you, get to know you."

"So he wants to be my dad now?" Jane asked.

Whatever Miss Carlotta paid me, it wouldn't be worth this, breaking a child's heart. And I knew what the break would be, because I'd grown up with one parent gone, her love absent.

"He wants to be your dad," I said slowly, trying to pick the words that would hurt the least. "But he didn't come himself because he's sick. He's in the hospital. He wants to see you, to say he loves you… before he has to go away again."

"Why is he going away?" she asked.

Beatrice answered, "Remember Quizze? She got old…and we had to let her go. It's like that for Damon…Daddy."

"Quizze went to dog heaven," Jane said. "Is that what'll happen to Daddy?"

"Maybe," Beatrice said. "He'll go to some heaven. But he's still around. He's in Memphis, so we're leaving to see him."

"Now?" Jane said, the simple happiness of traveling showing on her face.

"Almost now," Beatrice said. "We'll stay the night there, so we have to get packed."

"Can I wear my blue dress for Daddy?" Jane asked.

"Of course you can, honey. But you need to take a quick bath since you haven't had one yet. Then we'll pack and go."

Jane jumped up, dropping the coloring book on the floor. She stopped long enough to pick it up, then scampered down the hallway to the bathroom.

"Usually we have to go back and forth about getting clean. I've had to resort to bribes more than a proper parent is supposed to."

"She's not too bad," I said, with a smile. "I'd offer to swim in the bayou with the alligators rather than take a bath."

"You grew up in the bayous?" Beatrice asked.

"Yeah, one of those small towns between New Orleans and the Gulf."

She must have caught something on my face. "It's not there anymore, is it?" she asked softly.

"No…no, it's probably not," I said. We can't talk about me, I wanted to say. I can't think about my city, the place I grew up and lived for so long thinking my mother didn't love me. I can handle the sorrow I'm handing to Beatrice and Jane, but I can't handle it together with my own grief. I needed to keep my worries hidden away, as if they didn't exist.

"Hey, it's just us girls here," Beatrice said, handing me a tissue. "You can let down the tough private-eye persona."

"No, I can't," I said, blowing my nose. "It's against the rules."

Beatrice snorted, then said, "She's the butch, isn't she?" Adding, as both Shannon and I gave her a look, "I may be in east bumfuck Arkansas, but I wasn't always here. I assume you're lovers. And you're not as butch as you think you are," she told me, handing me another tissue. "My best buddy in the English Department is the Visible Dyke on Campus."

I blew my nose again. I was a coward and let Shannon handle this one.

"We've been working together a lot," Shannon said, "and there's nothing like evacuating jointly to draw you close."

"According to the requirements for licensure in Louisiana, private investigators don't cry. They don't discuss their private lives, and even the femmes have to be butch," I clarified. With that I gave my nose a final blow and finished. "We'll go with you to Memphis. How about we meet you back here in an hour?"

"Good save," Shannon said in a bad stage whisper.

Beatrice laughed, then said, "Deal. I'll have one cleaned-and-packed daughter ready in an hour."

She let us find our own way out while she went to check on Jane and the progress of her bath.

As soon as we pulled away, I got on my cell phone and called Miss Carlotta. I was surprised that she had gotten through to me. She must have been using a real phone, or a cell that wasn't from the 504 area code.

When she answered, I said, "This is Micky. We'll be on our way in about an hour. Beatrice and Jane are both coming with us."

Our conversation was brief. She would make arrangements for us and call back with details. I gave her Shannon's cell number just in case. Her voice showed relief, even joy at my news, but had a deep edge of sadness as well. What had she lost?

It can't be Miss Carlotta, I told myself. She wouldn't be desperate enough to kill off her nephew. But a voice in my head—one that can be useful or ugly—told me to keep my guard up, even with Miss Carlotta. If it was her, or Jud, I was bringing Damon's heir right to them.

As Shannon was pulling into the motel parking lot, I said, "Alex updated me on Cordelia. Said she was okay. At the airport."

"She's evacuating?" Shannon asked, stopping in front of our room.

"Presumably. What do you think? New York?" Then, without waiting for her to answer, I said, "It doesn't matter. I guess all our lives have changed more than we ever imagined. I wanted her to be okay. I hope she's happy wherever she ends up." I wanted to think that I did hope she was happy, but that wasn't what I heard in my voice. Much as I tried to hide it, the ambivalence seeped in. I wanted Cordelia back. I didn't want to ever see her again. I wanted her to hurt the way I was hurting. I didn't know what I wanted. My emotions felt like a cacophony, jangling and jarring inside my head. Shannon is here. Cordelia isn't. That was all I had and all I could think about right now, beyond that it was too overwhelming.

"What about you?"

"I intend to be happy wherever I end up." I leaned over and kissed her, just hard and firm enough to make my intentions clear. Did I want Shannon or did I just want someone to hold me, a warm touch to keep away the hollow, howling place inside me? Then I realized it didn't matter. Shannon wanted me and I was too weak to say no to her nearness and warmth. I too desperately wanted someone to touch me, even if all of us got hurt—Shannon, Cordelia, and even myself. Then I pulled back and said, "Come on, we have to get to Memphis today." I got out of the car, but couldn't stop myself from a quick glance at my watch. Not enough time, I told myself. Not for the first time, at any rate.

Just as we got inside, my cell vibrated, telling me I had a message, and Shannon's rang. It was Miss Carlotta. She wasn't able to get through to me, so she was calling Shannon—who, as they were talking, signaled me for a pen and paper. Grabbing the ones near the hotel phone, I handed them to her. She was scribbling down directions.

When Shannon finished the call, she said, "We're staying at the Peabody. Ever heard of it?"

"Miss Carlotta must like us. It's *the* hotel in Memphis. The one with the ducks." I explained about the ducks that lived at the hotel and every day came down from their roost to swim in the fountain.

"Just ducky," she said when I finished.

"Pack" was my reply.

It didn't take us long to gather our things. It wasn't like we'd packed for what was looking to be months out of the city. For a moment, I had an image of traveling with Shannon to New York—and then the image of running into Lauren and Cordelia there. Damn her, I thought, throwing my underwear into the suitcase. I hoped she was happy. I hoped I would be happy, too.

As we pulled up in front of Beatrice's place, Jane came running out. She was in a fancy blue dress and carrying a small suitcase.

"We're going to Memphis to see my daddy!" she called to us, her exuberance overcoming her shyness. She grinned a big grin, the same killer smile her mother had. I hoped Damon at least woke up long enough to see that smile, to see the shade of hair that so perfectly matched his, to hear her call him Daddy with that joy in her voice and see the sparkle in her eyes.

Beatrice followed her daughter out at a more sedate pace, carrying a suitcase, a carryall with what looked like healthy snacks and water, and another carryall with books and the kinds of toys to keep a seven-year-old occupied in a hospital.

"Let me help you," Shannon offered. She quickly crossed the lawn to Beatrice.

After the suitcases were stowed in the trunk, Jane remembered that she needed to take Ms. Sweetie. Ms. Sweetie turned out to be her favorite stuffed animal, a big black panther that I wouldn't have named Sweetie. That done, we each got in our separate cars, with Beatrice in the lead. She knew the route to Memphis and her way around the city well enough to find the hotel.

Traffic was light once we got out of Jonesboro, with only a few signs for small towns on the way. It picked up when we got to West Memphis. We didn't talk much, listening to the radio for any reports of New Orleans. Beatrice led us to the downtown part where the hotel was. When we pulled up and got out, she seemed a little flustered, as if not accustomed to staying at places where uniformed valets were waiting to help her.

"We're checking in," I told them, indicating all of us. Their training was perfect enough that they were just as gracious parking Beatrice's dented Honda Civic as they would have been parking a Jaguar.

Miss Carlotta had reserved a room for Beatrice and Jane and one each for me and Shannon.

"We're used to traveling together," I said, canceling the separate room. I wondered if I was fooling anyone. And then I wondered if anyone cared.

From there, we agreed on fifteen minutes to unpack and then we'd meet again in the lobby and go directly to the hospital.

Shannon let me carry our suitcases to the room while she went to find newspapers, wanting to read rather than just see the television images of New Orleans.

Back in the lobby, we all arrived at the same time from different directions. Beatrice seemed subdued, as if still grappling with being here, about to introduce Jane to Damon. Jane was either tired from the journey or picking up her mother's emotions. Or both.

I drove, with Beatrice up front reading a map and remembering how to get around the streets of Memphis. We were going to another hospital named Memorial. I had no idea if it was just coincidence that that's where Damon was in New Orleans, or if they were owned by the same mega health-care corporation, without the imagination for more than one name per city.

"Germantown," I muttered at Beatrice's directions, "why would a barbeque town have a German section?"

A glance in the rearview mirror told me that Shannon was working her charm with Jane. She had the child cuddled against her and they were both petting Ms. Sweetie.

As I parked, I said in a quiet voice to Beatrice, "Nervous?"

"No, perfectly calm and collected," she answered, running her hand through her hair. Quietly she added, "My best outcome is to be shunted aside while he wraps the daughter he hasn't seen in seven years around his finger...and the worst is a shattered little girl, her hopes raised only to be dashed one final time." She tried for a brave smile, but it was only in her lips. Her eyes were grim.

I reached over and took her hand, squeezed it and said, "I wish we could mold the future into what we want it to be." She squeezed back then we got out of the car.

CHAPTER TWENTY-TWO

Shannon was given the exalted task of carrying Ms. Sweetie as we headed for the hospital. I took the lead, asking at the desk for Damon's room number, then ushering them onto the elevator, being the first one off, leading the way to Damon's room. I was just glancing at the numbers when I saw the small group at the end of the hall. Miss Carlotta, Jud, and faithful George.

Miss Carlotta looked up and saw us. For a brief second, she looked confused, as if wondering what I'd be doing in a hospital in Memphis, then a look I was beginning to recognize among those of us spread across the country, the look that first said, "You're okay" and then "You live there, so you know what it's like." She rushed to me and gave me a big hug. It wasn't something I would have expected from her, at least not before the hurricane. Now it seemed necessary.

We held the embrace, then she let go and looked behind me. I heard her soft gasp of breath, joy almost turning to tears as she beheld Jane. "It's him as a child," she whispered. Then she tamped her emotions down and became the gracious Southern lady I had first met. "You must be Beatrice," she said, reaching to warmly clasp her hand. Then, "And you'll be Jane. I'm very pleased to meet you." She offered her hand to Jane as she had to Beatrice, giving her the respect of equal treatment. Jane shyly shook hands.

I watched the emotions as they played over both Miss Carlotta's and Beatrice's face. It was such a mix—joy, relief, and then a tinge of sadness—on Miss Carlotta's that told me Damon had not yet woken up.

The moment passed, Miss Carlotta introduced Jud and George. I gave both of them a hug. Shannon hugged them, too. We did a quick version of what was the new greeting among refugees. Where did you live? Was it flooded? Will you go back?

Jane brought us to the reason we were all together, as she innocently asked, "Where's my daddy?"

George reached over and grasped Jud's arm, his expression clearly asking if this was Damon's daughter. Jud gave a brief nod. I couldn't read Jud's expression, his face was almost blank. Too tired for emotion? Just a neutral detachment—let this play out as it will. Or doing a very good job of keeping something hidden? George first stared at Jane then, embarrassed by his curiosity, he turned away, his hand still clasped around Jud's arm as if he needed support to stand straight.

We were all silenced, searching for the words to explain how Damon was here and he wasn't. I knelt down in front of her and said, "He's close, but he's asleep right now. He's…getting old and everything that's happened has been hard on him."

She nodded, then asked the hardest question, "But he'll wake up soon?"

Beatrice knelt beside me. "We hope he'll wake up, but he's sick in the way old people get sick, and he was in New Orleans when the hurricane hit. They had to get him out through the flood and the heat…" She faltered.

"And that may have hurt him even more," I picked up. "Right now we just don't know if he'll get better or not."

Jane was silent, then she asked, "But he's here? Can I see him even if he's asleep?"

"Yes, honey, you can," Beatrice answered.

"Then it's okay," Jane said, as if knowing that her mother needed some assurance that that would be enough.

At least Jane can see her father, have a memory of him. It wasn't enough. All of us knew that. Cordelia being okay wasn't enough, I realized. It was just all I would get. We should be together now, instead of enduring this increasing chasm between us. I should have stayed with her at Charity. Or if that wasn't possible, we should have focused on reuniting with each other. Instead we were in different places and heading different directions. How had everything changed so quickly?

Was our separation irrevocable? That hurt too much to think about. All I could do was stumble through the next hour, the next day. Anything beyond that blurred into a frightening mist. At least some day I might be able to talk to Cordelia, I thought, as I looked at this young girl's face, the yearning in her eyes. She wanted Damon awake, alive, a father to hold his little girl.

"Why don't we visit him?" Miss Carlotta said.

I took the invitation to include me. Shannon, Jud, and George stayed in the hall.

Miss Carlotta led us into Damon's room. She evidently had the staff here charmed—or it was her money speaking—but no one objected to several of us entering his room. Or maybe they knew that little could harm him now.

From the diminished man I had seen before the hurricane, he had aged even further, his face tinged with gray. His hair had been washed recently from his ordeal in the heat, but even it seemed to have lost spirit and gained gray. The electric humming and beeping of the machines surrounding him seemed more alive than he did.

"Oh, Damon," I heard Beatrice murmur. She brought her hand up to her face as if to hide the emotions there from her daughter.

"That's my daddy?" Jane asked softly. She looked up expectantly at her mother.

"Yes, honey," Beatrice said, as they slowly approached his bed. She forced the brave smile back to her face. Her eyes were still sad. "Damon, it's Beatrice, love. Lot of years between us. I've got Jane here with me. She's got your hair and your eyes."

I hung back, watching the tableau, the light from the window on the far side of the bed ringing them with bright sunshine. Miss Carlotta stood at the foot of the bed, her hands resting on the footboard as if she needed to steady herself.

Beatrice bent down and gently kissed his forehead. Jane grasped her hand, then, safely anchored to her mother, she pressed against the side rail to get a closer look. Beatrice lifted her up, sitting her on the bed next to him. Jane took her father's hand in her small one, resting her head on his shoulder, the waves of her hair mixing with his.

Even as gone as Damon was and as vibrant and alive as Jane was, I could see the resemblance. Her hair color would have been his as a young man, her brow followed the line of his, her eyes a blend of his blue and Beatrice's gray.

Jane said, "Daddy, it's me, Jane. You remember me, but I don't remember you. But I'm glad to meet you."

I turned and quietly left the room. My heart was too close to breaking to keep watching.

It's all too close, I thought, as I carefully closed the door behind me, not wanting to disrupt them. The hurricane, the flooded and ruined city, the lost little girl. Every known landmark in my life had been torn asunder. Cordelia wasn't there, I couldn't live in my house, none of my friends were close, my damn cell phone wouldn't even work to call them. I only knew what I would do today, maybe tomorrow. Next week? Next month? I didn't know where I would be living, what I would be doing. Did I have anything left save for the one suitcase I'd packed? That, at least, was more than many had. And it wasn't enough.

All I could do was stay in today, I decided. If I thought about the days, weeks, beyond that, it was too overwhelming, too many days with nothing to anchor them.

Shannon had been talking quietly with Jud and George. She left them to come and put her hand on my shoulder. She said, "I just want to tell you that you're very good. At this. At what you do. You find the words when I know I'd be standing there with my mouth open. I thought this private-detective stuff was just reading records and watching people from cars. It is, but it's also being able to see people, what they claim to want, what they really want, what they fear. Helping them find their way. You're good at it." She kissed my cheek.

For this, I had no words, couldn't find any that she said I was so good at finding. The best I could do was mumble, "Thanks."

She laughed gently at my confusion. "Never thought you'd hear something like that from me, did you?"

Miss Carlotta, Beatrice, and Jane came out of the room. Jud and George joined them.

"Daddy will wake up, won't he," Jane asked.

Beatrice smoothed her hair and answered, "We hope he will, but it may take a while."

"He wants to see me, doesn't he?" she asked.

"Yes, he does," Beatrice said. "Remember, he got his friends to search for us, just so he could see you." Beatrice looked up at me for confirmation.

Okay, Shannon, let's hope you're right and I really am good at this, I thought. "Jane," I said, "I met your daddy when he wasn't quite as sick as he is now, when he was awake and could talk. I can promise you that, yes, he wants to see you. Please know that he wants to see you."

That seemed to give her the reassurance—for the moment—that she needed. "I'm hungry," she whispered to her mother.

Her simple request led to a complicated sorting out of adults. We finally branched off with Shannon taking Jane (and Ms. Sweetie) to find some snacks, of the usually forbidden kind. Miss Carlotta, Jud, and Beatrice found a corner to give Beatrice a quick overview of the legal details. George and I stayed near Damon's door, trying not to too obviously look like guards, although that's what we were.

I was glad for his presence; I could trust George to protect Damon. We were close together, our shoulders almost touching, as if we both wanted the comfort of closeness but were too stolid to actually ask for it. I wished I could say the same of Jud. I wanted to trust him, but, unlike George, he was clever enough to pull off playing the perfect friend while being the perfect criminal.

"How are you doing?" I asked George.

"Miss Carlotta takes care of me."

"She'll let you stay where you are?"

"Yes. A cottage behind her house." The Garden District where Miss Carlotta lived was close enough to the river that it probably didn't flood. George added, "She said we're okay, no water on our street. And I put things up."

"Did you have a lot?"

"Yeah, took a while. I collect comic books," he said with a smile that was half proud, half embarrassed.

"Wow, that's cool."

His smile became fully proud. I wouldn't look down on his collecting.

"I have some old ones, valuable. Maybe…when this is over, you'd like to come see?" His voice was hesitant, still expecting rejection.

"Comic books are cool. I think I have some stashed away where I grew up. I'd love to see yours. Maybe I could even bring mine by and you could tell me if they're worth anything."

George smiled. "Yeah, come over. As soon as we get back in town." His smile faded a little. "As soon as this is over."

A thought occurred to me. "George," I asked, "Can you tell me again who was there that day when Damon collapsed? Before we arrived," I clarified for him.

He didn't seem to think my question strange, but thought about it for a moment. "Jud was the first. Miss Carlotta was really first, but she was just dropping me off. She didn't see Damon or anything. Then Bruce came by. It was early for him. He comes by in the afternoon more likely, not morning." He paused. I didn't say anything, letting him sort it out without risking my leading him anywhere. "Bruce left, just missing Ambrose. Ambrose came and stayed until...until Damon got sick. Perry came by. Perry left. Then you came by."

"How long did Jud stay?"

"Not long. Talked to Damon, got him some water. Asked me if I needed anything. Then left."

"What time was this?"

"After Miss Carlotta, just after she dropped me off. I think maybe nine o'clock." He sounded relieved to have come up with the time, as if it were a hard task that he was afraid he'd fail.

I nodded. "Perry and Ambrose were there at the same time?"

George was again silent for his usual thinking time. "They don't like each other. I was about to pick up some of Damon's pills, about to leave, but Ambrose told me he'd do it instead. So he left after Perry got there."

"He left Perry alone with Damon?"

"Yes, until he came back."

"How long was Ambrose gone?"

"He walked to Royal Pharmacy, then back."

I nodded. Royal was at the corner of Royal and Ursulines, only a few blocks from Damon's house. Ambrose wouldn't have been gone long.

"When he came back, what did he do?" I asked.

"He went back with Damon. Perry left soon."

"Were you there the evening before?"

"Yes, his uncle was coming by and Damon wanted me there to help out."

"His uncle came by?" Uncle Raul, who supposedly didn't like coming to New Orleans. "How long did he stay?"

"A while. They had dinner. Miss Carlotta was there as well. Damon was tired afterward. He said listening to his uncle's country ideas wore him out." Then in a softer voice George said, "I think his uncle drank too much, he tripped walking out the door. He seemed angry, too. Talked about it being a damn fool thing, as I let him out."

"Were Damon's uncle and Miss Carlotta the only ones at the dinner?"

"Yes, just them. But two people came by during dinner. That AIDS guy…I don't remember his name."

"Kent Richards from the Crescent City Care Coalition?"

"Yeah, that sounds right."

"Do you have any idea what he wanted?"

"Something about money. Needed Damon to give him a loan to pay something back."

"Do you know if Damon gave him the money?"

"I think so, Damon asked me to get his checkbook. And I overheard Damon say he'd only give him five hundred dollars, not one thousand."

"What happened after that?"

"He left. Damon said he had to get back to dinner and told me to show him out."

"Who was the other person who came by?"

George hesitated. "Jud," he finally said.

"What did Jud want from Damon?"

"Not from Damon. He said he left something and he thought it was upstairs in the bathroom. He told me not to disturb Damon."

"How long was he there?"

Again, a slow response. "I'm not sure. I didn't see him go. I was cleaning up from the dinner and getting them dessert and stuff. And Miss Carlotta had to go, so she left right after his uncle did and she took me with her." He added, almost as if in apology, "That's all I remember." And then, his voice soft, as if speaking a fear he wanted not to have, "Do you think if I'd stayed with Damon the whole time it would have made a difference?"

"I don't believe so," I said, although I wasn't sure. "Someone put something in one of Damon's pills, so your being with him wouldn't have changed that." I wondered if my reassurance to George was true. It had to have been in something that Damon took on a regular basis, probably a daily medication, but often enough that his attacker could be sure that he'd ingest the doctored pill. That made it likely that the suspects were the people who saw him the day before he collapsed. It was all in the timing. And the desperation. But there were so many desperate men—and women—around Damon.

Shannon and Jane returned, a candy bar and soda for Jane, and an armload of drinks for the rest of us.

Then we waited.

And we waited.

I saw Jud slip into Damon's room. I followed him.

Jud was standing by Damon's bed. I angled around the foot of it so I could see what he was doing. He was brushing the hair back from Damon's forehead. Was that what he intended to do, I wondered. I hated having to be this suspicious, but I didn't feel I had any choice.

Still gently brushing the hair, he said, "Think I'm planning to rip out all his IVs? Smother him with a pillow?"

"Someone hurt him and might hurt him again." I saw no point in hiding my reservations about him.

"Not me," Jud said in a harsh whisper. He was angry. Angry that his friend was hurt, angry that anyone could think he had anything to do with it? Or angry that he wouldn't so easily get away with it?

"Too bad I can't see into your heart and know one way or another," I said quietly, to counter the sting of the words.

Jud shook his head, then bent down to kiss Damon on the forehead. "Too bad I can't open it up for you. Why would I want to hurt Damon?"

"He infected you with HIV and you get a lot of money when he dies. You're also a smart enough man to cover yourself as the faithful friend."

"So where does that leave us?" He turned from Damon to look directly at me.

"Here. Me watching you. I could apologize for suspecting you, but I doubt that you care."

"I would care. Better than you hating me, and I guess too suspicious is better than too trusting." He gave me a rueful grin that made me want to trust him. I already liked him and I didn't want to have my instincts so wrong. I wanted the bad guy to be bad.

"Jane and Beatrice are in danger, and I've brought them here. Until everything is settled, someone could get very rich hurting them."

He nodded. "So you'll keep watching me."

"I won't be following you to the men's room."

"Glad I've got some privacy." He was silent and turned back to Damon, then said softly, "I just wanted a quiet time to say good-bye." He bent again and kissed Damon on the lips.

I wanted to give him that quiet space, but I couldn't. I wanted the happy end—Damon to wake up, to see Jane, to have a smile of joy break out over his face, one that she would always remember. I wanted the murderer to be someone I hated, not someone I liked and wished I could be friends with.

Jud left the room. I followed him out.

We continued to wait.

And then it was time to go back to the hotel, to wait in another place.

Miss Carlotta, Jud, and George made plans to take turns staying with Damon. Beatrice asked to take a shift. They wanted to make sure someone was there with him all through the night.

"Should we offer?" Shannon asked me. "More as guards. Just in case…"

I suddenly felt an edge of despair. If it was Jud, he'd won. Miss Carlotta trusted him and she was willing to leave him here with Damon. And maybe, I thought, better to leave him with Damon, the dying man, than with Beatrice and Jane. Could he and Miss Carlotta be in this together, my suspicious voice asked? There was little I could do to keep either of them from Damon. The best I could manage would be to watch over Beatrice and Jane. And maybe they were both decent people and my instincts were right and I needed to be looking at Perry or Bruce or even the ex-boyfriend who just got out of jail.

"Whoever harmed Damon has to be someone they all know." I didn't add possibly someone here.

Also, as things sorted out, it seemed that George was staying all night. He felt it was his job, and both Miss Carlotta and Jud seemed to understand how important it was to him to do this duty. Maybe it's not him, I thought. Or maybe he's clever enough to know that if something happens to Damon, he's the most likely suspect here.

We were quiet on the drive back to the hotel. Memphis seemed to think this was a Saturday night, with lights, cars, people out. There were no lights in my city and I felt that I belonged more there than here. This normal Saturday night seemed almost a foreign land.

I was tired, I realized, the day long and now empty. My quest was fulfilled, I had brought the lost princess to see the dying king.

It wasn't enough.

CHAPTER TWENTY-THREE

Drink?" I said in a low voice to Shannon as we crossed the lobby.

She gave me a questioning glance before nodding yes. I quietly told Beatrice to double-lock her door and not let anyone in until she called me first. She nodded, although her look said it seemed I was being overly suspicious. Maybe I was. We bid a brief good night at the elevators. I lingered long enough for the doors to shut before heading toward the hotel bar.

Not that Miss Carlotta would care; New Orleans was enough of a drinking town that she would be used to the idea of a drink before bed. But I was ashamed, and I didn't want anyone to know. If I could have hidden my drinking from Shannon, I would have.

She got a beer, I opted for single-malt Scotch.

"Are you okay?" she asked as we settled ourselves in a corner.

"Okay?" I took a sip. "I'm so far from okay, I don't even know what it means anymore." I saw the hurt in her eyes, as if she should be enough for me and I'd just told her she wasn't and never would be. She's young, I suddenly thought, remembering that I had about a decade on her. Young enough to think that love could be enough.

"It's not you," I said, caring enough for her to want to take the pain away from her eyes. "It's…everything. It's so crazy. Yeah, I'm here in a nice bar in a nice hotel, but I'm still a refugee. They're saying two to three months to pump the water out. I no longer have a job, a business, maybe not a home. Everything is gone or changed. My friends are scattered, some may never come back. Even the people I used to pass everyday—the waiters, the store clerks. In New Orleans you see the same people, you say hi to them on the street. Every week they're there. Now they're gone. I'll probably never know what happened to them. Were they in the Superdome, did they get out, did they stay? Are they even alive?" I took a long drink. It felt too hard to talk about.

"What can I do?" Shannon asked.

"Nothing," I said, then to soften it, "Just understand that you can't do anything."

"Can I make love to you?"

I looked at her, then finished my drink. "Yes, you can do that."

We got up, she left her beer.

As we crossed the lobby, I wondered what it would be like to be with someone new. I never thought I would be; I had thought that Cordelia would be the only woman I'd ever make love to. But everything had changed, and there were no fixed points in my life anymore. Was Cordelia with Lauren? Were they making love right now? A searing fury coursed through me. The alcohol and the anger loosened what little control I'd had. Drinking and sleeping with Shannon wouldn't solve anything, but I didn't give a damn anymore. A small, sober part of my brain knew I was sleeping with Shannon to get back at Cordelia, but admitting how connected Cordelia and I still were and how little control I had—did she even want me back—only added a deep pain to the anger.

On the elevator Shannon asked, "Do we stay here until Damon wakes up?"

"What if he doesn't wake up?" I answered. "I don't know. I don't know where else to go, but I don't think we can camp out here on Miss Carlotta's dime for a couple of months. And I know my dimes won't cover it."

I let her lead the way down the hallway and open our room door. I watched her as she closed the drapes and turned on the lights.

"Or do you prefer lights off?" she suddenly asked, both of us realizing that we didn't know these basic things about each other.

"Let me brush my teeth and then we can figure out the lighting," I said as I ducked into the bathroom. I wanted to get the Scotch off my breath. I also washed my face, then quickly between my legs. I was nervous, both delaying and trying to be perfect for a new person. At least clean, I thought, looking at myself in the mirror. I seemed to have picked up a few more gray hairs in the last week. Maybe it was just the strong light, more suited for applying makeup than assessing sins. I rinsed my mouth with mouthwash and didn't look in the mirror again.

When I came out of the bathroom, Shannon was sitting on the bed reading one of the papers she had picked up. I watched her, the incandescent light making her hair golden, her face soft and young. Then I was looking at the swell of her breasts, the hint of cleavage showing, following the seams of her jeans to where they met at her crotch. And remembering the gentle way she held me when I could give her nothing, the simple kindness of making me something to eat while I was falling apart with a bottle of Scotch. Attraction is more than just a body, at least for me. Shannon was a beautiful woman, but I had come to know that there was much more to her than just an outward beauty. She was smart, she was funny. Many gorgeous women assume their beauty is enough, that kindness and consideration are only a one-way street heading in their direction. Shannon had proved herself an exception, showing me more kindness than I deserved. Certainly more than I was earning tonight with my drinking and anger and allowing this to happen when I knew my reasons for being with her were far from kind and selfless.

I crossed the room and took the paper out of her hands. Her knees were bent; I pushed them down, then got on top, straddling her. She looked up at me, her lips slightly open as if waiting to be kissed.

But not yet. I touched her cheek with the tips of my fingers, trailing them down to her jaw. I told her, "I'm drowning and you're a life raft. It's not how I'd choose to come to you…but it's all I can be now."

"It's enough," she murmured, lifting her face, her hands on the back of my head pulling me down to her. If I were a decent person, I would have said it's not enough. But I didn't.

Our kissing was fierce and passionate. I didn't stop as I undressed her, only moving away long enough to get her shirt and bra, one crumpled ball, over her head, moving next to her jeans, unzipping them, pulling them away. One hand kept working her jeans down and the other covered her, my palm against her mound. As I touched her, she made a sound halfway between a moan and a growl. Then her hips arched up, and she was helping me. I got her jeans as far as her ankles and then left them. I buried my face between her breasts.

She was pulling at my shirt trying to get it off. I paused long enough to peel it over my head, then I was back on her, sucking, kissing, biting.

I entered her with my fingers, pushing in deeply. It was fast, her hips arching to meet my hand, no words, just her gasps and moans guiding me. Her hand clenched in my hair, holding me against her breasts as she came. I kept fucking her and she came again. Then a third time.

Finally, "My turn," I murmured as I slowly took my fingers out, feeling her pulse beating.

"I don't…think I can move," she gasped out.

"You don't need to," I said, kissing her hard. I took off my pants, throwing them to the floor. Then told her, "Your head between my legs." I lowered myself over her, spreading my lips for her. She wrapped her arms around my thighs. Her tongue inside me was a bolt, beyond physical, almost too much.

I moved away, changed direction. I needed to be touching her. It was too much if it was just me. I again lowered myself over her, started kissing her thighs, running my hands along her legs.

Shannon used her tongue to spread my lips, then she was kissing and sucking me, bringing me close. But it ebbed away. A new person, I told myself.

My kisses moved where her thighs met her hips. A few of her outer hairs were a dark blond, the rest so slick and wet they appeared black. I found her clit and kissed it, holding it teasingly between my lips. Her hips arched up, and I both heard and could feel her growling moan. Her excitement brought me back and I began to get close again. But I still couldn't just let go. Another drink might have helped, I thought.

I spread her legs even wider and went beyond teasing. Her hips jerked against me, a hard rhythm of desire. But she wasn't content to just let me do her. Shannon spread my lips open, keeping them spread, keeping me tight.

Let go, just let go, I told myself. Still I didn't. Instead I made Shannon come again. Feeling her as she writhed under me, her heavy panting, brought me close again. She caught a breath and then was on me. This time it was enough. The long shudder coursed through my body, almost more relief than pleasure.

I rolled away from her, taking in the sudden cool of the air conditioner, our bodies no longer touching. Then I curled back around her, lying against her side, my arm across her chest.

We lay like that for several minutes, no words, just our bodies touching.

Then she murmured, "I'll be better next time."

I propped myself and looked at her. She was beautiful, her hair tousled, her face open and earnest. "It's not you, please don't think that. It's me. It's…" I couldn't find the words.

"You're not over things yet, are you?" she asked.

I was silent, counting the days. Not even ten days had passed since I had walked in on Cordelia and Lauren. It felt like forever, a yawning chasm. I needed to see Cordelia, I realized, have some resolution. Maybe if she apologized, I could get over her. Or maybe, somehow we could find our way back to each other, the years of being together long enough and strong enough to overcome her betrayal and my anger. Or maybe if she didn't apologize and made it clear that she wouldn't, I could get over her. Maybe I'd have to get over her no matter what, but I couldn't do it in eight days.

"There are too many places I hurt," I answered. "The shipyard, where we were, if there is anything left but piling, it'll be a miracle. I don't know if our cats are alive." Cordelia and I each had a cat when we moved in together, and over the years they had become ours. Hepplewhite, my cat, was old. Even if Cordelia had taken her, managed to keep her through the evacuation of Charity, it might be too hard for her. "I'm scared of what I'll find when I go back. My house, my office, what's left? All my friends, their houses, their lives?" I had seen the maps, the flooding. Where Cordelia and I lived, in Tremé, was near the edge of the water, but our house was raised, so it was possible it stayed above the water. I knew too many people who had to have been flooded, though. "When I go back I'll pass places where people died because they didn't have water to drink, didn't have medical care."

I couldn't get the haunting images out of my head and I couldn't say any more. I curled against Shannon and began to cry, heavy gasping sobs, the tears covering my face. Shannon wrapped her arms around me and held me.

It took a long time to stop. I rolled away from Shannon, muttered, "I'll be back," then headed to the bathroom.

I scrubbed my face as if the tears were stains that needed to be washed away. It took about half a roll of toilet paper to clear my nose. I glanced at myself in the mirror and almost didn't recognize the woman who stared back to me—there seemed to be so many broken hearts on my face.

Shannon was lying quietly on the bed, waiting for me to return.

"Sorry," I muttered as I climbed in beside her.

"For what? Finally letting go and crying?"

"I…I'm a bit of a mess right now."

"Kind of normal under the circumstances, don't you think?"

I looked at her. She had beautiful eyes, the blue of a sky on a clear fall day. I felt like I was in love with her and I felt like I had used her. I answered, "I guess, if you can call anything normal these days." I kissed her, a gentle, lingering kiss. Then said simply, "Let's go to sleep. Curl around me?"

Shannon held me as I fell asleep.

Chapter Twenty-four

When I woke, she was gone, the muted sound of the shower telling me where she was. I slowly sat up. For a second I couldn't remember where I was or even what day it was. Then Shannon came out of the shower in time to answer the phone. Beatrice was asking if we wanted to meet for breakfast. I nodded yes and headed for my own shower.

In fifteen minutes we were in the lobby waiting for them. Jane took a little longer to wake up than I did, it seemed. As I had suspected, Miss Carlotta had let Beatrice sleep rather than waking her to keep the vigil at the hospital.

"I'm not truly upset, I did get a good night's sleep, after all," Beatrice admitted to me. "But, we're such an odd family grouping, and just for Jane's sake, I need to fit in somehow."

From breakfast we went to the hospital.

Jane asked her question, "Is Daddy waking up today?"

"I hope so, honey," Beatrice said, holding her hand.

Miss Carlotta and George were there, in the same clothes from the day before. After greetings and hugs, and a quiet confirmation that Damon had not changed, they left to get back to the hotel for some rest.

Then we waited. One of us always stayed near Damon's room. Beatrice sat with him for a while. I couldn't do it; it was too hard to see him lying so close to death, a hastened, unfair death. I knew it was more than just him. It was a flash of the images of bodies floating in the flood water, neighborhoods with bare roofs showing above the oily black water, a lone black Lab standing on a car roof, the boats passing him by to save the people.

We took turns with Jane, trying to keep her occupied and shielded from how fragile her hopes, our hopes, were. I made sure that either Shannon or I was always with her.

Jud came around lunchtime. He cast a quick glance my way, opened his hands as if to say, "See, no weapons." George and Miss Carlotta joined us in the late afternoon. George looked like he'd gotten some rest, but if Miss Carlotta slept, it barely showed.

And again, we waited, the day slipping into the shadows of evening.

Finally, Miss Carlotta told us to go back to the hotel, get a proper meal, she'd call if anything changed. Jud and Beatrice started to protest, but I suspected Miss Carlotta wanted us away as much for herself as for us. She was the focal point, the one we turned to, and I think she just wanted some time when no one needed her, with only silent George and her dying nephew for company. I also wanted to keep Jud where I could see him.

I said, "She's right, we all need to take care of ourselves. A little food and rest won't hurt anyone."

As we walked out, I overheard Beatrice talking to Jud. She and Jane would stay another day, but would have to leave on Tuesday. Tomorrow was Labor Day. It didn't feel like it could be a holiday.

In the parking lot I noticed a car that looked familiar. It was black, a muscle car, but a few years old and with a few dents from less-than-perfect driving. The license plate was from Louisiana. On the bumper was the leathermen flag, part of it scratched and torn. I'd seen that car parked near Damon's bar, The Outer Limits, the one Bruce managed. Jud looked at me. It seemed that he recognized the car as well.

"I'll be right back," I said, and trotted back to Damon's room. I quickly told Miss Carlotta and George what I suspected.

"I'm hiring a private security guard," was her response. Seeing the look on George's face, she quickly added, "I know you can take him out with one swing, but I'd prefer to avoid that, and a uniformed guard plus you here will make Bruce behave."

I offered to stay as well, but she shooed me off, already on her phone. I slowly retraced my steps, taking time to check out places where Bruce might be lurking. When I got back to the parking lot, Jud and Shannon were still there. Beatrice and Jane had gone back to the hotel.

"No sign of him," Jud told me. "Should we wait around and see if he shows up?"

I told them about Miss Carlotta hiring a security guard as I pondered Jud's question. It might not be Bruce, just a coincidence. Black muscle cars tended to be driven by macho-turd boys. Maybe dents were more likely than not. Maybe it was Bruce, but he'd just ended up here by some bizarre chance. The car was messy, with fast-food wrappers strewn in the backseat, but nothing that offered proof that this car was his.

We waited for over an hour, but the owner of the car didn't show up.

Back at the hotel, Beatrice and Jane joined us and we all had dinner together, talking of anything save the reason we were here. At first it was the polite conversation of people who don't know each other well, but then we started telling stories of New Orleans—the New Orleans that had been. Outrageous costumes for Southern Decadence, leaving the house to get groceries only to hear the brass of a second-line band coming down your street, where to get the best oyster po-boys. And for a brief period we weren't strangers thrown together, but friends taking one of life's unexpected detours.

By unspoken agreement, Shannon and I headed for the bar afterward—or I headed there and she followed. We didn't talk much. I was glad to see that she didn't feel the need to fill time with chatter. We could just sit quietly together, holding hands under the table. This time I had two drinks, Shannon finished her beer.

When we got back to the room, I made love to her repeatedly, as if trying to make up for my reticence, letting her passion carry us. I both wanted her to touch me and was afraid of it. I had broken down so completely yesterday and I didn't want to do that again, but if I opened myself to her, I also opened myself to everything.

Maybe three drinks, I thought as I finally came. Maybe that would make it easier for me to let go.

My sleep was a mix of drunken dead-to-the-world, then restless fits as the booze wore off. I again woke to hear Shannon in the shower. I guessed her leaving the bed was waking me up. Even as small a thing as it was, it felt like a routine, and I clearly needed some anchors to my day.

When she came out, she asked, "Should we go to the hospital today? Would I be derelict if I took advantage of some of these Labor Day sales to get a few more things to wear?"

"I think you can go shopping. We're now at the level of spear carriers."

"We're what?"

"Theater. The actors who come on stage, say, 'What, ho, sire, a message,' and then leave. We should probably make plans for what to do next." Then I added, "Not that I have a clue what they might be."

"We could go to New York," Shannon offered.

"What, and stay with Lauren? I don't think so. You two share lodging, don't you?"

"Yes, we do...we did. But we do keep a small studio in Manhattan."

"The two of you?"

"It was. But I can use it until I find something else."

"Let me think on that," was all I said as I headed for the shower.

After breakfast, I let Shannon head off for her shopping. I wasn't up to joining the shopping hordes, people living their normal lives. That existence was too far away from me.

I also needed to give myself time to think. Since that moment in Cordelia's office, all I could do was react to what was happening, with no time to take it in, to work out what I wanted and what was possible to have.

I went back to the room and sat looking out the window, more at the sky than the people. I didn't think Miss Carlotta would hustle us off, but, as I had noted to Shannon, our role was done here. I didn't want to go to New York, although on a practical level that made sense. If Shannon and I did stay in their small apartment, Lauren would probably have enough sense to steer clear of us. If not, I could also stay with my mother. I would have to talk to her at some point, but I wanted to put off as long as possible the "Hey, Mom, my forever lover dumped me and I ended up with her new girlfriend's ex-girlfriend" talk as long as I could. I told myself that it was a big enough city, that even if Cordelia was there, we probably wouldn't run into each other.

Probably wouldn't, but it was possible and I'd always be aware that she was around, in a way that I had no control over. I could turn a corner and she would be there. Perhaps walking down the street, laughing and holding hands with Lauren. That thought was a stab. I felt the anger curling out of me.

Why didn't she talk to me? Where the fuck was she now?

The room phone rang. I jumped out of the chair, jolted by its timing.

It couldn't be Cordelia, she didn't even know I was here. As I picked up the phone, I did consider that if she didn't know where I was, then it would be kind of hard for her to meet my unspoken demand to talk to me.

"Micky?" It was Alex. I had e-mailed her telling her I was here.

"Yeah, it's me."

She was silent. Alex is not often silent. "I'm sorry, but I'm falling apart and needed someone to fall apart with. Is this okay?" Her voice broke.

"Yes, it's okay. Talk to me."

She took a deep breath. "It's been a shit morning. I woke up with indigestion. At least I hope it's just my stomach complaining from all the damn fried food served at my uncle's house."

She tried to make a joke of it, but I could hear her palpable fear. She said, "Then I talked to Joanne. She went by our house. In a boat. Eight feet of water. Everything downstairs… Oh, hell. It's all gone…every single goddamned book I've carted around since my undergraduate days, that stuff I just had framed two weeks ago, my grandmother's green chair that is now blue, but it was green for so long we always called it the green chair. Oh, fuck, it's just gone." Alex started to cry.

"Honey, I'm so sorry," I said. Alex doesn't cry much. She's always the calm, levelheaded one.

She caught her breath and said, "I'm at a goddamned coffee shop with a prepaid phone card because I can't stand being with my uncle and my cousins. You know what one of them said to me? 'It'll be a good chance to redecorate.' Fuck. I don't want to redecorate, I want my home back. And I couldn't tell Joanne…that I don't feel good. It's too much, just too much."

I now knew what Shannon felt like, watching me. There was nothing I could do for Alex. I wanted to reach out and hold her, but I could only grip the phone. I said, "Suggest that she turn a fire hose on her house, so she can redecorate as well."

Alex snorted. "Damn, Micky. It'd take a dredge pump from the slimiest part of Lake Pontchartrain to come even close." She let out a long breath. "I need to get out of here. I'm already so tired of this city. All my uncle and cousins can do is complain about the traffic and the crime and 'those people' coming here. Like I'm not one of 'those people.'"

"Where do you want to go? Road trip? Will Joanne be okay with that?"

"I want to go home," she said softly. "But we can't, can we? Joanne will be okay as long as I'm okay. So I couldn't fall apart on the phone with her or tell her how shitty things are here. She's in hell down there. Her voice is so hoarse I could barely recognize it."

"You talked to her today?"

"Yeah, just a bit ago. She borrowed a reporter's satellite phone. She's so tired she even said 'I love you' to me in front of the media. She just had enough time to tell me about the house, that she saw Cordelia, and that I can't come home for a long time."

"She saw Cordelia? I thought she left town."

"You did?"

"You told me she was at the airport."

"Oh. Right. God, I can't keep track of whom I've told what to. She's been working there."

"At the airport?"

"They've turned it into a triage center. They're taking all the sick people there. You know what a do-gooder Cordelia is. She's not leaving town while there's a temperature to be taken."

"I thought she'd left to go to…"

"As of this morning, she was still there." Alex and Cordelia had been friends for a long time, long before we met. If Cordelia had talked to anyone, it would be Alex. "This is so crazy. The two of you need to talk."

Oh, hell, Alex, I wanted to say, let's talk about you and your problems. I can deal with your emotions, I can't deal with mine. "I don't know if I'm ready for that yet."

"In normal circumstances, I'd give you a year. But nothing is normal now. Let her at least say she's sorry."

"Is she?" The anger flared in my voice.

"Yes, she is," Alex stated.

I couldn't come up with a response. I changed the subject. "Hey, Alex, didn't you call me so you can fall apart? How many more minutes on that card of yours?"

"Oh, God, Micky, we're all falling apart. We just have to pause long enough to help each other out. Yeah, falling apart. My mother's two biggest fears have come true—I'm pregnant and homeless."

"With a lesbian father. Who is also homeless. I bet she didn't have that in her biggest fears."

Alex let out a guffaw. We'd cried so much the only thing left to do was laugh. The phone call ended with me promising Alex that I'd be in Baton Rouge by the end of the week and we'd figure out something from there.

I glanced at my watch. Unless Shannon was unusually lucky in her clothes shopping, she'd be a while yet.

Cordelia was sorry. As if I didn't have enough to think about, now I had to add this into everything. I suddenly wanted to see her. To just be able to touch her hand. To yell at her and fight and hear her say that she was sorry. It hurt too much to have all these swirling emotions, to have to keep them contained until I could see her and let them out. To fall in love with Shannon, I'd have to finish with Cordelia.

She was in the city, about a six-hour drive from Memphis. I thought of just getting in my car and driving there. But it wouldn't be that easy. I didn't know if I could even get back in, as closed off as it now was. And even if I did, could I find her? And even if I did find her, it might be in the midst of chaos, with no time or space for the kind of conversation we needed to have.

I just stared out the window. I couldn't make any life decisions, they were all too jumbled. I couldn't even decide what to do next. Turn on the TV, take a walk, read the paper, check e-mail.

Alex is right, I thought, we're all falling apart.

I grabbed my room key and decided to just get out and walk for a while. Fifteen minutes of walking in the heat made TV, e-mail, and reading seem like better choices. CNN was just cycling through to repeat the top stories when Shannon returned.

"Anything new?" she asked.

"No, not really. More pictures of more displaced people. Any luck in the shopping?"

"Underwear, socks, two pairs of pants, some shirts, a duffel to carry everything in." She took them out of the bags, taking off the tags, then putting everything neatly away.

I told her about the call from Alex, at least the part about meeting her in Baton Rouge at the end of the week. I left out what she told me about Cordelia.

Shannon nodded, although she didn't seem thrilled at the idea of picking up Alex and taking her with us. She was probably as happy about having Cordelia's best friend along as a chaperone as I was at the idea of staying in a place that used to be hers and Lauren's.

We left it at that and then departed for the hospital. When we got there I drove around the parking lot, but didn't see the black car. I felt like we needed to be doing something for Miss Carlotta as long as we stayed, so I at least needed to check in and see if she wanted anything from New Orleans.

It turned out that she did.

"I know exactly where they are," she explained. "They have always passed down to the women in our family, and I think it only right that Beatrice and Jane have them." Two rings, a brooch, and a necklace, the jewelry that Miss Carlotta's grandfather had made for her mother for her début. "I'm worried they'll be stolen…or lost."

"I'm not sure we can get back into the city," I told her.

"I can get us in," Shannon interjected.

I looked at her. "You can? How?"

"Press pass. I've been e-mailing some editors about doing stories, so it would even be legit."

I had to admit that I wanted to return to New Orleans. If my home and office had been destroyed, at least I'd know, instead of waiting weeks and wondering—and hoping.

"Okay, we can try. I'll need something from you that authorizes us to be doing this, Miss Carlotta."

Jud was still a member of the bar, and he could notarize papers. He'd even brought his notary seal, just in case. "Thought there might be a few things to take care of," he said as we worked out the wording with Miss Carlotta. He also offered to let us stay at his place on the north shore. "Don't think there's power there yet, but other than a few shingles and some downed trees, it's okay."

He pulled me aside. "I'll tell Miss Carlotta in a moment, but I got a jumbled e-mail from Ambrose. He's in Houston. Said his briefcase was stolen. Had the only version of Damon's new will in it." Jud made a face. "He didn't sound terribly upset about it, went on about how it seems that the previous will is now the one that'll stand."

"But I—" I started to say, then caution caught me.

"What?"

I quickly covered. "But I thought I saw it in Damon's office, at his house."

"Ambrose must have taken it with him," Jud said.

"Why did he e-mail you and not Miss Carlotta?"

He gave me his charming half-smile. "Oh, c'mon, you know Ambrose is a sexist pig. Why would he e-mail a frail old woman when there's a man about?"

I had other questions, but I knew Jud would just give me the answers he wanted me to have. He and Ambrose weren't that friendly, so why did Ambrose even know his e-mail address? If that car in the parking lot was Bruce's, who had told him where Damon was? Jud was being helpful, but I had to wonder if he wasn't letting us use his place as a way to know our whereabouts.

But I didn't ask those questions. Instead I focused on how to return to my ruined city.

It was activity. Getting keys made for Jud's place, Miss Carlotta's, and Damon's. That was where I'd left one of the copies of the will. Another important reason for us to get back to New Orleans. We also had to pick up supplies, from several cases of water to bottles of bleach, for a city flooded but with no safe drinking water.

"Can we even pee or do we have to hold it until we're somewhere with a working sewer system?" Shannon asked as I loaded things into the trunk. Jud had been kind enough to store a number of our things, what I'd taken from the shipyard, in his truck so we'd have space. I wondered if I'd ever see them again. But I couldn't think about that any more.

"You can pee in the water. You can't pollute it any more than it already is," was my less-than-reassuring answer. I also got knee-high rubber boots—if the water was higher than that, I wasn't wading in it—breathing filters, a box of latex gloves, and some heavily minted ointment to rub under our noses.

"This looks serious," Shannon said as she appraised the load in my trunk.

"It is serious. You have to go back to the Civil War to get another city as destroyed as New Orleans is today."

"And it survived the Civil War intact. I hope New Orleans doesn't come back with the sterile towers of Atlanta."

"I hope New Orleans comes back."

We left early the next morning.

Chapter Twenty-five

Hernando, Mississippi, is the dangerous part," I told Shannon. She was driving, glanced briefly at me, but was passing a semi and wisely kept her eyes on the road.

I continued. "Both my friends Greg and Jean had car breakdowns on the interstate just as they were passing through Hernando. What are the odds? Two queer New Orleanians, two breakdowns, same small town in northern Mississippi?"

"I suggest we beat the odds," Shannon said, as she accelerated smartly to leave the truck behind.

We did, passing the treacherous Hernando early on our trip. Signs for towns I didn't recognize flew by. I'd lived most of my life in the South, but it wasn't this South, the red clay of northern Mississippi. We didn't stop until we were through Jackson, and then it was only briefly to get gas and a quick bite to eat and to switch drivers.

We were passing a rest area when I noticed a black car with a few dents parked there. What the hell, I thought, then did something stupid—except that fate was on my side and no cars were exiting as I pulled a U turn and entered the rest stop the wrong way.

Shannon gave me a worried look.

"Black car," I said.

She looked around the parking lot and saw it. I quickly parked, glad not to hear any sirens coming after me. We both got out and headed for the black car. It was the same one we'd seen in Memphis.

Bruce Payne came out of the men's room a minute later. He paused to light a cigarette, then absentmindedly adjusted the family jewels—cheap paste in this case, I'd say—as he passed several young girls.

"You can take the boy out of the bar," Shannon muttered.

"But you can't take the bar out of the boy," I finished for her.

He almost dropped his cigarette when he saw us. He recovered enough to blow smoke into my face as he came up to us. "Fancy meeting you here," he said, blowing another puff of smoke my way.

"Not fancy at all," I replied. "Just doing my job and following you from the hospital in Memphis. Guess George and the security guards foiled your little plot."

"Fucking dyke," he muttered.

"Careful, Bruce, you're not in a French Quarter bar anymore, but a rest stop in rural Mississippi. Might want to watch your language."

"Fuck you, bitch. I wasn't in Memphis and I don't know what you're talking about."

"Funny, because your car was. All those dents make it very distinctive. Plus I did write down the license number."

"So what if I was in Memphis? It's a free country. Can't exactly stay in New Orleans right now."

"It's a free country. Just awfully suspicious for you to be there, where Damon is, just when someone is trying to kill him."

"Wasn't me." He threw his cigarette butt on the ground, then lit another one. "Don't matter anyway. Ambrose told me someone stole Damon's will. Only got the old one to go by now."

"Ambrose told you what?" First I was surprised at Bruce's information, then had to wonder if he knew about it because he'd been the thief.

"Say, who was that woman and kid I seen with you? Damon's little bastard?"

"So you were in Memphis and spying on us." This didn't make sense. It couldn't be coincidence that Bruce was here, but was he really acting on his own? He wasn't as dim as Perry, but he was still a few sandbags short of a proper levee. Maybe someone needed to know if Damon was still alive, and if his daughter had been found. It worried me to think that more than one person could be involved.

"Didn't say that. Just that someone saw something and passed it along. So there is a kid?"

"Lots of kids in Memphis, Bruce. Maybe your source isn't as good as you think he is."

"Not too many that look like Damon." He blew more smoke in

my face, then made an exaggerated circle around me to get to his car. "With the will lost, something happenin' to that kid would make a lot of people happy."

"That a threat, asshole?" I grabbed his arm to stop him.

"No, bitch, just an observation." He shook my hand off, threw his still-burning cigarette on the ground, got in his car, and zoomed away.

"Damn," I muttered.

Shannon picked up Bruce's butts and disposed of them properly.

I had a copy of Damon's will in my office, if it survived, plus the copy I'd put in Damon's desk. Had Bruce stolen it? But Ambrose was in Houston and Bruce was clearly here. Or had Ambrose "lost" it on purpose? Or someone else? What if they had all gotten together? Bruce, Perry, Kent, even some others. Some searching for the will and some for the child? The thought chilled me.

I made two phone calls. One to Danny and Elly in Shreveport to see if they could shoehorn two more people in somewhere.

The next was to Beatrice. "You need to be out of sight for a while," I told her. "You and Jane. Rent a car, don't drive yours, leave at an odd time. Tell Jud and Miss Carlotta that you're returning home." I gave her directions to where Danny and Elly were. They weren't connected to her, so I was hoping that no one would think to look for her and Jane there.

That was all I could do—except get to New Orleans and find the supposedly lost will.

As we got closer to the Mississippi/Louisiana border, we began to see the effects of the storm. Trees broken, the side of the highway still littered with fallen limbs. In some places whole stands of trees listed, as if pushed by a giant hand. I wondered if they would ever grow straight again.

When we exited the interstate at Hammond, the damage was even more evident. In a direct line, Hammond is about fifty miles from New Orleans, longer if you want to stay on roads and dry land. Many of the signs had been blown down, roofs peeled back.

I had first thought of driving the back roads to Jud's place in Abita Springs, but clearly a good bit of the displaced population of New Orleans was up here. Traffic was almost at a standstill and every place that was open had a full parking lot. The local burger thing had only drive-through service, and the cars were backed onto the main road.

"Tell me this isn't normal," Shannon said, as we moved two car-lengths before the light turned red again.

"Nothing is normal anymore." My great plan had been to take the old highway from Hammond over to Abita Springs instead of catching the interstate. I was guessing that all the new people in the area would stick to the big roads. Plus we'd need some food and ice for the evening, and I thought we would just drive by some suitable mom-and-pop grocery and be all set. "I'd suggest you jump out, get what we need, and meet me at the next stop light, but if you buy ice, it'll just melt before we get to where we're going."

It took us twenty minutes to drive through the small town of Hammond, Louisiana. But at least I was right—once we got beyond the town, the back road was relatively clear. That changed once we got close to the next "big" city, Covington. I wondered how long before this massive influx of people would wear on everyone's nerves.

We did manage to find a small grocery in Abita Springs that was open.

"Sorry, no beer," was the greeting as we came in. The shelves did seem rather bare.

"Ice?" I asked.

"Got that."

"The Brewhouse open?"

He shrugged. "Came down from McComb to help my uncle. Not from around here."

But the store had ice and sandwich makings, which would do us. Plus chips, candy, all the essentials.

"It's weird, isn't it?" Shannon said as we got back in the car. "Now that I know how hard it is to get food, I feel like I need to be on the lookout for it at all times."

"How quickly hunting and gathering comes back."

Jud had been right; the power wasn't restored where his house was.

"Good thing it's still light out," Shannon commented as we entered.

"Find your way to the bathroom now," I advised. "Get it in your head, so you don't fall and break your arm in the middle of the night."

"Cheery thought," she said, walking back out to unload the car.

I'd insisted on leaving early so we could get here well before dark. I didn't want to be hunting for an open store, or coming to an unfamiliar house after dark with no lights.

It was still hot, so I opened some of the windows to catch the breeze. The air had the smell of pine sap, from all the trees broken by the force of the wind.

Jud had already cleaned out his refrigerator. Otherwise I would have done it for him. He'd said he didn't know if he would stay for the next storm. "Listening to that wind, I just kept expecting it to take my roof off, or bring a tree down on top of me." He'd lost a good number of trees in his yard, including an oak that looked like it had been around for a long time. Abita Springs is a good thirty miles farther inland than New Orleans, about ten miles north of the shore of Lake Pontchartrain itself.

Once we settled in, there was little to do—no TV or computers or e-mail. Even Shannon's cell phone didn't work. Probably most of the cell towers in the area were out. We took a walk around sunset, making sure to get back inside before dark. I'd bought several flashlights, but their beams were feeble against the immense blackness of a place with no lights anywhere.

We made love in the first cool of the evening, then sat on the porch and watched the stars, no lights to diminish their brightness. Even the trees thinned to let them shine through.

Nature can handle this destruction, I thought. The trees grow back, the islands lost will re-form. But we humans don't live on that scale. We need our houses, our roads. We can't wait the stretch of years for regrowth.

Shannon and I kissed under the stars, then made love on the porch, with them as our only light. We lay in each other's arms until the bugs drove us back inside. Then a cold shower, with no power to heat the water. But we were hot and the water was tepid, so it was no great privation.

We made love again. I was still slow, still learning to respond to her touch, but I was beginning to feel that this was my future and not some aberrant path—or a dream that I would wake from.

Shannon fell asleep in my arms. I held her for a while, but sleep didn't come easily. I couldn't stop thinking of what we would find tomorrow. When I'd left New Orleans, the day before the storm, it had been whole, intact. Now? They hadn't even begun to count the dead yet. They were still finding the living, still pumping the water out.

I eventually dozed and woke to the morning light. It seemed to so change the world, from the utter dark of the night before to this perfect day, the sun bright and shining, the sky blue. Even a few birds were calling to each other. They, at least, had survived the storm.

I gently roused Shannon. "We've got a long day ahead of us," I said, then kissed her between the tousled strands of hair on her forehead.

We showered together but it was more prosaic than romantic.

"We should try and get in and out of the city before it gets dark," I told her as I soaped her back. "And it'll be a journey just to get in or out."

From where we were, the usual way would be to take the Lake Pontchartrain Causeway, a twenty-four-mile-long bridge—supposedly the longest in the world—that crossed the lake into Metairie, the suburb just outside of New Orleans proper. It was near the floodwall, the 17th Street one that broke, and had the New Orleans side not given out first, then Metairie would have been the flooded city instead of the dry one.

The Causeway had been damaged, although not badly, but I wasn't sure if it was open. The next closest way was I-10 from Slidell into New Orleans, but that would not be passable for months. That left heading back the way we'd come in, backtracking to I-55, and taking that down to I-10 and then into the city.

We took everything we'd brought and locked up Jud's house securely. It was possible we wouldn't be able to get back into the city at all, in which case we might want to head back to Memphis—or Baton Rouge for Alex. Or we could end up staying the night there. I wanted to be flexible.

"One advantage to being this early," I told her as we pulled out, "is that we may miss the worst of the morning rush hour."

"Any chance of coffee?" Shannon asked. She was clearly missing her caffeine.

I was, too. "Everything's changed. If we can get back to where there's power, we might find some. Just remember what it'll do to your bladder."

She just grunted at my advice.

We found coffee, ice for the ice chest, and even managed to gas up before we got back on I-55.

Most of the traffic traveling south with us was official, with a fair smattering of army or national guard vehicles. Even the cars tended to have official logos on them, including one from the NYPD.

I wondered how Joanne was doing. And then I wondered if Cordelia was still in the city.

As I-55 neared I-10, most of the traffic was diverted to the right and away from the city.

"Let's try our luck and your press pass," I said to Shannon as I moved into the left lane.

We were stopped at a checkpoint.

As Shannon was showing her press credentials, I momentarily wondered where I was. No, I knew where I was, but this didn't seem possible. I was an American citizen, traveling into the city I live in, yet being stopped at a military checkpoint and the guards could turn us away. The man examining Shannon's pass had a gun slung over his shoulder, one that could easily rip this car apart.

"You part of the press, too? You got any ID?" he asked me. He had checked Shannon's press pass and her driver's license, and I clearly wasn't getting through on her credentials.

I pulled out my private-investigator's license and my driver's license.

"She's traveling with me as a guide and as security," Shannon explained.

He gave the two of us a dubious look. Or perhaps a woman with gray in her hair wasn't his idea of security.

Shannon said, "I'm doing several stories on first responders, like you guys. I think it's important that people know how many heroes there are down here. All of you are doing a great job. My brother's in the marine corps and I know what he's had to go through."

She gave him a big smile. He smiled back and waved us through.

After her window was safely rolled back up, I had to ask, "You have a brother in the marines?"

"If I had a brother, I'm sure he would have been. Checkpoint Chuck didn't look like the type who's into fact-checking."

Then the broken trees gave way to the sparkling waters of the lake. We were traveling over the Bonnet Carré Spillway. This elevated section of the interstate, narrowing down from three lanes to two, is usually crowded, but today we were one of the few vehicles there. It was eerie. Familiar, but so different. The swamp held few landmarks, but the fishing shacks that had always been there, gone. Debris in the water, trees splintered or toppled. That was all that was left.

The lake and the swamp gave way to land, the suburbs, the airport. Again, familiar but changed. No planes were hanging low, either leaving or coming in for a landing.

Briefly I wondered if Cordelia was still there. Or maybe she would be on the next plane out.

The damage we'd seen on the north side of the lake was here in greater force. Signs gone or twisted to the ground. Some buildings had sides or roofs missing. Blue tarps covered many of the other roofs that we could see.

"Good God," Shannon said, looking at a building ripped in half. "It'll get worse, won't it?" she said.

"Much worse." I'd seen hurricanes before. The signs down, siding torn off, while dramatic, were common aftereffects from most hurricanes. The wind can be bad, but it's the water that does the most damage, and the water had taken the city of New Orleans.

We drove on in silence.

Finally I said, "We need to get down toward the river. That'll be the best way to get into the city. Take the next exit. Then let me drive."

Shannon did as she was instructed, pulling into a closed gas station.

I took the side roads down to Jefferson Highway. That slowed to a checkpoint and I decided to go around it. Not to avoid the checkpoint so much, but I knew these roads and I didn't feel like waiting behind all the out-of-towners who were feeling their way around with only maps to take them to streets they'd never been on before.

I detoured around Ochsner Hospital and got on River Road. It runs beside the Mississippi levee. I stayed on that until we reached the bend in the river where St. Charles and Carrollton Avenue meet. From there I got on St. Charles. I was guessing it had already been cleared, plus it was probably the best way to reach Miss Carlotta's house.

The scenery was jarring, familiar yet irrevocably changed. Power lines down, trees lying beside the road, no streetcar. It was quiet, save for my car. Shannon had taken out her camera and was shooting pictures. I felt a jab of anger. I wanted to say, this was a living, breathing city, not just a story. But I had lived here, she was a visitor. She didn't remember riding the streetcar up St. Charles, watching the stately mansions, Audubon Park, the universities, Tulane, Loyola all rush by the window. She hadn't known it year by year, learned it so well that a certain oak limb was a visual cue to turn. If the color of one house changed, I knew it. But that graceful oak branch was now on the ground, and debris still sat on the streetcar tracks. Everything had changed.

Shannon took another picture.

No one in America knows what this is like, I thought. No one, no city, no place in living memory has endured this. Let her tell her stories, take her pictures. Maybe it will help those who can't see this understand the enormity and the horror of what has happened.

Block after block. Everything had changed.

We found our way to Miss Carlotta's house, having to drive the wrong way down a one-way street to get around a fallen tree. But few cars were visible, and those we saw were driving slowly. No stoplights were working, debris was everywhere.

We got out, Shannon armed with her camera. I had the notarized paper with Miss Carlotta's permission written on it.

One of the military patrols came by and asked us what we were doing. But it seemed they didn't think a woman with gray in her hair could be a looter. Plus Shannon had her press pass and I had my PI license, the note and keys to the house. I had been a little uneasy about not having my gun—somehow I had neglected to pack it for what I thought would be a weekend runaway. I was rather more assured than worried at being asked what we were doing here. I didn't need my gun if the boys—and girls—in green had plenty of firepower.

Miss Carlotta's house looked okay. The yard was scattered with tree limbs and some shingles, but, at least from the outside, it seemed to still be intact.

Waving good-bye to our friendly Humvee, we let ourselves into her house. She had had her windows boarded up, so despite the clear daylight it was dark and gloomy inside. Shannon went back to the car and fetched several of the flashlights.

I traced the slightly sour smell inside the house to the kitchen. Something was oozing from the refrigerator. And Miss Carlotta had thought she'd be back soon enough not to bag up the trash still in the kitchen trash can. I found her supply of garbage bags, triple bagging what she had left. I considered opening the refrigerator and also bagging whatever was in there, but the ooze decided me against it. Miss Carlotta and her insurance company could afford a new one, and I wasn't up to getting that dirty in a city in which it was a risk to even wash my hands. The waterless hand sanitizer would be fine for a little mud or dirt, but not decomposing food.

I found the stairway and followed Miss Carlotta's instructions on where to find the jewelry. They were where she told me they would be, in her bottom drawer, hidden in an old pair of socks. Maybe when this was all over I'd have a chat with Miss Carlotta about security. When this was all over, I caught myself thinking. Would this ever be over? I quickly glanced at the jewelry—two rings, a brooch, and a necklace—to make sure it was all there. One of the rings and the brooch were Mardi Gras gaudy—green, purple, and gold—the Carnival colors. But even those pieces showed the care and workmanship put into them. The other ring and necklace, also a pair, were delicate white gold, understated and beautiful. I could almost see Jane growing into a woman, putting these on and feeling the touch of a family she would only dimly know. I suspected that image is what made Miss Carlotta so want to pass these on to her, to enlist my aid in returning to this wounded city to retrieve them. It was also, I suspected, a grasp to make sure that not everything was lost—not the monetary value, but the memories held in the gold.

Or maybe it was just a plot to get me away from Damon and Beatrice and Jane. I hate this, I thought as I hesitated in the doorway of a room that seemed to be a home office. I hated being suspicious of people I wanted to like and trust. I hated having to constantly remind myself that smiling faces could hide evil thoughts. I was frustrated that I was no closer to knowing who had tried to kill Damon than when he first collapsed in his courtyard. Could it only have been a few weeks ago? It seemed like years.

Think, I told myself, wanting a solution that would make it easy to bypass rifling though Miss Carlotta's papers. Perry and Bruce had easy access to cocaine, something not true for Miss Carlotta and probably not Jud either. First rule of medicine and detecting—when you hear hoofbeats look for horses, not zebras. Perry, Bruce, and Kent Richards were horses, and Bruce was a horse that was too close for comfort.

"Oh, shit," I heard Shannon call from downstairs.

I hastily tucked the jewels back into their sock home, thrust them into my pocket, and hurried downstairs. I gave one backward look at Miss Carlotta's desk. On top was something marked Past Due.

Shannon was looking out the back door. I joined her and looked over her shoulder.

"Damn," she said. "And it seemed that everything was okay."

George's place, the cottage in back, was crushed under a tree, its contents strewn across the lawn.

"Can we get a tarp?" Shannon was asking as we crossed to it.

But as we got closer, I could see the already-growing mold. The roof was totally destroyed, ripped first by the tree, then the tattered pieces blown by the wind. I looked at the sodden mess that had been everything George had ever owned.

"Too late. Might be better to let things dry out. If it stays sunny, he might be able to save some of it."

"Just leave it?" she demanded.

"No, take a picture. Tell George's story. And remember that George will be taken care of by Miss Carlotta. Many have lost as much or more and no one will take care of them."

"Fuck," Shannon said, wiping away a tear.

"You angry at me?"

"No, I'm angry at...this." Her arm swept from the destroyed cottage to the whole city. "Maybe a little at you," she admitted. "Guess I want you to fix it. You're the expert. There should be some way to dry things out, make them okay."

I shook my head. "Too much water got in, and now the mold. He might be able to save anything plastic or metal that doesn't rust or pottery."

"But no pictures or letters or comic books?" She pointed to the sodden pile by her feet.

"No. I'm sorry."

She wiped her eyes again. "I'm not being an objective reporter, am I?"

"Hard to be objective here."

"It's just that...that George seemed to have so little, and now he's lost what he has."

I put my arm around her and hugged her.

She returned the embrace, then pulled away. "Tell the story. Let me take some photos."

I left her to her picture-taking and went back into the house. It was still and quiet, save for the occasional roar of a helicopter overhead or a truck on some nearby street. I quickly checked out the rooms. As far as I could tell, the roof had held; there were no leaks. The house seemed to have escaped being looted, the boarded-up windows perhaps preventing that.

I'd done my duty and I didn't want to be in Miss Carlotta's home anymore, wondering if she'd ever be able to return, knowing that George would never show me his comic books. I went out on the front porch and waited for Shannon.

She joined me after a few minutes. "Sorry," she murmured, kissing me on the cheek.

"You're supposed to be the crusading reporter," I told her as I carefully locked up.

"Hey, Micky," she said, taking my hand. "You know I love you, don't you?"

"Yes, I know that," I said. I kissed her on the lips. "I…" But I faltered, and then another Humvee was passing by and asking us what we were doing here and the moment was gone.

Did I love her? I wondered as she answered their questions. Not the way I loved Cordelia, but that was a love of years and years together. It was unfair to ask Shannon to meet that standard before I'd tell her I loved her in return. I cared for her, I liked being with her. We'd been together constantly for weeks, and I didn't feel I needed a break from her. Admit it, Micky, I told myself, I could fall in love with Shannon. Or did I just desperately want someone to hold me? And Shannon's arms were willing.

As we got back in the car, I thought about just telling her I loved her, but it would seem too much like I was just saying it because she'd said it. Better to wait until some time when it had more meaning than that. Maybe on the porch with the stars as my witness.

"Let's head for Damon's place," I said. "We told Miss Carlotta we'd check on it if we could. Plus it's pretty close to my house and I'd like to look it over as well. Maybe even snag some more underwear."

I made our way back to St. Charles, taking it down to Lee Circle—

the General was still there astride his stone horse. But everywhere was the jarring sense of the familiar with the strange, like some apocryphal New Orleans dreamed up by a movie studio. The mechanical growl of the helicopters overhead and the smell of sewage, the rotten and stagnant water permeated the city as it would no movie set. Trash of a city blown apart littered the streets—branches, shredded leaves, clothing, even a wheelchair, empty now. Had its occupant been saved? Or lost?

I took Camp Street to the Central Business District, then carefully headed up Poydras, wondering where the water had stopped and if it would block our way. I only went as far as O'Keefe, taking that downtown. That would turn into Burgundy Street when it crossed Canal into the Quarter. The changing street names were a legacy of the animosity of the French to their new American compatriots—none of the names of the streets in the French Quarter continued past Canal Street.

We saw more people, although they seemed more occupiers than citizens, most in uniform, save for those in front of or behind cameras. I almost felt like holding my PI license, paltry as it was, out the window, so it would seem I had some official reason for being here.

With no stoplights, and some of the roads obstacle courses of abandoned cars, blown trash, and downed limbs, it was slow driving. A dump truck coming down Canal seemed like it had no intention of stopping or even slowing and, in my little Honda Accord, I wasn't going to argue. We finally got across Canal and into the Quarter.

It was the same and it was utterly different. The buildings stood. But with no power, no people, they seemed abandoned, left to an indifferent occupying army. Windows were boarded up or taped, the sidewalks and gutters still filled with the flotsam and jetsam of the wind.

"I feel like I'm in some alternate reality," Shannon said quietly as we drove by the empty streets.

About two blocks ahead I saw a group of people. Even though they were walking away from us, one of them looked familiar. Everything is so changed, I thought, that the recognizable stands out. As we got closer I realized I was right, I could recognize her walk from the back. Parking in the French Quarter, for once, was easy. I pulled over and got out.

"Joanne!" I yelled, even though she was now only ten feet away.

She turned slowly, as if unsure she'd heard me call her name, or rather that she had heard it but wasn't sure it was real. A few weeks ago running into me in this part of the French Quarter would have been likely and normal. Now it was almost so bizarre as to be unbelievable.

"Micky Knight?" she queried, clearly still trying to fathom my being here.

She was now facing me. I could see the exhaustion on her face, her hair matted and dirty, mud caked on her pants, her dark T-shirt showing the sweat stains.

"Joanne," I said again, as if proving that I was real.

"What the fuck are you doing here?" Then she wrapped her arms around me, gripping me tight. I returned her hug. She finally broke free, saying, "I stink."

"So does the rest of the city."

She was with two other cops I didn't recognize. One had on a shirt that identified him as from someplace in California. The other looked as bleary as Joanne and I guessed he was NOPD.

Shannon had gotten out of the car, so I did quick introductions. Joanne seemed to not know who she was, which seemed to mean that Alex hadn't updated her on my relationship status. I decided that now was not the time or place, so I just gave Shannon's reporter position as our reason for being here.

"First responders, huh?" the California guy said. "You can follow us around."

Shannon cast me a look that was almost "Mama, may I?"

"Can't do better than New Orleans's finest," I said. "And their allies," I added for Mr. California.

Joanne looked at me, then at my car. "I hate to be rude, but do you have any water? Enough to spare us a bottle or two?"

"Plenty of water," I said, walking back to it and opening the trunk. I took out three bottles of ice-cold water and handed each of them one.

Joanne rolled hers across her forehead, then neck, before drinking any. The other NOPD cop guzzled half of the bottle in one long pull. The California guy didn't seem as dehydrated and managed only a third of his in his first gulp.

I gave them each another bottle and offered more, but they couldn't carry them. I also gave them some of our snack food—cracker packs and small bags of raisins and nuts.

As Shannon was talking to the other two cops, Joanne pulled me aside. "Have you heard from Alex?"

"Yeah, we've been e-mailing about every day. Phones when we can find any that work."

"I've only talked to her once since… How is she? Damn, I am so worried about her." Joanne took another swig of water to cover the emotions threatening to come out.

"She's okay. She's worried about you. Once I leave here I'm heading to Baton Rouge to get her. Then it's the girls-do-a-road-trip."

"Good." Joanne nodded, again rolling the bottle across her forehead. "Take care of her. I can't. I'm so worried," she repeated. "I just want to be with her. Even if just for a day."

Joanne had to be worried if she not only said it, but said it twice.

"I'll take care of her. We'll be fine. The biggest problem is figuring out where the gas station is or where to get groceries."

"Oh, hell, Micky, this is insane. How could they not come for so long?"

I just shook my head. I didn't have an answer to that.

"I had to walk by people stealing TVs to pull people off roofs. And wade past bodies to save the living." She took another drink. "Sorry, too much to tell. Try and let me know where you end up. Cordelia promised to pay to get me wherever I might need to go."

"You've seen her?"

"Yeah, a couple of times. I borrowed a boat to help with the Charity evac, met up with her once at the airport, so I could take a shower and eat real food. She's okay." Joanne looked at me. "She's worried about you."

"Well, I'm obviously okay," I got out. "Do you know where she is now?"

"I think she's still around, probably at the airport. She needs to get out and take a break. You might get her before you get Alex." Joanne was still looking at me. It was clear she knew something was going on.

"I'll…uh—"

"You know we'd get there faster if we had a ride," one of the other cops said loudly. He was eyeing my car.

"Gas is scarce," the other cop, the NOPD one, said. "So we walk if we can."

Five adults, three of them rank, wouldn't fit comfortably in my car. I tossed Shannon the keys. "Go get your story," I told her. "I can easily walk to Damon's and from there to my house. Meet me there. Joanne can direct you from wherever you end up."

"Will you be safe?" Shannon asked me.

The NOPD cop answered, "Now? Hell, yeah. More cops and soldiers in this town than anyone else. Houston's got our crooks."

"I'll be fine," I assured her.

"Thanks. See you soon." Shannon got in, letting the other cops into my car's air-conditioned splendor.

I grabbed a water bottle from the trunk, then shut it.

Joanne wrapped me in another bear hug. I held on to her just as tight.

"Love you," she muttered in my ear, low enough there was no chance any of her fellow cops could hear.

"Same," I said, as we pulled away. We're two such emotional butches. I gave a quick wave as I watched my car head down to the lower part of the Quarter.

Chapter Twenty-six

I was only five blocks from Damon's place in the Quarter. It was even more disconcerting to walk than to be sealed inside my car. The rolled-up windows and air-conditioning had cut some of the smell. Now I got it in full force.

I was on Burgundy, a mostly quiet residential street, with the quirky pronunciation of the accent on the second syllable instead of the first, as in the wine. Once my car was out of sight, I was alone. Burgundy is a block off North Rampart, the dividing line between the French Quarter and Tremé. At one of the side streets I got a glimpse of the still-flying rainbow banners that had been put up on the light posts on Rampart in anticipation of the upcoming Southern Decadence festival and Pride in October. I took a quick jog up to Rampart. All the rainbow banners were still there, the storm had left them intact. Interesting that the gay and bawdy sections of town were the parts least damaged since some of the so-called religious people were claiming this to be God's punishment for our sinful ways. Perhaps they believed in a god of poor planning.

Every block brought another jarring feeling of seeing the familiar changed. The French Quarter is never this empty. Even late at night its streets are jammed with parked cars, the off-key carousing of revelers.

As I walked along, I finally resolved to stop at the airport. I needed to see Cordelia, even just to tell her, "I don't want you hurt. I don't know if things can be the same, or where we'll end up, but right now isn't the time to sort it out. Let's go to Baton Rouge and get Alex." Maybe to tell her I still loved her, because I did. But love wasn't enough.

That should qualify us for the lesbian romantic Olympics—picking up my ex, with my new girlfriend who was her new girlfriend's ex, and driving cross-country. If we took all our cats with us, we would win the event.

That thought caught me up. I wondered about Hepplewhite and Rook, our two cats. I couldn't just leave them if they were still at our house. I'd have to see if they were there and come up with a way to carry them with me, I decided.

I turned the corner, heading for Damon's place. On the way, I passed one boarded-up window that said, "Looters: shoot to kill. Locked and loaded." I was slightly relieved to see no bloodstains on the sidewalk.

Another block and I was in front of Damon's house. I stood for a minute, just looking at it. He would never return here. I had probably known that when I saw him in the hospital in Memphis, but it was only here, in front of the house where he lived his life, that the weight of the loss hit me. At times I had pictured the scene. Meeting him in his courtyard, introducing him to his daughter, the happy ending. Damon having the chance to show her the French Quarter, his city. The six months he should have had would have been enough. Maybe not enough to be the father Jane longed for, but enough to give her memories for a lifetime, pictures she could cherish and show her children. It was not to be.

"Goddamn you," I muttered to the killer of a dying man.

I swung open the wrought-iron gate and climbed the stairs to Damon's house. Inside was still and dank, the same fetid smell I'd noticed at Miss Carlotta's. If the floodwalls hadn't failed, we'd all be back here by now, all the garbage cleaned up and put out.

I didn't want to stay here long, in a dying man's house that he'd never return to. I quickly climbed the stairs to the top floor, checking the rooms for any water or roof damage. There were signs of leaking in the guest bedroom, but it seemed more from around the window than the roof. One of the windowpanes had been broken. The wall was plaster, still a little soggy to the touch, but, unlike Sheetrock, it should be able to dry out. I found a plastic trash bag in the bathroom, and using Band-Aids, I taped it over the broken window. I moved the furniture in the room as far as I could from the window. That would have to do.

The rest of the top story was okay.

I next checked the second story below the leaking window, but it seemed to be dry. Unlike the neutral upstairs guest room, this was where Damon had lived. Everything seemed left as it had been the day he collapsed and was taken to the hospital.

Holding my breath, I went into his office. I was fearful that the mere mortals could easily confound the gods—that Damon's nemesis would have somehow found the copy of the will. There's a copy at your office, I told myself—if my office was there. I slid open the drawer. Bills and invoices. No will. I took the papers out and sorted them one by one. There, mixed in near the bottom of the stack, was the will. I let out a long sigh of relief, then shuffled it under some other papers and again left it. If there had been electricity, I'd have made ten copies.

Now knowing what to look for, I found the HIV medications that Cordelia had named. The Kaletra was open, half-empty. Damon had been taking them, and when someone slipped him cocaine, the combination had pushed his weakened body too far. I glanced at all his meds, still sitting next to his bed as if he might indeed come back. I didn't see any capsules, which would have been easier to doctor.

I remembered the garbage I had gone through. I first looked at his nightstand, but couldn't find what I wanted. Then I went to his bathroom. They were there, the anti-nausea suppositories. I looked at the date on the prescription. It was the day Damon had been poisoned. I opened the box. Two of them were gone. But there had only been time, at best, for Damon to have used one. It seemed that someone had experimented with opening one and lacing it with cocaine. Now I knew who the killer was. And he was a killer, someone who knew what giving cocaine to Damon would do.

The downstairs door thudded open. And me without my gun—or even my trusty sidekick to yell for help.

It was either some of the cops or military checking up on things—although they would probably have called out by now—or looters.

I quickly stashed the suppositories behind the toilet, then headed out of Damon's bedroom and across the hall for the office. Looters were probably looking for drugs, and I didn't want to be between them and Damon's stash.

I quietly closed the door, hoping that it had a lock, then wondering if a locked door would be a signal that something worthwhile was behind the door. However, the choice was taken from me; the door had no lock on it.

I heard no voices and, after listening for a moment, could discern only one set of footsteps. One lone looter? Or a killer using the chaos of the hurricane to cover his tracks?

As quietly as I could, I did a hasty search of the desk drawers, hoping to find a hidden gun. The best I could come up with was a letter opener. Enough to keep me off a plane perhaps, but not enough against one man if he was armed.

As I continued to listen, I realized I didn't hear the kind of noises that would usually accompany a ransacking, instead just someone walking around. Was it possible the killer had returned to the scene of the crime?

It was stifling in the office. Whoever this was seemed in no hurry. Footsteps for a bit, then quiet, then the steps again. A heavy thud as something was moved. I barely stopped myself from jumping at the sudden noise, for in this old house with its creaky floors, that would give me away. I finally decided it would be better for me to surprise him than to wait for him to discover me. It didn't sound like anyone making a quick grab for the TV, but instead someone methodically checking the place out. That meant he would eventually find me. It was so still and hot in the closed office I was beginning to feel like I couldn't breathe. I could at least be a lot closer to the front door than here on the second floor. As I slowly opened the door, I wondered if my reasoning was based more on impatience and the heat than rational thought.

I paused at the top of the stairs, but heard nothing that indicated he'd heard me or was coming this way. As best I could, I peered over the banister, but could see no one.

As silently as possible, I made my way downstairs. At the foot of the stairs, I paused again, looking first at the locked and bolted front door, the burglar chain secured. The intruder was a cautious man, clearly making sure that no one would surprise him here. Or was he trying to keep someone in?

I cautiously looked back into the house. Then I spotted him out in the courtyard, cleaning up the fallen branches. The keeper of the flame. I knew I had no choice but to confront him. He didn't hear me as I went to the open French doors to the courtyard.

"Hello, Ambrose," I said quietly, as if this was a normal meeting. The ugly duckling who would never be the swan.

He jerked upright, dropping the armful of debris he had gathered. "What…what are you doing here?" he gasped.

"Miss Carlotta sent me to check up on things."

He brushed his hands on his pants, then adjusted his glasses, composing himself. "Well, as you can see, I'm taking care of things here."

I remained in the doorway, watching him. "I found out who did it, who killed Damon."

"Oh? The butler? The ex-lover?" He looked startled, not quite in control. It wasn't on any of his lists for me to actually find Damon's killer. I was silent. He cleared his throat and finally asked, "Who?"

"Oscar Wilde was right; we kill the thing we love. What do you have left now, Ambrose, now that it's all spiraling out of control?"

"I don't know what you're talking about," he blustered.

"The lawyer did it." We were alone in the courtyard, but I was unafraid. A quick, violent murder would be too uncontrolled for him. "What lawyer?" he said, still trying for vestiges of control.

"You. One of his drugs, Norvir, increases the potency of other drugs. Including cocaine. You killed him, Ambrose, took away a life that he desperately wanted."

"You don't know what you're talking about." His face was turning red.

"Want to hear my list, Ambrose?" I taunted him. "Bruce wasn't lying when he claimed you were at the bar—that's where you got the cocaine. You used him, didn't you? To get the cocaine, to spy on Damon and report back if there was a child. You just thought that no one would believe him over you. That might have worked, if you hadn't been so careless otherwise. So sure a 'girl' like me wouldn't figure it out. You and Perry hate each other, yet you left him with Damon to do an errand that George usually does. The only possible reason was to get your hands on the suppositories so you could doctor them with cocaine. You got the prescription that morning, yet two are missing. You used the first as a practice run for putting the cocaine in it. The second you gave to Damon. That's pathetic, Ambrose. The only way your god would let you touch him was to administer anti-nausea anal suppositories."

"Damon liked me…helping him," he blurted out. "Said I had gentle hands."

"You were useful. And you were getting to be a lot less useful. Damon was set on finding his daughter, finally doing the right thing and being as much of a father as he could be. But that child and her mother would have quickly become more important to Damon than you ever could be. You were desperate to keep him from signing that will. Damon knew that, that's why he arranged it so that Shannon and I were there, two disinterested witnesses. Damon would listen to you over the likes of Bruce or Perry. But not his aunt, and especially not his aunt backed up by his daughter and her mother. Once he signed the will and I found Jane, you were nobody to him. That's why you were so desperate to stop him."

"You're making this up," he retorted. But he was out of control enough to add, "And there is no way to prove any of it."

"Actually there is. Miss Carlotta gave me keys and permission to enter, so everything I've found is legal evidence. Like the box with the suppositories. Before the storm, I also collected the garbage. In that I found one of the wrappers. If your fingerprints are on that and there's any trace of cocaine, it's good-bye law practice and hello Angola for you."

I knew my chain of evidence was a lot shakier than it sounded, but Ambrose wasn't a criminal lawyer. Plus, he would be blinded by his guilt—or fear. I didn't know if he was capable of feeling guilt, but he could clearly worry about losing what he had—or thought he deserved.

He was trembling, his hands visibly shaking. "No, this can't happen."

"Oh, yes, it can. It is."

"You don't understand," he said. "I was doing what Damon really wanted. He would have wanted to see that brat for two minutes, then he'd have been tired of her."

"I get it. Damon really wanted you to kill him, so he would never even see his child for those two minutes. And you would have sacrificed all the power and control gladly, but you knew that Damon really wanted you to have it. He was just teasing you with changing the will."

"He should have listened to me!"

"Maybe Damon thought he knew what he really wanted. And maybe he was tired of you pretending that you knew what he really wanted."

He turned from me, reached down into the briefcase he was improbably carrying, the one supposedly stolen in Houston. Then he turned back with a gun in his hand. His hand was still trembling, and it was all I could do not to laugh out loud at him.

But he was pointing the gun at me. "No, this isn't happening. If you want to live through this day, the evidence will be destroyed."

"I've already given it to the cops. They're on their way here now."

"You're lying! There's no way to call the police."

"Saw them on the street. Told them what was up and to meet me here in half an hour."

His hand was still shaking; he used his other hand to steady the gun. "Then I'll have to kill you now. Once you're gone, they'll have too much to do to bother with me."

I walked toward him. "You're a better lawyer than a criminal. You're really not thinking this through."

He backed away. "I'm not kidding. I will kill you. Stay where you are." He pointed the gun directly at me, as much as he could with his trembling hands.

I kept coming. "You're not going to kill me. A good lawyer might get you off with Damon, argue that you didn't know the effect the cocaine would have."

"I will pull the trigger. Stay away from me!" Ambrose was out of control.

I took another step closer, almost close enough to touch him.

He pulled the trigger.

"You have to chamber the bullet first," I told him, contempt in every word. The gun made an impotent clicking sound. I grabbed his hand, pushing the gun aside, pointing it away from me.

Then I kicked him as hard as I could in the balls. He crumpled to the ground, dropping the gun. I punted it across the courtyard. I kicked him again in the groin and was about to do it again, but stopped. I was no longer protecting myself, but letting out my anger at him, at what he'd done. And my anger at all the men like him, those who put their self-interest and comfort above the lives of others. "You wretched piece of humanity. You're just a greedy, grubby murderer, and your fancy suits won't fool anyone anymore."

A thin line of vomit dribbled out of his mouth.

I bent down close to him. "I lied about the cops and I lied about the evidence. But now I don't have to lie. I can tell Miss Carlotta what you said and about you pulling the gun on me. In fact, I'll act on her behalf." I dug in his pockets and took all his keys, then checked the briefcase. As I guessed, Ambrose was controlled enough to have duplicates. The original of the will was still here. I took it. "You're getting kicked out of the kingdom right now. I made copies of the will Damon signed, so your fake theft wouldn't have worked."

I grabbed him by the belt, dragging him through the house and out the front door. Ambrose was a slight man, and between that and the adrenaline of my anger, I managed the feat. Other than a wailing moan, he didn't even fight. I quickly retrieved his briefcase, then tossed it after him, not even bothering to latch it. The contents spilled over the sidewalk and into the street, some of them coming to rest on Ambrose and his pool of vomit.

I locked Damon's door and started to walk away.

"Wait, my keys," he gasped out. "You have…all my keys."

"Get a locksmith," I said, and kept on walking.

At the corner I turned, casting one last glance back to him. He was still lying on the sidewalk, his pants pulled halfway down his skinny butt from my dragging him, showing his cheap, white underwear, his glasses skewed on his face. What a pathetic little man to have murdered a god.

Then I spun away from him and kept walking.

Chapter Twenty-seven

Cordelia and I had bought our house in the Tremé section, just off Esplanade, a few years ago. It was bigger than the place we'd had in the Marigny, a camelback shotgun double that we'd converted to a single. We had both a dining room and a separate TV room, plus a study for Cordelia and even a nook I used as a home office. Cordelia had piles of medical books and journals, and it had gotten to the point that I, at least, wanted the piles in a room with a door that could be closed so I didn't have to see the teetering stacks.

As I got closer, I could see that the water had been here. Cars showed dark lines and there was still mud in the street, a line of debris where the water had stopped. Some of the streets were still blocked with tree limbs, and the odor of sewage, something rotten and foul, was stronger here.

Then I was in front of my house, the place I'd lived for the last four years. The water had been here, flooded the street. I just stood there. If I had stayed, I would have watched my street turn into a bayou, the tree across the street shorn of its limbs, cars floating so that one ended up with its back tires on the sidewalk. But I could also tell that the water had only been deep enough to cover the street and creep onto the sidewalk. There had been no water inside my house. A wash of relief hit me, then guilt. So many people had lost so much, and I was happy that the water hadn't gotten high enough to reach the shrubs planted in front of our house.

Wherever Cordelia had gone, she had taken her car. I didn't see it around.

"Rook? Hepplewhite?" I called. No cat answered. They never did, save when I had a can of food in my hands, but I thought that at this point they might be so grateful to hear a familiar voice they'd come running.

I climbed the stairs to the porch, pausing at the top step to listen, mainly for any cat meows. The neighborhood was silent, in a way it never had been before. All the bustle of daily human activity—voices, cars, and cats—all were absent.

I glanced at my watch. I didn't know how long Shannon would be pursuing her story, but we needed to be on our way out of the city before dark. I could think at night when I couldn't sleep, but now I needed to check out the house, fix whatever I could fix, get anything I wanted for the next few months, and then leave.

I opened the door and went inside. The first thing I noticed was a stack of mail on the small table we kept near the door. It was all addressed to me, the few pieces that came after I had gone. Cordelia had left them for me. I'd get them on my way out.

The next thing I noticed was that I wasn't alone.

I almost didn't recognize her. I hadn't expected to see her here, but like everything else, she was the same yet different. She seemed almost to have aged in the time we'd been apart. Like years instead of weeks, it felt as if the chasm was that deep.

"Micky?" Cordelia called out softly. The cats were beside her on the couch.

I wondered if she had been dozing when I'd come in. "Yeah, it's me," I answered. As I got closer, I could see the lines of exhaustion on her face; her hair was dull, hastily brushed back. She was wearing an old faded yellow T-shirt and cut-off shorts, the bottom-of-the-barrel laundry, we called them. Her arms were bruised, one hand wrapped in an Ace bandage. "You were at Charity?" I asked.

"Yeah. Until they finally came and got us. Those of us still alive. We left…left the bodies on the stairwells. The morgue flooded."

With no lights, the windows shuttered, the room was dim, but now I was close enough to see that she'd been crying. "Are you okay?" I asked.

She rubbed her hand over her face as if trying to rouse herself. She sat up, her elbows on her knees as if she needed to prop herself up.

"Yeah, I'm okay. I'm…oh, hell, Micky, I'm so sorry for…I'm…damn, I'm…I'm…" Then she broke down crying, gasping out, "I'm not… okay," before the sorrow engulfed her, long rasping sobs, her face wet with tears.

I'd rarely seen Cordelia break like this. I'm more likely to cry, the more outwardly emotional of the two of us. The last time I'd seen her fall apart this way was when her mother died. I was beside her on the couch, not even thinking, my arms around her, holding her tight, stroking her arm, her hair, just holding her.

Slowly she was able to talk again and the words came out. "The stench of the bodies, we tried to move them as far away as we could… but the heat, being trapped there. One man could do nothing but watch his wife die. We couldn't save…no power, no ventilators, no dialysis, no medications. We were shitting in plastic bags and throwing them out the windows. No food, no water. My arms…I've got IV marks on my arms because that's how we fed ourselves. No sleep, too hot, a few hours on the roof, but no one could sleep. No coffee, we all had splitting caffeine headaches by the second day. Couldn't sleep, couldn't eat, couldn't shit…couldn't save lives."

She talked and cried. The horrors she had faced as they waited for rescue that came days too late for too many. I held her, let her cry, let her talk. She finally pulled away, saying, "I can't breathe."

I got up and found a box of tissues and let her blow her nose until she could breathe again.

"Damn, can't wash my face either," she said. I offered her my half-full bottle of water. She first drank a swig, then dabbed some on a tissue and wiped her face. But even soap and water wouldn't have taken away the ravages of her crying. Her face was red and raw, her eyes swollen and bloodshot.

She's okay, I told myself. As okay as she could be. That was all I wanted, wasn't it?

"Are you going to New York?" I asked.

She looked at me, confused for a moment, then she understood what I was asking. She slowly shook her head. "I'm…I don't know what…to say."

"How about you're sorry for cheating on me after lecturing me for years about fidelity and monogamy?" Then I caught myself. "I'm sorry. I'm very angry at you…but this isn't the time."

"You have a right to be angry," she said.

I looked at her, her exhausted, tear-stained face. Not now, I told myself. I wanted my anger pure, not tinged with guilt at berating a drained and battered woman. "Glad we can both agree on that," I said curtly.

A car door slammed.

I stood up. "That's Shannon. I told her to meet me here."

Cordelia didn't meet my eyes. She just said, "I understand. You're with her?" She flicked her eyes to me, then, as if unable to look at my face, away again.

"Happenstance," I said. "At first. Then choice. There didn't seem any reason not to," I added.

Cordelia understood my meaning, a bare nod of her head. But all she said was, "I'll take care of the cats. I was leaving today. Came back to get them."

I heard Shannon call my name. I didn't want her to see Cordelia, as broken as she was.

"I'll be okay," she said. "Just go." She turned away, picking up Rook, her cat. She carried him toward the cat carrier.

"Take care," I said as I walked out.

Shannon was coming up the front steps. I took her hand and led her back to the car.

"Cordelia is there," I said. "She's getting some things."

"Are you okay?" Shannon asked.

"Yeah, I'm okay. As I can be." I led her back down the steps. I looked back at the house, then at her. I kissed her. I kissed her long and hard, then said, "I love you."

She gripped me tight and close. "And I love you." She looked at me, held my eyes for a long second, then pressed her cheek against mine. "Enough for this. You're going back to her, aren't you?" Her arms tightened around me.

"I don't know. I just can't know right now. I only know I can't leave her here like she is now."

"What do you want from me?"

"I don't know that, either. Time? Let me take Cordelia out of here, get Alex, put my life back together. It's a…lot to ask, isn't it?"

"It's not love if it's just about me." She let go of me.

"You can take my car. Give it back to me someday."

"You'll walk?"

"Cordelia has a car." Cordelia had Danny's and Elly's second car. It was parked down the block before the waterline.

"Call me in a day or two and let me know you're okay?" Shannon asked.

"I will. You do the same."

She kissed me again, one last time. Then, without looking back, she got in my car and drove away.

I went back in the house.

Cordelia had only made a pretense of being together enough to get organized. The cats were still free. She was back on the couch curled up in an almost fetal position, crying as if her heart was breaking in every place it could break. She didn't hear me come back in; she had heard the car drive away.

I watched her. I had a flash of regret for not going with Shannon, just leaving, walking away from her and the mess she'd made of my life. Our lives. Whatever my anger and whatever our futures, right now I couldn't leave her alone and crying like she was.

I knelt on the floor next to her. "We need to pick up Alex in Baton Rouge as soon as we can get there." I wiped the tears off her face with my fingertips, then put my arms around her.

Through her crying, she managed to ask, as if I wasn't real, "Micky? You came back?"

I gently kissed her forehead, then said, "You're in no shape to drive. We need to get Alex and get her out of Baton Rouge." Beyond that, I didn't know, either for her or for me.

CHAPTER TWENTY-EIGHT

The waters of the bay sparkled in the bright sunshine, the shimmering light slanting in through the living-room windows. I printed out the boarding pass for my flight back to New Orleans tomorrow. Even as the pages emerged from the printer, I had to push away the urge to tear them up. To not return, keep going without looking back. Yet just when I thought I could do that, memory and connection pulled me to my damaged city.

I would return. I just didn't know if I'd stay.

Alex hadn't had indigestion. Cordelia and I got to Baton Rouge just in time to rush her to the hospital, where she miscarried. I drove to New Orleans the next day and took Joanne back. She could only stay long enough to get Alex out of the hospital, long enough to hold her and tell her she loved her.

Cordelia and I ended up staying in different places while we were there, partly because of necessity, partly because it seemed easier. She was exhausted, a weariness beyond physical; she had fallen into a fatigued slumber as we drove from New Orleans, not even waking when I stopped for gas. Even when we got to Baton Rouge, she was barely awake as I sorted out where to stay, only responding to direct requests. She woke again only when Alex called and we were on the way to the emergency room.

Events pulled us away and neither of us pushed to be together. We were kind and polite with each other, but something had been lost and I didn't know if we could get it back. Or if I wanted to. Her affair, of course, was a jagged, sharp edge, but the time apart had made a difference; it wasn't long, but dense and heavy, a cataclysm when I needed and expected her hand—even at a distance—to be there to hold. It wasn't. Something I thought I knew so well, that Cordelia would be there for me, wasn't true anymore.

Two days after Alex got out of the hospital, she said, "I can't stay here." Her uncle and his family were terse and livid. Unmarried, pregnant, lesbian, Alex got what she deserved. Something in her had been broken; she seemed fragile and withdrawn, and it was time to get her away from this toxic atmosphere. Andy's brother had a friend who was in Europe and was willing to let us use his place. The next day we were on a plane to San Francisco.

Cordelia was to stay with her sister in Boston, driving there, taking the cats with her.

"Keep in touch, please," she said at the airport. She was dropping us off, hesitating to hug me good-bye, as if afraid to find me stiff in her arms. I pulled her close and held her, then my plane was called and we were apart.

Alex and I spent the next few days in blissful, desperate denial, being tourists in the Bay Area, from Chinatown to the wine country. It wasn't healing, but it was breathing room.

"I hate Houston," Alex had told me, but after a week in San Francisco, she was flying there. "But at least I can see Joanne, and right now that's more important than location. Besides that it doesn't feel right to be in a nice, comfy place in California, when Houston seems to be such a part of the Katrina experience." She said it with a smile, but I could see the sadness in her eyes.

It was now mid-October, most of the water pumped out, the cameras gone, a promise to bring "this great city back" made—and yet to be kept—and people's lives went on.

Danny and Elly had already returned. They had some roof damage, but they lived in the Irish Channel, close to the river. Danny's comment was, "Who knew we were rich and white? Not only did we not flood, we managed to evacuate just like all the well-heeled folks." Danny had also grown up down in Bayou St. Jack. Her brother had gone down there to see what was left of their parents' home.

"Gone," she told me. "Everything gone, only marooned boats and piles of debris." The shipyard, my childhood home, wasn't there. A few scattered pilings and nothing else.

Hutch and Millie had lived in Lakeview, near the breach. "Half a wall and the foundation, nothing else," I found out from Joanne. Hutch had just sat in the street and cried for an hour.

It was a long time before I finally found out what had happened to Sarah Clavish. She had planned to evacuate, but her brother and his wife weren't leaving. "Lived there all my life, thought nothin' could happen. Had a boat," he told me before breaking down. Sarah had tried to talk them into going until it was too late. They had lived in Poydras, the lower part of St. Bernard Parish. The waters had come, he and Sarah made it to the boat, his wife slipped as she was climbing in, Sarah grabbed her. But the water was too strong, and Sarah didn't let go. "I saw Ruby's head above for a second, but when Sarah went over, they were just gone. Water took 'em totally," he said, and again broke down. He could barely get one sentence out before crying again. I was angry at him, wanting to scream, "Why the hell didn't you leave?" but he would ask himself that question for the rest of his life.

Emma Auerbach's house had survived the flood only to be burned down. She and her partner Rachel were living in their place across the lake. They planned to stay there, to not come back to the city.

"All the gay bars have already opened," Torbin told me. "Drag queens can't be far behind. And as for Andy, you can do computers just about anywhere. We'll be back. I'm even planning my contribution to refrigerator art. It will be crowned with a cheap tiara, a slash that proclaims 'Miss Levee Breach 2005, the queen who dragged New Orleans into the sewers.'" He then added that Andy was leaning more toward, "The Army Corps of Engineers Gets Me Wet."

I told Miss Carlotta about Ambrose. "I wish you'd filmed it," was her comment. "I'd have loved to see his expression when you dragged him out to the street."

She had decided to press charges, even though I told her it might be a difficult legal battle. But so far the police had been unable to locate him. I think we were both hoping he was enough of a coward to put a bullet through his head. Bruce wasn't as clever, he was easily apprehended. His story was that he had no idea what Ambrose was up to. He claimed he hadn't actually given him cocaine, just mentioned where he might get some. He said that Ambrose asked him to check on Damon, paid him decent money, and that was why he was in Memphis.

No one believed Bruce was that innocent, but he was looking at accessory-to-murder charges and would certainly spin his story in the most self-serving way.

I had to get rid of all the liquor in the place I was staying, giving it all to Torbin and Andy to safeguard. Before Katrina I had been okay, now I wasn't. My control was too fragile. I could live with having slipped up and taken a drink, but what was hard was how much I wanted another drink. After all these years I thought I could be stronger than this, but I wasn't and that was difficult to know.

Shannon called, we talked every few days. I still needed time, needed to know what was left of my life before changing directions. When she was close, loving her had seemed possible, but she wasn't close anymore. I was lost in a limbo of indecision. Leave New Orleans? And Cordelia? Return? Make a new life with Shannon? Or find my way back to Cordelia? Each choice both pulled me to it and pushed me away, so the days ended and I still had no direction. Some days I felt like I had just used Shannon. She was close and convenient and she offered and I was desperate and too consumed with my own needs to not take advantage of her. But in my more lucid moments, I knew that I did care for her, love her even. She had been there, with her kindness and open arms, to help me through a horrific time. For that, a piece of my heart belonged to her.

"I feel guilty," she said. "I'm getting a lot of work because of Katrina and what happened to New Orleans. It doesn't feel right to make this kind of money off a city destroyed."

"Tell the stories. That's important." I'd read some of her pieces. The one on George, how he'd collected comic books since he was a kid, made me cry.

She had seen Lauren, had to separate their joined lives. She summed up Lauren by saying, "She's charismatic and reckless. Part of me still loves her. Part of me hates that I do." Shannon seemed to make it a point not to know if Lauren and Cordelia were still seeing each other. I made it a point not to ask, only slipping once. The answer I got was, "I don't know," said in a way that made me wonder if Shannon did know, but didn't want to hurt me. I didn't ask again.

Cordelia and I talked a few times, but I felt too brittle to call her, too uncertain of what I wanted, too afraid of how angry I was. Days, then weeks slipped by. Finally she'd tentatively call me, but everything save the safe topics—the weather, updates on friends—remained unspoken. I'd go from one day being so infuriated that I didn't want to see or speak to her again to the next day desperately wanting to be with her, talking over the mundane details of our day, having her stand beside me, her hand rubbing my neck while I cooked.

Neither of us mentioned Lauren, so I didn't know whether they were still involved or not. Boston and New York weren't that far away. I wondered if that was part of Cordelia's decision to go there. On the days I wanted her back, I couldn't ask that question, couldn't dare risk finding out that those times in the kitchen were no longer possible. When I was angry, I didn't ask because I was afraid I'd so lose my temper that I'd go too far.

She was returning at the end of October—I'll see her then, I told myself. Face-to-face will be better than over the phone. I didn't know if that was true or not, but it was another excuse to put off the talk we had to have. Between the anger and the longing, I was numb, everything felt overwhelming, too hard to make a decision, too hard to know what I wanted, so I shoved it aside, read, watched TV, took long walks, anything to distract myself. But the numbness was penetrated with an understanding that no matter what I did, I had to return to New Orleans. If I left, I'd have to cut the ties that had so long bound me there. If I stayed, I'd have to find ways to repair them.

Damon died three days after we left Memphis. Beatrice had to tell Jane, "Even if he didn't wake up, he knew you were here." Her voice broke as she talked to me, and that was all I could bear to know of how much his death hurt Jane. I hoped that somehow he did know she was there, that I'd found his daughter, the young girl with his hair.

I had liked Damon and I didn't like Lauren, but I had to acknowledge that they were alike. Flames who took little notice of the moths burning. Beautiful, charming, alluring, but inexcusable nonetheless. Damon, at the very end, had at least sought redemption. Lauren? Her soul wasn't my worry.

I had the soul of New Orleans—its ravaged streets, torn lives, friends, and strangers—to worry about. My own soul as well. It, too, was ragged and battered, torn in ways I didn't know if I could ever mend.

About the Author

J.M. Redmann has written five novels, all featuring New Orleans private detective Michele "Micky" Knight. The fourth, *Lost Daughters*, was originally published by W.W. Norton. Her third book, *The Intersection Of Law & Desire*, won a Lambda Literary Award, as well as being an Editor's Choice of the San Francisco Chronicle and featured on NPR's Fresh Air. *Lost Daughters* and *Deaths Of Jocasta* were also nominated for Lambda Literary Awards. Her books have been translated into German, Spanish, Dutch and Norwegian. She currently lives in New Orleans, just at the edge of the flooded area.

Books Available From Bold Strokes Books

The Lure by Felice Picano. When Noel Cummings is recruited by the police to go undercover to find a killer, his life will never be the same. (978-1-60282-076-0)

Death of a Dying Man by J.M. Redmann. Mickey Knight, Private Eye and partner of Dr. Cordelia James, doesn't need a drop-dead gorgeous assistant—not until nature steps in. (978-1-60282-075-3)

Justice for All by Radclyffe. Dell Mitchell goes undercover to expose a human traffic ring and ends up in the middle of an even deadlier conspiracy. (978-1-60282-074-6)

Sanctuary by I. Beacham. Cate Canton faces one major obstacle to her goal of crushing her business rival, Dita Newton—her uncontrollable attraction to Dita. (978-1-60282-055-5)

The Sublime and Spirited Voyage of Original Sin by Colette Moody. Pirate Gayle Malvern finds the presence of an abducted seamstress, Celia Pierce, a welcome distraction until the captive comes to mean more to her than is wise. (978-1-60282-054-8)

Suspect Passions by VK Powell. Can two women, a city attorney and a beat cop, put aside their differences long enough to see that they're perfect for each other? (978-1-60282-053-1)

Just Business by Julie Cannon. Two women who come together—each for her own selfish needs—discover that love can never be as simple as a business transaction. (978-1-60282-052-4)

Sistine Heresy by Justine Saracen. Adrianna Borgia, survivor of the Borgia court, presents Michelangelo with the greatest temptations of his life while struggling with soul-threatening desires for the painter Raphaela. (978-1-60282-051-7)

Radical Encounters by Radclyffe. An out-of-bounds, outside-the-lines collection of provocative, superheated erotica by award-winning romance and erotica author Radclyffe. (978-1-60282-050-0)

Thief of Always by Kim Baldwin & Xenia Alexiou. Stealing a diamond to save the world should be easy for Elite Operative Mishael Taylor, but she didn't figure on love getting in the way. (978-1-60282-049-4)

X by JD Glass. When X-hacker Charlie Riven is framed for a crime she didn't commit, she accepts help from an unlikely source—sexy Treasury Agent Elaine Harper. (978-1-60282-048-7)

The Middle of Somewhere by Clifford Henderson. Eadie T. Pratt sets out on a road trip in search of a new life and ends up in the middle of somewhere she never expected. (978-1-60282-047-0)

Paybacks by Gabrielle Goldsby. Cameron Howard wants to avoid her old nemesis Mackenzie Brandt but their high school reunion brings up more than just memories. (978-1-60282-046-3)

Uncross My Heart by Andrews & Austin. When a radio talk show diva sets out to interview a female priest, the two women end up at odds and neither heaven nor earth is safe from their feelings. (978-1-60282-045-6)

Fireside by Cate Culpepper. Mac, a therapist, and Abby, a nurse, fall in love against the backdrop of friendship, healing, and defending one's own within the Fireside shelter. (978-1-60282-044-9)

Green Eyed Monster by Gill McKnight. Mickey Rapowski believes her former boss has cheated her out of a small fortune, so she kidnaps the girlfriend and demands compensation—just a straightforward abduction that goes so wrong when Mickey falls for her captive. (978-1-60282-042-5)

Blind Faith by Diane and Jacob Anderson-Minshall. When private investigator Yoshi Yakamota and the Blind Eye Detective Agency are hired to find a woman's missing sister, the assignment seems fairly mundane—but in the detective business, the ordinary can quickly become deadly. (978-1-60282-041-8)

A Pirate's Heart by Catherine Friend. When rare book librarian Emma Boyd searches for a long-lost treasure map, she learns the hard way that pirates still exist in today's world—some modern pirates steal maps, others steal hearts. (978-1-60282-040-1)

Trails Merge by Rachel Spangler. Parker Riley escapes the high-powered world of politics to Campbell Carson's ski resort—and their mutual attraction produces anything but smooth running. (978-1-60282-039-5)

Dreams of Bali by C.J. Harte. Madison Barnes worships work, power, and success, and she's never allowed anyone to interfere—that is, until she runs into Karlie Henderson Stockard. Aeros EBook (978-1-60282-070-8)

The Limits of Justice by John Morgan Wilson. Benjamin Justice and reporter Alexandra Templeton search for a killer in a mysterious compound in the remote California desert. (978-1-60282-060-9)

Designed for Love by Erin Dutton. Jillian Sealy and Wil Johnson don't much like each other, but they do have to work together—and what they desire most is not what either of them had planned. (978-1-60282-038-8)

Calling the Dead by Ali Vali. Six months after Hurricane Katrina, NOLA Detective Sept Savoie is a cop who thinks making a relationship work is harder than catching a serial killer—but her current case may prove her wrong. (978-1-60282-037-1)

Shots Fired by MJ Williamz. Kyla and Echo seem to have the perfect relationship and the perfect life until someone shoots at Kyla—and Echo is the most likely suspect. (978-1-60282-035-7)

truelesbianlove.com by Carsen Taite. Mackenzie Lewis and Dr. Jordan Wagner have very different ideas about love, but they discover that truelesbianlove is closer than a click away. Aeros EBook (978-1-60282-069-2)

Justice at Risk by John Morgan Wilson. Benjamin Justice's blind date leads to a rare opportunity for legitimate work, but a reckless risk changes his life forever. (978-1-60282-059-3)

Run to Me by Lisa Girolami. Burned by the four-letter word called love, the only thing Beth Standish wants to do is run for—or maybe from—her life. (978-1-60282-034-0)

Split the Aces by Jove Belle. In the neon glare of Sin City, two women ride a wave of passion that threatens to consume them in a world of fast money and fast times. (978-1-60282-033-3)

Uncharted Passage by Julie Cannon. Two women on a vacation that turns deadly face down one of nature's most ruthless killers—and find themselves falling in love. (978-1-60282-032-6)

Night Call by Radclyffe. All medevac helicopter pilot Jett McNally wants to do is fly and forget about the horror and heartbreak she left behind in the Middle East, but anesthesiologist Tristan Holmes has other plans. (978-1-60282-031-9)

Lake Effect Snow by C.P. Rowlands. News correspondent Annie T. Booker and FBI Agent Sarah Moore struggle to stay one step ahead of disaster as Annie's life becomes the war zone she once reported on. Aeros EBook (978-1-60282-068-5)

Revision of Justice by John Morgan Wilson. Murder shifts into high gear, propelling Benjamin Justice into a raging fire that consumes the Hollywood Hills, burning steadily toward the famous Hollywood Sign—and the identity of a cold-blooded killer. (978-1-60282-058-6)

I Dare You by Larkin Rose. Stripper by night, corporate raider by day, Kelsey's only looking for sex and power, until she meets a woman who stirs her heart and her body. (978-1-60282-030-2)

Truth Behind the Mask by Lesley Davis. Erith Baylor is drawn to Sentinel Pagan Osborne's quiet strength, but the secrets between them strain duty and family ties. (978-1-60282-029-6)

Cooper's Deale by KI Thompson. Two would-be lovers and a decidedly inopportune murder spell trouble for Addy Cooper, no matter which way the cards fall. (978-1-60282-028-9)

Romantic Interludes 1: Discovery ed. by Radclyffe and Stacia Seaman. An anthology of sensual, erotic contemporary love stories from the best-selling Bold Strokes authors. (978-1-60282-027-2)